CW00662060

THERE'S SOMETHING WRONG WITH THE CATS

C J POWELL

Copyright © 2023 by C J Powell

All rights reserved.

No portion of this book may be reproduced in any form without written permission from the publisher or author, except as permitted by U.S. copyright law.

MOUSEBANE

They call me The Night. The Shadow That Stalks Behind. The Dark One.

My brother and I go to war.

I hunt as if my life depends on it, for I know hers does. And she is my everything.

My prey, you ask?

Probably the old man in the suit. Or maybe that blonde woman over there. Or perhaps The Disappearing Ones.

Definitely that squirrel.

Trifle with me squirrel, and you will rue the day you ever crossed my path.

Oh, running away? I thought as much.

The street calls for my aid once more.

In a thousand anguished voices it cries my name.

Mousebane.

Jammy. Little. Bugger.

The printer jammed another copy of the poster up into its insides and cranked to a stop. Dan refrained from launching it through his third-floor window and out onto the street.

But only just.

Instead, he gave it a good hard squeeze with both hands. *Stuuupiiiddd priiiiinterrrr!*

How was it that a man could fly a rocket to the moon, or a surgeon could remote pilot scalpels on the other side of the world to perform delicate brain surgery, or an automated biscuit factory could churn out perfect custard cream after perfect custard cream, but as soon as it came to getting a bit of bloody ink on a bit of bloody paper, all human capability in engineering and science went flying out the flipping window?

Printers. Never. Worked.

Especially when you needed them most.

Helping your mum make invites for her birthday party? *Error! Ink cartridge running low.*

Printing out a boarding pass for a flight and you should have left ten minutes ago? *Error! Printer speed settings are not within an acceptable range.*

Making a poster because your poor little cats have been missing for four days straight and you're worried sick? *Haha, not today you son of a mother! No paper.*

"I know there's no bloody paper," spat Dan, not caring if anyone outside could hear his bitter tirade. "You've just sucked it all up into your stupid brain, you absolute cretin."

He had the urge to headbutt it. But instead closed his eyes and began to count to ten. Stopped at four. Felt better enough. Anger didn't often get the better of Daniel Dixon, but when it did, you would not want to be on the receiving end.

A soft breeze blew through the open window into his tiny home office. The net curtain, with its concentric swirls of lace, danced slowly as the room filled with the sweet, musky air of the cool autumn day that was beginning outside. He took a deep breath. Held it.

Two huge cardboard boxes, one labelled 'old band stuff', sat stacked beneath the window. He leant both his forearms on the top one and gazed out at the street. Pigeons cooed hypnotically on the roof opposite. Crisp husks of leaves swept by on the pavement below.

He breathed out. Looked at the picture of the cats on his desk. Where were the little buggers?

It wasn't like them to go missing.

Catman had spent maybe two nights outside before now. Roaming around the block, culling the local rodent and bird populations, and causing general havoc, no doubt. But as far as Dan knew, The Flash always came in early for his dinner and never left the house again until the following morning.

He looked up and down the road, hoping to see them waltzing up the pavement.

Nothing.

Last week, the street had been all go. The couple from across the road, the ones who'd leant him that strimmer he still had in the shed, had moved out, and an older gent had moved in. Lorries and removal men had busied themselves outside all day.

Perfect procrastination fodder.

He'd passed the new neighbour on the street a few times since. A funny old fella. Always wearing an expensive-looking suit and a large, wide-brimmed hat like some 1920s gangster.

He and Amy had nicknamed the man Gatsby.

Dan didn't know his real name. Small talk wasn't his forte, especially with old people, so he didn't go out to introduce himself. Didn't want to get caught in a conversation about the war or cricket in the 1930s or something.

But since moving day, the street had been dead.

Now, instead of seeing his cats, he saw a lanky man in a parka ambling confidently in the direction of his house. Feet aimed in almost opposite directions as he walked, as if he were about to plié. Didn't look the ballet type, though. More like he was about to belt out Wonderwall to a packed pub, punch a granny, and down another Carling. His arms swung wildly at his sides. A strut that was all elbows and knees. A strut that ever since school, Dan had associated with danger. If someone walked towards you like that on the playground, you were about to get decked.

Parkaman was familiar. The parka gave him away. As did the gaudy walk. He'd been loitering on the road outside their house a few weeks ago. Dan always noticed a loiterer, but rarely remembered one unless he saw them again.

That time, Parkaman had taken something from his pocket and placed it next to their garden path. The guy had no idea Dan had been spying on him from behind his net curtain. When he'd moved on, Dan had crept out to take a look and found a small pile of little stones stacked neatly against the wall. At the time he'd thought it strange, but had soon forgotten.

This time, Parkaman walked straight past without stopping. Maybe just the faintest of glances up.

"No creepy little stone piles to dispense today, huh?" Dan whispered to the empty room. "You still look super shady, matey boy. What are you up to? Some sort of drug deal? Looking for cars to steal? I've got my eye on you." An eye, which he narrowed in judgement.

Parkaman threw odd jerky glances over his shoulders, as if he were about to surprise the road by crossing it, and continued on his way

Dan took a deep breath. He was getting himself worked up. His heart had begun to dance to rapid drum 'n' bass in his chest. He gave his head a little shake.

Amy would have said, "you're just being overly creative again."

His wife liked the term "overly creative" for his imaginings. She'd picked it up from his mother.

She would be able to come up with a plausible reason for Parkaman's darting, furtive glances. "The man's probably just got a nervous tick," she'd say.

A tick?

He sighed. Catman had a tick once. Dan had to remove it with tweezers. Its little black legs kicked as he squeezed it flat and washed it down the sink. Revolting. Bugs made his back itch. Ticks, both kinds, made him nervous.

When Catman and The Flash hadn't come home last night, he'd considered calling the police, but Amy had just made fun of him, coming up with an idea for a TV show called Cat Cops, where a ginger tom in a police uniform hunted down cat-nappers to a funky 70s backbeat. She'd strutted around the living room strumming an imaginary guitar singing, "Cat Cops - chika wowwow". He'd laughed, licked his thumb, and added some gnarly slap bass.

If Amy said the cats were fine, they probably were.

Not including the leaf that he'd adopted for a week, aged three, with the unorthodox name of Stick, Dan's boyhood pet history consisted of a single goldfish. And that mother flipper had only ever run away once, before dying an untimely death twitching on the kitchen rug.

It was The Flash he worried about mostly. He and Catman were binary opposites. Catman liked nothing more than to chop a baby bird into tiny bits, and hide the remains in the tumble dryer. That cute little murderer would be fine on the mean streets of Walton. The Flash, on the other hand, just wanted to sit and chill out on the sofa, watching TV with his mum and dad. He wasn't cut out for the big wide world with its fast cars and tail grabbing children.

Dan hoped Catman would take care of his brother. Catman could hunt down mice and birds if they needed food, and would likely punch any tail pulling toddlers square in the face.

A clap of wings caused him to look to the roof opposite. The trio of plump pigeons perched there had been startled into flight. A shadow moved behind where they had just been.

Catman and The Flash darted out from behind the brick chimney, and across the tiles like four-legged ninjas on a covert mission across the rooftops of a Japanese stronghold. They moved quickly, Catman's pitch black coat almost hidden against the dark slate. The Flash, as ginger as a fluffy orange, stood out like a flamingo at a funeral.

He edged closer to the glass to get a better look, careful not to twitch the curtain. Although technically he was one, it would be his worst nightmare to get a reputation as a curtain twitcher.

Something was different about Catman. After four nights away, Dan had expected him to come back thinner, perhaps with his fur in a tangle. The opposite was true. He looked chunky and sleek.

Must be a trick of the light, he thought. Black fur on charcoal slate making him look bigger.

Dan squeezed his thumbs with his fists. The pair of them were bloody high up. His heart popped an E and continued its D'n'B rave from earlier.

The cats sat on the edge of Gatsby's roof and looked down for a moment.

Catman turned, gripped the gutter with his claws, and dangled his tail over the side. The Flash caught hold and swung down to the window ledge on the third storey.

Um... Dan peered closer. That wasn't normal cat behaviour.

He squeezed his thumbs harder. Felt like a mother watching her only child fool around in the top branches of a giant redwood. Realising his mouth was hanging open, he shut it with a snap of teeth.

The Flash balanced on the ledge like a tight-rope walker then disappeared through the top of Gatsby's glazed window.

He gasped. Jammy. Little. Bugger.

Catman clambered down the drain pipe after him. In the light of day against the brick front of the house, Dan could see he was definitely bigger. Not fatter, but more muscular, like he'd been getting beach body ready for the summer. In his mind's eye, he saw an anthropomorphic steroid pumped Sylvester the Cat in speedo's flexing some impressive biceps.

It was definitely strange. Dan had been going to the gym for years and had put on nowhere near as much weight. And here Catman was making some serious gainz in just four days. What had he eaten?

From his window ledge vantage point, Catman scanned the street. What was he looking at? Parkaman had moved on. The place was deserted.

Dan leant closer to the window. "What are you up to?"

GATSBY

D an pressed his laptop lid closed and hurried downstairs. Flapped his arms into his hoody like a panicked bird. Although it was usually his prerogative to avoid social interaction whenever possible, Gatsby might be in, and he had no way to tell what the old man might do if he caught uninvited cats in his house. Might have a heart attack or something.

He slipped his socked feet into flip-flops — a bold look deeply shunned by everyone of his generation, but strangely held in high esteem by the kids of today (and in his mind's eye, ninjas) — then shuffled up the garden path.

By the time he arrived at his rusting garden gate, Catman had disappeared too. Gatsby's bathroom window was now wide open.

He stretched up on tip-toes, trying to see the ground beneath the window, hoping Catman hadn't been knocked from the ledge to his death, but his garden hedge was a little too high to see over. They say cats always land on their feet. Not so comforting if they fall from such a height that their legs shatter on impact.

What was the terminal velocity of a cat?

He opened his creaky garden gate, flecks of black paint embedding in his palm as he gripped it.

I must remember to repaint and oil that, he thought. Amy had mentioned it in passing several thousand times. And he'd said he'd do it several thousand times.

He started to cross the road, picking tiny pieces of rusted metal from his hand.

He wouldn't remember.

He'd been so lost in thought that he hadn't noticed Parkaman, back already, and standing just outside Gatsby's gate. Gatsby was on his doorstep clutching a newspaper to his chest.

"What are you gonna do about it, you old fuck?" Parkaman spat, whilst violently shaking a finger at the old man. He hadn't noticed Dan.

Dan stopped in the middle of the road wondering, gallantly, whether or not it would be best to just creep back home and maybe come back later, considering that at the present time Gatsby appeared a little busy.

The old man, to his credit, looked more angry than sad or afraid, but he didn't say anything. His lower lip trembled slightly.

Parkaman moved to open his new neighbour's gate.

"Hey, stop it." The words just popped out of Dan's mouth. No thought behind them.

He almost didn't hear his own voice, but Parkaman clearly did. He wheeled around on the spot, lips pulled tightly across his yellow teeth, and suddenly he was off the curb and in Dan's face.

"You neighbourhood watch or something, mate?" Behind him, Gatsby quickly hurried inside and shut the door. Parkaman was his problem now. He glanced past Dan, quickly inspecting the houses behind him. "It's a nice street. Which one's yours?"

"Um..." He swallowed. Thought quickly. "No, I was just walking through." He pointed feebly up the road, away from his house. It wouldn't do to have someone like this know where you lived. "You know, you shouldn't—"

"Shouldn't what?" Parkaman leant his head to one side. Stared.

Dan held his arms rigid by his sides. "Shouldn't talk to people like—"

Parkaman jabbed a long finger forward and prodded him roughly on the nose. "You wanna keep your nose out of things that don't concern you, or else you might end up in a lot more trouble than a stupid old man is worth, yeah?" He continued to glare. His eyes were creamy marbles, wide and glassy.

All Dan could think was whether or not the guy had blinked since the altercation had begun. Any normal person should have blinked by now. Did he have eyelids? Where were his eyelids?

"You hearing me or are you some sort of fucking idiot?" Parkaman lifted a disgusted nostril. Then blinked.

Dan looked at his feet. "Sorry."

"Next time, you will be." Without another word, he strutted off towards the main road.

Dan watched him go as nausea blossomed in his stomach. Why was it that whenever you tried to help someone, it was always you who ended up in the firing line?

He took a slow inhale to try to calm himself. "*You're* the flipping idiot," he mumbled under the exhale, whilst staring daggers into Parkaman's retreating back.

It took another moment for him to remember why he'd left home in the first place.

He glanced up at Gatsby's bathroom window. The cats hadn't reemerged.

Gatsby's gate opened silently despite the slight shake in his hand as he pushed it. The paint was even, un-cracked, impressive. A gate even Amy's dad would have been proud of.

He entered the front garden beneath the bathroom window. Catman wasn't in bits on the well-groomed lawn, so he guessed he must be inside.

There was a plastic sign on a wooden post in the hedge: "Shields Properties".

He had met Gatsby's landlord, who also happened to be the man's son, Marty, or Matt Shields. Dan hadn't properly heard the name, and was too English to ask again. They'd had a strange conversation, the details of which were fuzzy. All he could really remember was that Marty Matt was weird. Not someone he'd want another chat with if it could be avoided. But to be honest, there weren't many people he could think of actually wanting to have a chat with.

He flip-flopped up the garden path, admiring the clean line of the hedge, the short trim of the grass. You had to have a lot of spare time on your hands to keep a garden like this. Or a lot of money. Dan lacked both.

I must remember to trim our hedge when I get a spare moment, he thought. Cut our lawn too. Maybe I'll get around to using that strimmer I borrowed.

Whose was that again?

He wouldn't remember.

Both trimming the hedge and cutting the lawn resided permanently on the mental to do list that he imagined Amy kept for him. This also included: oil the gate, empty the bins, clean out the cat bowls, and don't be such a forgetful idiot.

There were other things, but they'd slipped his mind.

He raised his hand, hesitated — stole himself ready for the interaction — and knocked on the door. A sleek PVC number in a dashing shade of olive.

Nobody answered. Not really surprising.

He stepped off the porch. Looked up at the bathroom window again. The boys hadn't come out.

Next to the front door was a bay window. Most of the houses in the road were based on the same design, meaning Gatsby's living room probably lay beyond. He put his head to the glass and cupped his hands to his face to shield the reflection. As he did, the front door opened.

"Can I help you?" said a wavering voice. Gatsby had a slight Cornish accent, which made Dan, having grown up in the Surrey suburbs, think unfairly of farms.

He jolted away from the window and ummed while he figured out what to say.

Gatsby stood on the porch dressed in a navy pinstripe suit. Atop his head sat a matching fedora. A speckled feather was held in place by a white band that ran around the outside. He was tall and thin and old. But not the sort of cuddly old that you associated with a nice Werther's Original-wielding grandad. More the old of someone who has found a very serious problem with little girls taking up football and boys, ballet. He cleared his throat and raised an impatient eyebrow.

"Are you OK?" asked Dan.

"Yes, why wouldn't I be?" His lined face trembled slightly.

"Sorry about that guy. Not everyone round here is like that. We're actually all pretty nice." He scratched his chin. "You don't know him, do—"

"No."

"No, of course not."

Gatsby frowned. "Don't worry about me. I can handle myself." He moved to shut the door.

Dan put a hand out. "Sorry, that's not the reason I'm calling by."

"What then?"

"Um... I think my cats have snuck in through your upstairs window." He pointed upward.

Gatsby looked him up and down. Clearly a little suspicious.

"I live across the road," he continued, jabbing a thumb back towards his house, his other hand resting on his hip.

Realising he looked rather like a little teapot, he folded his arms.

Gatsby glanced past him and frowned, no doubt at the lumpy hedge row that surrounded Dan's over-grown garden.

"It's not much, but it's home." He cleared his throat, not sure what to say next. With a flash of inspiration, he spread his arms wide and smiled. "Welcome to the neighbourhood."

"Some welcome." Gatsby squinted with one eye. A bushy grey eyebrow lifted, nearly disappearing under the brim of his hat. He twiddled his wire thin moustache. "I ain't seen you around." The word "I" came out more like "oi".

"Oi don't get out much," said Dan, who had a bad habit of taking on other people's accents. He crammed a few more teeth into what he hoped was a winning smile, praying Gatsby hadn't noticed.

Gatsby's eyes darted to and fro as if he were trying to remember something. His eyebrows sunk together into a frown. "Well, there aren't any cats here."

Behind him, Dan saw a blur of orange zip across the landing, followed by a large bolt of black.

"There they are." He pointed over the old man's shoulder, almost jumping up and down.

Gatsby looked behind him, coat tails swinging with the motion, then turned back, resting his hand on the wall for support. He gave his head a little shake. "I didn't see nothing."

He leant backwards, putting some distance between them. His gaze travelled down the undulating hills of his nose, making Dan feel as if he were impaled on a spear of ice.

"They are upstairs." Dan stepped forward and pointed again.

Gatsby retreated through the doorway and coughed into his gloved hand. "'fraid I shan't be having any visitors today."

"Oh, but—"

Gatsby slammed the door, the olive PVC narrowly missing Dan's nose.

"What about my cats?" Dan's body sagged.

Wow! That was some thanks for putting his life on the line with Parkaman. He scratched his head and looked back up at the window.

Well, at least they were alive. Amy would be pleased. They were just hanging out at someone else's house. They were fine. Catman had grown, and The Flash was weirdly good at climbing, but they were fine.

His brief moment of relief turned to anger. Slamming the door in his face had been a tad rude. He considered knocking again, became anxious at the thought of the resulting confrontation, and instead decided to stomp back home. But not before throwing open Gatsby's infuriatingly silent gate and then shutting and latching it with all the mumbling rage he could muster.

"If they want to be in that crotchety old man's house," he huffed. "Then let them. Aaaand next time any parka wearing oiks come calling, he can deal with them himself."

Crossing the road, he recalled an urban legend of a duo of crooks that preyed on OAPs. One would stand at the front door pretending to sell double glazing, or do some kind of survey, while the other snuck in the back and stole anything they could.

His shifting river of emotion turned to a trickling of guilt.

Did Gatsby think he was trying something on? That maybe he and Parkaman had been in cahoots.

The old 'Oh! My cats are in your house,' ruse.

Likely story.

He stopped, turned to face Gatsby's house, and watched for a twitching curtain. He could picture poor, old, fragile Gatsby checking his back door, hoping that no one had snuck in. But there was no going back to apologise. That would seem even more suspect. He fanned his T-shirt. He'd suddenly got a bit hot in the pits.

A car beeped at him still standing in the middle of the road. He waved and continued on to the pavement. Opened his front door and entered, rubbing his face to try to remove the shame.

He trumped upstairs and dropped into his desk chair. A heavy lethargy gripped his limbs. There was nothing he hated more than hurting or worrying people, especially the older ones. The thought of doing someone harm, even with intent, made him sick to his stomach.

Why did he bother leaving the house? He always said and did the wrong thing.

There was that time, aged nineteen, when he'd snuck next door to his parent's neighbour's house in the middle of the night armed with a metal trampoline leg because he'd heard screaming in their garden and thought someone was being attacked. Turned out the neighbours had just been having a bit of alfresco fun and gotten carried away.

He'd come very close to hurting someone that night. Really hurting them.

It was always best not to get involved in other people's business.

Unable to clear his head, he leant forward and rested it on the cool wooden desk.

But that wasn't getting any work done, so he sat up and opened his laptop ready to stare at his unopened emails for a bit.

Something outside caught his attention once more. A shadow moving on the other side of the street. He stood to get a better view of Gatsby's house.

Catman clambered out of the old man's window and perched on the ledge. The Flash followed, but as he exited, Dan could swear he did something stranger than using his brother to abseil — he pressed the window closed behind him.

As Catman scaled the drain pipe, The Flash took hold of his tail once more. Then, when Catman had safely reached the roof, and was gripping the tiles for support, he swung out, using the tail as some sort of feline belay, and climbed up behind him.

Dan rubbed his face. What exactly was he seeing?

They skirted up the tiles and disappeared over the peak of the roof.

That was all pretty weird, right? Cats didn't do that sort of thing.

He imagined himself clinging to the roof of their house while Amy climbed up his own leg. The image ended with him screaming, "I can't hold on," and them plummeting to their deaths.

The Flash was climbing using Catman as a rope, and Catman had put on some serious weight and strength. How could that happen? Dan's 'overly creative' imagination jumped gears and sped off on its own.

Protein shakes. Plastic surgery. Cat inflating pump. Drugs. Steroids.

Hm?

Maybe they'd been at Gatsby's the last four nights, trapped while he fed them non-stop steroids and beef. The old man had slammed the door because he was guilty. Guilty of drugging Dan's cats.

That had to (probably) be it.

His nervous guilt dropped away. If there was even a remote chance that Gatsby was drugging them, then he had to find out.

The old man would have gotten away with it too, if it hadn't been for Dan working from home.

He scratched his chin, contemplating for the tiniest of seconds the ridiculousness of an old man beefing up cats with steroids. But he'd seen crazier headlines. Those magazines you got in the vet waiting room were full of them. And everyone knew those were all based on cold, hard fact.

He could see the cover now. A picture of him looking miffed, squashed beneath a Catman the size of a small lion.

My Neighbour Drugged My Cat to Create a Super Army Of Cat Henchmen and Now I Can't Afford to Feed Him.

He'd have to tell someone. The RSPCA. The police. But they'd want proof. And he knew the devious old man would never let him inside his house. If only he could see through the cats' eyes.

He lifted the lid of his laptop and googled 'camera for your cat'. The results showed an array of baffled-looking pets with cameras strapped to their heads.

After some research, he ordered two 'Collar Cams' from Amazon, along with a signal booster. Each camera could transmit over Bluetooth, uploading to the cloud when they were close enough, or saving the files to an SD card when out of reach.

It was more money than they could currently afford, but it'd be cheaper than the vet bills if the cats got sick.

Delivery was the next day, so as long as the cats returned home tonight, he'd soon get his answers.

He'd have to tell Amy. She'd think him mad unless he explained what he was doing. He would certainly think her nuts if she did the same thing. He would tell her about Catman and The Flash going into Gatsby's house. She would get on side, keen to find out why they were there too, but he would leave out any mention of drugs for now. She'd only brand him 'overly creative' again.

He rubbed a hand over his stubble and squinted thoughtfully at Gatsby's house. He'd get to the bottom of this.

MOUSEBANE

The old man was clean.

We will return to our fortress. The power that grows within me is like nothing I have experienced. It begs to be fed.

Then the hunt must continue.

IT MIGHT SOUND CRAZY BUT...

"Look who's decided to come home," said Amy as the cats followed her through the front door that evening. "You can't just swan in like nothing's happened. Daddy's been very worried."

Dan looked up from the sofa where he was snuggled with his laptop, a blanket pulled tight over his lap. She stood in the hall with her backpack still on. A finger wagging close to Catman's face.

Catman blanked her and sauntered into the kitchen.

"I was just about to tidy up," Dan said. His usual greeting.

"Sure you were." Hers.

He threw his laptop away and chased Catman into the kitchen. A pile of washing up leftover from lunch sat soaking in the sink.

Amy followed him in. Her bag thudded on the kitchen table. "Better late than never, I suppose." She patted his head.

The cats yowled at their food bowls. Chanting the incantations that would, as if by magic, fill them with mystery meat.

Amy pulled two pouches from the cupboard and filled each bowl. She had to jerk quickly back as Catman wrestled her out of the way. The Flash watched for a moment before joining.

"Hm? He looks well fed, doesn't he?" she said, turning her head sideways to look at Catman. "Must have caught something big out there."

"What, like a water buffalo?" Dan said, finally getting a good look at their black cat. "He's not just well fed. Check out those lats." Catman's back muscles rippled as he ate. "I've been working out in the gym four times a week for the last million years and I've nothing on him."

"We both know you're a hard gainer, honey." She gave him a knowing smile. "Or at least that's what you told me."

"Yes, I'm an ectomorph. It's a thing." It was a thing. He crouched for closer inspection. Held his thumb and little finger spread over The Flash's back and compared it to Catman. He'd almost doubled in size across the shoulders. "This is ridiculous. He's gone away four nights and come back as the cat equivalent of Mr Universe."

Amy stepped back. A finger placed on her chin. The cute little lines on her forehead were showing — the ones that made him want to kiss her all over her face — each one probably a result of stress caused by him somewhere along the line.

"You're right, Shrimpy." She poked him in the ribs. "So what's happened to him?" She knelt and ran a hand over Catman's head, clearly concerned. She looked back at Dan. "You don't think he's sick or something?"

He picked up a pan from the sink and started scrubbing. Where to begin?

"Not sick. But I have a theory."

She turned her head to look at him sideways. "Does this theory start with an 'it might sound crazy, but'?"

"No." He winked, pointed two finger guns, and, in an adopted American accent, said, "No crazy butts here except yours, hot stuff."

Amy tutted. The left side of her face raised in a half-smile.

He dried his hands, then knelt and stroked The Flash's back. He was the same size as he'd been before he went away. But even with him, something seemed off. Something about the eyes? Maybe his head? Whatever it was, Dan couldn't place it.

"The pair of them have been sneaking into Gatsby's house."

"The new neighbour?" Amy's forehead lines returned. "The old guy?"

"Yep. It might sound cra—" he started. Amy rolled her eyes, "—unusual, but I think Gatsby's doing something with them."

"Something?" She folded her arms and moved her weight to one hip.

"Feeding them up or something." No steroid conspiracy theories here. "I saw them climb through his bathroom window earlier today. I went over to ask. He didn't like me bothering him. Shut the door in my face."

"You didn't still have your dressing gown on, did you?" She held the back of her hand to her forehead in mock embarrassment. "Oh God. I know how you like to work in your PJs."

"Of course not." He blew up his cheeks and wiggled his head from side to side. "I was just in my pants."

Amy mimicked his movement and stuck her tongue out.

"Of course, I was properly dressed," he confirmed.

"He dresses very smartly, so even if you were wearing your best, I'm sure he'd have still thought you'd crawled out of a nearby drain." She cocked her head with a proud grin that was both infuriating and sweet.

"Whatever Trevor," he said, pretending not to be deeply scarred by her mega-diss.

"You'll need to keep an eye on them." She began to unpack her bag onto the kitchen table. "We don't want to be overfeeding them. Maybe tomorrow you could go over and have a word with him about it. He shouldn't be giving them treats."

Dan's stomach flipped. He would not be having another awkward bout of human interaction.

"I think I've got it covered," he said, in a way he hoped would fill her with confidence. He didn't say anything to elaborate.

"You could always lock the cat flap. Keep them in with you." Amy chewed the corner of her mouth. "Keep an eye on the old man too. See if you catch him with anyone else's cats."

SMASH FLAP

The next morning, when Dan came down to the kitchen, Catman and The Flash were already sitting patiently by the back door waiting to be let out. He ignored them both. Grabbed a box of Weetabix and shook out a trio.

They began to yowl.

"Shhh," he said, as he turned the kettle on for Amy's coffee.

Their cacophony intensified.

"You're not going out today," he said, then begun milking his 'bix.

A loud bang came from the back door. He turned, startled, poured coconut milk all over the kitchen top.

"Oh heck," he said, reaching for a tea towel and throwing it atop the spillage.

His immediate thought was that the bang had been someone kicking the door. But Catman was standing up, looking through the cat flap with one paw resting on the wooden doorframe. He glanced back at Dan — the look said, 'you're not the boss of me,' — then brought the other paw back and pounded it straight through the clear plastic. The cat flap exploded outwards.

"Woah." Dan dropped the carton. Its contents chugged out onto the floor. He grabbed Catman up. He was like a lead weight.

"What are you doing?" He turned him around. "How did you do that?" Those green emotionless eyes stared back at him, the pupils needle thin slits at their centre. The little hairs on the back of Dan's neck prickled. "What's happening to you?" he whispered.

Beneath his fingers, Catman's body was covered in large pads of hard muscle that Dan was sure hadn't been there before. And he seemed to have grown again overnight. Absurdly so. Almost too big to hold.

He scanned the kitchen floor for The Flash. For a moment, he thought he had escaped through the broken flap until he spotted that ginger tail curling out from under the kitchen table. He ducked and lifted the tablecloth with one hand, struggling to balance Catman in the crook of his arm.

The Flash was crouched low, letting out short yowls like he was trying to speak.

—Yow-yow-yow—

His eyes were wide. Staring directly into Dan's.

"Look what you've done, Catman. You've scared your brother."

He wrestled the beefcake under his arm and tried to reach out to The Flash. "Come on, little man."

At that moment, Catman chose to squirm so violently that Dan lost his grip. The second the black cat's feet touched the floor, he catapulted towards the broken cat flap and squeezed out. And before Dan could stop him, The Flash followed.

He went to stand, banging his head on the underside of the table, before racing for the door. But by the time he had the key in the lock, they had already clambered over the back fence.

He let out an exasperated sigh and planted his hands on his hips. So much for keeping them in today.

MOUSEBANE

D espite The Jester's best efforts, we have escaped. He knows not my strength.

The maned man has taken her. I am sure of it.

We must free her before she is taken to the pit.

Mousebane must not fail.

CAMERA ONE, CAMERA TWO

The cameras arrived by the time the cats returned home that evening.

Dan filled The Flash's bowl first and cornered him there. Removed his red collar and swapped it for the new one with integrated camera. Surprisingly, he didn't put up any sort of fight. His large, intelligent eyes watched as Dan turned the camera on. The circular lens lay flat on his chest, giving him the look of Rose from The Titanic wearing that blue diamond, while Leo drew her like one of his French girls.

The bulky long-life battery pack ran flush around the outside of the collar. Cumbersome, but The Flash looked like he could handle it.

Dan left him in peace with his food and installed the app that came with the camera onto his phone. He logged in and synced it. When near enough, the video capture would come straight to his phone over Bluetooth or WiFi. Currently, the app showed a closeup of glistening meaty chunks in jelly as The Flash ate.

Catman was harder to pin down. He was definitely in the house somewhere. The cat flap barricade Dan had constructed with duct tape and cardboard once they'd both come in for dinner still stood.

He checked the black cat's usual haunts. Top of the sofa. Top of the washing machine. And last, top of the stairs, where two green eyes peered out of the darkness. He tried enticing him down with a felt mouse attached to a piece of fishing line. His own invention, and usually a firm favourite, but today Catman wasn't into it. *'That's the mouse I deserve, but not the mouse I need right now.'*

Dan pretended to ignore him. Busied himself by setting up the Bluetooth boost box at the front of the house. Wanted to cover as much of the road as possible. Especially Gatsby's house.

In the end, Catman came of his own accord while he and Amy sat on the sofa watching TV. He hadn't been paying much attention to what was on. Was more interested in The Flash Show on his phone. It was strangely addictive seeing everything from a cat's view.

Moments before Catman had entered the room, The Flash had visited him at the top of the stairs. It looked like they had been having quite a serious conversation.

Catman hopped up onto the sofa between them and rested a paw on Dan's leg as if to say, *'I am ready'.*

He attached the camera collar. The black lens camouflaged against his chest.

"You're getting big," he said, as he wrapped a thumb and forefinger around Catman's thigh. They no longer touched. "What have you been up to today?"

He ran a hand over his silky fur, wondering how it was possible for a cat to grow so large in such a small amount of time. Smoothing back the fluff on his cheeks, he stared into those mesmerising emerald eyes. A tiny tooth poked down over his bottom lip, making him look like a vampire, or a puma ready to pounce.

Amy paused the TV. "What are you doing?"

"Look." He opened the app on his phone. Passed it to her. He waved into Catman's camera. "Cool, hey?"

Amy looked down at the screen, down at the cat, then down on Dan. "How much were those?"

"Um..."

"Is this what you meant when you said you had it covered?" She leant her head to the side.

"How else am I going to find out what's going on over there? Our cats' lives might be at stake."

"Hm," she said, taking another look at the shot of the side of Dan's face, which Catman had expertly captured. "Have you thought about just asking him?"

Dan blew a long and annoying raspberry to indicate that he hadn't, and wouldn't. "That'd just be weird."

She wiped her face with her sleeve. "You know, I always thought when I married a wannabe rockstar that you'd actually enjoy talking to people."

"Quite the opposite. We musicians sit in our rooms and practice on our own for years. We work only at night. We get jobs making so much noise we can't hear anyone." He grinned. "For me, it's perfect."

"You can't go through life avoiding people, Dan."

"I can try."

She looked again at the view on his phone, then rolled her eyes. "Well, if this is how you want to wind up in jail... Don't come running to me when someone knocks on the door accusing you of being a peeping Tom."

He laughed again. "Peeping Tom — good one."

"What?" She gave him a sideways look.

"Tom." He waggled his eyebrows. "Tom cat."

She tried to hide her smile. "Don't explain my own jokes to me." She looked back at the TV, then winked at him. "You know I'm the pun master."

He wrapped an arm around her as she leant against him and tapped the phone over her shoulder to show her The Flash's cam. The Flash was now under the kitchen table. The top half of the shot was cut off by the red and white chequered line of the tablecloth. In the background was the cat flap, blocked off with card and silver tape.

"Was that like that when I came home?" Amy asked, holding the phone up to get a better look. As she did, Catman sat up and peered at it too. The glow of the screen lit his shadowy features.

"I'm afraid to say it's been like that since this morning." He ruffled Catman's head. "This little bugger smashed it."

"And you somehow forgot to tell me they'd been out all day?" She narrowed her eyes. "You said you'd keep them in."

"I know. I know. But now we've got these," he shook his phone, "we can keep track of them."

"Just make sure the flap's blocked off properly before you go to bed. We don't want anything else sneaking in through the hole."

"Anything else?" said Dan.

"Yeah, I found a gross frog behind the bin." She visibly shuddered. "I thought perhaps Catman had brought it in, but maybe it hopped in on its own."

She turned her head to the television for a moment, then turned back. "Oh, I was going to tell you, you know Vicky?"

He shook his head.

"She owns Crystal."

He shrugged, not sure who either of these people were, or why one would own the other.

"Vicky lives up the road. Blonde. Owns that beautiful white Persian."

"Ah, Pretty Pretty Princess," he said. That was his name for the fluffy white cat that lived in one of the houses nearby. He often saw her in the window shining like a Hollywood starlet with wind machine wafting her fur in slow motion.

"I spoke to her on the way back tonight, and the poor little thing has been missing for a few days. She's very upset. I told her Catman and The Flash had been missing, but they've come back. Do you think they've all been in the same place?"

Gatsby's, thought Dan. The Pretty Pretty Princess could be in his secret underground lab right now being pumped full of steroids. Perhaps she'd turn up soon, ripped like Schwarzenegger in his prime. Perhaps Catman wasn't his first. Perhaps he moved from town to town, under the guise of a feeble old man, unleashing an army of super cats upon the unsuspecting suburbs. Perhaps—

"Dan?"

He shifted in his seat to face her, excitedly taking up one of her hands in both of his. "Did you tell her about Gatsby?"

"I'm not going to start spreading your rumours."

He tapped his chin with one finger and glanced away in thought. "No. Probably best not to tell anyone in case it alerts him." He stared into space for a moment, then returned his focus to the phone to look at The Flash's view. "Hopefully with these, we can figure out what he's up to."

"If he is indeed up to anything. I think you need to calm down a bit, Danny. I don't want you bothering the poor old man. He looks frail enough as it is."

"That's just what he wants you to think." He stood and crossed the room. With one finger, he peeled the curtain back a fraction. The light in Gatsby's upstairs room was on. "A poor, helpless, lonely old man. Everyone knows it's the ones you don't expect."

Amy made an uneasy sound in her throat and resumed her programme.

He returned to the sofa and watched some of it with her. One of those reality shows where a bunch of ridiculously good-looking people swan about on an island. They didn't seem to wear much and spent some of their time snogging or sunning themselves, but most of it arguing.

When it finished, Amy kissed him on the cheek and went to bed. Catman trotted off, too.

He watched an episode of one of his superhero shows, then headed to the kitchen to fix a snack before he started another. Shredded duct tape and cardboard covered the floor. The cold evening air blew through the gaping black hole where the cat flap used to be.

They were out.

MIDNIGHT STROLL

Dan checked the cat-cams. The Flash's view was too dark, so he flicked to Catman's. A glass patio door stood before him, a dim rectangle of dancing light, possibly from a television further into the house, surrounded by darkness. Near black silhouettes of jagged grass rose up from the bottom of the screen. He didn't recognise the house. But then he couldn't see much.

He checked The Flash's feed again. He could now see Catman standing in front of the patio doors, with the faint flickering light behind. The Flash closed in, then cut a right towards a back door with a cat flap.

The view jolted as he entered the house, stepping through onto the chequered lino of a shadowy kitchen.

Gatsby's house? Was there anywhere else they could be? The feed was live, so they were in Bluetooth radius. It had to be one of the houses on either side of his own, or the three adjacent. The cat flap suggested a cat owner, a number of whom lived on the street.

He grabbed a hoody and rushed outside.

The night air was close, damp. Misty coronas of amber light surrounded the street lamps. No one else was out. It wasn't the sort of suburb for midnight walkers.

A slim cycle path ran behind the back gardens of the houses on Gatsby's side of the road. If the cats were in Gatsby's garden, Dan would be able to see them from there.

He jogged to the end of the road and round to the path, temporarily losing the feed as the Bluetooth went out of range.

The path was dark. As he slipped past a pair of bollards topped with reflective blue bicycle icons, he pulled up his hood. A wooden fence, roughly head height, ran along the backs of the gardens to his right. On the left, a shallow ditch, then shadowy woodland.

The path took a meandering route, parallel to the road, through to the nearby industrial estate.

The hairs on the back of his neck prickled. His nervous insides wobbled. It was unusual for him to be out walking alone in the dark. And the open wood to his left gave him the willies.

As he followed the path, he realised that he himself, scurrying in the shadows with a hood over his head, could be quite willie giving. He was probably the scariest thing on the back alley tonight. Which definitely said something about the lack of scary things.

He checked the app. A little icon told him the feed was still coming direct from the camera rather than the boost box. They were close.

The Flash was inside a small kitchen that was laid out similarly to their own. Catman still stood guard outside. Maybe he couldn't fit through the flap.

Dan jumped up to peek over the nearest fence. Beyond it, the patio windows were lit up, and the doors were a different design. Not here then.

He moved further down the path. Pulled himself on tip-toes at the next fence, careful not to shred his musician's fingers on the splintered wood. No lights this time. He checked his phone again. The light of a TV definitely flickered somewhere. This wasn't the house either.

At the next, he jumped up to look again. A quick scan of the garden while in mid-air revealed a pair of dimly lit patio doors and another back door with a cat flap. A patch of impenetrable shadow sat next to the door. Within it, two emerald eyes followed him as he rose and fell.

"Catman," he hissed, his breath coming out in a faint cloud. "Come out."

He rubbed his hands together. Pulled his sleeves down over them before stretching on tiptoes to see over the fence. Lights from the room beyond continued to flicker. The Flash was clearly visible inside, standing atop the kitchen table.

The fence had a gate, so he pulled himself up, leant over, and unlocked it. He got stuck as it swung open and threw him around, flopped over the top like a worm on a stick. The hinges creaked like a wail of distorted feedback in a hushed concert hall. He jumped down. Held it still. Letting out a shaky breath, he crossed the knee-high grass.

His heart beat heavy in his chest. He could no longer see The Flash through the kitchen window.

Suddenly, a bright light flashed on above. He raised a hand to cover his dazzled eyes.

"Oi, what you doing?" came the shout of a man at the window. "Get out of my garden. I'm calling the police."

The cat flap clattered, and Catman and The Flash blasted past either side of his legs. He panicked. A voice with a Scottish accent screamed into his ear as they brushed past. "Run!"

Dan turned and fled, flip-flops clapping like the wings of a bird as he lolloped down the red cycle path.

"Yeah, you better run," shouted the man at the window.

He didn't look back. Couldn't stop running if he tried.

He reached the street that ran perpendicular to his. A car sped past, shaking him from his frantic sprint. He skidded to a halt. Looked left and right. There weren't many cars on the main road. He took a deep breath as his heart slowed.

"Idiot," he growled, and shook his head.

The voice he'd heard hadn't been Gatsby's. It must have been someone else's house.

He had to get back home quickly. If whoever it was phoned the police, it wouldn't be long before they pulled up. He didn't want to be walking the streets when they arrived. But getting home could be difficult. The flip-flop and hoody combo were a dead giveaway, and the house owner might be watching the street.

In an irrational tizzy, he ripped his hoody off, and stuffed it into the wheelie bin closest to the end of the road.

His teeth rattled with the cold.

Calm down. He tried to breathe deeply, the way they taught in the yoga class Amy had taken him to. *Just get home.*

He peered down the street. This late on a school night, it remained unsurprisingly deserted. Parked cars packed the right side of the road. He could probably make it if he stayed low.

He crossed the road. Steadied himself on the first car in a low crouch, and with a half-waddle, half-crawl, headed home. His calves and thighs screamed the whole way: *Walk properly, you maniac. We can't go on. You've neglected leg day for too long.*

As he reached his garden path, blue lights flashed from the main road. He looked back. The lights cut off as the police car cruised up the road. A shark gliding above a coral reef.

His heart stopped. He fumbled for his keys. Hands shaking so badly it sounded like jingle bells. The house key jigged around the keyhole before sinking in. The police pulled up to a house two doors down from Gatsby's. He fell through the door and eased it shut behind him. When he knew he was safe inside, he slumped to the floor.

First thing he did was bury his flip-flops under a pile of shoes on the rack. Light-headed, he lay at the foot of the stairs and strained his ears for anything outside. He had no social connections with the people who lived two doors down from Gatsby. Didn't even know what they looked like. They couldn't know it was him. But that didn't stop the rising nausea.

He'd never had a proper run in with the police before. Not unless you count that time when he was young and he and a few friends had snuck out during a sleepover and been caught moving temporary road signs to block off a main road. They'd been let off with a warning, but even that had been terrifying. A man of his age caught sneaking into gardens wouldn't get away with just a warning. He was looking at a one-way ticket to juvie.

Adult juvie.

Which was prison.

It would be fine. He would just tell them the truth. His cats were in some guy's house. He had footage to prove it. If anything, *that* guy had some explaining to do. Yeah. What was he doing attracting cats?

The butterflies in his stomach calmed. The need to vomit subsided. It would be fine.

He walked into the kitchen, both relieved and furious to find the cats sitting next to their bowls, looking at him expectantly.

"Do you know how much trouble you nearly put me in? No food for you." He wagged his index finger at them. Their heads followed it up and down. Then they began to yowl.

Dan saw red. He grabbed the duct tape from the breakfast bar and, mumbling expletives, wrapped the whole roll vertically around the entire back door.

"Let's see you get out of that."

He left the kitchen. When he passed the front door, he listened once again for voices outside. It took all of his willpower not to peek through the curtains.

It would be fine. He'd laugh about it in the morning — although very privately. Amy was never to know.

Not wanting to wake her, he changed on the landing. Left his clothes on the radiator. Tiptoed into the bedroom. Paused for a moment to listen for her breath. Just knowing she was there calmed his nerves.

He slipped under the sheet. The bed was warm. It was a king-size. Amy had bought the biggest she could find. Her idea being that when he got home late from gigs, he could slide in without waking her. Still, he rolled over and placed a careful hand on her smooth hip, kissed the back of her neck, and closed his eyes.

The knock came just as he'd begun to drift off. For a moment, he ignored it, the sound blending into his dream.

Amy sat up, rigid, and shook him.

"Was that the door? What time is it?"

Instantly awake, as if someone had punched him out of sleep, he looked at his phone. 12:35 a.m. He'd been down less than ten minutes.

"Wait here." It was a struggle to get the words out.

"Dan?" she asked as he left the room.

He pretended not to hear her. Grabbed his trousers and T-shirt. Fumbled them on as he stumbled down the stairs. Another knock came and he almost fell to his death.

A look through the peep-hole sent his stomach squirming. Two tall policemen in high-vis jackets stood at the door. With a deep breath, he undid the latch and eased the door open.

He rubbed his eyes and feigned a yawn. A difficult task when your mind was working at light speed. "Oh? Hello," he said, doing his best to sound surprised, and fixed a confused frown on his face. "Can I help you?"

The policeman on the left studied him for a moment, then nodded at the other.

"May we come in, sir?"

Dan searched for words. They didn't come. He nodded and held the door open. The first officer stepped in and scanned the entrance hall. Dan backed into the living room and they followed.

"Is anyone else in?"

"Just my wife." He felt like he couldn't breathe, like he was wearing an undersized shirt and someone had forced the top button closed on his neck. "She's asleep."

Both policemen stooped as they entered the living room. Their heads snaked to the side like cobras as they passed beneath the door frame, allowing for their tall forms. Before them, Dan felt like a cornered field mouse.

The second officer brought out a piece of black material. "This yours?"

His hoody. Someone must have seen him dump it. But how did they know it was his? He was long past the days of having his name sewn in the collar.

"Uh huh." He moved his tongue over the top of his mouth. The dryness released a click.

"And this?" The other policeman handed over his wallet. It must have been in the hoody pocket. His address was on his driving licence.

"I can explain."

Which he did. The whole truth. They didn't look overly impressed.

"And where are the cameras now?"

"Still on the cats. Still out there somewhere." He hoped that was a lie. Hoped they were hidden somewhere safe in the house. But he didn't want the cameras confiscated. He needed to continue his investigations.

"As soon as they come back, you are to remove the cameras and cease all use of them outside your home."

He nodded.

"I'm sure you're aware there's been a spate of missing pets in this area." The police officer looked at him with hard eyes. "So we have to make sure we follow up every suspicious event. And the way you've behaved tonight is suspicious, to say the least."

He nodded again and looked between them. Their faces remained stern. He'd never had many telling offs as a child, so he didn't know how to react. Where his mother could be bought with sweet apologies, the police just presented a united front of cold indifference. For some reason he felt the need to make a joke, like he needed to be funny to survive this excruciating moment.

Lucky for him, the police weren't like the superheroes on TV, who would likely just punch you until you stopped committing crimes. But, in a way, the weariness in their expressions was almost worse. It said, "You aren't special. We see idiots like you all the time."

And he expected they did.

One studied his notepad before folding it away into a top pocket. He rubbed his face, clearly exhausted. "I expect what you've told us is the truth. You'd have to be stupid to rob someone who lived on your own road. But we're going to be keeping an eye on you."

"I'm sorry. I didn't mean to scare anyone."

The officers headed for the door. He held it open, apologising profusely. Shut it as soon as he possibly could without seeming rude. Took a deep breath. His hands were shaking. It had been fine, though. He wasn't in trouble.

"What was all that about?" Amy sat near the top of the stairs, arms folded across her lap.

Scratch that, he was in big trouble.

He swallowed. Walked up three steps, trying to piece together an excuse. She cocked her head and raised her eyebrows.

"What did you hear?"

"Most of it."

"I was trying to get the boys in. Didn't want them going into Gatsby's house again. I was—"

His throat caught and he stopped. Hung his head. He couldn't take a telling off from her, too.

She reached out and took his hand. "You're a lovely idiot, you know that?" She stroked the back of his hand with her thumb.

"I do know that."

"Thank you for looking out for them." She stood and tugged at his hand. "Come on. It's late. You're going to have to get up real early tomorrow. You're making me a yummy breakfast so that I can forgive you for stalking the neighbours."

He let out a relieved sigh.

She turned and led him back to bed. His whole being relaxed. As long as she thought he was OK, then he was OK. The best thing about being in love with your best friend was how easily they could take the heaviest weight from your shoulders.

Sometimes, nothing else mattered.

OLD BAND STUFF

D an awoke to Amy poking him in the ribs. He smiled as he opened his eyes.

"Get - me - coffee. Get - me - coffee," she said, in time with each prod.

He poked her back in the spot he knew she was most ticklish. She giggled and kicked him until he fell out of bed.

"A big sugar please, Big Sugar," she called as he left the room.

It wasn't every day they got to wake up together. He was often up until at least midnight working on his entertainment agency or playing a gig, so she would let him sleep in. Leaving her in bed while he went downstairs to get them a hot drink reminded him of when they were younger. Back then, before all the stress brought about by living in the material world, they could spend all morning lying in bed. They'd read comics with coffee while a cool breeze blew in through the window. The sun shining, warming their naked legs beneath the sheets.

These days it was almost instinct for him to pick up his phone as soon as he woke up and scan through work emails and gig enquiries. Not that he wanted to. It was just impossible to switch off. He was so intent on making the agency work. His goal was to create a job for Amy so she could leave the one she hated. The grind was addictive.

Today, instead of scrolling through mail, he loaded up the cat-cam app.

Watching them go about their lives was just as compulsive. Like those mind numbing phone games. You didn't gain anything from them, but you couldn't tear your eyes or thumbs away. He was willing to bet that the average productivity per person on the planet had dropped significantly since the release of gaming on phones.

The phone was struggling to connect. And when he entered the kitchen, he realised why. Despite his best efforts with the tape, there was a large cat-shaped hole where he'd covered the flap. Once more, the floor was covered in shreds of silver tape. He gathered them up and binned them.

He looked out the back window at their garden, saw the little shed and the two chair seating area where, in the summer, they'd have breakfast, and refreshed the screen on his phone. Catman's view finally loaded. It showed a pixelated close up of asphalt. White lines stretched out ahead, and cars lined the curb to his right. He was walking in the middle of the road. Dan changed camera to find that The Flash was following close behind — a little too close. The view, on the whole, wasn't pretty.

They crossed onto the pavement.

Someone walked just ahead of them. It was the same awful man he had run into the morning they'd gone into Gatsby's. Tight blue jeans. Wide-armed strut. Over-sized parka. In one hand he held a cat box. Dan couldn't tell if it was occupied.

He bounced along the pavement a few metres ahead, with Catman and The Flash in hot pursuit.

Were they following him? No longer content with cat burglary, had they taken up cat stalking?

He grabbed a notepad from the little tray by the fridge. Jotted down, *'7:45 a.m. - Parkaman - following - cat box?'*

Stuffed the pad in his pocket.

Amy came into the kitchen. She was already dressed for work. "Where's my coffee, Handsome Dan?" She wrapped an arm around his shoulder and looked at the phone. "Misbehaving again?"

"I'm not— oh, you mean the cats. They escaped." He pointed to the back door.

"Blimey, you wrapped the whole thing?" She walked over with her hands on her hips to inspect the tape covered door. "What a mess."

"I got a little overwhelmed last night."

She narrowed her eyes. "Were you mad at them?"

He held his thumb and forefinger a centimetre apart. "I may have been a little annoyed."

She checked the cat flap. "They must have really wanted to get out. Not in someone else's house, are they?"

"No, but," he pointed out the man just ahead of them on the phone screen, "I think they are following this guy. Do you recognise him?"

She peered closely at the phone. "I might have seen him around." She looked up. "Are you sure you aren't being a little overly creative?"

Dan silently pondered the possibility that he was, whilst at the same time, just as silently, quashed the little prick of annoyance at his mother's words coming out of his wife's mouth.

Parkaman stopped. Held a phone to his ear and looked around. The Flash's front paw shot out and pulled Catman away, presumably into cover. The screen was filled with a closeup of white painted brick.

"Are they hiding?" he asked, surprised.

Amy filled her flask with what was left in the coffee pot. Tucked it into her bag.

"Oh, you aren't going now, are you?" He glanced up at the wall clock. "I thought we could read comics or something..."

"I thought, seeing as I was up, I could go now and get my work done for tomorrow. Then, I can have a half day and we could go out for dinner?"

"I'm in," he said, hiding his disappointment with a smile. "I can't wait until the agency is paying enough so you can quit, then we can get off whenever we want."

She smiled at him, though it didn't quite meet her eyes. "Yeah, sure. Me too."

What did that look mean?

She moved to kiss his cheek. He turned. Caught her off guard. Let his lips brush hers. She laughed, then headed for the front door.

"Don't spend all day watching the cats," she called back. "Love you."

The front door closed behind her.

He moved to the breakfast bar with his Weetabix and propped the phone up against a vase filled with drooping flowers. The cats were still watching Parkaman. Perhaps they could smell something nice in his box.

Parkaman gesticulated wildly as he spoke on the phone. The cat box was on the floor by his feet. He kicked it in frustration.

Dan remembered Amy's words about Pretty Pretty Princess going missing. Perhaps there really was a conspiracy afoot. Not one involving an old man drugging cats in a secret laboratory beneath his house, but something more realistic, like chavs in parkas stealing cats away in the night. Had Catman and The Flash uncovered something?

His spoon hovered inches from his mouth as his mind raced. He wasn't being overly creative at all. Yes, he often grasped concepts that weren't exactly tangible and then ran with them. Hey, he was a musician. He'd spent his whole life chasing a dream that was statistically never going to happen. But you couldn't be awesome without being a little creative. Did Mrs. Einstein ever chastise Albert for being too much? Doubtful. No one ever discovered anything without taking their imagination for a spin.

He was on to something. Catman and The Flash were following this guy for a reason.

He rubbed his forehead with the back of the hand still holding the spoon. Soggy cereal splattered down his T-shirt.

"Oops."

He pulled the cloth to his mouth and sucked it before it stained, only managing to make it worse.

Parkaman picked up the cat box and resumed walking. The cats crept out from their hiding place and continued to follow. The screen started to go blocky and judder, then cut out completely. They were out of range.

Bugger. Cat-cam had just been getting interesting.

He opened the mail app on his phone. Twenty-two unread mails. This was a good thing. But today was going to be busy. He had to stop procrastinating.

He microwaved his coffee and jogged up the stairs two at a time.

He glanced through his window. Gatsby was in his front garden, fully suited, booted and hatted, and was shaking a brown paper bag. The old man looked up and down the road, his face sullen. Every few seconds he would open his mouth and say something, but from here on the third floor, Dan couldn't hear.

With one last sad shake, Gatsby headed back to his door. Head down, shoulders slumped, and tottering from side to side. He looked over his shoulder, then disappeared inside.

Dan's heart sank. The poor guy looked so lonely. Maybe he was just looking for a friend.

He took a sip from his coffee, opened his laptop, and checked his emails. There was an enquiry for his band for a wedding in Cannes, which looked exciting. One of the nice parts about his job was being able to visit places you wouldn't otherwise. Dan could imagine the glamour. He looked around his bland, spare room office with a rising bubble of jealousy.

Back in his early teens, long before his parents' divorce, the family had gone on holiday to Fuerteventura. Whilst lounging by the pool in the hot sun, he'd spotted a young, beautiful woman not far into her twenties. A goddess in his eyes. She had been rubbing sun cream into the hairy back of a man older than his dad. He hadn't been able to take his eyes off her, and that night, much to his embarrassment, his dad had brought it up over dinner.

"Saw you looking at that girl with the old geezer today," he'd said, pointing his fork at him, almost in accusation. "You know who he is, right?"

It turned out he was some pop star from the 80s. Some guy whose name Dan hadn't known, and even now, couldn't remember.

"He's got all the money in the world to pay for a woman like that," continued Dad.

At that, his mother had quite rightfully given his father a good, hard flick on the ear, and accused him of having drunk one too many cervezas.

"Ow," he'd said, covering his head with his hands. "I don't mean she's a prostitute — and there's no problem in that if I did... I mean, like, she'll have needs other women don't."

Mum hadn't looked impressed, yet Dad kept digging his own grave.

"She'll want jewellery, yachts. I'm just saying a woman like that wants nice things. If you want a woman like her, you'll need the money to pay for those things."

And there, deeply buried in his father's self-limiting belief, was one of the main reasons why Mum had left him.

Before that particular conversation, Dan had always dreamed of becoming a detective. Sniffing out clues. Unearthing facts. Stopping the bad guys. But as a result of being young and impressionable, and deciding he did in fact 'want a woman like that', he had grabbed a bass... And, without reading the fine print in the contract he was about to make with the four-stringed devil, signed up for a lifetime of unattainable dreams and increasingly crushing disappointments.

Despite what he had been led to believe in his teens and early twenties, the life of a musician was not glamorous. It was not sex, nor was it drugs. And rock 'n' roll, if you wanted to pay the bills, was far from the equation. The life of a musician was fending off micro sleeps on a late-night drive, lugging heavy equipment until your back ached, and getting changed into a creased suit in a drizzly car park, before fighting off drunken wedding guests whose primary aim in life seemed to be to get you to play Mr Brightside so they could passionately scream the wrong words into the faces of their friends whilst simultaneously covering them in overenthusiastic sprays of spit.

It wasn't a bad job. It was often joyous and beautiful. Playing wedding after wedding taught you a lot about people, like how at a basic level everyone was pretty much the same. They all loved their kids and their friends. They all wanted to be happy and to feel safe. They all went nuts for jangly indie songs about jealousy.

He reached out and stroked the strings of his favourite bass, which sat on a stand in the corner sadly collecting dust. A Gibson Thunderbird. It looked absolutely killer, but the neck was a little heavy, so he'd stopped performing with it when he'd started playing weddings. Standing there for the hour long sets with a heavy block of wood around his neck had been wrecking his back.

The guitar must have been worth over £1500, but he'd never had the heart to sell it. He liked having it nearby. It was like some sort of oversized barbarian club.

He looked at the box labelled 'old band stuff' next to it.

At some point his music career had shifted from living the dream, to working to pay for the dream, to putting the dream in a cardboard box and labelling it 'old'.

Eventually, he would go through it. When the pain of failure wasn't so raw. He half-hoped Amy would throw it away herself and save him from having to reopen the old wound.

Once at a big family party, Dan had sat in the living room playing piano while his family and their friends gathered in their large, open-plan kitchen, drinking, eating, talking, and generally having a great time. He didn't want to be with them. The loud talk and social interaction gave him a headache. The lonely calm of the subtly muted piano was an oasis in an arid desert, a quiet, air-conditioned hotel room in an overpopulated, heavily polluted capital.

"Why are you in here playing piano?" His sister had asked when she found him alone. "Everyone's in the kitchen."

It was difficult to explain to her how well she'd answered her own question, so he'd reluctantly joined the party.

That was what it was to give up on a dream. It was leaving your oasis. Leaving behind the thing that made you, you. The thing that made you calm and happy.

But the dream can only fade. It never disappears completely. A dream unfulfilled is like an ex-girlfriend that broke up with you, yet continues to ring every few weeks to check how you are. She might even question whether she should have broken up with you in the first place. You feel the hope spark. You open your heart to her, and then she breaks it all over again.

Whenever he heard a great new album, he'd feel that hope rise, like a siren calling him back to the stage. When one of his cover band's YouTube videos received a few thousand hits, he had to force himself not to get too optimistic that maybe the video would go viral and some record company would whisk him away into superstardom.

Would it have been better to have never tried? To never have dreamed in the first place?

Maybe.

He sifted through the rest of his emails feeling depressed. He'd always wanted to avoid the nine to five grind, but with the agency and the cover band, he was putting in longer hours than anyone else he knew. He'd work until the next meal, the next sleep, or the next gig, then start the process all over again in the hope that something magic would fall from the sky and save him.

THE SQUAT THICKENS

D an always scheduled his gym trip for around midday. It was good to stay active, and he liked to split up the day.

The leisure centre was only a ten-minute walk from the house, and on sunny days like this, he ran.

During his jog, he would often pass quite a few other cats along his road. He had taken note of their usual haunts to make sure they didn't cause trouble for the boys. Didn't want them getting into fights. Although Catman would likely be the one to emerge victorious.

He had names for all of them.

Hitler was usually the first cat he saw. A female. Completely white, save a small black patch on her head that looked like a side parting and another just beneath her nose that looked like a tiny moustache. She would perch on the wall that bordered Gatsby's front lawn, but she wasn't there today.

Then there was The Pretty Pretty Princess, who, according to Amy, was missing.

Another regular was Dimitri, who he liked to think of as Catman's arch nemesis. There had been a few hissing matches between them. Nothing serious. It was a shame they didn't get on. Dimitri was cute. A fluffy brown ball. It would have been nice if they could be friends, but alas, their love for Hitler would forever make them bitter rivals.

He only knew Dimitri's real name because he gave his owner bass lessons every few months. Andrew was a strange cross between a hipster and a posho. A hippo. The first time they had met, Dan had made the mistake of calling him Andy. He had been quickly corrected.

Andrew had lived on the road for a couple of years, having previously owned an artisan cheese and craft beer cafe in Shoreditch.

Whenever Dan saw him, a strange and warm feeling of pride welled up inside. The guy wore the craziest combinations. Pink flamingo T-shirts with brown safari style shorts and pointy brogues. Long-sleeved jumpers, braces, and leggings. Andrew was someone not afraid to be who he truly was. Dan often wished he had the nerve to live like that.

Together they would have made a good band. Andrew the style. Dan the talent.

Every couple of months, Andrew would call him up and invite himself over for a bass-based-space-jam and cheese evening. It was Dan's only proper social engagement outside of the gigs with the band.

Together, they'd get all freaky on the craziest of cheeses and, with Amy happily hidden behind a pair of sound cancelling headphones, record horrific bass noise into his computer, until the early hours of the morning, laughing and generally having a lovely time. If only they saw each other more than a handful of times a year, they might become great friends. Amy kept telling him they should meet up more.

As he jogged, he realised there were no cats in their usual spots today. Was that strange? He slowed, removed the pad he had written his previous note in — all good detectives had notepads — and recorded the fact. Perhaps he was making something of nothing, but it was worth noting down.

He stuffed the pad back into his pocket and looked up just in time to stop himself from walking crotch first into the head of a woman bent at a right angle on the pavement. She had her eye to the viewfinder of a Canon SLR camera and was pointing it directly at the floor.

He stumbled to the side to avoid tripping over her and mumbled something like an apology.

She squinted at him for a moment. Then moved closer.

"Look where you're going much?" she said, pressing a hand to his stomach and giving him a shove.

She then stuffed her hands into the pockets of her knee-length navy coat and looked at him with intelligent eyes. Curly dark hair fell to her shoulders. It had a sort of blue tint to it that matched her coat. She didn't look the sort to start a fight in the middle of the street, and for a moment actually shrunk away while she waited for his reaction.

"It takes two to tango," he replied with a frown. It'd sounded cooler in his head than it did out loud.

He glanced down to where she had been aiming the camera. There was a trail of luminous purple splotches on the pavement. It looked like someone had broken a glow stick.

She didn't say anything else, just watched him and slowly backed away.

He turned and jogged on before she could do anything else weird.

After the short run, he arrived at the leisure centre. The gym wasn't one of those big chains. It was small and worn out, and its free weights section left a lot to be desired, but it was enough for a casual curler like him.

He had enough equipment for a half-decent workout in his shed, but the gym was a welcome break from the monotony of sitting at home answering emails. It also acted as a safe space for some semblance of a social life.

He would nod at the other tough guys in feigned social interaction, as if they knew a secret no one else knew. That was enough fraternising for him outside of Amy and the band.

The lunch rush was always busy, so he aimed to be out just before. More often than not, it was just him and the retirees.

Stood in the weights section were three older ladies, each wearing fingerless gloves. He knew them by name.

"Afternoon ladies," he said with a friendly wave, then headed for the exercise bikes that lined one wall.

"Afternoon, Dan," said Helen, who was spotting a squatting Sandra. Out of the three she'd been rocking the gym the longest and had envy-worthy calves. "Little late today."

"Busy morning. Enjoy." He gave her a nod. She returned it. *We know the secret no one else knows.*

As he began his routine, he couldn't help but overhear the ladies' conversation over the inane pump of the gym radio pop.

"Apparently, another one of hers has disappeared," said Sandra. "It was all she could talk about yesterday at the coffee morning."

"Poor Deirdre," said Helen. "That's the third one in as many weeks. Wonder where they're getting to."

"Serves her right for having so many. She can hardly look after herself, let alone five cats," said Mary, beginning a set of forward lunges. "Well, two now."

Poor Deirdre, whoever Deirdre was.

Did it have anything to do with the disappearance of The Pretty Pretty Princess, and Catman and The Flash's unexplained hiatus? He wondered whether Deirdre lived on his street too.

This was getting serious. How deep did the conspiracy go? Would the other cats appear in a few days overgrown like Catman? Perhaps if he could find the others, he might be able to find out what had happened to him.

"But hers aren't the only ones," continued Mary, between gulps of air.

"Mm." Sandra nodded as Helen helped her remove the barbell from her shoulders. "You know what I heard?" she said, pressing her hands into the small of her back and stretching. "My grandson, Trent, said he and his little friend were playing out on that big field by the industrial estate. Said they saw a large black cat. Said it was The Surrey Puma. You heard of it?"

Mary shook her head. Helen scoffed. Dan's stomach jumped. The Surrey Puma was a local cryptid. A big cat that supposedly roamed the countryside and filled local school children with dreaded fascination. A big *black* cat.

"I reckon he's been at the local pets." Sandra held a straight face.

Mary wrinkled her nose. "The Surrey Puma, what's that?"

"Stupid local legend," said Helen, re-racking Sandra's weights. "Sandra, you don't—"

"Ha, no!" Sandra's face cracked into a smile. "Nearly got you!"

"Oh, top bantz," said Helen, somewhat youthfully.

"Oh, don't say bantz, Helen," said Sandra, rolling her eyes. "If anything, it just makes you look older."

"Whatever."

"Megalolz," added Mary. "Right, on to calf raises."

The women laughed as they got stuck in.

Hmm? Megalolz indeed. But all bantz aside, had Sandra's grandson spotted Catman out near the industrial estate? He sure was getting large enough to mistake for a puma. It hadn't crossed his mind that Catman could be the cause of the other cat's disappearance... Because that thinking was clearly stupid and wrong.

As he cycled, other unanswerable questions came thick and fast. Could Parkaman be the one responsible for the other cat disappearances? If so, how could he prove it? If not, then where were they all? And who was Parkaman? And why had Catman and The Flash been following him? And why had they been in Gatsby's house? And what was there to have for lunch when he got home? Had he run out of oven chips? Was there any of yesterday's quiche left?

The questions just kept coming. A cascading waterfall of mystery. The answers out of reach.

The safest thing to do would be to keep his boys inside for a while. At least until cats stopped going missing.

But that was going to be difficult at the rate he was getting through duct tape.

THE INCIDENT

Three of Dan's questions were answered as soon as he returned home and opened the fridge. No chips. No quiche. Lunch was to be lentils and rice again. That was his go to 'Amy's forgotten to leave me anything' meal. And because she worked nine to five, five days a week, and had herself to worry about, it was a meal he had most days.

Stick lentils and rice in a pan. Boil it. Bosh! Maybe stir in frozen peas and sweetcorn for a soupçon of indulgence. It was very cost effective and you couldn't fault the simplicity. An additional benefit was that particular delicacy could be eaten straight out of the pan with the spoon you used to stir it, giving it five out of five on the minimal washing up scale.

As he filled the kettle ready to boil, he caught a waft of something truly distressing. More so than the smell of lentils and rice. It was as if someone had drunk the entirety of a stagnant pond, held it in for a few days, and then farted directly across his nostrils.

He blew hard through his nose to exorcise the stench. It conjured up images of murky, stagnant water and rotting trees.

He scanned the floor for evidence of cat deposits — the usual suspect — but there were none. He did find a series of muddy little paw prints dotted along the floor leading from the battered cat flap to the cupboard where he kept his protein bars and shakes. Either something inside had gone very bad, grown sentient, and then crawled out through the cat flap, or the cats had left him a little present.

When he opened the cupboard door, he saw the edge was slick with dripping brown mud. The swampy smell intensified, and his stomach lurched. Something rose in his belly. He threw the door shut and took a few deep breaths of cleaner air.

When sure he wasn't going to throw up, he pulled his T-shirt over his nose — the smell of slightly soured milk and weetabix from this morning's breakfast better than that of rotten swamp — and, while facing away from the cupboard, opened the door once more. The stench pressed through his T-shirt, but he endured it by breathing shallow and quick.

Something glistened at the back of the cupboard, lurking behind his tub of protein powder. He pushed the tub aside. Whatever the thing was gave off a soft blue glow, much like a black light. He reached in. His outstretched hand grazed something cold, wet, and slimy. He recoiled. A brown-red mix of dirt and blood clung to his fingers. It smelt of stagnation and rot.

He quickly vomited all over himself.

Everything had already left him by the time he reached the sink. For a few minutes, he leant his forehead against the cold tap and spat stringy dregs into the drain. He took off his T-shirt and placed it in the basin before sticking his head under the tap and washing his mouth out.

He grabbed a roll of kitchen towel and returned to the cupboard. With the paper between his fingers, he reached in again and caught hold of a long, thin appendage. Fighting his squeamish instinct to let go, he pulled the dead creature out. The tendons of his forearms twitched as the thing came into the light. Dangling from one spindly leg between his fingers, a large bulb of a frog pirouetted like an upside-down ballet dancer. Black wrinkles shaped like snakes peppered its dark green skin.

In a fit of disgust, and quite involuntarily, he flung it across the room. He retched as it splatted on the wall and slid down the white kitchen tiles, leaving a long brown skid. In a spasm of panic, he rubbed his fingers on his shorts, trying to grate away the feeling of slimy, bony frog.

This wasn't the first gift the cats had left him. But it was definitely the worst. As it lay there sprawled on the laminate flooring, he noticed the glow again. He moved closer. It was some sort of bioluminescence. Like a jellyfish or glow worm.

He thought to take a picture, but in that moment couldn't find his phone. Probably best to just get rid of it. The smell was unbelievable, and he didn't want it to start permeating the rest of the house.

He picked up an expendable tea towel — an old one covered in drawings of the pupils in his year at infant's school — and scooped up the frog. Gave it a quick tester sniff. Retched again.

Oh God.

With the towel held out in front of him, he ran to the back door, threw it open, and flung the whole disgusting package as hard as he could. The frog came away from the towel, clipped the top of the back fence, and went spinning off into no-man's-land beyond.

He left the tea towel where it lay at the end of the garden. It was a write-off. There was no saving it.

He took a quick look around at the houses that overlooked the garden. No one was in view at the windows, potentially watching him. No twitching curtains. Most people would likely be at work anyway.

With several deep breaths of clean afternoon air, he headed back inside. His appetite for lentils gone entirely.

TIMELINE

D an flicked through the video files that he'd just downloaded from the cloud. The old ladies in the gym had him worried. Cats seemed to be going missing every day, and if he had a lead, then it was his duty to do something about it.

He nibbled a rice cake (about all he could manage after 'the incident') and started with a video time-stamped as 6:55 a.m. These events had occurred before he'd seen the cats stalking Parkaman.

He hit play on both their videos so he could see each viewpoint in unison.

The two ran alongside a corrugated panel covered in peeling red paint. A wall stretched out of view above the camera. The image wasn't clear, but it looked like a warehouse or a shed. The ground was cracked grey tarmac interspersed with patchy areas of powdery brown earth and unhealthy yellow grass.

They turned a corner. Two 4x4s sat parked up ahead. A man was leaning against the nearest one, talking to someone through the window.

It had to be somewhere in the nearby industrial estate. You could get there via the cycle path he had used yesterday.

The jiggling motion of both screens as they ran made his stomach lurch. He tried not to think of slimy green frogs.

They didn't spend long at the warehouse. Just walked around it a few times. Sometimes right up close. Sometimes further away. Something about the old building seemed to interest them. But what?

Perhaps they'd found something they liked to eat around there. Maybe it used to be a fish market. That would be a total pussy magnet.

He picked up his pen, turned his notepad landscape, and drew a line. Placed a dot on the left-hand side and wrote *'6:55 a.m. at warehouse'*.

Next, he skipped forward to the part where they were following Parkaman. It was time-stamped 7:45 a.m. He put another dot roughly halfway along his timeline and noted this down, too.

He followed the videos. Marked what he saw on the timeline. They left the warehouse at 7:15 a.m. First saw Parkaman at 7:26 a.m.

When they spotted him, the cameras shook. They were moving fast. When the image finally steadied, they were behind a mound of brown leaves in the woods, still watching him. He was carrying his cat box along the red cycle path. The door of the box was open.

Parkaman stopped at one garden, stretched on tiptoes, and peered over the fence, just as Dan had the other night. Maybe the best time to peer over fences wasn't in the dark when you thought no one could see you, but in the day when everyone was at work. This guy was a pro.

He looked left and right, checking whether the coast was clear, then twisted the gate latch and entered the garden.

The screen went wild with another flurry of movement as the cats sprinted after him, brown as they scaled the fence, and then green as they leapt down into the garden. The grass was clipped short. Not the same as the garden from last night. A wooden shed sat next to the fence on the right side. A side gate led around to the left.

Parkaman had disappeared. Either the cats had scaled the wrong fence, or he'd used the side gate to come through to the road.

With another burst of speed, and a flash of red brick, they were on the roof with the whole of Walton stretched out before them.

He had to pause the video, not believing what he'd just seen. They had scaled the drainpipe to the top of the house in a matter of seconds.

They remained on the roof for several minutes. He skimmed the video forwards. Another flurry of movement and they were in the middle of the road. The video met up with where he'd tuned in that morning when they were following Parkaman. The cat box he was carrying was now closed.

He thought back to that morning, when he'd seen Gatsby outside with cat treats. Did the video show Parkaman having just stolen Gatsby's cat?

It was time to get the police involved. This was the evidence he needed. Parkaman was clearly the guy they were looking for. But what had he done to Catman to make him grow so large?

He rang 999. When they answered he told them about the footage. Maybe embellished it a little, but of course there was no denying it showed what Parkaman was up to. If you knew what was going on, it was plain to see. They agreed to send someone around to collect the files before the end of the day.

The video files continued to run while he was on the phone.

A car pulled up next to Parkaman and he got in.

Dan skimmed the video forward again. The cats had returned to the warehouse. They were in a shady alley, presumably around the back of the building, framed by stacks of pallets and breeze blocks. To the right, overgrown trees pressed through the gaps in a chicken wire fence.

He paused Catman's video and expanded The Flash's footage to fill his screen. In it, he could see The Flash enter the warehouse through a back door.

The camera fought to expose the darkened interior. It was hard to see, with the only light coming from outside and behind the camera, but he could make out a short, slim room. A line of desks on one side, and shelving on the other. The floor was dusty and covered in litter. At the far end of the room, a beam of light reflected from a crisscross of wires that looked like cages. The beam moved. A torch. Its illumination widened as its bearer came closer. Two pinpricks became visible in the darkness behind the wire, but before he could make out what it was exactly, The Flash had turned and fled.

Dan held his breath. Knowing that this must have happened some hours ago, and that the cats were fine as they had delivered him his froggy present since, did nothing to calm his nerves.

He rewound the footage and paused it. The two shining objects reflecting the light of the torch, and locked behind a cage door, were cat's eyes.

He checked Catman's footage to see if there was a better angle, but it showed something very different. He hadn't followed his brother. Instead, he'd moved closer to the fence.

There was a woman there, in a long navy coat. She looked familiar. She studied Catman from outside the fence. He moved closer. She reached out. In her hand was a small black circle. Her hand came towards his collar. The footage blurred momentarily, and when she took her hand away again, the circle was gone.

She looked up. Catman followed her gaze to show The Flash running out of the warehouse.

A bright flash turned the screen white, and when Catman looked back towards the woods, the woman had disappeared.

He paused the video. Scanned the forest. Scratched his brow. She should have been right there, but she was nowhere to be seen.

"Creepy."

A loud bang from downstairs shook the house, causing an almost painful jolt of nerves to shoot through him. He calmed a little when he realised it was just the front door.

It seemed a little too quick for the police to be here already. There were no deliveries coming, and Amy wouldn't be back for another few hours. No one ever visited in the day, except Jehovah's Witnesses and conservatory salesmen, and neither of them ever knocked so hard.

What if it was the neighbour whose garden he had invaded? What if they'd come to give him a firm talking to? He could just pretend he wasn't in. But what if it *was* the police?

He closed his laptop and jogged down stairs. The door banged again, rattling the chain.

He opened it. A large man in a tight white T-shirt stood on the front step. His head was completely shaven. His arms covered in tattoos. Streaks of colour wrapped up from beneath the collar of his shirt and spiked up his neck.

Probably not a Jehovah's Witness.

"You live here?" The man's head cocked at a menacing angle, his enlarged pecs flexed under his shirt.

"Um... yes, I live, do," Dan stuttered. If this was a conservatory salesman, then Dan was about to spend a lot of money — fascias, guttering, a new front door, solarium spanning the entirety of the garden, the works. "I mean, I live here. How can I help you?"

"Got something for you," he snarled. His head was becoming more and more like a tomato. Large veins popped, embossing the skin under his tattoos.

He reached a hand the size of Dan's face into his back pocket.

Dan's stomach clenched. He took a tentative step back.

Oh God, he thought. He's going to knife me. Right on my doorstep. Poor Amy. She'll come home and find me cold and dead on the front step.

He raised his hands non-threateningly, in an 'I just want to talk' gesture. A defensive stance he'd learnt as a teenage Ju-Jitsu student.

When the man brought his hand back, Dan was surprised to see something he recognised. His previous thoughts of self-preservation were washed away, replaced with a sickening dread. The muscle man on the door step was holding a thick red collar in his hand. It belonged to The Flash.

DAN'S WHAT PALACE?

"Where did you find that?" said Dan, reaching up to take the collar. The man pulled away.

"On your cat, along with this." With his other hand, he fished in another pocket and brought out the camera. His nostrils flared. "You been spying on my bird, mate? Sending your cat round to perv, have ya?" He looked as though he was about to spit on Dan's bare feet.

His toes curled under themselves. Heat bloomed in his cheeks and under his arms. "No, no, no. You've got it all wrong."

"Well, then you better help me get it all right?" The man stepped forward and placed his hand on the door frame. "How did you do it? You been training them to sneak in through people's windows or something?" He was almost a foot taller than Dan and brushed him easily out of the way, then pushed through into the hall, like he was looking for something. "Bet you've got these linked up to your TV. Like some sort of wank palace."

Dan stuttered. "No, I... I haven't." Words wouldn't come. "I don't have a... a what palace?" He followed the man through to the lounge. "Listen. I can explain. Let me explain."

The man strode through their downstairs searching each room. He didn't seem interested in what Dan had to say, but he carried on regardless.

"My cats went into my neighbour's house the other day. You know the old guy who's just moved in?"

"You spying on old men too?" said the man, whirling round, nostrils expanding in disgust. "You're weirder than I thought."

He strode to the stairs, taking them two at a time.

"I didn't make them do it. They just did it. I was trying to monitor their movements. Make sure they weren't getting into trouble. I promise, that's all."

"Unless you can prove it, I'm calling the police, or beating you to a pulp." He drummed his fingers on the wall. "I ain't decided yet." He pointed an accusing finger down at Dan. "Either way, everyone on this street is going to know you're a dirty perv."

"I'm not, I promise." How could he prove his innocence? "I know. I'll show you on my phone. You can see when I downloaded the app for the cameras. I have the receipt for them. They only came yesterday when I saw Catman and The Flash in Gatsby's house."

His hands shook as he patted himself down for his phone.

"What the hell are you on about?"

"Sorry, Catman and The Flash are my cats. And Gatsby is—"

The man raised a hand to silence him. "Show me the app and the receipt."

Dan showed him the app. The Flash cam was still in the guy's meaty hand, so the stream showed a sideways view of Dan's wide eyes and pale face. He didn't like the way his cheeks had sunk, nor the quiver in his bottom lip. He cleared his throat and tried to stand a little straighter.

The man pulled the phone from his hand and studied the app while Dan stood on tiptoes, trying to see the screen. He tapped the app and flicked to Catman's camera.

"You've got another one?" His cue ball eyes fixed on Dan before turning back to the phone.

The view showed Catman's paw stretched out in front of him on some sort of flowery fabric. A bed sheet. A blonde lady sat a foot or two away, dressed only in a towel.

"Ah," said Dan.

The video didn't show the woman's full face, but it did show that The Flash was also there, curled up in her lap. She was absentmindedly stroking his fur, but her attention was not on him. The angle of her chin suggested she was looking away from him at the floor. Lips parted. Was it Vicky? Amy's friend. Pretty Pretty Princess's owner.

"I'm so sorry—" Dan began.

"You're going to delete everything. Where's that laptop?"

"No. I—"

The man drew a head-size fist back. Dan cowered against the wall.

"I'll get it." He passed the man, hunched like a whimpering Igor-shaped mess, and jogged up to the office, where he grabbed the laptop. He couldn't lose all his evidence. Not now he was so close.

He quickly scrolled to the folder to try to make a copy of the files, but the man had followed him to the third floor.

"What are you doing?"

"Uh..."

The man shoved him aside and snatched the laptop away. The videos were still open, and the folder containing everything was all there on view.

"You creepy little bastard." He selected every single file in the folder and hit delete, then opened the recycle bin and removed them for good.

With a violent snap, he clapped the laptop closed, and threw it back at Dan, then held up a fist. "If you saw anything—"

"I swear, I didn't. And anyway, I couldn't have trained them to sneak into your house, even if I wanted to."

The man's jaw tightened. Eyes glared.

"Which I don't. I haven't tried. I've only just got the cameras because of the other cats going missing. I wanted to keep them safe. Let me show you the receipt. Please."

"Go on." The man's shoulders relaxed slightly. He held Dan's phone back towards him, though he still kept it tight in his grip. Reaching up on tiptoes, Dan flicked to the Amazon email.

"See? I've only just got them. I haven't been spying. Honest."

The man turned the phone back around to inspect.

"Alright. Alright." He waved a hand and pushed past Dan to get back downstairs. His anger seemed to have shifted to impatient annoyance.

Dan hurried after him, his curiosity getting the better of him. "Have they been in your house before today?"

The man glanced back. "I bloody hope not," he said, then stepped out through the open front door.

"Hey, my phone?"

The man turned and flung the phone back through the open doorway like a frisbee.

Surprisingly, Dan caught it.

"I better not catch them in my house again," the man said, poking a rigid finger into Dan's chest, "or they'll be coming back through your letterbox. If the wife didn't love cats so bloody much, they'd already be on their way first class."

He dropped The Flash's camera, and without taking his eyes from Dan's, crushed it into the garden path with his heavy Doc Martin boot. He raised a middle finger and stomped away without another word.

Dan collected up the pieces of camera from the floor, trying to process what had just happened. He pressed his cold fingertips to his burning cheeks. His stomach was bloated. He felt like he was going to throw up again.

His first thought was of Amy, and that 'I told you so' that he knew was waiting in the wings. She would be so embarrassed.

Surely people would talk about him after this. He'd be branded a pervert up and down the street. Up and down Walton. Up and down the country.

Mothers would hurry their kids past him on the street. "Don't talk to him sweetheart, he trains his cats to spy on naked ladies and old men."

In this Surrey suburb, gossip spread like the plague.

The muscle man had known exactly which house to come to. That alone said something. At least two homes on the road already knew of his garden invasion. The people at the end of the street, the ones who'd found his wallet in their bin, they would know what he looked like. You can always trust people to have a good nose through a wallet. Despite the long hair on his driving licence, he was easily recognisable. And then the police would have taken the wallet to the guy whose garden he'd invaded. He expected they'd all had a good rummage around through Dan's private wallet stuff.

Was he now the resident psycho? The Boo Radley, dining on raw cat?

He sat down on the porch step and rubbed his face.

He had to prove to everyone that it was Parkaman. Parkaman had taken the cats. Dan was just trying to stop him.

At the light clicking sound of claws on the garden path, he looked up.

"Oh, so you do know where you live then?"

Catman ran past him without acknowledging his existence. The Flash stopped for a moment. His head moved from side to side, almost as if he had never seen Dan before. Then he continued after his brother.

He shut the door and followed them through to the kitchen, fists clenched.

Catman sat by his empty bowl. The Flash by the cupboard where Dan had found the frog. He looked at Dan expectantly. His little orange chest puffed out in pride.

The anger washed away.

"Stop being so ruddy adorable, you." He walked over and patted The Flash on the head. "So it was you who left me that lovely green surprise. I'm sure you guys love them, but I'm not going to lie, frog isn't really my cup of tea."

Catman started yowling. Hungry again.

"It's not dinnertime yet, Billy Beefcake." Dan shook his head. Hands on hips.

The Flash moved closer to his brother and meowed. The pair of them glanced up at Dan, before Catman proceeded to the cupboard where the food was kept, walked his feet up to the handle, and pulled it open. Dan's mouth fell agape as his cat grabbed a new 3kg bag of dry cat food with his jaws and lifted it out onto the floor as if it were nothing.

"Uh, what are you doing?"

Catman ripped the side of the bag open with his teeth, spilling the little pellets over the floor, and began feasting.

The Flash moved over to eat too.

"You're not supposed to do that," he said, moving in to stop them.

Catman glared up at him and hissed. The muscles on either side of his jaw clenched.

"Um." Dan froze, hands raised. Maybe a little snack wasn't out of the question.

He leant back on the breakfast bar and watched them lap it up. They were really going at it, like starved lions feasting on a carcass.

Catman's back muscles rippled beneath his fur as he ate. His increasing size and strength really was abnormal. He must be getting to a record-breaking size now. It couldn't just be the amount of food he was eating. This was something unnatural.

Dan took out his phone and googled *'massive cat growth'*. The results weren't really what he was expecting — and actually pretty disgusting — so he tried a different term. *'Fast cat growth'*. The first link was entitled *'Fastest Way to Grow A Cat'*, which led him to a body building forum populated by meatheads who were trying to get their cats *'proper swole'*.

This wasn't something he had ever considered.

Suggestions included:

-*Tying a weight plate to a cat's harness and letting it run around.*

-*Making it jump higher and higher for treats.*

-*Taking it for runs.*

He looked at the two of them. Both had now finished eating and were staring at him, nonchalantly licking their chops.

Catman really was strong, but how strong was he?

There was only one way to find out.

"Wait here you two," he said, not that he had much choice in the matter if they did, and headed for the attic.

MOUSEBANE

The Princess has been taken. Red Mist now knows my pain. How many more do they need for their barbaric games?

Hello Guys, I Love You

B ack when the boys were young and wanted a bit of outside time, Dan used to stick them in a pair of cat harnesses attached to a long washing line that spanned the length of the garden. This gave them space to burn off all that youthful energy without being able to escape over the fence.

After a short dig through his obnoxiously stuffy attic, he found both harnesses beneath a stack of homemade signs from his and Amy's wedding. They were in with a box of moth-eaten T-shirts sporting his band's logo.

Despite having been in the attic for a few years, both felt sturdy, with good room for adjustment.

He took them downstairs to where the cats lounged under the kitchen radiator, soaking up the warmth. Their eyes followed him as he entered.

He held up the harnesses. Catman backed away against the kitchen cabinet. The Flash remained where he was, allowing Dan to fit his without protest. Once it was on, he yelped at Catman, who reluctantly stepped closer and lay down. With a small amount of difficulty, Dan squeezed him in. Even at the biggest setting, it was tight.

He grabbed a bag of cat treats from the cupboard. Gave it a shake. "Who wants to go weight training?"

Hopefully, they were still hungry. The bag of cat food they'd stolen was still over half full. They began to purr. Rubbing themselves up against his legs and circling him like vultures.

They followed him out to the garden shed. Once upon a time he'd had plans for his own gym, and after convincing Amy of the massive savings they would reap from avoiding membership fees, had bought a barbell with about fifty kilos of weight.

In the end, the shed hadn't been suitable for his workouts. Too cold in the winter. Too hot in the summer. So the plates had been left to become homes for the spiders.

Net loss - £150.

"Time to get some use out of this," he said, as he wiped away the dirt from his custom made 'Dan's Gym' door sign with the bottom of his T-shirt.

It took a few minutes to set the weight plates in size order along the back fence and remove some of the dust and cobwebs. Then he took hold of the lead on Catman's harness, and threaded it through the smallest of the weights, knotting the end so it wouldn't come off. Not much to start, just one kilogram. About a quarter of the weight of your average cat. Like Dan tying eighteen kilograms to himself. He did the same with The Flash's lead, picked up the bag of treats, and headed back towards the house.

He didn't want to be cruel. Just wanted to test a hypothesis. Find out how strong Catman really was, and whether the same was true of The Flash. If not, maybe he could isolate what the difference between them was, and hopefully find out why Catman had changed so drastically.

He took out two treats and held them in his palm. "Come on."

He made that odd, kissy sound that you do when you want a cat to come to you. It doesn't really work, but it's the one you use.

Catman sprinted up the garden, clearly desperate for the treat. His weight plate skimmed along the grass behind him like a smooth stone on a flat green lake. He gobbled up both treats before Dan could even pull his hand away.

The Flash remained motionless.

He shook out two more treats onto his palm. Closed his fist as Catman dived for them. "These are for you, Flashy. Quick, before Catman gets them."

The Flash didn't twitch.

"Ok," he said, relenting under Catman's assault and giving up the treats.

The Flash's eyes thinned to jealous slits.

He gave Catman a little scratch behind the ear. If Catman could lift the 3kg food bag, then dragging 1kg was nothing.

"That seemed a little too easy. Do you want to take it up a notch?"

Catman bounded back down to the end of the garden, having seemingly understood and appearing happy to try.

Dan raised an eyebrow. "Ok?" Then followed.

He untied the first plate and replaced it with a five before returning to the house. As he was walking back, Catman overtook him, with The Flash trotting behind.

He expected to see that both plates had come loose, but instead, Catman had somehow tangled himself up in both leads, dragging his weight and the one tied to The Flash.

Dan untangled them from the leads and handed them both some treats. He couldn't help but laugh. He had been right. Catman was strong. Strong and fast.

But how? What had happened to them during their time away? What had Parkaman done to them?

Maybe he'd just been pumping iron with the rest of their missing pals down the industrial estate. Doing chin ups on railings. Squatting miniature barbells. A puss-in-boot-camp.

He wanted to try more. Needed to know what Catman was capable of. Ten kilograms was the next size up. Assuring himself that he couldn't hurt them, that they wouldn't pull the weight if they didn't want to, he added it to the leash, making the total fifteen. If it was too heavy, they would just have a lie down instead. That's what cats did best.

He took out his phone. Hit record. Maybe he would upload it to the band's YouTube page. Finally get some hits. Catman could be a record breaker or something. World's strongest cat. He could be a viral YouTube sensation.

"Here we have both my cats," he commented. "The black one on the left is attached to fifteen kilograms of weight." He filmed the weight plates up close for proof. "He weighs roughly five..."

He paused. If the average house cat weighed five kilos, then Catman must weigh much more by now.

"... roughly nine kilos. Let's see what he can do."

He returned to the house and poured out a pile of treats. Catman began to jog towards him, but as the lead pulled taut, The Flash yelped. Dan stepped forward, anxious that something had gone wrong and that The Flash was hurt. But no. Catman stopped and returned to his starting position. With a jerk of his head, The Flash lifted his own lead in his mouth and threw it around Catman's neck.

Dan stared. Then frowned. Then smiled. *Wow!*

Then, once again, Catman began to jog towards the pile of treats.

The leash tightened. Lines of sinew stood out on his legs, and his shoulders bulged through the harness. Dan had never seen anything like it. Like a lion or tiger in the wild.

A horrific image flashed through his mind. One of Catman straining so hard on his lead that his skeleton came shooting out of his mouth, leaving an empty bag of furry skin behind. Like something out of an Itchy and Scratchy cartoon.

Each of the plates, including The Flash's, slipped along the grass as Catman pulled. They clanked together as the cats trotted up the garden side by side. Catman pulled all of it. The Flash merely walked with him.

Dan wasn't sure who he was more impressed with. The Flash for giving Catman his weight to pull, or Catman for pulling nearly double his bodyweight.

"Well done, boys." His voice shook ever so slightly.

As they fed on the treats, he gave them both a tentative scratch behind the ears.

How was this possible?

He watched the video back to prove to himself he hadn't gone bonkers. It was all there. The cats. The plates. Catman pulling them without any hesitation. He sent it over to the band WhatsApp group. They all had cats, and the drummer was deep into weight lifting. They would love it.

This was real mutant, superhero territory, but how had it happened? Had Parkaman zapped them with radiation?

Maybe they had other secret abilities. Ones not visible on the surface. A secret healing factor? Super speed? Telepathy?

Dan looked at The Flash, so slim and delicate next to his bro. That had been extraordinarily smart to rope Catman in to help. Maybe something had changed in his brain. Maybe he was psychic. Was he reading Dan's thoughts right now?

They were watching him.

Hello, guys. I love you, he thought in their direction.

A knock on the gate brought him back to reality, and for a moment he almost laughed at the absurd rabbit hole he'd just taken himself down.

Super cats? Idiot.

"Mr Dixon, is that you?"

His heart jumped. He looked from the cats to the weight plates scattered around the lawn to the back garden gate.

"Y-yes. Who is it?"

"Officer Sternberg. We met last night. We knocked at the front but nobody answered."

"Hold on."

He scanned the garden. There was no way he could hide what he was doing, and Catman still had the camera around his neck.

"I've just got to find the key for the padlock."

He loosened the leads tied to the weights. Grabbed a bar out of the shed and lay it by the stack of plates. Hurried to the back gate.

As he fiddled with the latch, he remembered why the police were here. With everything that had happened this afternoon, he'd forgotten he'd phoned them. They were expecting evidence.

He opened the door. Tried a smile. "Sorry, I was just doing a spot of exercise... I expect you guys are here for that evidence I promised."

"We understand you have a lead on the cat disappearances."

"I did." He thought quickly. "But my computer crashed. I seem to have lost all the files."

He didn't want to tell them the truth. Didn't want them talking to the muscular guy from down the road. The files were gone. It made no difference how they'd been lost.

The policemen looked at each other. "You do understand that wasting police time is an offence. You can face up to six months in prison."

He rubbed his sweaty hands on his trousers. "It was Parkama— The man in the parka. It's him that's taking them. I caught him on video taking a cat from across the road."

"OK, Mr Dixon. And aside from the fact he was wearing a parka, can you describe the man?"

"Oh, I don't know, really. I've seen him around a few times. He walks like Liam Gallagher." Dan gave a short circular demonstration, turning his feet in opposite directions, with arms held out like he had sunburn on his ribs.

The policeman, looking less than impressed, held a hand up. "And facially. Did he have a face?"

"Yes." Dan rolled his eyes and wiggled his head from side to side as if to say, 'of course, silly.' "Big globy eyes, beaky nose. Doesn't blink much. He was very rude to the old man across the road, actually."

"Maybe we'll have a word with him." The policeman sighed. "Now, I understand you may be worried about the safety of your pets..." He surveyed the garden behind Dan with a straight lipped look on his face. His brow twitched as he took in the scattered weight plates. "But please just leave this up to us. No more filming. No more evidence gathering. And no more sneaking around in the middle of the night. Understood?"

Dan looked down. Nodded. They turned and left. He closed the gate, then pressed his fingers to his eyes. What must they have thought? Had they known he was lying about the files?

The skies had started to darken. A solitary star twinkled in an otherwise empty sky. He collected up the plates. Could feel the cats watching him as he stacked them by the shed. He glanced over. Their eyes flashed menacingly in the dying light of the day, piercing the gloom like emerald flames, reminding him of those Siamese twins from Lady and The Tramp, and how their eyes glowed when they were ready to cause havoc.

He wished they could speak. Spill the secrets that hid behind those mysterious eyes.

He let out a nervous sigh. Were they dangerous? You could never tell what cats were really thinking. Did they like him? He tried to remember the last time he'd been scratched or bitten. Or a time when he had shouted at them for something, like shredding the arm of the sofa.

Once, when he had been running late for a wedding gig, he had slipped on a pair of smart brogues only to discover a gutted mouse mashed inside. Hadn't known at the time that the dismembered body was actually a lovely little present like the frog they'd brought him. He grimaced at the memory of stringy mouse intestines wrapped around his toes. The grimace quickly faded to a wretched frown as the extent of his past anger returned. He had been livid.

All energy left his body. He sighed, remembering with regret the way he'd roared out of the house to get to work.

If he had left someone a present, and they had reacted in a similar way, would he hold a grudge?

He eyed them in his peripheral vision while he dumped the plates on the floor of the shed. Maybe, from now on, he should keep the bedroom door closed at night, just in case.

He wiped his cobwebby hands on his jeans and, nervously turning his back on them, set the padlock. Knowing they were watching sent a chill up his spine.

Night was coming in fast, and as he fumbled the shed key under the rock where it lived, he aimed the same telepathic thought at them again.

Hello guys, I love you.

MOUSEBANE

The Jester refused the amphibian. He appeared disgusted at the delicacy. Humans are a baffling species. Does he not know the elixir's potential?

We overcame his laughable trials. He is coming to understand our power and, justifiably, he fears it.

Red Mist believes soon we will be able to communicate, and then we will show The Jester what we are truly capable of.

SNOWFLAKES

D an screamed himself awake. The Flash, who had been perched atop his head, leapt off, sprinted across the bed, and dove through the open bedroom door.

He rubbed his face irritably. The tickle of hairs still itching his nose. They weren't supposed to come on to the bed. They hadn't done it in years. And hadn't he shut the door last night?

His temples throbbed. Remnants of the dream still clung to him. He'd been trapped inside a cage, or box, his vision greatly restricted. He couldn't really recall any specifics. It was the feeling that lingered. A sickening mix of fearful anticipation and confusion. A strange paradox of emotion — the desire to be free and home safe with Amy, but also the fear of being released.

Hungry beasts growled outside the prison, and through the small opening in the box, he could see their silhouettes moving with bright light behind. He didn't want the door to be opened. In the strange way you do with dreams, he knew that meant death.

He pulled the cover up to his chin. Bad dreams weren't a rare occurrence. Once every few months, he'd wake in the middle of the night moaning or screaming, body coated in sweat. It had been the same since childhood. His mother had put it down to that "overly creative" side. He put it down to watching *The Exorcist* when he was eleven. Google put it down to stress. But what did Google know?

Amy always knew how to save him from the nightmares — a calming hug, a whispered 'there there' in the dark — but today she was no longer in bed. He checked the clock. 9:10 a.m. She would have already left for work.

He looked up from his pillow. The memories of the faded dream left a residue of bad vibes, like dried white rings of sweat salt on a black T-shirt. A coffee mug sat on the bedside table with a post-it note stuck to the side. *'Be home at 2, be ready to go out - A. XXX'*

He smiled. Even though she wasn't there, Amy always knew how to save him.

It was one of those personalised mugs. Beneath the post-it was a picture of them a few years ago on her birthday. Dan had surprised her with a short trip to Disney Land Paris. She'd always wanted to go. In the picture they were wearing the Mickey and Minnie ears he'd made out of card and black hair bands.

He took a sip. Already cold, but no less welcome.

Going out that evening was a good idea. He owed her a good time. She'd been so understanding the other night when the police had come. And she'd been working hard too. Really hard.

He already had an idea of what she might like. Nothing too fancy. He typed out a to do list on his phone. Didn't want to forget anything.

-Shirt
-Flowers
-Book restaurant
-Wine?
-Taxi???
-Ice cream
-Bath things - face mask, bomb?

That done, he checked his mail to see how much work he had to get through. His thumb hovered for a moment over the cat-cam app. It took a great deal of willpower not to look.

Over breakfast, his resolve waned and he found himself checking in on the boys. Catman's feed showed both him and The Flash scampering around another person's home. He had no idea whose. He and Amy had kept themselves to themselves since they had moved in, so they didn't really know the neighbours. Must be within Bluetooth range, though.

Still, it wasn't his problem. The police were on it.

He left the house and headed for his van. A big white ford permanently filled with band gear.

"Alright man," came a watery voice as he stepped out into the road.

Dan blew air through his teeth. He wasn't really prepared for talking to people this morning.

"Hello Andrew."

"How you doing?" Andrew's well-groomed beard parted around a wide yawn, revealing his previously hidden mouth.

Andrew was slim, like Dan, but sported a rocking Viking-style beard that made Dan's facial failure look prepubescent in comparison. Although it was particularly hot for an autumn day, Andrew wore a large woollen hat that looked like an arthritic Nana had knitted it after four or five decent sherries. Little beads of sweat stood out on his brow. He looked a little pale. A pair of red braces held up some outrageously short purple shorts. His T-shirt read 'Vegan Warrior', which Dan thought a little hypocritical for someone who used to run a cheese shop. It was probably ironic, but would explain why they hadn't had a bass and cheese night in a while.

"Sorry, I'm in a bit of a rush." As he spoke, Dan noticed the heavy bags under Andrew's bloodshot eyes, and immediately jumped to a judgemental conclusion. "You haven't been eating that feta from Marrakech again?"

"Nah, I don't do that stuff anymore, man." He spoke slowly. "I was just going to ask you if you've seen Dimitri. He hasn't been home all week. I'm starting to get really worried."

Dan's stomach fluttered. Another one? He decided to play it cool. "Sorry, not seen him. My boys went away for a couple of days at the start of the week. They're back though."

"It's not like him to stay out overnight. He's been gone since Monday. I did put up a post about it on Facebook. Not had anything back, so thought I'd venture into the real world." He opened up the satchel on his hip and handed Dan a flyer. "Maybe if you see anyone you could show them this?"

'Missing Cat' was stencilled in funky eye-catching graphics that made Dan feel a little embarrassed about the violation of graphic design he still had jamming up his printer. Beneath this was a black and white photo of Dimitri wearing a bow tie. And beneath this, it said, *'Can be a bit scratchy.'*

"Will do," he said looking past Andrew. Every single lamp post up the street had a flyer taped to it. Some had two. "You've been busy." He folded the flyer and stuck it in his pocket. "Have you asked around the road?"

"Yeah, I saw a few people this morning. Don't know if you know that big tattooed guy who lives just up there?" Andrew pointed, but didn't take his eyes from Dan's. Was there something in that look?

He nodded. Jaw tense. "We've met."

Andrew cleared his throat. "Frank's his name, his girlfriend is Vicky. Her cat went missing last week as well."

"Amy mentioned it."

Was he implying something?

A door banged and Dan looked across the road towards the noise.

A light shaking sound and someone saying, "Come on. Come on."

He peered through the windows of his van to the other side of the road. Gatsby, dressed in perfect pinstripe, stood at his gate shaking a bag of cat treats.

Andrew raised his hand to wave. "Good morning, sir."

He crossed the road. Dan followed reluctantly.

Gatsby coughed when he saw them and lowered the treats.

"I was wondering if you've seen my cat." Andrew handed him a flyer.

Gatsby took it in his large, gnarled hand. Looked it up and down. Shook his head. "Nope. Not seen him."

"Are you looking for a cat, too?" Dan nodded at the bag in Gatsby's hand.

The old man looked at him for a moment. His eyes narrowed. Then his face softened.

"You're the boy who came to see me, aren't you? Sorry, I was having a bit of a morning. Before you'd arrived that strange man had been quite rude." He cleared his throat. "Did you find your cats?"

"I did, thank you." Dan tried to smile whilst showing sympathy. "You lost one as well?"

Gatsby nodded. "A tortoiseshell. You know, black with bits of orange." He patted himself down with shaky, clawed hands to indicate patches. Then turned to Andrew. "Where have you looked?"

"I've just started. It looks like a few have gone on the run."

"Hm. How'd you lose 'em? You boys are always in, ain't ya? With your computers, no doubt. I'd understand if you were in there with a woman." He pointed at Dan; his arm didn't straighten fully as if he was throwing a granddad-style mock right hook. "You're not though. Yours goes out the whole day, doesn't she?"

Um, what? Dan cocked his head. Had Gatsby been spying on them? Should he be questioning him on that? Sure, he watched the road too, but that was different. His was 'making sure everyone was safe' neighbourhood watch, not 'creepy spying on your neighbour's wife when she goes out' neighbourhood watch. (Although the muscle man from down the road might beg to differ.)

"Yeah, I work from home, but I do other—" He paused, not really knowing what he did other than work, and worry about the cats, and watch the neighbours. "Stuff."

"Well, if I was you, I'd be careful. A woman like that doesn't just hang around. One day she'll be all yours, snuggled in that nest you've made for you both. The next she'll up and leave ya."

This was the very reason he avoided talking to anyone. Either he or they always embarrassed themselves. Like that time he'd rushed next door to save his screaming neighbours, and they'd been doing it... and oh Jesus... the horror!

"I don't think Amy's going to leave him because he's working too much," said Andrew. Dan looked at him, thankful for the support.

"You'd be surprised," said Gatsby, giving him a strange look. "You should keep a closer eye on your pets."

Dan raised an eyebrow. What did he mean by pets?

Gatsby grunted. "You know what the problem is with you young men these days?" He pointed a finger at them. Wobbled a little on his feet before his other hand gripped the wall to steady himself.

Dan didn't, but expected he was about to find out.

Gatsby squeezed his hand into a fist in front of his reddening face. "You've got all the vigour that young men should, but no reason to get up in the morning. And it festers. You've got no dragons to fight. My boy calls people like you snowflakes. You've got your computer jobs, your internets, your cushy living. You don't know you're alive and you melt at the first sign of any real heat." He pointed at Andrew's vegan shirt and shook his head. "That's exactly what I mean. You're offended by everything, and it's spoilt you."

Gatsby looked at them expecting a reply, the way a racist does after telling you "what we should do with all the immigrants". On the surface wanting your agreement, but secretly willing you to argue.

Dan didn't know what to say, and judging by Andrew's open stare, neither did he. They shared a glance, but their attention snapped back to Gatsby as he started up again, like next door's lawn mower at 7 a.m. on a Sunday.

"My father's dragon was the Nazis. My son—" At this, he looked down at the ground, almost sad. "He has his own. And me, my wife left me with a young son when I was working full time. That quickly made a man out of me. Back in my day, we were carted off to fight before we'd even left school, and before that we'd work our backs sore in the fields."

What was going on? A minute ago they all had a commonality. Cat lovers worried for the safety of their feline friends, but somehow things had turned and Gatsby had gone off like old milk.

"I—" Dan started, hoping to calm the situation.

But Gatsby didn't stop. "We got a taste for life that you kids will never understand. If I was your age I'd be out there looking, but you're not going to do that, are you? Not going to get your pretty, snowy hands dirty."

For a moment there was silence. Dan wished the ground would swallow him. Why did he ever leave the house again?

"But I've got flyers," said Andrew, holding one up.

Gatsby snorted. "You boys will always be boys until you find your dragon to fight. No matter how old you get."

His rheumy eyes caught Dan's and he chuckled. There wasn't much humour in the sound. And with that, using his white-knuckle grip on his garden wall, he turned and headed back up the path to his house.

"Bloody hell," said Andrew, his cheeks a blossoming red above his beard. "Some people."

He raised an eyebrow and looked at Dan for agreement.

"If anything, he's the snowflake. All I asked was 'have you seen my cat' and then he started kicking off on me because I'm a vegan. Carnist dinosaur. They're all the same..."

Andrew seemed to need affirmation, so Dan nodded. "Mm."

"And what was he on about dragons?"

"I think he was being metaphorical."

Despite Gatsby's delivery, and his growing dislike for the man, Dan couldn't help but feel he was onto something. It was true. Sometimes he had no reason to get out of bed in the morning. He had the agency, but it wasn't like he was busting his nuts to make it work. He had no big goal. No dragons to fight. Not since the band had stopped writing their own music.

This wasn't news to him. Gatsby's words had only peeled away a blindfold that he liked to hide behind. He needed a purpose. Something exciting to galvanise him. Something to achieve.

Maybe now he had one.

He made a snap decision. "Andrew, I'm going to show you something, but please don't judge me until I've explained."

Before he could say anything, Dan had taken out his phone and held it up. It showed someone's living room. A TV and a pair of bright red sofas were clearly visible in the shot.

Andrew craned his neck to see. His eyebrows lowered. His lips drew so tightly together that his mouth was fully hidden by his bushy moustache. He looked at Dan, a trace of anger there.

"Why the hell is my living room on your phone?"

BETTER THAN NOT BEING TALKED ABOUT

Dan explained about the camera and Andrew's expression softened. He looked away, nodding as if he was coming to an unknown realisation.

"Do you think they know where Dimitri is?" he asked.

"They might. But there's not much battery on Catman's cam. We should hurry."

Andrew held his hat down as he broke into a run. Dan followed, answers beginning to knit together. His cats had visited Gatsby, Vicky and Frank, and now Andrew, all of whom were cat owners themselves. And all of whom hadn't seen their cats in a few days. Were Catman and The Flash on the hunt for the missing cats?

Inside Andrew's home, the air was thick with the smoky cinnamon smell of incense.

"Catman," Dan called out as they entered the lounge.

The house was spotless, with minimal decoration. On the mantle piece sat a picture of Dimitri in a silver frame. There were two red sofas arranged in an L-shape, facing a retro-looking black and white television. Behind them, the living room opened straight into the kitchen. Dan felt a slight tingle behind his eyes when he spotted a full cat bowl on the laminate floor there.

"Dimitri," called Andrew.

Dan checked his phone. Catman's camera had died.

The light pitter patter of tiny feet crossed the ceiling. His eyes met Andrew's and they hurried to the stairs.

"Sounds like they're in my room."

Dan had to muffle a gasp as they entered. Despite the sleek minimalist look of the downstairs, Andrew's bedroom was a mess. Clothes strewn across the floor. Bass buried under more. And a half-eaten packet of Oreos lay crumbling on the overturned sheet of the unmade bed. On the side table next to the bed were several blister packs of pills. The room had a fusty stench, which would have been much worse had the window not been open.

The centre two slats of the blind were bent in a cat-shape. He crossed the room and drew them up. Looked out to the street. The cats weren't to be seen. Through the jungle of dummy chimneys and television aerials, he could see the industrial estate. Beyond that, the motorway.

"Are they there?" Andrew's voice was light. Eyes wide. Hopeful.

"No," he said. The shortness of the word a muffled gunshot. He wanted to say more to make Andrew feel better, but couldn't think of anything.

Andrew's shoulders sunk.

"The battery on Catman's camera is dead. We won't find them."

"But you've been watching them for the last few days, right? You know where they've been? Perhaps they've seen Dimitri. Can't you check the footage on the cloud or something?"

"I have some of today's footage saved on here." He held up his phone. "But I... lost the rest."

"Lost it?" Andrew narrowed his eyes. Dan sensed doubt.

"Yeah, it was corrupted on my laptop. I had to delete it." He was starting to believe his own lie.

Andrew's nostril lifted questioningly. "But isn't there an SD card in the camera?"

Yes, there was!

If it hadn't been recorded over yet, the footage would still be on there. There was hope. The evidence he needed to nail Parkaman was right there around Catman's neck. He needed that SD card.

Andrew folded his arms as he waited for him to answer.

"There is." He moved to leave, but Andrew side stepped to stand across the doorway.

"Where else have they been?"

Dan didn't want to tell him. Didn't want Andrew and Frank talking about him.

"A few other houses on the street."

Andrew removed his hat. Rubbed his hands across his bald head. "Look, I know they've been to Frank's. I know Crystal is missing, too."

Dan's stomach lurched. They'd already been gossiping. He clenched his fists. Showing Andrew had been a bad move. This was just wasting time. He moved to leave again.

Andrew's face creased into a snarl. "Stop. Why won't you tell me? You think that brute Catman and his little friend have something to do with Dimitri and Crystal going missing, don't you?"

That was out of the blue.

"What are you talking about? They're just cats." He threw his palms to the ceiling.

"Murderers always return to the scene of the crime," Andrew blurted out. He pressed his lips together tightly, then looked down.

Dan glared at him, but couldn't hold the stare. That sense of foreboding he'd felt after last night's training session returned. He had almost come to terms with the idea of having super cats, but not super villains. He pointed a shaking finger at Andrew. His lips parted, but there was no way to explain why Catman and The Flash had been following the missing cats around.

He had to find them. Retrieve the SD card before the footage was lost, and before Frank told everyone else in the road. What would Amy say if she found out the whole road thought her husband was some crazy cat controlling voyeur?

Andrew, powerless to stop him, moved aside as Dan strode from the bedroom. A faint whine emitted from his throat. He clearly wanted to say something as he followed Dan downstairs.

"Look, man, I want to give you the benefit of the doubt, but people are talking."

His chest tightened. People? As in, not just Frank. People that talked quickly became angry mobs that accused. Came round with pitchforks. Burnt you at the stake.

"Dude!" said Dan, raising his palms in a 'what gives' gesture, hoping to remind Andrew of the entirety of their bass and cheese relationship, and also express his disbelief at Andrew's distrust with a single word.

Andrew appeared to get it.

"Sorry," he said. "I know you're cool and everything, but you have to admit it's weird." He stepped back. "Will you just call me when you get the SD card?"

"I will."

Andrew glanced up and down the quiet street, and without another word, shut the door.

The Warehouse

L eetwood Industrial Estate had been there for most of Dan's life. A sprawling mass of warehouses. Most still operating, but a few abandoned and fallen into disrepair.

It took almost twenty minutes for him to find the hulking red building that he had seen on the cat-cam.

To the truck drivers that passed, kicking up dust, he must have looked strange walking up and down the dead ends of the estate. Back and forth. Back and forth. Eventually finding the right building, tucked away in a corner furthest from his street.

The warehouse stood in an overgrown lot. A high chain-link fence topped with nasty looking barbed wire surrounded it. Ragged plastic bags and other wind-carried fodder hung from the barbs like torn pennants. Out back, the fence bordered a small forest. The motorway hummed beyond that.

To the right stretched a large area of open wasteland. Sandy soil broke the green in patches where grass would never grow. It had once been land-fill, and Dan and his friends used to play there as kids, jumping the strange humps and bumps on their bikes. The undulating ground made an excellent stunt track. Many times he had limped home after mangling his front tyre on one of the patches of concrete that jutted up from beneath the ground. His mother regularly told him that if he ever came crawling home impaled by rebar, she would not drive him to the hospital.

There had been a strange vibration that would conduct through the handlebars of his bike and into his hands, as if the very ground there were emitting strange electrical signals. He could feel it again now, very faint, coming through the links of the fence into his fingers, like the weird buzz you sometimes receive when you touch a laptop or phone on charge.

He could remember this warehouse then, but the building had clearly been unoccupied for several years. Many of the windows that circled the roof were smashed, and the cracked red paint had peeled back, revealing dirty grey corrugation beneath.

Most of the industrial traffic would never come around this way, so the warehouse was secluded and quiet. The drone of the motorway added to the eerie, isolated atmosphere.

A plastic bag drifted like tumbleweed across the lot. A cold shiver ran up his spine.

Inside, tyre tracks criss-crossed the dirt, originating from a large gate that rolled open on a small worn-out tyre. The tracks suggested the place wasn't as abandoned as it looked. The gate sat parallel to the long wall of the warehouse and perpendicular to the fence where he stood. It was chained shut with a padlock. From here, he couldn't see any other way of getting through without bolt cutters. He scanned the perimeter. Maybe there was somewhere the fence had broken or been cut by someone else.

He skirted around towards the field, lifting different parts of the fence to see if there were any gaps at the bottom. All the while, the strange buzz from the metal tingled his fingers.

Out of the corner of his eye, he spotted movement. At first he thought it a large black bin bag blowing in the wind, but as it moved again, its shape became more apparent. Catman, his black coat terrible camouflage against the red warehouse, crept towards a closed door.

Even from this distance, Dan could see he had grown again, coming closer to the size of a puma. He spotted The Flash skulking a little further ahead, almost invisible against the red paint. He looked like a kitten compared to his brother.

"Hey!" He shook the fence.

They stopped dead. Like creepy animatronics, their heads swivelled towards him. Even in the daylight, their green eyes glowed. Catman hissed.

"Hey?" Dan repeated, shoulders dropping. "Come on, guys."

Neither moved.

He shook the fence again to see if it came away at the bottom. Despite its age, it still looked very secure.

"I've got food!" That usually got them running. "Chicken!" He didn't, but they didn't know that. Or did they? *I've definitely got chicken,* he beamed telepathically.

A few awkward seconds passed. It looked almost as if they thought he'd forget they were there and leave if they just stayed still long enough.

"I can see you." He wiggled his fingers through the fence. "I'm not going anywhere until you come out."

Before they could respond, a door flew open at the side of the warehouse. It crashed against the wall. A man wearing a black tracksuit with the hood up lunged through and looked around. The cats scattered. They moved so fast Dan lost track of them completely.

"Oi mate," he shouted when he spotted Dan, then strutted over briskly with arms flapping at his side. He had a wobbly, chunky look about him, like sand stuffed into a misshapen sock.

He pointed two fingers at Dan as if they were a gun, his arm held high, and made his way closer to the fence, stopping just on the other side.

"Oi mate," he said again, his red face screwed into a grimace. "Who you callin' a chicken, you mug?" He glared through the fence.

"Um, sorry," Dan replied, his voice coming out uncontrollably high and uncharacteristically plummy. His mouth dried as he tried to speak. "Sorry, I saw my cat on the other side of the fence. I was trying to get him over here."

Hoodyman shook his head, snorted, and spat something thick into the dust at Dan's feet.

He retched. Couldn't help it. Hoodyman turned to inspect the warehouse, then gripped his side of the fence. The warm chip fat smell of greasy body odour crossed the threshold.

"No cats in here, mate." Hoodyman's bottom lip drew tightly over his teeth. "Got that?"

Dan nodded. "That is got." Then his mouth ran away with itself. "Well, no, actually, my cats were in there." He pointed tentatively, wrinkling his nose. "Just by the warehouse a second ago. Would I be able to come in and get them... maybe, perhaps, possibly, please?"

Hoodyman turned towards the warehouse again. When he finally looked back, his face had softened into a smile.

"Wait there," he said with a wink. "I'll come round and we can both look for them together."

Great. Finally, some luck.

Hoodyman paused for a moment, one hand gripping the fence. "Actually mate, come and meet me by the gate. I'll get it open."

He made his way towards the gate through the centre of the lot, and Dan followed around the outside. Hoodyman took out a mobile phone, tapped the screen, and held it to his ear. He spoke, but from where he stood several feet away from the fence, Dan couldn't hear the words.

Something about this was off. He started to sweat.

Hoodyman noticed him slow. Gave a thumbs up. Pointed once more at the gate and made a walking motion with his two fingers to indicate Dan keep going.

"I'll get the chain off for ya, mate." His voice echoed across the lot.

In the distance, Dan could hear a truck shifting gear and moving away.

He drew closer as Hoodyman unlocked the padlock and unravelled the heavy chain, then wrenched the gate open with a screech.

The warehouse door opened again. Another man exited and headed towards the gate. He was slimmer, wiry. Wore tight blue jeans, a grey and pink striped polo neck shirt, a peaked cap. He looked familiar.

They both stepped through the gate and headed in Dan's direction.

"You know what? I've changed my mind," he said, recognising the man in the polo shirt. He looked different without his trademark parka. This wasn't a good idea. Caught inside a barbed wire fence with these two was not the way he wanted to spend his afternoon. "I'll just wait for them at home. Don't you worry yourselves."

The dirt crunched beneath their feet as they broke into a run.

He turned and ran, sprinting away across the cracked tarmac towards the open field.

Despite all his efforts at the gym, he had never been a fast runner, and Parkaman, with his long legs, was gaining. The only hope was to get to the forest. Lose them there. Dense vegetation covered the ground. He'd spent long summer holidays in amongst those trees playing manhunt with friends. There was always somewhere to hide.

He skirted the corner of the fence. Sprinted past the spot where he had stood shouting at the cats moments before. He was moving too fast over the uneven ground to risk a look back to see if the men were giving chase.

The flat tarmac ended, giving way to the hazardous moguls of earth that marked the start of the landfill, and he nearly lost his balance. His ankle bent awkwardly in a small ditch, shooting pain up his shin.

He pushed off the fence, managing to keep himself upright. Stole another glimpse back. Parkaman had already turned the corner.

His knees quivered, as he raced across the hard, bumpy ground. His ankle ached. He'd twisted it.

How could he outrun them now?

He launched into the wood where soft mulch muffled his footsteps. Branches whipped across his face.

"Oi. Stop."

Unsurprisingly, he did not.

A glance back told him they still hadn't entered the woods. He abruptly changed course. Threw himself into a bramble bush, landing on his back hard. Narrowly missed a faded polythene bag filled with old, broken beer bottles and cans. His bottom lip caught between his teeth as he landed and his mouth filled with the warm taste of blood.

At least he was hidden.

His heart thumped as if a living thing was burrowing out of him. He held his breath to try to slow it, and to hear what was going on around him.

Thorns dug deeply into his skin through his T-shirt. Why did he have to pick this particular bush to hide in? Every nerve was on fire, torn between flight or fight. Fight was looking all too probable. He'd never been in a real fight before. Sparring in Ju-Jitsu when he was younger didn't count.

He accepted the fact that he was going to get hurt. Pictured Amy's face. Would they be lenient if he gave himself up? If he told them he had a wife? Someone to miss him if he didn't turn up later. They might let him go. This certainly hadn't been on his to do list for the day next to ice cream and wine. If he survived, he'd give her the best night out she'd ever had.

Fallen leaves rustled and sticks snapped as one of the men entered the forest. They stopped, and it went quiet. Dan couldn't see him, but he could picture him surveying the woods, locking eyes directly on the bush where he lay, perhaps seeing a scrap of clothing or a shoe still on show. He squeezed his eyes shut as if that would make him invisible.

"What's the matter?" Parkaman. His voice was slow and drawn out. The auditory equivalent of an eel slinking out from a dark watery hole.

"Didn't want to find your cats?"

He tried to picture where Parkaman was. The image in his mind suggested he was close.

"I know you're in here. Just come out. I'll help you find your little pussies." A snigger.

That did sound reasonable. Perhaps he was overreacting? Maybe Parkaman genuinely wanted to help him find the cats. Maybe he was a cat tracker and knew how best to locate them? That's why he'd been skulking about the street for the last few weeks. He was doing the same as Dan.

But then, nice people never used the 'p' word when referring to cats, not out loud.

And another 'but then' — and this was a big 'but then' — people don't tend to give chase when you run away from them unless they have bad intentions for you. They tend to just watch you go and leave you to your running off.

He couldn't hear Hoodyman. Perhaps he'd given up altogether. He hadn't looked particularly spritely.

He shuffled hoping to get a better view. Long thorns dragged across his back. He bit the corner of his mouth to stop himself from crying out. Through the brambles, he could now see Parkaman's thin, blue jeans.

"There you are." Came an exhausted voice from the other side of the brambles: Hoodyman. He must have come into the woods from a different angle. He gripped a small penknife.

"Get him," said Parkaman.

Dan jumped to his feet. Hoodyman was two arm lengths away. He tried to pass, but the guy mirrored his every move, blocking off all escape.

"You know what, fellas," he said, shuffling from side to side like a crab to avoid them with eyes fixed on the knife. "It's OK. Really. I don't need to find my cats anymore. I'm sure they've just gone home. I can go and wait for them there."

He pretended to look at his watch. Jabbed a thumb over his shoulder back towards home.

"Actually, my wife is probably waiting for me. She knows I'm here... by this warehouse for, um... jogging... reasons. She'll be expecting me back."

Parkaman shook his head. "Nope." A cold smile crept onto his gaunt, almost yellow, face. He drew closer. "Didn't I tell you to keep your nose out of things that don't concern you?"

"What are you going to do?" said Dan, raising his hands in his 'I just want to talk' stance. "Please, don't hurt me."

Parkaman grabbed his raised fist and turned him around to face Hoodyman, pinning his arm behind his back. Splinters of pain flared in his shoulder. Hoodyman tucked his little knife in at his side ready to thrust it forward. It glinted like a mirror in the light through the trees. Somehow, it being so small made it all the more threatening. A knife like that took a while to kill you.

He held his breath. Didn't want to close his eyes. Looked everywhere, breathing fast, frantic for a way out. His knees buckled beneath him, but Parkaman held him up as Hoodyman crept closer with that knife.

A harsh hiss came from somewhere close by, followed by another deeper one that was more like a growl. Hoodyman hesitated and looked around the thigh-high vegetation that surrounded them.

Parkaman's grip loosened on his arms.

"Was that... a snake?" said Hoodyman. "I fucking 'ate snakes."

"Na! You don't get snakes in this country." Parkaman tightened his grip once more. "Just do him. He saw us with the cats. Martin'll—"

A silent black shadow suddenly flew from the bushes to their left and knocked Hoodyman to the ground. The shape disappeared back into the undergrowth.

Parkaman let go of his arm. "What the hell was that?"

Hoodyman groaned as he got up. "Looked like a—"

The shape reemerged, slipping quickly through the ferns that surrounded them, lunging for Parkaman before Dan lost sight of it again. Could it be...?

Parkaman gasped and went down with an audible thump.

"Leeroy?" Hoodyman's voice rose.

"My leg," shrieked Parkaman. He sat up and raised a blood covered hand. What little colour he had in his cheeks drained fully.

Dan took his chance and bolted.

"Stop him," he heard Hoodyman shout, but he was already gone.

As he sprinted onto the dry, patchy earth of the field, two blurs — one orange and one black — converged on his position like star fighters returning to the mothership. Catman and The Flash ran at his side.

"Yes boys."

Elation filled him. He punched the air like a cheesy eighties rock star, the fear completely blown away with the cool air rushing past his face.

The cats pulled ahead of him, but only slightly, as they bound with ease across the uneven ground. It was clear that they could have run faster. He did his best to keep up. The rush was intense.

He glanced back. Smiled. Couldn't stop smiling. The two men weren't chasing. Catman had seen to that.

"Wait," he panted as they reached the path back to his street. His lungs were on fire. He leant his forearms on his knees and caught his breath.

The boys stopped and returned.

What had just happened? He'd been so close to being mincemeat and Catman had saved him.

They gazed up at him. He sensed disappointment in their eyes. Disappointment at his feeble attempt at running? Or at the fact that he'd allowed himself to get into such a ridiculous mess in the first place?

"I'm sorry, guys. Some owner I am. I really got myself into a pickle back there, and if it wasn't for you..." He grimaced at the thought, then rolled his eyes. "I mean, you can't understand me, so why am I even talking to you?"

Catman sprinted away. Back up towards the far end of the path. There, he scanned the vicinity, as if keeping lookout while Dan caught his breath.

The Flash came to him and licked a deep thorn wound on his shin that was visible through his torn joggers. A mixture of blood and mud had run a rusty path down his leg. Dan knelt and ruffled his fur before pulling him close.

"Thank you," he whispered.

Catman trotted back, apparently satisfied they weren't being chased. He wrestled his way into Dan's arms beside his brother. Dan lay his hands on the nape of their necks and looked into their eyes.

"Thank you," he said again, trying to simultaneously push out the word with his mind and hold in the tears of relief that were starting to fill his eyes. He hoped they understood what they had done for him.

"I wish you could tell me what's happening to you."

He sat down and leant against the fence. His back ached. Stinging lines crisscrossed it from the brambles. He inspected his legs. Several cuts laced his shins and calves, and his trousers were shredded from the knee down. He'd come away relatively unscathed.

Despite the lack of physical harm, his hands were shaking. He felt heavy. Pressed into the earth as the events of the last few days returned heavy on his shoulders. It was suddenly all too much, and right then, alone on the path, he just wanted to curl up and cry until Parkaman and Frank and the police didn't mean anything anymore.

But he held it in.

He looked left to right. Very aware that someone might see him. A muddy thirty-something-year-old man crying alone on the cycle path. The gossip would burn from both ends of the street. From one, a creepy stalker garden invader, and the other, a mud-covered alleyway dweller. Or, perhaps worst of all, an emotion expresser.

"How am I going to tell Amy about this?"

Should he tell Amy about this?

He could just about handle the stress on his own, but the addition of her knowing, of her worrying about him, would be too much. He couldn't cope with both.

Calling the police was out of the question. After the last two nights, they wouldn't take him seriously. He could imagine the conversation: "I was chased into a wood by two men, but it's OK my cat beat them up. I am unharmed, but my trousers are ruined, and I have a few scratches where I threw myself into a bramble bush."

"Sure sir, we'll send someone over immediately with a sewing kit and a plaster. What's the address? Number 2, Stop-wasting-police-time Avenue?"

The Flash gazed up at him with those mysterious unblinking eyes.

"What were you doing there in the first place?" Their keenness to make sure he was safe was adorable. "Let's go get something tasty to eat. You've earnt it. I said chicken, didn't I?"

Their eyes lit up, and together the two cats skipped off down the path towards home. He followed.

As he walked, he saw Dimitri's face plastered on every lamp post, reminding him that he said he'd text Andrew.

He took out his phone and was surprised by the number of notifications that covered his screen. He scrolled down. Most were from the band's YouTube and Facebook pages. The top one read, *"Just tried this with my cat. He couldn't even pull the 1kgs."*

He scrolled through to see more of the same. Some nice comments, as well as a variety of others.

"Faaaake, this ain't real people."

"Guy talking sounds like a fag."

Classic YouTube.

He opened up the band's YouTube account as he walked. A new video had been posted on the channel entitled, *'World's Strongest Cat'*. Paul must have uploaded the video of their gym session in the garden. It already had over forty thousand views.

He felt that familiar twinge of hope. The energising feeling he got whenever one of the band's videos started to make waves. Like a stream of excitement running down his back, into his limbs making his fingers twitch and his toes wiggle.

Maybe it would go viral. Maybe thousands of people would flood to their channel to check out the band. Then Franky Sharp of Sharp Records would be in touch with the record contract ready to make every one of his wildest dreams come true. He could stop answering emails and stressing about weddings for a living, and start doing what he'd always dreamed of.

Amy could leave her job.

He texted Andrew.

'Found Catman n Flash. Any luck with Dimitri? Going to check out footage on Catman's SD card. Will tell you what I find.'

Catman's new size and The Flash's strange behaviour was definitely mysterious, and, near death moments aside, something magical seemed to be happening.

He couldn't wait to see where it took him.

Mousebane

The Jester has also found the pit. He is more resourceful than we gave him credit for. Granted, he was nearly killed, but perhaps he may be of some use.

Tonight, we return.

Tonight, we fight.

MEMORIES

Dan didn't let himself get comfortable at home. Knew that if he stopped for a minute the gravity of the situation he'd barely escaped would hit him and he wouldn't be able to do anything.

He kept thinking of Amy. Of her reaction if he'd... He swallowed. It didn't bear thinking about.

It was stupid, but the events at the warehouse made him all the more determined to show her a good time. They had each other. That was all that mattered. And she deserved better than what he'd been giving her.

He grabbed his keys and headed to Tesco. She was due back in a couple of hours; time was running out.

The security guard gave his ripped and mud stained trousers a long once over as Dan collected a basket.

He felt jittery. Not just because he'd nearly been stabbed. He'd pressed those almost tectonic jitters down deep beneath his crust, where perhaps one day they would erupt as some volcanic mental breakdown.

The current anxiety was caused by the shops. He was always worried he might spot someone he knew and have to talk. He knew he looked bad, so readied an excuse. Trousers ripped? Blood clotting on his leg? Hair like a bird's nest? Obviously, a gardening accident.

It was never a good idea to enter a supermarket without prepped small talk just in case he bumped into someone he half knew, so he had his three favourites ready.

That weather, hey?

How's -insert relative name here- *doing? (Default to your mum.)*

Have you seen the price of -insert nearby product that seems expensive here-*?*

One of his deepest fears was seeing someone and then having to have that awful "we need to stop meeting like this" conversation as they repeatedly crossed paths up and down the aisles.

Usually, when he saw someone he knew, he'd hide, or pretend he was too interested in whatever was in front of him to notice them, hoping that they would do the right thing and jog on.

Once home, supermarket and near murder survived, he showered. Stinging points all across his back lit up like fires as the hot water washed away the blood and mud. His thighs burned from the run, but he felt somewhat renewed.

As he dried off, he inspected his T-shirt. The back was covered in little tears and smears of blood. He put his PJs back on to give his wounds time to heal, not wanting to stain his smart clothes before dinner.

He hacked the cooked chicken he'd bought in half and split it between the two cat bowls. Once again, Catman lunged in, shoving him out of the way.

While Catman ate, Dan removed the camera from his collar. He was getting a little big for the collar, so Dan adjusted it as far as it went. He set his laptop up on the counter and opened the SD slot in the back of the camera.

Empty. The memory card was gone.

He let his head drop to the worktop and banged his fist so hard that the vase of wilted flowers jumped at the other end. He'd nearly died, and what did he have to show for it.

Could it have fallen out? Did Frank have it? Would he have taken it and left Catman's camera around his neck?

He glanced down at the cats, who had already finished eating, rubbed his fingers over his tired eyes, and decided to try something both impossible and stupid.

He pressed two fingers to his temple and squinted at The Flash. Pushed with every ounce of his brain, if that was even a thing... *Where is the SD card? And why is Catman so stupidly big? Am I a complete idiot for doing this? I'm glad no one is watching.*

The Flash glanced up at him as if he'd spoken, then leapt up onto the breakfast bar. Dan leant back on his chair. Uh, *did you hear that*?

The Flash bumped his forehead in the way cats do when they give affection. But on contact, a painful feedback-like buzz filled his ears and his forehead tingled with that same sensation you get when you accidentally snort up a load of pool water. Suddenly, it was as if he could see through The Flash's eyes. He briefly saw a close-up of his own face before his view changed to something else.

The sensation was alien. His senses were enhanced, but beyond his ability to process, like watching a 4k video on an old cathode TV. He could feel more going on around him than he could comprehend. More sounds. More colours. More smells.

Above, sunlight splashed through swaying branches. He was standing in a dark alley, with the warehouse on his left, the chain-link fence on his right. It was the moment he'd seen in the video. On the other side of the fence stood the woman in the dark blue coat. Seeing her like this reminded Dan of how he knew her. She had been the woman he'd bumped into on the street. The one taking pictures of the glowing stains on the pavement.

A few paces behind her was a man. Shorter than her. Slightly hunched. Dressed in chinos and a white coat. He'd been out of shot before. He rubbed his hands together nervously. Glancing around as if he didn't want to be there. Keeping watch while the woman tried to coax Catman closer.

Was this a memory? Was he hallucinating? He wanted to move away, but it felt as if his body was not his own, as if he were in some sort of VR simulator.

The vision continued as The Flash entered the warehouse through the door at the back. The room was dark, but he could sense the presence of someone coming towards the doorway up ahead, almost like he could see them through the wall. The torch flickered just as it had in the video he'd seen, and this time he could clearly see the two pinpricks of light in the cage. They were eyes, wide and afraid, trapped behind the door of a locked cat box. It was Dimitri.

The sound of keys jangling dragged him away from the warehouse and back to his own lesser senses. He felt a strange sucking sensation in his ears. Then he was back in the kitchen. Fur tickled his forehead as The Flash leapt off the counter and onto the floor.

The front door opened. Keys dropped to the floor.

The room span around him. His breathing felt shallow.

"Bugger. Dan, I'm back. Can you help me with the shopping?"

Amy was home. Like a whirlwind, she entered. Several bags of groceries wrapped around her arms. The fizzing hiss of the plastic was almost too much for him to bear as she dropped them to the floor in front of the fridge. "Sorry I'm a bit late. Needed to get some things."

She huffed and rolled her eyes when she saw him.

"You're still in your pyjamas?" She shook off her shoes, flinging them behind her. "We're supposed to be going out. What have you been doing all day?"

He couldn't really hear her. Couldn't really see her. He blinked several times, unable to compute what had just happened. His whole body felt slow and heavy.

"Are you alright?" She stepped closer and touched his arm.

Dizziness overcame him, and he slipped from his stool.

Her mouth moved, her words coming out as a muted hum. She managed to grab him before he hit the ground.

"I'm OK," he said, hoping his voice didn't waver. It sounded strange, like it was coming from another room.

"Are you dizzy? You didn't work through lunch again, did you?"

He shook his head. Not a lie. He hadn't been working. He'd been fleeing death. "I don't know what happened."

The room stopped spinning and the achy tingle in his head melted rapidly away to nothing.

She steadied him on his stool. Then grabbed a loaf from the bread bin and slathered a thick slice with a dense coat of peanut butter. "Eat this now." She handed it to him. "Oh honey, you're shaking."

He took a bite. It helped.

"I'm OK — I promise."

Her concerned look shocked him back to reality. He scratched the back of his head. She would never believe what had just happened. He couldn't believe it himself, let alone understand it. Were those The Flash's memories he'd been reliving? Or had the events of the day just got to him?

She was right, he often got a bit faint when he hadn't eaten; he didn't have much in the way of reserves. Had it just been a stress induced daydream?

He looked around. Catman and The Flash were watching him and Amy from the other side of the room, curious expressions on their little faces. Amy followed his gaze.

He cleared his throat, trying to appear normal. Any explanations could wait until he'd had time to process.

"I've booked a table for seven at Truffles. I was going to run you a bath, but—"

"We can't go out with you like this." She paused. "You don't look yourself."

"I wouldn't miss taking you out for the world. This has sorted me right out." He shook the slice of bread at her sincerely.

She watched the crumbs fall and shifted her weight onto one hip.

He pulled a guilty face and scooped the crumbs from the breakfast bar into his hand. "I bought wine."

Before she could protest, he'd unscrewed the cap and gathered up two glasses from the cupboard. "It's good stuff. I googled it." He poured a glass. Handed it to her.

"As long as you promise you're alright." She took his empty glass before he could pour himself one and placed it down along with her own. "I'm worried about you."

He waved a hand. "Just a dizzy spell. A little daydream."

"OK." She nodded. Rubbed her hands together. "Go get that bath started. I'll put the shopping away."

PROMISES

The mirror behind the bar made the restaurant look bigger than it was. Resting upon the shelf above, and twirled around a row of dust-covered wine bottles, soft yellow fairy lights radiated a warm glow. Non-offensive instrumental jazz serenaded them beneath the sound of several other couples chatting and clinking forks on plates.

Truffles held a special place in their story. It was where he'd brought her before he'd taken the knee and proposed. It should have been a place where he could forget about the day's events, but he was finding it difficult to stay present.

He caught Amy watching another younger couple. They were leant in close, holding hands. The flickering orange light of the candle on the table cast shadows on their features. He reached under the table and took hold of her hand.

"Do you remember the first place you ever took me to?" she said.

"Yeah, sorry about that." Their first date had been at a gig venue around the corner that had since been shut down due to more than a few health code violations.

She smiled and gave his hand a squeeze. "It was OK. I never really needed anything flashy. Just you and me."

"It's coming up to ten years since we played there last." He poked at his gnocchi. Didn't have much appetite for it. "Closed now. Obviously, they couldn't top our last performance. Why stay open?"

"Well, I must have enjoyed it, otherwise I wouldn't have let you take me home."

"I thought it was something to do with me pretending to be your boyfriend." He stabbed a pepper with his fork.

She laughed. "We had to leave together, otherwise that guy wouldn't have believed the ruse."

"That guy was awful. He wouldn't leave you alone. I had to do something." The pepper glistened green in the candlelight, a little like something swampy he'd recently found in a cupboard. He placed it back down.

"Well, how did you know I wouldn't think *you* were awful?"

"I wasn't really thinking about that. I just saw you weren't having a good time."

"Do you still pretend to be girl's boyfriends to rid them of lecherous idiots?"

He puffed out his chest and looked dramatically to the corner of the room as if a cape were billowing behind. "A hero's work is never done."

She laughed. "Oh, it better be." She sipped her mojito.

"To tell you the truth, I don't watch many girls that closely."

"Many?" She raised an eyebrow.

"Any." He corrected, picking up a hunk of bread from the basket that sat between them.

A brief silence hung, and he let his mind wander. That thing with The Flash, what was it? Had his brain just rehashed something from their video? Or, as crazy as it sounded, had The Flash been trying to communicate?

She put her fork down. His mind returned to the table, sensing she was building to something.

"Do you have to do the gigs you've got coming up this month?" she said. She glanced down, then back up at him. "We don't get to see each other much anymore. And you've been working hard on the agency. Don't you want a break?"

He looked at her, trying to get a read on what she really meant, but he wasn't really present. In his head, all he could see was Dimitri locked behind that cage door in the warehouse. And the woman and the man stood in the woods. It had been so real.

"Dan?"

Maybe he did need a break, but—

"We need the money," he said. He didn't mean for the words to come out as flat as they did, but surely she knew.

She reached her hand across the table towards him. He took it, palm up. Her eyes widened when she saw the deep thorn scratches that ran up his forearm.

She traced a finger from his wrist to his elbow. "Did Catman do this?"

"Yeah." He pulled back. Scratched the itchy skin.

"Is he still attacking you whenever you play bass? I thought he'd grown out of that."

He had, but it felt easier to lie. It was the best cover. "Yeah, must be something to do with the way my fingers move."

He pretended to inspect the scratches before hiding his arms under the table. She appeared not to notice his urgency to conceal them.

"You don't still think that man is over feeding him, do you?" she asked.

Couldn't they talk about something else?

"No," he replied, honestly. While Gatsby was not his favourite person, Dan just felt sorry for him. But the old man's missing cat wasn't his problem. None of the missing cats were his problem.

She looked at him. Her lips pursed as she chewed the inside of her cheek. "I saw the video on your YouTube. It looked like you had Catman pulling weights in the garden."

The candle light reflected in her watchful brown eyes. She didn't look angry, but there was something there.

"I've only done it once," he said, feeling the need to defend himself. He shuffled the vegetables around his plate. "I googled it before I did it and I tested with smaller weights first. Other people train their cats."

"It's OK. I'm not cross." She touched his hand. "But there's clearly something wrong with him. You shouldn't be exploiting that."

"I'm not—"

"We should take them to the vet."

"I think they're OK."

She withdrew her hand.

"Catman's sick, Dan."

Was he?

"I'll get to the bottom of it. I'll find out what's the matter with them."

"How? I don't want you using those cameras. The police told you to get rid of them."

"I've already chucked The Flash's." He leant back. It was like she didn't trust him.

She frowned then rubbed a hand over her eyes. "I'm just worried about you. You're spending all day in your office. And there was that dizzy spell earlier."

Those words, "I'm just worried about you", were some of the hardest to hear from a loved one's lips, especially when you think your actions are perfectly sane. They make you reassess everything. If someone else was worried about your behaviour, and you weren't, then what did that say about you?

He made a decision.

"I'm fine. Don't worry. I'm not going to look into the missing cats anymore."

But he might try to track down that woman from the video. Find out what she knew.

"You promise?"

He looked past her. Perhaps he needed to investigate the woods behind the warehouse.

Amy gripped his hand, tightly. "Promise me, Danny."

He promised.

Promises Broken

"Follow us," said The Flash, with a low Scottish tone.

It reminded Dan of his old Ju Jitsu sensei.

It was cold out. He didn't want to go. But before he could move away, something sharp dug into his back.

He jerked awake with the same nervous impression of being trapped that he had felt the previous morning. Had he had the same dream? No, this was different.

He sat up. Hadn't screamed this time, but he was cold. Cold to his bones. His side of the duvet sat in a heap around Amy. Most nights, she would roll over and over while she slept, twirling herself up like a wooden stick in warm, fluffy candy floss. Most nights, he didn't mind.

An amber line cut across the bedroom floor from the streetlight outside. He looked at his phone. Just after one. He waited and listened. Amy's breath maintained its soft and steady repetition. He hadn't woken her.

A sudden sting under his right shoulder blade caused him to gasp. He eased his hand up his back. His finger caught something embedded in his flesh. Something sharp. Something foreign. Pain forked across his skin. He bit the inside corner of his mouth, forcing the hurt out through his nose as a silent breath.

Stiff from the earlier chase, he stood. His legs were iron rods. He limped across the hallway to the bathroom. Closed the door. Tugged the light pull over the medicine counter mirror. His wan skin glowed milk-white in the pale fluorescent light. He looked ill.

He turned, his eyes watering as he strained to see his back in the mirror. It was a mess. Shallow red gouges of various lengths covered it. At the top, in the place he felt the pain, was a black mark that looked like a hole. He eased his fingers up his back and plucked out a long spike. A thorn.

He turned on the cold tap, washed it — and the spatter of blood that came with it — away.

Everything was suddenly too much. He dropped onto the closed toilet lid, buried his face in his hands, and let out a long sigh. His face creased into a sob, but he suppressed it. Pushed it down into his stomach.

He had been lucky today. What would they have done to him if Catman hadn't been there? Killed him? Buried him in that forest — never to be seen again.

How would Amy have coped if he'd just disappeared? He knew he would go mad looking for her if she went missing.

His mouth filled with salty saliva. He swallowed, fighting back the panic induced nausea that rose in his stomach like a balloon filled with putrid air. He dropped to his knees and lifted the toilet lid. Closed his eyes. Willed the sickness to subside.

Slowly, it receded.

Once he had regained control, he slid to a seated position, bare back against the bath, legs stretched out in front of him. The cold plastic soothed his stinging back.

He closed his eyes. If they wanted to hurt him, that meant he'd been close to something. It meant that whatever secret they were hiding was worth keeping.

Something clattered, followed by a slow creak from downstairs. As if air had moved somewhere in the house, the bathroom door gently opened. Beyond the threshold was darkness. He held his breath.

The creak had sounded like the front door.

He froze in place, trying to concentrate on every sound in the house. Was someone inside? He was sure he'd locked the front door, but he'd been slightly buzzed from the two or three glasses of wine he'd had over dinner. Was it the men again? Were they here?

He grabbed a pair of nail scissors from where they sat next to the toothbrush cup on the window sill, then slid his index and middle fingers through the loops, and held them, blade out, like a viscous knuckle duster. He wouldn't use them, but they might discourage a would-be attacker.

He turned off the light and stood for a moment in the darkness so his eyes could adjust. No other noises came from downstairs. He edged open the bathroom door, hoping it wouldn't creak. The landing was still. Quiet. A ghostly blue glow rose up the stairs. He crouched low to see as much of the ground floor as possible through the bannister. At the foot of the stairs, the front door was ajar.

Squeezing his fist tightly around the scissors, he descended. When he reached halfway, he crouched again, taking shallow breaths so he could listen better. From here he had full view of the hallway and into the lounge. The house was empty.

A flash of orange flitted across the wooden boards of the hallway floor and out through the front door, making it swing further open. He readied himself for whoever may be there, but the doorway was empty. The Flash sat in the middle of the garden path. When he saw that Dan had noticed him, he bound away through the gate and disappeared on to the road.

Thoughts of home invaders forgotten, he hurried down the stairs, pulled his black hoody from the pegs by the door, and jammed his feet into his trainers. He stuffed his keys into his pocket and pulled the door shut behind him.

He ran to the end of their path. Looked right towards the industrial estate. Streetlights illuminated the tail end of The Flash as he disappeared into a shadow a little way up the road. Catman's stocky silhouette moved into another arc of street light ahead of him. They were moving fast. Heading back to the warehouse.

He should stop them.

Squashing the backs of his shoes with his heels, he shuffled along in hot pursuit.

"Hey," came a hissed whisper from above. "What are you doing?"

He looked up. Andrew sat with both feet hanging out of his bedroom window. He held a cracker in one hand and a plate in the other.

"I just saw your cats run past. Where—"

"I know," Dan hissed back, as he hoofed past like a duck in stilettos. "I'm getting them back."

He quickly reached the path that led back to the industrial estate. At the far end, in the monochrome orange of the estate road, The Flash paused, watching him, before moving off once again.

Were they trying to lead him back to the warehouse?

He took a deep breath and began to walk the path.

"Where are they then?" came a voice from behind.

Dan's frayed nerves blew sky high, and as a reflex, his fists flew up. A ghost stood behind him in the darkness. A billowing white sheet glowing in the pale light of the moon. Andrew stood before him, in socks, sandals, and what appeared to be a long white nightgown. He looked like a funky Jesus.

Andrew jumped back at Dan's sudden movement. "Sorry, I didn't mean to frighten you."

"You didn't." His arms dropped to his sides.

"Where are they?"

"They've gone to one of those warehouses in the industrial estate."

"Is it just me or was Catman massive?"

"Yeah... he's um... had a growth spurt. You should stay at home. This might be dangerous."

"Dangerous?" Andrew folded his arms and stiffened like a child who doesn't want to leave the park. "Do you think Dimitri will be there? Because if he is, I'm coming."

He wanted to tell him that Dimitri wasn't there, and that this had nothing to do with his cat, just to get him to go away. But he couldn't. Dimitri was trapped behind the bars of that cage.

Andrew's eyes widened as he noticed the glint of bright moonlight on the nail scissors held in Dan's fist.

"What's going on?" His voice wobbled. He clasped his hands in front of his chest and scratched an index finger with the thumb of the other hand.

"I'll fill you in on the way." He started to walk, but Andrew held back. Dan didn't stop. "Come if you're coming, just be quiet."

After a moment's pause, Andrew caught up. Dan increased his pace and Andrew matched it. As they jogged, Dan filled him in on the events of the day since they'd parted. The trip to the warehouse, the encounter with the two men in the woods (with a few embellishments to make him seem braver), and the way Catman and The Flash had saved him. To Andrew's credit, he didn't turn back and run when Dan told him about Parkaman and Hoodyman, though his features seemed to have sunk, and his face was the same pale orange as his robe under the radiance of the street lights.

Andrew now knew more than Amy, but Dan still left out the telepathic image share that he'd had with The Flash. That was perhaps a step too far, even for a cheesehead like Andrew.

Concluding that a skinny guy in his PJs and funky Jesus on a late-night stroll through the industrial estate might look somewhat out of place, he led Andrew along a cycle path and directly on to the land-fill field behind the warehouse.

Funky Jesus and PJ-boy positioned themselves behind a particularly lumpy mound in the shape of a large toad. It squatted roughly twenty metres from the back fence of the warehouse. The mound was covered in tall grass that felt dry and dead to the touch. He lay down to try to scope out the lot, avoiding the worn blocks of concrete that erupted from beneath the soil. The field behind was a large, open mouth at their backs, ready to swallow them whole. Anyone could have been out there hidden in the darkness, watching. The muscles in his back twitched, and his skin prickled as if someone was delicately plucking his neck hair like a harp.

A few hundred metres behind where they lay, the motorway roared with the occasional stream of white or red light. Between the sound of each car or lorry, the buzz of a crowd could be heard on the still night air, like hissing static between radio stations. It came from the warehouse.

The line of broken windows that circled the top of the building was illuminated from within by a strong white light.

Crouching low, they moved closer until they were at the fence within the tree line of the forest.

The sounds from within became clearer. Cheering and shouting, coupled with the occasional harsh bark.

A high almost inaudible whine came from Andrew's throat. It seemed to clear the way before he began to speak. "What's going on in there?" He nodded towards the warehouse.

"I don't know."

Dan placed his fingers through the chain-link fence. The strange vibration he'd felt earlier buzzed through his hands. He pulled away. Rubbed his palms on his trousers to try to alleviate the sensation.

Andrew looked up; something had caught his eye. He pointed to the roof. "Look."

A broad black silhouette stood on top of the building, watching them from above. At first Dan thought the warehouse had a gargoyle, like some old cathedral, but then its eyes flashed green.

Catman.

The Flash stood behind him just as still.

A harsh series of barks followed by a squeal broke the night's silence. What was happening in there?

Above, the cats turned back towards the roof. They crouched low and crept towards the line of shattered windows. They were going in. Without a sound Catman crawled through, followed by The Flash.

Dan didn't want to follow, but his curiosity had the better of him. His cats were special, and more than anything, he wanted to find out why.

THE PIT

Careful not to rattle the chain links, Dan edged along the fence further into the forest. Andrew followed close behind. To cut him off earlier, Hoodyman must have left the compound directly into the woods. The exit had to be back here.

He felt a soft tug on his elbow.

"We can't go in there." The beads of sweat on Andrew's brow glinted in the moonlight.

"What about Dimitri?" The hard metal scissor dug into Dan's knuckles as he squeezed his fist. "What if he's in there right now waiting for them to experiment on him like they did Catman?"

"You're crazy."

Dan shook his head. He wasn't — was he?

He was going inside. Andrew had to either stay here and be quiet, or go with him and be quiet.

"We'll just have a look to see what's going on, see if Dimitri's there. There's a back way in somewhere here." His arm shifted to point deeper into the forest. "If anyone spots us, we'll make a break for it through the woods. But we'll make sure we don't get spotted."

"Ok." Andrew's mouth, almost hidden behind his beard, drew into a tight line. "For Dimitri."

"First though, are you wearing anything underneath that robe? You're hardly camouflaged in that."

Without a word, Andrew untied the rope around his middle and pulled the robe over his head. Beneath, he was wearing a white vest and linen trousers. He folded the material and gently placed it over a tree branch.

Dan raised his eyebrows.

"It's vintage," said Andrew, hugging himself and rubbing his arms. "It'll crease."

They found a gap where the metal fence had rusted and snapped. He pulled it aside and helped Andrew through, before crawling after him. Sharp slivers of glass from the smashed windows above littered the tattered tarmac. Fragments bit into his hands, but tetanus was the least of his worries.

They reached the narrow alley that ran behind the warehouse. It was strange seeing it in real life, like when you finally meet someone you've only ever spoken to on the internet. Broken pallets, breeze blocks, and retired goods trolleys had been left to rot.

They followed the alley to the door through which The Flash had entered in the video. He passed Andrew the nail scissors, steadied his shaky hands, and showed him how to hold it in the knuckle duster position, blade out.

"What's this for?"

Dan picked up an old wooden broom that was leaning against the wall, stood on the brush head, and gave it a twist and pull. The handle broke free. The wood felt comforting in his hands. Heavy enough to do some damage if it came to it. Please God, he thought, don't let it come to it.

Maybe all those seemingly pointless kettlebell swings he'd grimaced through at the gym would finally come in handy.

"You said we'd run if anyone spotted us." Andrew cast a wary eye over the broom handle.

"Yes, we will. But," Dan gave the broom a tester swing, "just in case."

The window in the door ahead was not glowing like those above. He remembered the video. The room that lay beyond was not part of the main warehouse. They could get in without drawing attention.

Readying himself, he pulled the door open sharply. It squeaked like a fork on a plate and he could feel the sharp electric taste of panic on his tongue. He held his breath and listened to the sound inside. It was strange. It sounded like cheering.

The thin room stretched along the width of the building. Above them, the ceiling opened up to the eaves. The floor was littered with chunks of plaster from the roof, as well as crisp packets, plastic bottles, and old files left behind by whatever business had once operated there. He picked up a file from a desk as they crept by. It was faded. Only 'Shields and Son Ltd.' remained visible. Not much help.

The sound coming over the partition from the other room was unbearable. A generator grumbled just the other side of the wall. Growls and barks of dogs and the laughter of men almost drowned it out. An intense cacophony of pleasure and pain that threatened to overwhelm his nerve. It took all of his will to quell the rebellious urge to run.

The stench was the worst part. A sickening mix of sweat, faeces, and a raw meaty smell that he couldn't pinpoint, but which conjured up dark images of dirty, tiled abattoirs. The air was rotten, festering, hot.

A bright light from the room beyond reflected in the jagged remains of the windows above. Dark shadows of men danced on the ceiling like cavemen revelling around a sacrificial fire.

His mind twisted towards the occult, to dark, depraved desires, sacrifice, blood magic. He shook those thoughts away. Damn whatever idiot had let him watch The Exorcist when he was eleven.

A row of shelves on his right held five cheap looking cat boxes. Each was about the size of a small footstool. The doors were open. Andrew peered inside. He looked at Dan and shook his head. The corners of his mouth drew down like an unhappy clown.

They were empty but had clearly been used.

They pressed on. The force pulling him onward was almost unnatural. Every part of him wanted to run, but he had to see what these people were doing to those poor animals.

At the end of the room, several more cat boxes were stacked high on a sagging wooden desk half-hidden in shadow. There was no door in the frame there. To check the boxes, he would have to step out into open view of the main room.

As they reached the door, a terrible howl cut through the jeers of the crowd. It was followed by another cheer. Dan's stomach wrenched. Before he lost what little nerve remained, he stole a quick glance around the edge of the door frame and caught the moment like a photograph.

A group of roughly twenty men stood around a four-foot high wooden fence. Several halogen lamps surrounded them, standing tall on industrial bases. The lights were connected to a humming generator that sat behind a bar-like counter roughly a metre or so from the doorway. The connecting cables ran over the top.

The men were too busy watching what was going on in the centre of the room to notice him and Andrew. And what they were watching was immediately and horrifyingly clear.

"It's a dog fight," he whispered.

Andrew stared. "No. People don't do that sort of thing anymore."

He nodded. The idea was alien, but it was true.

"We should call the police?" said Andrew. "Do you have your phone? Mine doesn't fit in the pocket of my linens."

Dan patted himself down. He'd left it by the bed.

He looked back to the centre of the room. His stomach knotted. He couldn't believe, with all the technological advances of modern times, that man could still lower himself to this. Forcing things to fight for his own enjoyment. Just get a PlayStation and fight it out on Mortal Kombat, or join a boxing club if you're that way inclined.

He tensed, rigid with fury. How cowardly, how cruel, how selfish could people be?

He tried to imagine the sort of men that could take pleasure from this. The image scared him and he ducked back into cover.

But Andrew stayed in sight of the other room. His focus was on the cat boxes on the nearby table. They were arranged in a pyramid. Four of the doors were closed. Shrunken shadows huddled inside. He inched towards them.

"Hey?" Dan hissed. He glanced around the doorway — no one was watching — then back to Andrew. "Stop."

Andrew opened the second from the top and put a hand in. He recoiled and let out an audible whimper. Dan held a finger to his lips. Pulled him into cover by the back of his T-shirt.

He motioned for him to wait in the shadows and then reached inside the box, thinking himself less noticeable dressed in black than Andrew's white. It contained the body of a cat. He pulled it out carefully. A pressing tingle behind his eyes caused them to water. It was Hitler. The white one from their road with a little moustache and black patch on its head. Her body was deflated. Limp like a piece of cloth. No longer the family pet she had been. He placed her gently on the desk by the cat boxes.

There was slow movement inside the other closed boxes, but before he could investigate, the noise from the main room filtered down to the sound of general chatter. They'd finished. He dived back into the shadows, hoping he hadn't been spotted. After a moment, he glanced around the door again.

Those around the pit had dispersed into smaller groups. At the far end of the warehouse, Hoodyman was sitting at a table illuminated by a desk lamp. In front of him was a large holdall. Roughly a quarter of the men were heading towards him. Each held a slip of paper in their hands.

Behind him stood Parkaman, leaning to one side with one hand resting on the back of Hoodyman's chair. The lamps highlighted the matted fur around his hood but his face was hidden in shadow.

As the men approached, Hoodyman unloaded a few wedges of cash from the holdall. Placed them on the table. He took each slip, studied it carefully, and handed out some notes to the man who had given it to him. When he had given money to all of the men, he zipped up the bag and dropped it under the table. It still looked heavy.

Two men jumped into the pit where a badly injured dog lay, its mouth dripping pink foam. Together, they tethered it. The dog lunged erratically as they dragged it towards one of the side doors and out. Another two men were arguing over another dog, which lay to their side, bleeding out on the dirt floor.

Its ribs rose and fell slowly. The men gestured wildly as it died. One of them gave it a hard kick. It didn't make a sound.

Dan looked to the ceiling. He didn't want to see anymore.

In the rafters above, he could see two sets of green eyes glowing. Catman and The Flash were perched above the largest group of men, close to the centre of the room, high up near the corrugated roof. They were well hidden. Two black shadows. Only their emerald eyes and the tips of their ears caught in the light of the halogen lamps gave them away.

They looked like they had a plan.

Their heads bobbed. They were judging the distance to the floor. The eave where they stood was roughly six feet above the head of the tallest man. Could they make the drop?

If their plan was to attack, he had no way of stopping them. But maybe he could help. God knew these men deserved whatever was coming to them. And he was angry enough to try something stupid.

He glanced at the humming generator. Men couldn't see in the dark, but cats could.

"Andrew." He leant closer. "I'm going to shut off the power."

Andrew's mouth worked silently. He shook himself. "We should just grab these cat boxes and go. Call the police."

"No. I can do this."

Andrew backed away. Dan let him go. He didn't blame him. It wasn't stupid to be afraid.

He turned his attention back to the generator. For the first time in his life, he prayed. *Please let my confidence in my pets not be totally misjudged.*

He took a deep breath, hurried through the doorway, and dropped behind the counter where the generator rumbled. In his haste, he almost knocked over two large jerry cans. They reeked of petrol. He paused for a moment to listen to the room. No noise to indicate he'd been spotted.

He placed the broom handle on a shelf in the back of the counter and investigated the generator. He'd never used one before. Heavy fumes piped out as it rumbled on.

After a brief search, he found the off switch. He raised his hand, hesitated, his finger hovering like a humming bird at the mouth of a flower. If Catman and The Flash didn't do anything when he turned it off, then one of the men would just come over, beat him to a pulp, and turn it back on. Or it would be his turn in the pit. There would be no escape.

He looked up. Though their bodies were now blanketed fully by shadow, he could tell they were watching him, waiting. They'd had long enough to get ready. Please let them be ready.

Inside his head, he heard that deep Scottish voice as if on the wind. "Push."

A wave of confidence washed over him, accompanied by a feeling of strength and of purpose. This was the right thing to do. This would work. Just push the button.

He closed his eyes, took a deep breath, and without another thought, jabbed his finger forwards.

It was like someone had pulled a bag over his head. The sound of the generator choked off and the whole room went black. The talk and the laughter stopped dead.

"Wooo," said one of the men. "SpoOoky." Some laughed. Most didn't.

The low rumble of their merriment hit Dan like a punch in the gut.

"One of you mugs go get the gennie back on. I'm tryna count here. If we're out of petrol again, Leeroy, you can say bye bye to your pay tonight."

"I'll get it."

Someone began to shuffle blindly towards the counter. The scraping sound of their feet as they edged closer cut through him like knives. He couldn't breathe. Each intake of air, shallow and uneven. *Come on boys, now's your chance.*

It dawned on him that maybe he'd put too much faith in them. They were cats. They were never going to do anything.

He'd been a fool to think they had some kind of telepathic link, and now he was going to pay for it.

THE SURREY PUMA

D an tensed. He retrieved the broom handle from the shelf. Squeezed it
tightly with both hands. Shards of the wood dug into his sweating palm,
but he didn't feel it.

He crawled towards the end of the counter as those scraping footsteps edged
closer. There was no chance of escape before whoever it was came and cut him
off. They were nearly at the far end of the counter now. They'd spot him if he
tried to slip out. He closed his eyes as his mind raced. There was only one option.
He'd have to hit them. Hit them hard and run.

Something thumped in the centre of the room, and the quiet air was split by
a throaty scream.

Then another.

"What the hell was that?"

"Something's got Carl."

"My ear!" The voice faltered, then cut off with a gargle and a thud.

For a fractured moment, the room went silent, save the hushed breathing of
the men as they tried to listen.

"Carl?" Came a whisper.

Another scream.

"Jesus Christ, it's a puma."

Panicked movement exploded in the room as the men tried to flee from
the unknown horror attacking them from the shadows. Scream after scream
sounded as Catman cut through the crowd.

Dan crawled to the end of the counter. Glanced out from behind it, his head
almost coming into contact with the knee of the man who had come to fix the

generator. He looked up, but the man had turned back to watch the madness, his hands clasping tufts of hair on either side of his head. He twitched from side to side, clearly unsure whether to stay or run.

Dan rose up behind him, watching the room over his shoulder. Frantic shadowy movements filled the space beyond like some sort of post-modern dance piece. Silver moonlight shone down through the windows above like spotlights on the heads of the men running to escape.

"Someone get the generator back on. Now."

The man turned. He smelt of sweat and dirt, and despite having the strong build of someone who regularly partook in manual labour, he jumped back when he saw Dan. His black eyes widened, clearly startled to see someone standing face to face with him in the dark. An angry scowl spread across his face as he realised it wasn't a friend.

He raised his hands and stepped forward, aiming for Dan's throat. With little more than reflex, Dan swung the broom handle like a baseball bat and caught the man across the head. He stumbled, dazed, and Dan hit him again, this time bringing the broom down katana-style on top of his head. The old wood juddered in his hand. Dan was surprised it didn't snap. The man fell to the ground where he stayed.

A primal and exhilarating wave of satisfaction the likes of which he had never felt before washed over him, coupled with the desire to dive forward and start wildly swinging at others. The feeling reminded him of the hungry confidence that comes after two beers. But was quickly replaced with the sickening taint of regret (like when you've had seven).

He looked down at his fallen enemy. Don't let him be dead.

Engines roared to life outside. The screech of rubber in the dirt. A few men continued to circle the pit. Either too stupid to run, or too scared to move.

Before anyone spotted him, Dan ducked back to floor level, where he was hidden in shadow. He searched the man on the floor, patting his pockets until he found a phone, then crawled back behind the counter. He hit the button to make an emergency call. Like Batman or Daredevil, he'd done his part and it was time to call in the authorities to bag 'em and tag 'em.

As soon as the operator picked up, he spoke in a hushed whisper. "I need the police. I'm at Fleetwood Industrial Estate in the abandoned warehouse nearest the motorway. The big red one at the back." As he spoke, he heard someone shout from the middle of the room.

"Hear that? Someone's behind the count— aaaaah!"

He was rumbled.

"I've stumbled upon a dog fighting ring. I am in immediate danger—" his voice unintentionally rose.

"Get him!" came a shout from the shadows. Several scowling faces turned in his direction.

"There's still a few of them here. Send help, quick."

He ran back for the door to the narrow room. Caught his elbow on the frame as he passed through, almost knocking himself off balance.

Andrew had gone.

The operator started to answer, but he had already dropped the phone into his pocket and was at full sprint towards the back door. Behind him, the sound of his pursuers became more frenzied as they entered the confines of the thin room.

With his lungs screaming for air and his heart pounding so hard he could hear the blood in his temples, he slammed the door shut. He raced around a wooden pallet that was stacked high with cobweb-covered breeze blocks.

Straining with his legs, he pushed hard, relieved when it started to topple. The blocks came crashing down in front of the door just as the handle jerked from the other side. The door rattled on its hinges as the men banged against it.

"You can't escape us," one of them said. He sounded unnervingly calm. "You activists always get what you deserve in the end. Mark my words, he's not going to let you get away with this."

"Phil," came another voice from behind the door. It was high and breathy. "What's that?"

"Just one of the bait cats. Must've of got out of its box. Let's go round." The door jumped as they pounded on it. "We're coming for you."

A piercing hiss, which grew into a high growl came from behind the door. Dan could sense the fury in it.

"Phil, that ain't a bait cat."

"Oh God."

The door slammed on its hinges. A number of the breeze blocks tumbled away, but it did not give. Screams came as the door handle flapped up and down as uselessly as the broken wing of a bird clipped by a car.

"Let me out. Please, let me out."

Instinctively, Dan began throwing breeze blocks aside. It couldn't be Catman and The Flash in there. He imagined terrible cat-like beasts with all-seeing headlamp eyes. Jaws sopping with blood, tearing the men apart. He had to help them.

Breaking several fingernails in his haste, he frantically dug the last remaining blocks away from the door. No matter what the men had done, he couldn't have their deaths on his conscience.

When the door was almost clear, he grabbed the handle and wrenched it open. The last of the blocks scraped across the tarmac, and he fell back as two men scrambled out. They pushed each other down in their panic to get away. They didn't look back.

The Flash sauntered out of the darkness. Pressed himself affectionately against Dan's legs. In the pale light, it looked like the cream fur around his lips was flecked with dark spots.

Roughly halfway up the corridor, he could just make out a pair of black boots sticking up from the ground. Mostly hidden in shadow, flat on his back, was an unconscious man.

He stepped through the doorway, aware that anyone could appear from the next room at any minute. Catman sat atop the desk at the far end of the room, next to the stack of cat boxes.

"Come on," Dan whispered to him. "We have to go."

As he eased himself closer to the desk, around the body of the man (*unconscious-not-dead, unconscious-not-dead, unconscious-not-dead*), he realised what Catman was doing. He had one paw on Hitler, the white cat, shaking her gently.

Dan's heart broke. He placed a hand on Catman's back. His head whipped round. He hissed and bared his teeth. Dan flinched away.

"I'm sorry buddy. There's nothing we can do for her."

The Flash brushed past. Hopped up to the desk. Catman hissed again, this time at both of them. The Flash stepped forward with caution and bumped his forehead lightly on Catman's. There was a brief moment between them. Dan's mind flitted back to when The Flash had done the same to him. Was he showing his brother something?

Catman seemed to sigh. Then he turned, dropped from the table, and left through the back door. Dan and The Flash followed.

He was surprised to see Andrew a little further down the alleyway, standing with a bundle wrapped protectively in his arms. At his feet, watching Dan from behind Andrew's skinny legs, were Pretty Pretty Princess and two other cats he didn't recognise.

"Sorry I left," said Andrew, his voice sounded small.

"You rescued them?"

"Yes, I checked the other cat boxes while you distracted those men." Andrew stroked the thing in his arms. The shadows cast by the trees were darkest where he stood so Dan couldn't see clearly. It looked like an old towel.

"But I couldn't save him." His voice cracked over the words.

He sniffed and stepped forward. Dimitri lay there lifeless and flat. His paws hung limply over Andrew's hands.

"He's still breathing, but I don't know what to do." His face creased up on the last word. He sniffed again and let out a blubbery breath. "I think he's going to die."

The Flash bounced towards Andrew's feet. He stood on his hind legs and leaned against Andrew's thigh. Then he motioned with his paw.

"I think he wants to look at Dimitri," said Dan.

With a slight frown, Andrew obliged, leaning over to hold the cat closer. The Flash's nose wiggled. A slight rise and fall in Dimitri's chest, slow and unsteady, showed he still clung to life.

The Flash turned to face Catman, who sat next to the back fence. There seemed to be a moment's communication between them. A look. Or something more? Something in their thoughts? Catman slunk out of the darkness. His large paws crunched on the broken tarmac as he passed Dan and Andrew, then through the gap in the fence into the wood. From there, he looked back, clearly wanting them to follow.

In the distance, the sound of sirens grew steadily louder.

"I think they want us to go with them," said Dan as he moved to do so.

"Shouldn't we wait for the police? They'll know what to do." Andrew held Dimitri out as if Dan hadn't already seen how hurt he was. "Maybe they can help Dimi?"

Pretty, Pretty Princess and the two other cats followed Catman and The Flash through the fence.

"We should follow them," he said decisively, then moved to the gap in the fence.

Something curious was afoot in the woods. In Gatsby's words "a dragon to fight", or at least, one to discover.

"No." Andrew stamped his foot. "This is ridiculous. I am not going to follow your stupid cats into a dark forest."

Dan stepped closer and placed his hand on Andrew's shoulder. The poor guy flinched as if he were about to be struck.

"My stupid cats just took down a dog fighting ring. My stupid cats just found Dimitri for you. My stupid cats know something we don't." He looked over Andrew's shoulder into the black of the wood. "There's something in there. Something we don't understand. It might help."

The tell-tale flash of blue and red lit up the field as police cars approached the warehouse.

Andrew hugged Dimitri closer to his chest. His eyes glazed over.

"And if we stay here, and we get seen, what do you think those men from the warehouse are going to do to us for spoiling their evening once they get out of prison?" He looked back. Did you go to prison for watching dog fighting? "That is if they even get sent down. If we go out there and show our faces now, they'll know it was us who called the police. We'll go straight to the top of Walton's Most Wanted's most wanted."

Andrew stared at him. His lip shook. He didn't speak.

"Aren't you curious to see where The Flash is going? They might be able to help Dimitri." He applied a slight pressure to Andrew's shoulder, moving him towards the gap in the fence. "Come on, Vegan Warrior, let's try it."

Andrew nodded. His head wobbled slightly as if it were too heavy for his neck. He followed Dan as Catman and The Flash led them into the heart of the wood, stroking Dimitri all the while, comfort for himself more than anything.

THE FOREST

The overgrown vegetation was almost impenetrable in the dark. It made the going tough, but Dan was too afraid to turn on the torch of the phone he'd taken, aware that men from the warehouse could be lurking back here. Though if they were, it would be to their detriment. Catman didn't look in the mood for an ambush.

The going got tougher as they moved further into the wooded gloom. All shapes became one. Arm-like branches clotheslined at head height, and thick ferns and brambles covered the forest floor, stabbing through his pyjama bottoms and clawing at his legs.

He held his arms in front of his face as he moved. Conscious of how Andrew was faring, clutching Dimitri in both hands behind. He tried to be extra careful not to let any branches ping back and whip across his face.

The night air was cool and still. A mellow juxtaposition to the sweaty brutality of the warehouse. The only interruption of the calming silence was the low rumble of lonely cars passing on the nearby motorway, and the odd angry shout from back at the warehouse. The sirens had ceased blaring, and when he looked back, he could no longer see the red and blue light at all.

As they proceeded through the all-encompassing black, a strange glow appeared in the centre of his vision. He blinked hard, but it didn't go away. Perhaps a trick caused by his tired eyes adjusting to the darkness.

A few more steps and he realised the murky glow was outlined by finger-like branches. It wasn't a trick of the dark at all. Somehow it was getting lighter as they progressed deeper into the undergrowth.

The light came from behind a large group of firs that blocked the path up ahead. The trees stood like monolithic doormen guarding the entrance to some eerie nightclub. Thick black branches thinned as the trees tapered up, filtering the ghostly glow that radiated from behind them.

Catman and The Flash meowed, calling him from the other side having already passed through.

A slight breeze rustled the branches carrying with it a faint, but awful stench. He recognised the earthy rotten smell as the fetid odour of the frog The Flash had left him.

He drew back the dark green curtain of needles and followed the boys through.

Beyond was a clearing, roughly the width of a road and, in the very centre, a pool of glowing water. A soft blue light radiated from its depths.

He moved closer, stumbling slightly as the soft, fudge-like mud around the pool's edge gave beneath his feet. The water looked somehow thicker than it should. Like a giant luminescent jellyfish had dropped from the sky and burrowed into the ground, lighting up the surrounding trees with its pale light.

He knelt and tried to wave away the fine mist that hung over the pool. The source of the light was not the water itself, but a great swathe of frogspawn writhing beneath the surface.

That earthy rotting smell was thick. It gave substance to the air. It was strange, horrible, but something you could get used to. After a few deep breaths, he had forgotten it completely.

The air above the pool vibrated with the heavy sound of buzzing insects, and when he looked up to the canopy, he found it alive with dancing shadows. If they were flies, they were some of the biggest he'd ever seen.

In the centre of the pool was a small island. Several frogs sat in the slimy mud. Their skin glowed brightly, like the spawn in the pool. Whenever they inflated their pouches, it looked as though bright blue lightbulbs were illuminating below their mouths. They were just like the frog he'd found in the cupboard.

Andrew stood in stunned silence as he cradled Dimitri.

Catman and The Flash edged close to the water's edge, their concentration fixed intently on the pool. With a violent slash of his paw, Catman dragged a large kicking frog out by one of its legs. With a twist of his jaw, the frog's neck crunched, and it ceased its squirming. He dumped it next to The Flash on the muddy ground and walked away to curl up in some grass at the foot of one of the firs.

Dan watched this display wondering how any of it fit together. The dog fight, Catman's growth and strength, the strange memories The Flash had somehow shown him. His head buzzed with questions like the flies in the canopy above.

The Flash picked the frog up by its neck and carried it in his mouth towards Dan. Its lifeless legs flopped either side of his mouth like a long Fu Manchu moustache. He dropped the frog at his feet, the blue glow still emanating from its lifeless form. The Flash then moved towards Andrew, who hadn't yet taken his eyes from the pool. Standing on his hind legs, he pawed lightly towards Dimitri before returning to the frog.

Dan shook his head slowly, not quite believing what he was seeing. The Flash's meaning was easily discerned. He was amazed to find the level at which the cat was able to communicate.

"I think he wants you to put Dimi by the frog," he said.

Andrew knelt and lay Dimitri on the soft mud next to The Flash. The Pretty, Pretty Princess and the other two cats stood nearby watching.

With a snap of his strong jaws, The Flash ripped a piece of flesh from the frog's bloated stomach, and pushed it into Dimitri's mouth with his paw. Dimitri's eyes fluttered as he began to chew. Surely a reflex. Only seconds before he had been at death's door.

The Flash took another piece, this time leaving it next to Dimitri's head. He repeated this process several times until Dimitri had a little stack of raw frog bits piled near his mouth.

Understanding what The Flash was trying to do, Dan took the next piece and held it up to Dimitri's mouth. After swallowing the first, he grabbed and pulled it in with his teeth. His eyes remained closed.

"Feed him as much as he can eat," Dan said, resting his hand on Andrew's shoulder to make sure he was listening.

"What is all this?" Andrew said, gesturing to the pool. He picked up Dimitri with one hand and scooped up some of the frog pieces in the other. Already the cat's breathing had steadied and he was chewing more voraciously.

"I have no idea. I'll have a look around. Wait here for me."

Andrew continued to feed Dimitri while Dan surveyed the pond. From here, he couldn't see any indication as to what made the frogs and their spawn glow. He skirted around the pool edge, taking it slow so as not to slip.

The water thrived with life. Fish, newts, and insects swam and skittered across the constantly writhing pool. It was a biologist's dream. Only the frogs and their spawn glowed. Something had made them special. He didn't think it was the water itself otherwise the other creatures might glow too.

It couldn't be a natural phenomenon, could it?

He scratched his chin. If this was common of English woodland, there would have been reports of similar glowing bodies of water, especially being situated so close to an English suburb. Explorers had gone deep into the forests and jungles of the Amazon, and he had never heard about anything like this — and he watched a lot of BBC nature documentaries. No, this was something new. Maybe man made?

Although the estate and the motorway were nearby, there wasn't really any other civilisation out this way. Just woodland and a few country roads.

Could radiation cause a glow like this? From his extensive comic book knowledge, Dan was all too aware of the side effects of radiation.

Was this caused by some hazardous dumping in the woods by one of the local businesses? Perhaps a top-secret lab was hidden amongst the tyre fitters and warehouses somewhere on the industrial estate? The estate could house all sorts of crazy secrets, and with no reason to search them, no one would ever know.

He walked around the pool until he was adjacent to Andrew and the cats. On this side there were fewer insects so it was quieter. His ears picked up a new sound. A ring, high and almost inaudible at first, like one of those devices shopping precincts used to deter kids from loitering. A high pitched whine.

The sound came from further into the wood, so he stepped away from the clearing, and once more into darkness.

ORIGIN

The glow of the pool had ruined Dan's night vision, but he decided that he was probably far enough from the warehouse now to use the phone as a torch.

As he moved away from the light of the clearing the eerie whine grew louder. He held the phone by his side so that the light only pierced the gloom around his feet. Wet, mulching leaves covered the ground, and as he traipsed through, following the sound, he noticed the occasional spatter of a glowing liquid on the ground. He was reminded of the scene in Predator where Arnie manages to injure the monster and tracks it through the jungle using its glowing green blood.

"If it bleeds, we can kill it," he said to himself, hoping the power of a Schwarzenegger one-liner would dispel the creeping dread of walking through the dark forest alone.

It didn't.

A closer inspection of the liquid revealed nothing. It was unlike anything he'd ever seen. Though it appeared to be dry, it still had a vibrant blue luminescence. The closest comparison was the goo you get inside a glow stick.

He blinked. He'd had a similar thought recently when he'd bumped into the woman in the street. The one with a camera. The one who'd been in The Flash's memory. The one who'd disappeared in the woods. She'd been taking a picture of similar splotches on the pavement.

The high drone led him close to a dark country road that ran almost parallel to the motorway. He recognised it. He'd driven down it once or twice before when the motorway had been closed. Narrow, with tight corners, it was an unpleasant road, even in the daytime; there was always the risk of a startled deer running out from the forest.

A few metres from the tarmac, he found the source of the noise. A round metal crate about the same size and shape as a beer keg, blanketed by a pile of rotten fallen leaves. It was tucked in behind a sprawl of large tree roots that erupted out of the ground like tentacles. It was difficult to spot. If it had been silent, he would have missed it.

Was it safe to touch? He kicked the leaves away with the toe of his trainer. Held the torch up to get a better view. The top was split and the torchlight glinted off a long crack running down the outside. A logo was embossed in the dull grey metal of the keg. A large S with a thunderbolt cast through it, almost like a dollar sign. He didn't recognise it.

On the tree above it, at roughly head height, was a large split in the bark. Long splinters of wood jutted out at right angles.

It could have been thrown from a truck.

He pulled his T-shirt up over his mouth like a cowboy's bandana, as if that would ward off any radioactivity. Leant closer to inspect the split in the crate.

Hanging limp just inside the opening, its head crushed, was a small dead frog. Although it had a slight blue tinge to it, if it had once had a glow like the others back at the pool, that had since faded.

He rolled the crate with his foot and the cracked lid fell open. The box was built like a corridor with ten small cells either side. The cells on one side were matt black, and on the other, a clean silver.

He raised the light to look at the road that was only a few metres away. Red and orange slivers of plastic glinted in the churned-up mud at the roadside. Maybe there had been a crash. A vehicle had skidded in the road, bumped a tree, and somehow the crate had come flying off, cracked open, and spilt an army of mutant frogs into the wood. It didn't surprise him. Well, the frogs did, but not a skid. It *was* a dangerous road.

But where had the crate come from? And why were the frogs glowing?

Feeling brave, he rolled the crate over with his hands. The interior colour pattern of silver and black ran to the outside, almost like a yin yang, with the black interior corresponding to a silver exterior and vice versa. The keg was almost weightless, considering the thickness of the metal. There were no other markings on it. Not even a serial number or company name. Just the S. He kicked it closer to the tree, behind the roots, and threw some leaves over it. He wasn't going to get any more answers now. Best to come back, and have a look in the day.

He turned his hands over as he returned to the pool. An almost unnoticeable glow covered his fingers where he had touched the crate. He rubbed them on his trousers.

When he arrived back at the clearing, Dimitri was up and on his feet. All of the cats except Catman were chasing each other around the pool. Andrew beamed as he watched them.

"It's amazing," Andrew said, and span around, palms turned to the night sky. "What is this magical place?" Not waiting for an answer, he continued. "Look at him, Dan." He gestured towards Dimitri. "For a moment I thought it had made him worse, but he's better. You were right."

Dan didn't know what to say. It was strange to be told you were right about something.

The cats raced around his feet and he smiled, but inside anxiety was beginning to squeeze his chest with its strong, inexorable fingers.

"We shouldn't stay here long," he said as he made his way back around the pool. "It might not be safe."

He caught himself itching the scratches on his arm which sent his mind into a spin.

Was hazardous radiation seeping through his skin, changing his cells, mutating him? Or was it all in his head, like when you see a wriggly bug on the TV, and start to feel one on your neck?

"Not safe?" Andrew span again, turning his head to the sky with a look of fanatical glee. "But it's wonderful. Look at Dimitri."

Dimitri, The Flash, and the rescued cats were now cuddled up in an adorable carpet of orange, white, and brown fur.

"We need to tell everyone about this place. Think of what it could do for people."

"We'll talk about it tomorrow. We'll make sure some good can come of it, but let's not make any rash decisions. It's late and we've had a bit of a night of it."

"Too right." Andrew leant back with a giddy sort of wobble.

Catman led the way home. Dan made sure to stay just far enough ahead so that Andrew couldn't engage with him. Fawning over Dimitri kept him preoccupied anyway.

He felt uneasy, and not just because of the obvious reasons. It crossed his mind that if Catman and The Flash had been affected by the presence of the frogs, then what of other wildlife? Could they have been contaminated? If contaminated was the right word. If the frogs had been there some time, and judging by the state of the crate, they had, there was no way to guess what other animals in the forest had also been exposed.

He didn't see any other animal life as they walked, and except for the noise he and Andrew made as they battled through the undergrowth, the forest remained eerily quiet. No birds. No deer.

A legion of super-strength squirrels could be watching them silently from the tree tops and he would never know. He looked up, unable to see much of anything in the dark, and shivered.

Ahead, The Flash and The Pretty, Pretty Princess walked side by side, with the other two rescued cats just behind. Neither was like the cat Gatsby had described. Perhaps that poor little one was already gone, like Hitler.

Catman, barely visible ahead of them, travelled alone. Dan's heart felt like a cold stone in his chest. He sighed. Blinked. His eyes began to tingle again. The whole night had been a rescue attempt. For Catman, the attempt had failed.

When they reached the industrial estate, he made sure they gave the warehouse a wide birth. Police officers still worked the lot. Red and blue lights whirled and several heavy-duty floodlights had been set up to illuminate the building as they moved in and out.

He and Andrew returned down the path to their street. As they passed Frank and Vicky's house, The Pretty, Pretty Princess broke off from the group and dashed home. The Flash followed her before returning to the pavement a few seconds later. Though not fully, Dan smiled.

"I'm sorry I accused you," said Andrew when they arrived at his house. He stroked Dimitri, who had fallen asleep in his arms.

"That's OK," he said, toeing a piece of gravel back on to Andrew's path. "I was acting weird. I get it."

"What are we gonna do about the pool? It could help so many people," said Andrew.

Dan stepped closer and looked him in the eye wanting to make sure he understood what he was about to say. "I'll call you in the next few days. Don't talk to anyone until we've discussed it. We shouldn't go anywhere near the warehouse or the pool until we know what we're going to do."

He'd watched enough sci-fi shows to know that unusual science experiments, the type that resulted in outbreaks of mutant frogs and cats, were just the sort of thing people disappeared over.

"We talk too soon and the shady men in black suits and Ray Bans will come knocking."

Andrew pressed his lips together. "I don't think that's going to happen."

"Well, there's also the shady men in black tracksuits and parkas to worry about," he said. Andrew's Adam's apple bounced as he swallowed. "We can't be seen to have been anywhere near the warehouse tonight. We should wait until the heat's off."

"I suppose that makes sense." Andrew nodded. "Night Dan."

"Night."

Dan led Catman and The Flash home. The other two rescued cats came too. He felt sorry for them. They were probably nowhere near home. Lost and scared. Perhaps they belonged to the woman he'd heard about at the gym. If they let him, he'd try and give them some food and somewhere safe to sleep tonight, and look into getting them home tomorrow.

Once back, he put out another two bowls on the plastic mat in the kitchen and filled them all with as much food as he could. He also filled a few bowls with water. The two newcomers were very thin and appeared happy to be there. They dived in.

His hand shook as he poured himself a glass of water and raised it to his lips. Before he spilt it everywhere, he put it down. He leant his elbows on the kitchen worktop and held his head in his hands. In the cool quiet of the kitchen, the events of the night flooded back like a cinematic montage.

"Why did you go?" he whispered, although he wasn't sure if he was talking to himself or Catman and The Flash. Looking back, he'd been stupid. That's twice in one day he could have been killed. Three times if you included the possible radiation poisoning.

He didn't want to think about what might happen if someone found out they'd been there. He couldn't tell anyone, not even Amy. They'd never had any secrets before, but now, the skeletons in his closet were mounting up. He wouldn't be able to keep this all from her for long, she was too smart.

She always aired her grievances. Always confided her worries and fears. But he just couldn't tell her the things that worried him. While doing so might ease some of his burden, it would only give it to her, and she didn't deserve that. This would scare her as much as it scared him.

He had to keep it inside, handle it alone.

He slid into bed next to her. Pulled himself close. Let his hand rest on her hip. Hearing her breath in the darkness, and feeling her warmth was always a comfort. His taut muscles relaxed. He closed his eyes. The collection of tears that had built up, but hadn't yet spilled over, rolled down his face.

He didn't sleep.

MOUSEBANE

I failed.

DANNY DIXON & THE NEWS

O nce more, by the time he'd woken, Amy had left for work. He felt like he hadn't seen her at all lately.

He ventured downstairs to see what sort of mess the four cats had left the house in, but the kitchen door was slightly ajar and the two newcomers had gone, clearly keen to find their own way home.

Wrapped in Amy's fluffy blanket, he planted himself on the couch. Catman and The Flash perched behind on the sofa-back, although Catman no longer really fit. The previous night's events kept returning to him in flashes and strobes. The memories had twisted themselves into nightmare scenes of blood and screams.

He tried to work. Really wanted to just plough on and forget it all. Pretend it had never happened. But it had. He couldn't think. Couldn't concentrate. It was like he had an ugly black balloon tied around his neck, which floated behind him wherever he went. If he really focused on something and moved quickly, he could forget it for a moment, but, stop long enough and eventually it would creep back into his periphery.

The same question kept cropping up. Had he been seen? The guy he'd hit could have seen his face. Would he remember? Had he, or the ones Dan had freed from behind the door, been able to get a good enough look at him in the dark?

By that evening the media had a hold of the story. It was the local news head-liner. He tried to watch it whilst Amy talked to him about her day, pretending that his eyes were not completely glued to the screen. The report on the raid included some shoddy overhead footage of the warehouse taken from a drone earlier that morning. The police in their luminous jackets moved in and out of the building. Seeing them working the scene with such purpose helped calm the butterflies in his stomach.

After Amy had gone to bed, he sat with Catman and The Flash on the sofa and scoured the internet for any mentions of the story. Facebook had one or two posts from local news sources. An old school friend had shared one and written, *'Sickened by this. Can't believe it still goes on in this century. Sounds like they got what they deserved though. Bunch of scum bags. I'd like to shake the hand of the legends who cracked it.'*

At this, his mood brightened. It was good to know his unintentional good deeds were appreciated, even if no one knew it was him. This must have been how it was for Batman. Knowing you'd done some good in the world, but unable to tell anyone. With a renewed warm feeling inside, he read the article that had been shared.

"The group at the warehouse were part of a larger dog fighting and drug trafficking ring that Surrey police have been watching for some time. Authorities seized over £25,000 in cash, but are baffled by the condition of some of the men they arrested at the scene."

"I'd've been pretty baffled too," he said to Catman.

'Some of the men found on site were unconscious, covered in bloody scratches and bite marks. One was missing an ear. Another, part of his nose. There were mentions of a large black creature lashing out in the darkness. Police weren't able to comment as to any relation to The Surrey Puma sightings that have been reported over the last week.'

"Looks like you're famous." He gave the fur on Catman's head a scruffle.

Catman climbed on to his lap, squeezing the air out of him with his weight. He laughed.

In the comments section a number of people mentioned having seen a large black cat in the last week or two, and a number of others echoed his school friend's sentiments. Dan smiled. The three of them had done some good at least. That ugly balloon deflated a little.

His thoughts turned to the pool. He'd put off ringing Andrew all day, unsure of how to approach the situation. On the one hand Andrew was right, if the frogs could be used to heal people then they had to tell someone, but his doubts from the night before still lingered. There was a chance the men in black (tracksuits and parkas) were still at large and looking for *the legends who cracked it*. Then there were the actual men in black (suits and Ray Bans), the ones from the mysterious "S" company, who might show up and threaten to chop Catman and The Flash into little bits for experiments.

Whatever mysteries the pool concealed weren't worth giving up their anonymity for. Not just yet. It would be better to see the place in daylight. Re-evaluate it. Pretend they had stumbled across it whilst out walking.

In the meantime, he needed to lay low and keep Catman out of the spotlight. Despite the history of the local legend, there was likely only one real Surrey Puma, and Dan was pretty sure some very bad people would be looking for him now.

CAPTAIN FROGCATCHER

Dan called Andrew that Saturday morning with the plan to meet up and head to the pool. He had a gig that night and was planning to head straight to work once they'd checked it out. Andrew had texted him a few times over the last few days, and Dan sensed he was getting itchy to go and investigate. He was aware it was still a little soon after the warehouse incident, but better they go now than Andrew go on his own and get in trouble.

Amy spooned a pan of pasta into a Tupperware and handed it to him. "What are you and Andrew up to again?" She threw a pretend punch at his face and made an explosion sound with her mouth. "I wanted to spend some time with you this afternoon. Thought we could take Catman to the vets. Get him properly looked at."

"Oh, very romantic." He dodged the blow. "Andrew just wanted a bit of help with some scales." Returned with a slo-mo right hook. "I've told the band lads I'm going to have next weekend off. Got Adam in to cover me."

She grinned and grabbed the lapel of his jacket, pulling herself in. Her breath hit him. Dizzyingly warm and sweet. "Really? That's great. Can I plan some things?" She let him go and rubbed her hands together like a super-villain.

If he was honest, he'd wanted a bit of a break to sit and do nothing. "Yeah, if you want. Relaxing things."

She ooooh'd. Eyes alight. "Maybe a spa?"

"Can we afford it?"

She winked. "I've been working on a big project. And it's payday soon. I'm sure we can find space in the budget."

He kissed her goodbye, patted the cats on the head, and went to leave.

"What time should I call the police?" she said, looking at him expectantly.

A startled cough escaped his throat, and he stared at her for a moment, before remembering this was her normal jokey way of asking what time he'd be home — what time should she call the police to come find him if he didn't arrive back? He caught himself. Tried to act normal.

"2:30 a.m.? So, give them a call at 3ish?" He held her hand and planted another kiss on her cheek. Their fingers pulled apart with a reluctant snap as he left.

He dropped his bag and tupperware off in his van, then headed towards Andrew's. It was a little later than he'd hoped to start, and there wouldn't be much time for a debriefing, but Andrew hadn't answered his phone until midday and then he'd had to wait until Amy came home from coffee with friends so that she could watch Catman and The Flash while he was out.

As he approached, he spotted Andrew staring out from behind the curtains.

"What took you so long to text me back?" was the first thing Andrew said when he opened the door. Above his beard, his cheeks were rosy. And he seemed to stand a little taller. "Come see Dimitri." He stood back and let Dan enter.

Dimitri sat on one of the red sofas, head held high like a miniature Aslan. His coat had a stunning, almost golden, sheen to it, and he was a little stouter around the shoulders.

"Wow," said Dan, concluding in certainty that it was something in the frogs that had changed both Catman and The Flash, and now Dimitri. "He looks amazing."

A grin lit up Andrew's face. "He does, doesn't he? But he's not stopped eating."

Behind him, in the kitchen, the drying rack by the sink was covered in empty and washed tins. Both cat food and what looked like beans and soups.

"I think they just eat a lot after... whatever happens to them must take a lot of energy, you know?"

"Yeah, I guess it does. We ran out of cat food. Twice." Andrew held two fingers up. "We're going back, right? To the pool." He rubbed his hands together. There was a Gollum-like tone to his voice. *My precious pond.* "Now?"

"If you want to."

"We have to." Andrew's eyes were wide. "I was thinking of going over myself, but I wanted to wait, like you said." He grabbed a long coat from the stand by the door. "I— I wasn't sure I should go alone. You don't think those men from the warehouse saw us, do you?"

Dan sighed through his nose. "I don't know. I think we need to be careful, though."

Andrew grabbed a backpack from beneath the coat stand. It clinked with the sound of glass as he hefted it onto his back.

"What's that?"

"Kilner jars," Andrew said. "For samples."

"And you had that ready by the door?"

"I've been waiting for you." Andrew looked over Dan's shoulder. "Come on, Dimi. It's adventure time."

Dimitri jumped off the sofa and jogged towards them.

Together, they set off on the path that lead around the back of the warehouse and onto the field. The sky was a smoky grey blanket, and the air held a fine mist which clung to Andrew's beard. Dan could barely make out the motorway and the back half of the field in the fog.

He kept his eyes trained on the warehouse as they traversed the uneven ground, with Dimitri trotting just in front. There was no one on the lot, so they hiked past the fence and into the woods.

"Oh man, my robe."

Andrew hurried towards the white robe that still hung from the tree branch.

It looked floppy and damp, and when he picked it up, the bark had left a lengthy brown stain where it had been folded.

He held it up and sadly studied the stain. "It's my favourite piece of leisure wear." He tucked it into his bag.

The gap in the fence wasn't far, but Dan had no idea where to go from there. He stopped. The woods all looked the same.

"Any idea what way we went before?" he asked.

"I was just following you." Andrew crouched down. "Do you know where it is, Dimitri?"

Dimitri stepped further into the woods, then looked back.

Andrew smiled. "This way."

Together they skirted along the edge of the chain-link fence outside of the warehouse.

Seeing it now, Dan still couldn't believe they'd made it out. The whole evening, before they'd reached the pool, was now a horrible, violent blur.

They didn't speak much as they trudged through the misty wood — it was difficult going through the dense brush and he was surprised they'd both made it in the dark without injury — but it wasn't long before he saw the familiar dark green shape of the fir trees.

He sped up to a light jog and pressed through them, with Andrew close behind. Cool droplets of dew flicked off the branches and on to his face. The pool was still beyond. He was almost surprised to see it. Insects buzzed, frogs croaked, the water fizzed with life.

"Hm," said Andrew, his shoulders slumping slightly under his bag straps. "It's not as impressive in the day, is it?"

He was right. In the dull light of the foggy afternoon, the glow wasn't as impactful as it had been.

Andrew set his bag down on the bank and opened up one of the kilner jars. Dipping it in the pond, he collected a sample of water, along with several wriggling tadpoles.

"What are we going to do with these samples?" asked Dan.

"I don't know." Andrew's attention remained on the jar in his hand, then he looked up. "Don't you have a friend at the university?"

"Why would I have a friend at the university?" He stepped closer to the water and knelt at its edge to examine its murky depths. "And what university?"

"I don't know." Andrew held the jar up and examined the squiggly little blobs in the faint sunlight coming through the canopy above. "People in situations like this usually have a friend at the university."

"You've been watching too much 80s sci-fi."

"You can never watch too much 80s sci-fi." Andrew moved to stand by his side and passed him the jar.

A silvery blue sheen seemed to radiate from the tadpoles' tails.

"Do you think it's the water that's special, or the creatures?" Dan was sure it was the frogs, but wanted to know if Andrew agreed.

"Definitely the frogs."

"I found something a little further into the woods." He passed back the jar. "A box. I think they came from inside. I think that's the source."

Andrew looked up over the pool as if he knew where it was, then sealed the top of the jar and put it in his bag.

That droning whine from beyond the trees had stopped.

"So if the cats ate the frogs and became mega, what do you think would happen if we did the same?" Andrew gave Dan a strange sideways glance.

Dan studied the other frogs nestled on their little island in the centre of the pool and wrinkled his nose. He hadn't considered that. Probably because eating a cold, slimy little frog was the most disgusting thing he could think of and nothing in his wildest dreams could make him do it, not even the thought of attaining superhuman strength.

"Do you think we'd grow like Catman or something?" continued Andrew. "How long did it take for him to grow like he has?"

"They were missing for a few days, but he was already a little bigger when he came back. I'd say eight until he reached his full size. It seems to have stopped now, though."

"Mm." Andrew twirled the tip of his beard.

"So, we're agreed, the frogs have changed them in some way?"

Andrew nodded. He motioned to Dimitri. "He was at death's door and now he's looking stronger than I've ever seen him. And your boys took on a bunch of hardened criminals. It's not natural. It has to be some sort of magic, or... I don't know."

Magic? Like witches. His thoughts turned to the mysterious woman from The Flash's memory, the one who'd pushed him in the street.

"Oh, look." Andrew's eyes lit up at something by Dan's feet. He pulled another jar from his bag and knelt.

The half-eaten body of the frog that had saved Dimitri was touching Dan's right foot. He hadn't spotted it when he'd knelt down. The remains were covered in several unusually long and fat slugs. Dan gagged and bolted upright.

Andrew picked it up by one of its legs and dropped it, slugs and all, into the second jar. "It's dead, don't worry." He sealed the lid and placed it next to the other jar in his bag.

"I know, sorry, I'm just not very good with bugs and things. When I see them there with their slime and their legs, I just feel like somehow they'll end up inside me."

Andrew raised an eyebrow. "You what?"

"Like they'll try and get in my ears and mouth or something."

"Oh, I see. Fair enough." Then he thumbed his chest. "I've got guts of steel." He gave Dan a friendly elbow. "Must be all that casu marzu."

Dan gagged again, this time remembering the evening Andrew had invited him over for maggot infested Sardinian sheep's cheese.

"We should try to get a live one, too," said Andrew, glancing over at the little island. He clearly didn't mind getting his hands dirty.

"Be my guest." Dan held up a palm invitingly.

Andrew took out a third jar and approached the side closest to frog island. It looked quite the jump, but Dan thought he could probably make it from the closest point.

"You'll have to be quick to get one before they all hop away," he said helpfully.

"Thanks for the pro tip, Captain Frogcatcher." Andrew removed his long coat, placed it on his bag, and moved to the edge. The mud squished under his feet. It looked slippery. "But how do I get there?"

"Can you jump?" Dan tried to recall how his old PE teacher had drilled a standing long jump into them at school. "Swing your arms, bend low, and go for it!"

"Sure."

Andrew fixed his eyes on the island. He swung his arms, bent low, and the mud beneath his feet gave way. His sandals slipped, and before Dan could do anything to help, Andrew was face down in the pool. The almost jelly-like water covered him fully.

Andrew pressed himself up, gasped and said something like, "Bleargh!"

He scraped his front teeth over his tongue and spat the water from his mouth, then stood, drenched from head to toe. Dan tried not to laugh as Andrew combed a handful of squiggly tadpoles from his beard.

"Are you OK?"

"Mm, yep, all OK." Andrew gave him a thumbs up, then scooped up the dropped jar floating on the surface of the water, and waded towards the island. "Everything is going swimmingly."

"Ha. Swimmingly. Good one."

Andrew gave him a less than enthused eye roll.

Dimitri had somehow found his way to the island already. He had two of the smaller frogs pinned beneath each forepaw. He watched his owner with little sympathy. If cats had eyebrows, one would have been raised in mild exasperation.

Most of the frogs had already scattered, but some remained, eyeing Dimitri uneasily. Andrew cupped his hand over one paw and picked up the first pinned frog. He dropped it carefully into the jar, then did the same with the other, before closing the lid.

"Well done, you two," said Dan.

Andrew squelched back to his pack, and put the jar inside, then closed the bag and swung it onto his back grumpily.

"What about that box you mentioned?" he said. "I'd be keen to see it."

"Maybe you should go back, stick the kettle on and get dry, and I'll come find you in a mo'. We'll chat about next steps before I go out to work." Dan held up his phone. "I'll take some video and pics of the box for you." He glanced in the direction he thought it was in. "If I can find it."

Andrew looked a little reluctant to go, but finally, through teeth that were beginning to chatter, he agreed. He gave his arms and legs a drying shake, then jerked his head towards Dimitri. "Come on, Dimi."

With ease, Dimitri leapt from the island to the side of the pool, and together the pair disappeared through the line of firs.

Dan tapped his fingers on his chin. Without the sound, it was going to be difficult to find the box. And light wasn't on his side. Though there was a slight clearing of canopy above the pool, the forest on the other side was dense and blanketed by tall, thick pines.

The mist that had hung over the field had also permeated the forest, giving the trees a ghostly grey quality. He stood with his back to the firs that marked the edge of the pool, hoping that would give him an idea of the direction in which to go. He could hear the crunch of Andrew's footsteps as he headed away, the muttered grumble of his voice as he complained to Dimitri.

He drew back the curtain of needles and looked through the firs to see if he could still see them. They were nearly out of sight in the wood.

Slight movement in the shadows caught his eye and Dan froze. Someone was heading towards his unsuspecting friend from an area of the forest a little way from the pool. She made no sound as she tracked him carefully through the woods. A shadow, half-camouflaged in her navy blue coat.

The woman.

As far as he could tell, she was alone. He swallowed, his mouth suddenly dry, and allowed the soft green needles to fall across his face so that if she looked, she'd be hard-pressed to see him.

He should follow, right? What if she meant Andrew harm? She was either working for the men in the dog fighting ring, or against them. And, there was always the possibility that she could shed some light on what had happened to Catman and The Flash.

He swept through the firs and, picking his route as carefully as he could, gave silent chase.

The Disappearing Woman

Andrew didn't spot her, and she did not spot Dan, with her eyes always fixed ahead. He suspected, although he could not tell from his position behind them, she was perhaps focussed on Dimitri. Even from here, he could see Andrew's cat had an unusual gleam about him. A golden hue that shone, sun-like, from every strand of fur on his densely covered back.

He lost track of them as they moved through the tree line and onto the field. At that point he risked speeding up, hoping the sound of his advance might be hidden beneath the noise of the screaming cars on the motorway and the clanking, groaning industrial estate.

When he reached the forest boundary, he paused for a breath behind a thick oak tree, and looked out over the field. Andrew had already moved out of sight, likely onto the pathway that lead back to their street. She strode purposefully after him, knees high through the long grass. She had that same camera wrapped around her shoulder. She gripped it firmly across her chest with both hands.

He waited for her to disappear onto the path, then sprinted across the field to the wooden fence that marked the field's boundary. From there he peered down the path only to see Andrew turn the far corner seemingly oblivious to his pursuer. When he disappeared, she put a phone to her ear and broke into a run after him. Was she calling for back-up?

He waited for her to turn the corner, took a quick breath, and again gave chase. Who was she? And how much did she know about the pool? And about the frogs? Was she the men in black? If so, both Andrew and Dimitri were in trouble.

He sped up, sprinting now, to the end of the path. Stopped again at the far end and looked down the street towards home. Andrew was nearing his house. She still had her phone pressed to her ear, but had fallen back slightly, likely watching to see which home he went into.

Dan crossed the road so that he was on the same side as Andrew's house and the opposite to the woman. He slowed his pace in time with hers, whilst keeping a good few metres behind. She hadn't spotted him, and the cars lining the road meant he was somewhat hidden.

Andrew finally turned onto his garden path and she sped up once more.

He ducked behind a car as she reached Andrew's path, crouching low so that he could only see her feet between the wheels. She turned a full three-sixty — likely surveying the road — then disappeared through Andrew's gate.

Aaah! This was it. She was going to get him, or Dimitri, or both. Aaah!

He pushed himself up, and jogged to the high bush at the end of Andrew's garden path. Didn't dare peek around it for fear she might be looking this way. He heard her knock. There was a long pause in which Andrew didn't answer. He imagined him fretting inside, soaking, trying to find something to dry himself, oblivious to what awaited him at the door.

What exactly did await him at the door?

She knocked again.

Even from here, Dan could hear the muffled sound of Andrew from inside. "Coming."

The door cracked open.

"Sorry," Andrew said. "I was just about—"

"Where did you get those?" Her voice snapped. Short and to the point.

"Ikea. They're nice aren't they. I usually keep lentils in—"

"Not the jars," she said. Dan heard a click. "The tadpoles."

"Um."

"Simon. I'm going to need extraction in ten. I've found them."

"What? Look, sorry, I've just fallen in a pond, and I need to have a shower, so thank you, but I'm not buying anything today."

"Me and one other. Teleportation radius one metre on my position."

Another click. Followed by a strange sound — *fwutung*.

Dan hazarded a brief look around the corner. Andrew stood just inside his house with another, this time brightly coloured, robe wrapped around him. Something was sticking out of his chest. A silver dart of some sort. His eyes were wide.

"Whaaaaat?" Andrew looked down at the dart and his eyes dropped closed, before he fell forward into the woman's arms.

"Got him," she said, as she struggled with his lifeless form in her free arm. "Do it now."

The ground beneath Dan's feet thrummed with that strange sensation he'd felt in the fence at the warehouse. He looked down as a low bass note started to rumble seemingly centred on the pair.

"Andrew?" Dan hurried forward around the bush.

The woman's eyes flashed to him. "Simon, wait, there's two of— aah."

Dan shouldered her out of the way, and into Andrew's garden hedge.

"Sorry," he said — feeling an odd sense of guilt for bush pushing this woman — but she seemed unharmed. Andrew's lifeless form fell against him. He dragged him through the front door.

The woman struggled to pull herself out of the hedge while that weird rumbling bass intensified. But before she could get up, it cut out, and she disappeared into thin air.

He stood there for a moment closing his eyes and opening them again, wondering if it had somehow been another weird vision. The air felt thick with the stench of molten plastic that reminded him of overused electrical appliances. He gripped Andrew under the armpits and willed the woman back on the front step. What was happening? Part of him suggested that if he blinked hard enough he might wake up sitting at his breakfast bar earlier that morning having dozed off while getting ready to go out.

He lay Andrew down on the ground. The weird dart was still sticking out of his chest. He plucked it free and threw it away.

"Andrew?" He gave his friend a gentle shake. "Andrew, I need you to wake up."

Something brushed past him. He nearly fainted with shock. Dimitri climbed up to stand on his owner's chest. He butted heads with him, and Andrew gasped awake as if slapped.

"Oh, what happened?" He rubbed his head and looked up at Dan.

"Some woman shot you with a dart. She... she disappeared." But he bet she would be back soon. "We have to get out of here."

Dan helped Andrew to his feet, then moved into the living room. They should head out the back way.

"Who was she?" Andrew followed.

Dan shook his head. "I don't know." He rubbed his head. It had to have been another vision. People didn't just disappear.

Dimitri led them through to the kitchen before hopping up on to the side next to a six pack of condensation covered IPA cans. Andrew's bag sat on the floor containing only the jar with the two frogs jumping about happily inside. He picked it up.

"Where's the other... oh." Assuming the beers had come from the fridge, Dan opened it. The top shelf was clear except for the jar containing the dead frog and slugs. Holding back a gag, he stuffed that in the bag, too.

A very small but primal part of him, some long dormant survival instinct that had seemingly reared its ugly head the night he and Catman and The Flash had assailed the warehouse, told him, in its underused but aggressive little voice, that he shouldn't stay here, that he should get the hell out of dodge. He threw the bag over his shoulder and hurried to Andrew's back door.

"Come on."

He paused with his hand on the handle. That same strange electric vibration buzzed from the metal into his palm, and suddenly he could feel that low bass hum start to build once more. It wasn't a sound that could be heard, more felt in the pit of his stomach.

Someone's coming, that primal part of him said, *you should leave.*

He pushed open the door as the hum cut dead, coupled with the sense of movement at Andrew's front door and the sound of someone trying to be quiet. Dimitri bolted past them and out into the back garden.

Dan did not wait to see who or what had arrived in Andrew's front garden. He ushered Andrew out and pulled the back door closed. They hurried after Dimitri, who scrabbled quickly over the back fence and onto the path that led behind the houses on this side of the road.

Andrew fumbled with the rusted bolt at the top of the gate as the back door was thrown wide open behind them. "The bolt's stuck." His voice rose.

"Wait right there." The woman's voice from the back door.

Then *fwutung* and something slammed into the fence on Dan's right.

He risked a sideways glance. Another silver dart stuck roughly an inch into the wood juddering with the force of impact.

"Damn it," she said.

"Come on, Andrew." Dan slapped the bolt with his palm and it sprang open. He shoved Andrew out onto the muddy back path. To the right Dimitri was sprinting away towards his home, towards Amy. They couldn't go that way.

To the left was the suburban maze of Walton's crescents and footpaths. Best to lead them as far away as possible. Dan began to make his way along the path.

"Dimitri!" called Andrew running after his cat.

"Wait," said Dan, but as Andrew rushed past his garden gate the woman emerged. She had been joined by a man. He wasn't in a black suit nor Ray Bans like Dan had imagined. In fact, he was dressed rather conservatively in chinos, a shirt, and what appeared to be a knee-length lab coat. He didn't seem particularly spritely, already appearing a little red in the face from the chase.

"Get him," shouted the woman pointing after Andrew. The man looked reluctant, but began running after Andrew and Dimitri. Then she turned to face Dan and raised that camera to her chest. "We just want to talk to you," she said, before firing another dart that went whizzing past his ear.

He jumped back and sprinted. Yeah right, "*Talk*," with hot blinding desk lamps shining directly into my eyes, whilst tearing out my finger nails, and chopping my cats into pieces, and never letting me see my wife again.

You can talk to my arse, is what his brain might have said had it not been screaming the word, *RUUUUN!!*, at the top of its brain lungs.

He ran like his life depended on it, because it probably did. Wound his way through the paths and streets, taking random turns here and there, as his pursuer fell further and further behind. He must have run for an hour this way and that, near and far, only stopping when his body finally gave up and he could not take another physical step.

Heart pounding, he leant against a lamp post to catch his breath. He had intentionally brought himself, albeit via a very indirect course, to the gym. No one would come looking for him here, right? Not with all these people around. And the place was open 24hrs. He could stay here indefinitely if needed.

He hoped Andrew had managed to get away.

The jars in his backpack clinked together as he stepped briskly across the car park. He was briefly aware of the condition of the two living frogs still inside, but it sounded like the jars were at least in one piece.

With a nod to the guy on the door, he beeped his gym card. His head felt numb and strangely silent, like all the questions he should be asking had tried to force their way into his consciousness all at once and got wedged in the doorway.

He pushed his way into the men's changing rooms and sat down in such an exhausted daze that he didn't think to remove the pack. The jars dug into his back, but still he didn't move.

He replayed the moment the woman had disappeared, again and again.

Had she really vanished right in front of him? Had she really then appeared once more with someone else?

What had she been planning to do with Andrew? With both of them?

A small grating thought told him that things had grown increasingly strange ever since he'd dragged that first frog from his kitchen cupboard, that perhaps just touching it had somehow pierced his body with whatever radiation (or magic) that had infected his cats, and since then he'd been spinning further and further into brain damaged delirium. A more likely story than cats attaining super-feline powers, him taking on a dog fighting ring, and an unidentified woman evaporating into nothing before returning and chasing him and his cheese-loving neighbour through the back streets of Walton.

The unsolicited sight of a recently showered penis entering the changing rooms snapped him out of his stupor before a towel fell to cover it. His eyes rose, following the intricate collection of tattoos and dense muscle, to meet the owner's. A beetroot-red face — this time through heat and exertion rather than raw anger.

Of course it was Frank, the guy who'd accused him of spying using the cat-cams. Of course it bloody was.

Dan tried a smile. Caught himself looking exceedingly deranged in one of the mirrors. Stopped.

Frank snarled and turned away to dry himself. "Just sitting staring at dicks in the men's changing rooms isn't doing much for that reputation of yours," he said after a moment's awkward silence.

"Sorry," said Dan. "I've um..." He didn't know what to say, so pulled his bag from his back and pretended to be looking for something. "Forgotten my shorts."

Frank glanced over his shoulder while he pulled on a shirt. He snorted. "Right."

Dan's phone pinged and he fumbled to take it from his jeans pocket.

A text from Paul: *Where are you?*

He slapped a hand to his forehead. He was supposed to be meeting him before their gig tonight. He was already ten minutes late to their usual rendezvous point.

His thumbs flew across the keypad: *Sorry P, can't make it, ill. Can Adam fill in?*

The reply was almost instant. *Bit late to let me know. Will sort. Get well.*

He didn't think any more of it. He called Andrew. It rang off. What did that mean? Was he running or caught? He didn't text him. If he was caught that woman might read it, might triangulate his position, might set up a cordon of super-soldier-agents outside the gym ready for him to come out.

He lay his head against the wall, and closed his eyes. That woman had seen his face. She knew what he looked like. Did she know where he lived, too? He guessed not. She'd have been over before now if she knew where he lived. Amy and the boys were safe for the moment he hoped, but for how long?

Frank finished dressing and left with another displeased grunt. Dan didn't even raise his head.

He could probably stay here for another few hours. Wait for the heat to die down. Amy would assume he was at work. She wasn't expecting him until gone two. He could wait here, but Frank was right, he couldn't just sit in the changing rooms like some crazy person.

He popped to the gym's kiosk and bought a pair of swimming shorts, some goggles, and a towel. When you can't go home because spooky disappearing women with tranquilliser dart firing cameras are after you, your friend, and your mutant super-cats because you've found a bunch of weird radioactive magic frogs in the woods, you might as well try to get some lengths in while you wait for the coast, and your head, to clear.

Plus there was a steam room.

BAD CALL

The night air was still and calm. The street always so eerily quiet so early in the morning. No birds sang. No cars rattled past on the main road. Everything had a purple-orange tint. It could have been another world.

Dan's fingers were prunes. His skin felt soft and his sinuses were clear. And while his body felt relaxed after his hours spent between pool, sauna, steam room, and gym, his mind had not quieted.

He'd gone over his options a thousand times and had decided he was going to come fully clean to Amy. He would wake her up as soon as he returned and tell her exactly what had happened. Everything, from dog fight to disappearing woman. She would know what to do. She always did.

He felt lighter for the decision.

As he passed Andrew's house, he considered whether or not he should knock. Instead, he crossed to the other side of the road and passed as quickly as he could. He cast a sideways glance. There was a faint light behind the curtains. He sensed a flicker of movement, a shadow.

Something told him that the place wasn't empty, that the woman or her man were in there now, watching the road, waiting in the dark. Waiting for him. Were they waiting for Andrew, too? Or did they have him?

He hurried past and crossed the road again.

There was a light on the second floor of Gatsby's house. The old man was up. Dan pictured him tottering around the house alone.

A sigh escaped him in a breath of mist.

The gate shrieked as he opened it.

"Oil," he mumbled, voice hoarse with a sudden nervous fatigue that dragged at his limbs. He trudged up the garden path.

The house was silent, still, dark.

Catman and The Flash would be asleep somewhere. Back when they were younger, they would bound up to him as soon as he came through the door after a gig. Now, they were used to him returning at ungodly hours, and were content to wait until the morning to say hi.

He headed straight upstairs and pushed open the bedroom door, shutting it quietly behind him.

He liked a bit of light in the room at night. Being able to see made him feel safe. But Amy insisted on heavy blackout curtains to block out the amber glow of the street. The room was pitch black save a sliver of orange down the middle that divided the room in two.

He closed his eyes and navigated his way along the wall to the bed. Sat down on the edge and stretched. His muscles twitched. He was nervous to wake her, nervous to begin. It was a similar feeling to when he'd asked her to marry him. He was asking her to trust him, to be with him fully in all things, good and bad.

"Amy," he said, whispering into the dark.

She didn't stir.

"Amy, I need to talk to you about something."

Nothing.

She must be tired.

He lay down on the bed and eased himself towards her. Careful not to pull the cover from her. Best to wake her gently. He stretched his right arm over to her side of the bed to give her a light shake.

"Amy?"

His hand touched down on cold duvet.

...

He stretched his arm further, suddenly aching to touch her warm, smooth skin. His fingers slid along the bed sheet until they curled around the far side of the empty mattress.

He sat bolt upright, tearing the duvet away from the bed.

"Amy?"

No answer. He couldn't breathe. It felt like he was being squeezed.

He stood up and smacked his hand against the wall, blindly groping for the light switch above the bed. Blinked as bright light filled the room. The bed was empty.

He jumped up, hands at his temples. Was he forgetting something? Had she gone to her parent's tonight? She sometimes stayed there when he was out.

But her car was outside. Wasn't it?

He sped to the window and ripped aside the curtains. There it was, her little mint green Fiat, parked in its usual place in front of the house. The sight of it winded him. She should be here.

He grabbed his phone from his pocket. She might have messaged him.

Out of battery.

His whole body tensed with frustration. His charger cable was in his bag in the van where he'd left it before going to Andrew's.

He ran downstairs. Turned on all the lights as he did. The house was exactly as it had been when he'd left.

With shaking hands, he grabbed his van keys. Threw open the front door. Stepped out into the cold night air.

Maybe her mum had picked her up. Maybe she'd hired a taxi. Maybe she was with a friend... but why couldn't he remember her mentioning it? He was liable to forget conversations, but in the seven years they had lived together, he'd never forgotten whether or not Amy was going to be at home after a gig.

He flung the van door open. Rampaged through his bag until he found the cable and jammed it into the charge point in the dashboard. Powered up the engine. Patted his knees impatiently while he waited for his phone to turn on.

"Come on."

The woman had come for him here, at home, and found Amy. That had to be it. She'd taken her just like she'd tried to take Andrew. And Catman and The Flash had been captured too. Were they being experimented on even now? Questioned. Tortured—

No. No. No. Now was not the time to let his brain run off on its own. Now was the time to think logically. Amy was safe. She had to be safe. That woman couldn't know where they lived. There were no connections between Andrew and him.

He banged his fists on the steering wheel, willing himself to remember if Amy had said anything.

The phone finally lit up in his hand, and two texts arrived. Both from her. Both around 7 p.m. The first a missed call notification. The second read: *Call me now.*

A huge weight descended on his chest. He felt like he'd been kicked by a horse.

He rang her number. No answer. He tried to push the panic back. Tried to concentrate, to rack his brain for any clues as to where she could be.

She'd gone to stay at her mum's before. She was probably asleep there now with her phone set to silent. But he checked the message again. *'Call me now.'* No kisses. No details. Nothing. That wasn't right. She would have left an answerphone message, or sent more information if plans had changed and she'd gone to stay somewhere else.

He ignored the sting of stone on the soles of his socked feet as he ran up the pavement to her car and tried the passenger side door. Unlocked. He leant in. Aside from the general clutter of boiled sweets, scattered old CDs she'd never had the heart to throw out, and various make-up things, there was nothing.

He backed out of the car and moved around to the driver's side. With his hand hooked on the door handle, he paused and looked up and down the road. Tried to imagine what she would have been doing.

Maybe she'd popped to the shops. And when she'd arrived home, she would have gone around the back of the car to the boot.

He stepped around to the back.

Next, she would have walked to the house with the shopping and used the remote to lock the car.

But she hadn't locked it.

The boot was slightly ajar. He opened it fully. Several bags of groceries sat inside. His stomach churned.

Something caught his eye in the gutter. A familiar object by the exhaust pipe. He bent and retrieved a bunch of keys from the mud by the drain. They were hers. The Lego R2-D2 that he had bought her hung from its little chain. Its white body flecked brown with mud. He rubbed the grime off on his trousers and scanned the road, half-hoping to see a neighbour watching from a window. Someone who could help. Someone with an insight.

He tried her number again. While the phone rang on and on, he let his eyes travel up the road to Andrew's house. It wasn't overly creative to think the ones who'd chased them earlier had also come for Amy. It wasn't crazy at all. She could be in there now. Or at least someone who knew where she was could be in there now.

The phone clicked to answer phone, and he stuffed it into his pocket. His hands balled into fists.

He ran back indoors and picked up Andrew's backpack. The live frogs inside the one jar were looking a little sluggish, but when he released the lid to let a little more air inside, and tapped the glass, they seemed to perk up a bit. They really were gross little things with the strange S shapes covering their backs. He'd give them back to The Disappearing Woman, tell her all about the pool, and they'd have to bring Amy back, right?

He hurried upstairs to his study. His bass sat silhouetted in the light through his net curtain. He picked it up by the neck. The club-like weight felt comforting in his hands. If there was someone still in Andrew's house, he'd get them to listen to him, get them to give Amy back. He slung the bass on his back and left the house.

First, he approached his van and removed the jar containing the dead frog leaving the live ones in the bag. He placed the bag in the driver's side footwell of the van, hidden by the pedals. The live frogs were his insurance.

He locked the van and hid the keys under the tyre, then strode to Andrew's house.

What would he do if no one was there?

He'd cross that bridge when he came to it. For now, he had to not think. For now, he just had to act.

His hand shook as he raised it to knock. And just like when he'd first knocked on Gatsby's door, and when he'd turned off the generator in the warehouse, he hesitated. Was this a good idea?

Amy was out there somewhere alone and scared, and he was her only hope. This was the only idea.

He thought of the way Frank had acted when he'd suspected Dan of spying on his girlfriend with the cat-cams. That was who he needed to be now. Angry. Unrelenting. He channeled that force.

With teeth gritted and shoulders set, he jammed his finger on the doorbell.

The chime cut through the silent night like an alarm. He placed the frog jar at his feet, gripped his bass in both hands, and stood back, ready. Muffled footsteps approached on the other side. One set? Or two? Who would answer? Some sort of suited Matrix-style Agent Smith? A super soldier pumped full of whatever Catman had running through his veins? He gritted his teeth and tensed. He didn't care, he'd whack 'em whoever it was. He'd take the moments following as they came. He just had to make sure whoever it was didn't disappear on him.

The door clicked open and he raised the bass and rammed it through the doorway like a snooker player striking a cue ball. With a low donk, it connected with the forehead of the small middle-aged man that had appeared on the other side. His bespectacled eyes fell shut and he flopped to the ground.

"Oh."

Dan raised a hand to his lips, unsure as to whether he'd just knocked out what could be Andrew's very normal looking older brother. But then he recognised him. He'd removed his lab coat, but he was definitely the guy from The Flash's memory. The man who'd been in the woods behind The Disappearing Woman and who had chased him earlier.

He wore an orange woollen jumper over a shirt, brown chinos, and a pair of plastic brogues that still had the sticker from the supermarket he'd bought them from on the sole. He was a little shorter than Dan and looked like he'd be more at home behind the counter of a comic book shop than heading up a unit of genetically enhanced super-soldiers.

Dan leant his bass against the wall, then knelt and checked the man's pockets. There was a phone in one. He took it. He also removed the man's watch, just in case it was some sort of sci-fi teleportation tech gizmo. Then he grabbed the man under the armpits and dragged him through Andrew's lounge into the kitchen. Once there, he dumped him onto a dining chair, spent a moment to make sure he didn't fall off, then filled a pan of water from the cold tap.

A large shiny bump had begun to form in the centre of the man's forehead. His skin hadn't broken. He hadn't expected him to fall unconscious. He'd not hit him that hard, had he?

He hadn't expected someone like this at all.

Dan returned to the front door, retrieved both his bass and the jar containing the dead frog, and placed both on the kitchen table next to a letter with an NHS logo on the top. Hanging over one of the other dining chairs was the man's white lab coat.

He took a short breath and blew it out to try to still his fluttering heart. He felt numb, cold, like he was outside of himself. His hands were shaking and he clenched both around the handle of the pan.

He threw the cold water into the man's face. "Wake up."

The man jerked in his seat

"What?" he spluttered, then raised his hand to adjust and wipe his glasses that still clung to his ears. "Oh, my head." He put his hand to his forehead where he touched the bruise that was starting to form. "Did you hit me with a guitar?"

"No. It was a bass," growled Dan. His lips twitched with an anger he'd never felt before. "Where's Amy?"

The man squinted his little beady crab eyes. "I thought his name was Andrew? Andrew Giles."

"The woman. My wife. You've taken my wife." Dan raised a fist and shook it, his fury guiding him. "Where is she?"

The man scratched his head and wrinkled his nose. "I'm... um..." He looked at Dan as if he were wrestling with a very difficult maths problem. "The man we saw you with earlier is your wife, Amy?"

"Are you stupid?" Dan couldn't help but shout. His fingers stiffened into claws.

"No, I'm gifted bio-chemist, Simon De Frain." He said it as if he were reading from a tele-prompter. "They say I'm one of the best in the world, but—"

"The man you kidnapped, Simon De Frain gifted bio-chemist, is my friend Andrew. You've also taken my wife."

"Andrew Giles escaped. But..." He shook his head. "...kidnapping's not right. Kidnappings not right at all. Pippa said we weren't going to do kidnapping. We were just borrowing. I lost some things and Pippa is trying to help me find them. Pippa thinks Andrew Giles knows where they are." Simon began to rub one hand over the back of the other repeatedly, creating a rapid hissing sound. "She says you know where they are, Daniel Dixon."

Dan took a few steps back at the sound of his own name coming out of this stranger's mouth. "Stop messing me around. So Andrew got away, but I know you have her." Although now he wasn't so sure. Somehow, he could tell the man wasn't lying.

Simon shook his head repeatedly. "No." His hands moved to his pockets.

Dan flinched, thinking perhaps he might have missed a weapon of some sort.

"Where's my phone? You've taken my phone. I can call Pippa and she can tell you. We don't have Amy Dixon."

"What will that prove? She'd just lie."

"You have my word, we don't have her." Simon's gaze shifted to Dan's pocket. "I just need to find the specimens and, with your help, I can. That's all I need."

"Then where is she?"

"I'm sorry, I don't know."

Dan sighed. He believed him. He reached forward and Simon shrunk back. Dan grabbed the jar with the dead frog from the table. The giant slugs were nearly finished with it. A milk white skeleton was all that remained.

"What are these?" He passed it to Simon.

Simon's eyes sparkled behind his glasses. "Those are arion hortensis. Wowee! Look at them—"

"Arion what now?"

"Slugs, and looks like they've been at my specimens." He pushed up his glasses and peered closer. "Fascinating. The effects of the serum have transferred. Never in my wildest dreams... uh." His eyes flicked to Dan and he stopped. "I shouldn't be telling you this." He paused, then, with a curious turn of his head, asked. "How did the cats assimilate the... um?"

"They ate them."

Simon's eyes widened. "Not the black ones, I hope. They wouldn't want to eat the black ones. That would be very, very ba—"

"Look, just shut up a minute." Dan took a deep breath. He could feel himself about to explode. "You said serum? What do those frogs contain?"

Simon shook his head. "No. I shouldn't be telling you."

Dan gripped his arm. Felt Simon's pudgy flesh squeeze in his fist.

"You're hurting me."

"Tell me what they are."

"You wouldn't understand."

"Try me." He loosened his grip a little.

"It doesn't have a proper name. I just call it..." Simon cleared his throat and lifted his head to look into his eyes. "I just call it the reptile."

"What?" Dan stepped back.

A shiver ran up his leg. Then again. He put his hand to his pocket. His phone was vibrating.

He took it out. Amy. Thank God. Relief flooded him.

"Wait here, we're not finished." He held up a finger to Simon and moved to Andrew's hallway.

His shaking hands fumbled to answer as he held the phone to his ear.

"Amy?"

The voice that answered didn't have the sweet, high timbre he'd loved from the moment he'd heard it. Instead, it was a male voice with a soft West Country twang.

"You owed us. Now we're even." It was smooth, almost calm, and despite having only said a few words, the malicious authority of it made him feel utterly inferior. "Unless you can think of a better way to pay us back?"

"What?" He tried his best to hold back the quiver in his voice, but the words came out high and shaky. "Who are you? Where is she?"

"She's right here with us, aren't you Amy?" There was a muffled whimper in the background.

"Whatever you want, you can have it. Just let her go. I can tell you where the frogs are. I can take you to the pool. We won't tell anyone."

There was a pause on the line.

"The fuck you talking about? You lost me twenty-five grand with your little escapade. You injured my men and you made me look bad."

Dan suddenly felt like he'd been thrown from his own body, as if he was hovering above it. Sickeningly high. The dog fight. The criminals from the warehouse. A soft moan escaped him. They'd found him. He half-fell, half-sat on the first of Andrew's stairs as his head span.

"And I can only think of two ways to get it back. Option A, you get it to me tonight in cash, or option B, I sell your little lady to a friend of mine." Another pause. "You still there?"

He mumbled a reply as a familiar low bass note compressed the air. He pushed himself up and stumbled to the kitchen. Simon had gone, but that no longer mattered.

He steadied himself on Andrew's red sofa as the man on the phone continued.

"I know which option you'd prefer, but this isn't about you. There's a little more in it for me with option B. I've sold far uglier English girls for fifty and our Amy has the best pair of legs I've seen in a while." He paused. His breath had a lecherous rasp that made Dan want to bite down on something. Whoever it was, was enjoying himself. "Yes, I suppose option B would be my preference."

His mind raced. £50,000 in twenty-four hours was impossible. He stuttered down the phone. No words came out. The man replied with a laugh that cut into him like a knife.

"Is there anything you can think of to swing my decision towards option A?"

"I can get you fifty thousand." He said it without thinking, and cringed with regret immediately.

"That's a lovely offer, but it'd be less hassle for me to just sell her." Someone laughed in the background. Dan was a puppet dancing at the fingertips of a cruel master.

"No loose ends if I do that. Except maybe one, but you shouldn't be too hard to snip." The glee was apparent in his voice.

"Please, I can't— One hundred thousand!" He didn't know what else to say. "I can do it."

He hoped the man couldn't hear the absolute lie. Hoped it would buy him more time to figure something out.

"That's more like it. Now I can tell you're really trying. A hundred grand sounds fair to me." He paused and Dan heard another whimper in the background. "I suppose we ought to arrange a meet up to get this little transaction sorted. You start the ball rolling on getting my money. Your offer is generous, so I'll give you a little extension. I'll call you in twenty-four with details."

Dan grunted in response. It felt as though strong fingers were wrapped around his throat. He couldn't speak.

"I don't think you're stupid enough to get the police involved. That would make Option B much, much more attractive." There was a pause. "Trust me, I'll know."

The phone cut off.

He stumbled through Andrew's front door and out into the middle of the street. Had to get away in case Simon returned with reinforcements. He didn't have time for the frogs, whatever they were. He had to help Amy, had to get money.

Money? Money! Shit. What was he going to do? The street lights span. His vision filled with streaks of orange as if he was revolving at warp speed. He was just a pair of eyes in a head. Everything else had shut down. His legs shook and he fell to his knees in the middle of the road.

He crawled to the kerb, if only to have somewhere to sit, torn in two as his thoughts raced between possibilities. Police. Money. The thought of never seeing Amy again was a blunt blade pressed hard into his forehead, threatening to split his skull. It blocked any sort of logic from getting through, but he gritted his teeth against the panic. Tried to think.

Where was he going to get £100,000? No one he knew had that kind of money. His and Amy's account had barely £15,000 in it. He'd have to hit cash machines all over town just to get that. The man must know there was no chance.

He pulled himself up in the filthy gutter and threw up. As he clutched the chipped concrete kerb with white-knuckled hands, his mind began to clear. He heard the light pitter patter of feet from his left. He wiped his mouth with the back of his hand and turned to sit on the kerb. The Flash clambered up and rested his paws on Dan's knees.

"Hey man."

He looked up. Andrew stood on the pavement with Catman and Dimitri. He was still wearing that brightly coloured robe, but had the hood drawn up over his head. He looked like some sort of shaman.

"Andrew? They've got Amy. The ones from the warehouse."

Dan picked The Flash up and hugged him, unable to hold back the tears. The Flash's fur was soft and comforting.

"The Flash told me," said Andrew.

Dan blinked. "What?" He felt like he might collapse. Everything was going wrong, and what hadn't gone wrong had gone really weird.

Andrew glanced around the empty street. "We should head to your house. Don't wanna be out here if they come back. Those two were whack jobs." He held out a hand and dragged Dan to his feet. "And..." He looked him in the eye a moment, then took a quick, nervous breath. "And I have something I need to tell you."

Gags

Dan sat on the sofa surrounded by cats. He was numb, cold, tired. Andrew came through from the kitchen carrying two mugs of steaming tea. He'd insisted. Said he'd needed a moment to gather his thoughts before he confessed whatever he needed to confess.

"I wanted to tell you this earlier," said Andrew, handing him a cup. "But I didn't want to disappoint you."

Dan let the heat of the mug warm his cold fingers, but didn't say anything. He eyed Andrew suspiciously and took a sip.

Andrew positioned himself on the armchair opposite. He looked nervous.

"I have cystic fibrosis," he said.

It took Dan by surprise. He almost choked on his tea. He had been expecting something to do with the men that had taken Amy.

"I'm sorry." He didn't quite know what that meant. Should he ask? Was is rude to? Was it rude not to? "How could that have disappointed me?" he said. He tried to offer Andrew a smile, but couldn't get past his own all-encompassing worry. "Is it bad?" He wanted to ask what it had to do with Amy.

"Sometimes. It's getting worse as I get older." Andrew smiled and took a sip of his drink. "When we found the pool, when Dimitri came back to life, I thought maybe it was something that could help me, you know? I—" He stopped. Thought a moment. "When you went off into the woods on your own that night I grabbed another frog. I squeezed it into the pocket of my linens and took it home."

Dan met his eyes. Andrew's face was alive, glowing. He didn't look ill. In fact, he looked better than he'd ever seen him.

"It took me a while to work up the nerve. But in the end I thought, what the hell, I don't have anything to lose, and I've tried weirder stuff, so I... um—" He held his hands up to his mouth and did a quick nibbling movement.

"You didn't..." Dan's mouth hung open in horrid fascination.

"I'm still a vegan, mind you. This doesn't change—"

"But they were so gross... Did anything happen to you?"

"Dude," Andrew raised his eyebrows and shifted to the edge of his seat. "What didn't happen? I thought I was going to die for a bit, then I had this truly psychedelic dream, crazier than any fromage induced fantasy. I was back in the warehouse with you and those bad guys, but it wasn't the warehouse, it was the doctor's office. The doctor was you, and then Dimitri, and then he was the doctor again." He gestured with his hands and stared wildly as if seeing once more. "But then you were there again, and you spoke to me, but you had these red eyes and these fangs." He put a clawed hand in front of his mouth and gritted his teeth. "When I woke up it was something like eight or nine hours later. But..." He blinked and Dan could see there were tears in his eyes. "I felt better than I'd felt in months." His lip trembled when he smiled. He took a deep breath as if to show Dan something. "I don't know, and I don't want to get my hopes up, but I think... I think I'm getting better."

Dan sat up in his chair. "Really? You think eating the frog cured you?" It truly was great news, but he just couldn't process it properly — not right now.

"It didn't just cure me. CF is a genetic disorder. The frog changed my DNA."

"But—"

"I'm telling you this because I think somehow the frogs know. They give you what you need. I know what happened to Amy, Dan." He nodded towards The Flash. "He showed me." Andrew blinked. "I think he's telepathic or something."

Dan leant forward mimicking his friend's posture. Andrew had seen what he'd seen. "He is. He is. I saw a memory too. Did The Flash see what happened to Amy?"

"He saw them take her. I saw them in his memory. I want to help you find her." He looked around to the other cats. "We're all going to help you." He reached out and ruffled The Flash's fur.

"But what can we do?

A devious smile lit up Andrew's face. "We've been back to the pool..."

"No." His stomach lurched.

Catman, The Flash, and Dimitri jumped down from the sofa and jogged around to the back.

"...and we grabbed a couple more frogs."

An involuntary groan left Dan's mouth as he turned to look over the sofa back.

Dimitri, Catman, and The Flash stood around a pile of three dead, glowing frogs. They looked like cowboys who had finished up for the day and were bedding down around a dying blue bonfire. The Flash picked up the biggest frog in his mouth. He carried it around and dropped it next to Dan's hand. With his nose, he nudged it towards him.

Dan looked at Andrew. "I can't..."

"Catman is massive, he's strong, The Flash is sending telepathic dream visions, Dimitri came back from the dead, and I'm healed. You'll get something. You'll get something that will help you here. You'll get what you need."

What did he need right now? Strength? Intelligence? The ability to vomit up mountains of cash?

The dead frog was the size of his fist. Its innards pulsed with blue luminescence. The Flash watched him inspect it as a young child might watch his mother assess a piece of fridge-worthy artwork.

Dan picked it up. Just holding it in his hand kicked off squirming movements in his stomach. It was cold, and wet, and heavy like a very well used hanky.

He swallowed but his throat was dry.

His gaze shifted between the frog and Dimitri. Andrew's cat should be dead, but by some kind of miracle he was full of life. And Catman *was* bigger and stronger than he'd ever been.

There was no way he was getting the money to get Amy back. Not in a million years. He pressed his lips together as anger bubbled up inside of him.

He had one option.

"You can do it," said Andrew.

What had Simon said? A serum. What had he meant by that? What had he meant by the reptile? Did it matter?

If there was a chance he could save her, he had to take it. Amy was alone and scared. He could only imagine what those men might be doing to her. The worst came to mind. The darkest images his brain could put forward. Horrifying magnifications of slasher films he'd seen in the past.

He looked to Andrew who smiled and nodded. "It hurts for a bit, but I feel so much better now... like so much."

As he was, he was powerless to save her. He was going to lose her. He couldn't change the situation. It was him who had to change.

He stood up quickly. The frog flopped with his movements.

"I'm-gonna-do-it. I'm-gonna-do-it." He was gonna do it.

He began to pace. Needed to move.

Andrew jumped up next to him and matched his stride like some sort of running coach. "You-can-do-it. You-can-do-it."

"Oh, I'm-gonna-do-it." He shook his head as he paced and repeated. "I'm-gonna-do-it."

"You-can-do-it." Andrew bunched his fists.

"Aaaaaah."

"Aaaaaah."

They screamed in unison. What in the hell was happening?

Dan's face curled into a snarl. The frog crumpled in his hand as his grip tightened. His arm shook and he could feel the bones inside the cold body crunch. There was a dull pop as the frog's guts, glowing like a black light, shot from its gaping mouth and hung on tendrils of flesh from its face.

"Aaaaaah."

"Aaaaaah."

Amy needed him now.

He pushed the head of the frog into his mouth. Cold entrails slapped wetly on his chin. He gagged, but kept chewing. He bit down, breaking bones between his teeth. He fought the urge to throw up. Another light pop as his molars cracked the skull and a bitter vinegar taste covered his tongue. He chewed as fast as he could. Within a few, what seemed like eternal, seconds, it was gone. Choked down, ready to do whatever it would in the pit of his stomach.

Andrew was staring at him. His eyes jumping from side to side as he studied Dan's face.

Dan raised his fists above his head. He roared to the ceiling. The cold weight in his stomach started to shift and squirm. No going back now. This had to work.

A cold tingle spread across his body followed by a sharp kick from within his abdomen. Andrew caught him as he fell to his knees. His stomach felt hard and bloated. He looked down; he looked pregnant. Andrew helped him to the sofa.

"I felt this. It will pass."

He wanted to ask how Andrew could be so sure.

He gasped as another stab came, so sudden and sharp that he was unable to scream. Spit clogged his lungs when he drew breath. He coughed hard and rolled onto his side, his head coming to rest on the arm of the sofa. A cascade of tears streamed across his crumpled cheeks.

Fur tickled his face and he opened his eyes. The Flash was close, leaning his forehead against his. Suddenly he was inside another vision, looking at muddy ground with the glowing pool in the woods just behind. Catman, thin and weak, lay next to him, the bloody remains of a half-eaten frog by his side. His eyes were screwed closed, his stomach distended. He whined in obvious pain. They had been through this too.

The vision faded as The Flash moved his head to lay on Dan's chest.

"Don't worry, Dan." Andrew's voice was fading.

His abs squeezed like a pump, but nothing came up. He couldn't vomit. It felt like something was blocking it. He tried to push himself up. There wasn't time for this. He had to save Amy. His arms gave way and he dropped back to the sofa. The searing pain in his stomach sapped all of his strength. The Flash's soft fur was the only comfort as his body was racked by stab after stab.

He closed his eyes. A cold wind blew over him and, as if carried by the breeze, he was somewhere else...

You Are In Control

It was dark, and Dan was afraid. He'd always been afraid. Afraid of the forest that surrounded his parent's old home, afraid of the unseen ones that hid and watched through windows while he stood inside vulnerable and visible in the light. The ones that waited for him to step out of the safe glow and into the night where they could reach him. The ones that only really existed in his head. He knew this to be true. It didn't help.

He'd come home late from a club. As the designated driver, he was buzzing off the back of several plastic cups of the dingy bar's alternative to Red Bull. He lay awake in bed counting the sheep to calm his overactive mind, too hot for the duvet, too scared of the imaginary demons that stalked the night to take it off.

It was always quiet at his parents. They had two neighbours — one on either side — but each house was at least twenty metres away from the next, with no others for at least half a mile in any direction.

It took him a while to realise he could hear something outside. At first, he thought it was his imagination humanising the sounds of a fox shrieking in the forest, or the creak of the old pipes that ran above the ceiling. But soon it became clear that what he could hear was the sound of someone in serious trouble.

The screams came to him as his mind buzzed and, innocent as he was, he didn't attribute them to their genuine cause. From where he lay, whoever it was sounded fearful and pained.

Something told him he'd been here before. He'd heard this before. It told him not to go outside.

But he swung his legs out of bed, his head filled with visions of a young woman being attacked by men. Men who'd managed to drag her up the gravel track to his neighbour's garden. An innocent brought against her will for the gain of others. A rush of heat ran through him and he wheeled himself out of bed. For some reason, he didn't think to wake his parents. Perhaps there wasn't time.

As he stepped out through the back door, dressed only in his flannel pyjama bottoms, he strained his ears for the sound of movement in the dark. The garden had been huge, a few acres of unusable scrub in the middle of nowhere, and with no light pollution, the grass and trees had a ghostly, silver pallor from the moon and stars. The screams had stopped, but a rustling came from the neighbour's side of the border.

He moved towards the line of large oak trees that split the two gardens. En route, he removed one of the heavy metal legs from the trampoline he and his brother used to play on as kids. Through years of neglect, it had rusted itself into a tetanus riddled oblivion, but was slim yet heavy enough to get a good swing. Sticks and stones covered the ground and stabbed at his bare feet as he crossed the border.

His stomach crawled with all matter of insects, not just butterflies. His skin, warm despite the biting cold of the night. Taurine fuelled fight scenarios and visions of conflict flew through his mind at a hundred frames per second. The weight of the trampoline leg felt comforting in his hands. Although he'd never fought anyone, his testosterone-filled teenage body wanted nothing more than to hurt people who were hurting someone else. His staring eyes, wide in the darkness, felt like they were trying to burrow out of his face, and he squeezed and relaxed his fist involuntarily on the rough pole. It felt almost wooden in his grip. Different to how he remembered, but familiar.

The neighbour was an older gent that had always reminded him of the BFG. Large ear lobes framed a long, kind face. He still cut his grass with a scythe. The screams may have woken him, too.

Dan imagined him at the window, scanning the darkness outside with worried eyes, questioning whether his aged body was up to the task of saving the girl in the garden.

The clouds shifted across the moon. Blackness fell. The screams hadn't resumed. Anyone could be hidden; what would he do if there were more than
one? It suddenly occurred to him how stupid he'd been to not wake his dad.
But there was no going back. Someone needed him.

He lowered his voice to a growl, hoping to sound bigger and older than he
was, and shouted into the night. "I've called the police. They are on their way."

The rustling in the bushes stopped, and he caught a glimpse of movement
to his left. A short, larger woman trotted towards him. Her form shifted as her
heavy body plodded along on the grass, changing between that of the woman
that was really there and a taller, dark-haired woman carrying a camera that
seemed to flit in and out of existence. As she came closer, he noticed that her top
half was clothed only in a bra, and the fly of her denim skirt was undone. He
looked over her shoulder towards the bush she had just come from. Someone
else lurked in the shadow. Another figure.

"Are you OK?" he asked, hiding the pipe behind his leg.

"What are you doing here?" She panted. She finally solidified into the form
he remembered.

He didn't answer.

"Sorry," she said.

"Sorry for what? Are you OK?"

It still hadn't dawned on him what he had interrupted. With the knowledge
of hindsight, his next question, asked because he thought the lady was in trouble
and couldn't say so, makes him curl up and die a little inside. It is the block that
has always kept him from putting himself out there.

"Do you want to come over for a cup of tea?"

Simon De Fraine came rushing out of the bushes towards him. He wore a vest
that glowed white in the night, his hair cut into a sloppy Mohican. Dan stepped
back. This wasn't quite how he remembered the event.

"Of course she doesn't want to come and have a cup of tea. Now piss off."
Simon looked him up and down. He noticed Dan wasn't wearing a top and
pulled his vest off, throwing it to one side. As he did, he seemed to grow back
into the punk from Dan's memory, and then into something taller, something

monstrous, with long arms and gangly legs, and a head buried inside a dark ring of fur. "You gonna be the hero, mate?" He stepped forward. "You gonna be the hero?" A small knife glinted despite the lack of any light.

Dan stepped back once more. If this guy decided to kill him here and now, then he couldn't stop him. Even if he had in fact called the police, they would never have made it here in time anyway. His hand twitched as it gripped the pole, which had somehow become a broom handle. In the dark, the man couldn't have known he had it hidden.

Someone spoke up inside his head. It wasn't his dad's voice, but it used his dad's words.

If you ever come up against someone bigger than you, you hurt them a lot, quickly. Before they know it. Hurt them so they can't get back up again. Otherwise, it'll be you going down, and they won't let you back up.

Words passed down from Dixon father to Dixon son, from small bodied man to small bodied man, for generations. An instruction manual to go with the genetics. Because, for the men in Dan's family, someone bigger or stronger usually meant everyone. In this moment, at nineteen years-old, the meaning of the words became suddenly clear. If this thing in the parka came any closer, he would have no choice but to swing the pole and swing for its head. If he was caught, he was in trouble.

"Don't come any closer." A warning. A plea.

"I'm OK, hun," said the woman, moving herself between them. The thing stopped its advance.

"If you're sure." Dan touched her arm. It was cold and wet with sweat. He sucked in the night air through his nose and sighed as the pieces came together. What he'd interrupted had definitely been aggressive, but entirely consensual.

Heat rose immediately in his cheeks.

He shook his head and, without a word, walked away, back through the boundary dividing the gardens and left the two of them to it. Luckily, he hadn't called the police. That would have been too embarrassing.

He knocked on his parent's room instead of going back to bed.

"Dad, can you come out here?"

He waited a few moments until his dad's sleepy growl came from behind the door.

"Everything OK?"

The door opened slowly. His Dad squinted in the light of the hall. His forehead wrinkled as he registered the broom handle gripped in Dan's hand. Hadn't it been something else?

He stepped out, immediately wide awake. "What's going on?" His eyes flashed a momentary red.

Dan told him.

"Are you alright?"

He shook his head. Couldn't answer with words.

"Do you want to check everything's OK over there?"

He nodded. Relieved at his dad's ability to know what he was thinking even before he spoke. Father's intuition, he called it. More like telepathy.

"Go put black on and we'll go over."

They stalked across the boundary together, hidden in the darkness. The light was now on in the neighbour's house, and the couple were arguing inside.

"Stuart's on holiday," said Dad. "That guy's his nephew. He sometimes house sits. Bit of a prick." Dad never minced his words.

Dan dropped his head. His cheeks, hot despite the cold night. Another moment in his life where it would have been better to have done nothing. A reassuring claw fell on his shoulder. It had talons, scales.

"You did the right thing coming out here, Danny. You must always do your best to look after those who need it."

He looked at his dad, at the black snout growing from beneath his hooded top, the glowing red eyes. Something told him to get away, but he was frozen to the spot. His heart beat fast in his chest.

"You must have scared the hell out of them." Dad grinned, revealing a mouthful of sharp teeth.

"What?" He could hardly talk through fear.

Dad turned and began to lead the way back, quickly disappearing in the dark.

Deep down everyone is afraid of the dark, son. The voice came from inside his head. His dad's words, but not his voice. *And seeing you, all skin and bone, like bloody Nosferatu, coming out of the shadows would put the willies up anyone. You remember that. When you're the one in the dark, and they're out there in the open, you're the one to fear. You are in control.*

He saw a flash of teeth, of red eyes in the darkness.

He was no longer scared. He didn't need to be. The reptile was smiling. It was happy to be free.

He was no longer scared. Not of anything or anyone.

Do You Know Ju Jitsu?

Dan rubbed his eyes as he woke. A long string of yellow bile stretched from his face to his hand as he did, and he flicked it away. He lifted his head from the sofa. Numbness ran the length of his face, and the right side of his neck ached from the unnatural position it had been in. Strands of yellow liquid oozed down the wall ahead of him. He must have thrown up, which was so unlike him. There was nothing substantial in it. No bits of half-digested frog.

Andrew wasn't there.

He sat up with memories of the dream already dwindling. The event had been real, a memory from before, but certain things had been different. He blinked as those changes faded.

Soft fur on his bare chest brought him back to the moment. The Flash's paws rested on his shoulder. He stroked his furry head, flattening his ears.

The Flash leant forward and butted heads once more.

A familiar scent of wood polish and sweat filled his senses as the ground beneath him softened. The cold laminate flooring of their downstairs hallway changed colour, becoming large tiles of yellow, then white, then green. Foam mats spread out around him in a square, each fixed together by puzzle shaped edges. The same ones he'd trained on all those years ago. He was a teenager again, back in the dojo.

At the far end of the mat stood Sensei Martin, his old Ju Jitsu instructor. Beyond was darkness, as if the mats were floating somewhere in space, deep within a black hole.

Sensei Martin faced away from him. Watching the void. Broad shoulders filled his red and white gi. Tufts of orange stuck up either side of his head, though Dan was sure his hair had been grey.

Dan pushed himself up into a kneeling position. He too was wearing a white Ju Jitsu uniform, just like the one he'd worn every Wednesday and Friday at his after-school lessons. It fit him perfectly. The badges he'd won fighting in the demonstration team and competitions, covered in Japanese writing that he'd never understood, were stitched along his right arm. And the black belt he'd earned after years of training was wrapped tightly around his waist. He touched the thick cotton, remembering how smooth it felt against his skin. How long had it been? Seventeen years?

Why had he ever given it up? Because for someone who hated the idea of injuring others, Ju Jitsu was a useless skill.

He felt nostalgic for the time he'd worn the belt last. A time when his biggest worry had been English homework. Not long before he'd picked up a guitar for the first time. Way before, his dreams of superstardom had been shattered and taken over by nightmares of mortgages and bills.

"Do you know why you are here?" Sensei Martin didn't turn. He continued to face away into the black abyss. His thick Scottish accent reverberated around the mat as if coming from all directions.

He paused. Sensei Martin would expect and accept only one answer. It had been years since he had been asked this, but he responded quickly.

"To learn."

Sensei Martin turned and held up a finger. He shook his bald head. "Not this time. This time you are here to remember."

There was something unusual about his face. Dan had not seen his Sensei since he'd quit training and couldn't remember exactly what he looked like, but he was sure he hadn't had pointed ears or whiskers.

As Sensei Martin came forward, his body shrank. His clothes too. Dan blinked, confused.

His teacher's hands touched the floor and became forepaws. A tail sprung from his back and his skin sprouted orange tufts of fur. The Flash, wearing the same white and red suit, leapt forward, landing several paces ahead of Dan on the mat.

He bowed.

"It is good to finally be able to talk to you as equals, Dan." His voice had the same Scottish twang as the Sensei. "It has been too long that we have dwelled under the same roof without the means to communicate."

He didn't know if it was an effect of the dream, or if his tired mind had given up trying to make sense of anything, but acceptance came easily.

"Flashy? But how? And why do you sound like my old Sensei?"

"We do not know how." The Flash sat back on his hind legs, his head held high. "But I sense a fighter in you. I have picked your sensei to open your mind once more to valuable teachings you have chosen to forget."

He looked inward a moment and found that he could remember much of his Ju Jitsu training from when he was a boy. The teachings were there as if he had attended the lessons yesterday.

"Is this all caused by the frog?" He nodded to the void in which they floated. A vision of a scaled snout with sharp teeth passed through his mind.

"Mousebane and Scratchtacular have their strength, and I have the power of thought. I have created all you see here from your memory. A conduit allowing you to unlock the lessons buried beneath time."

"Mousebane? Scratchtacular?"

"You know them by other names. Catman, Dimitri."

"And what should I call you?"

"I have many titles. My mother honoured me with the name Red Mist. The rabbits of the field call me Bloodstalker. The squirrels know me as Orange Death. And I am known by the little girl next door as Captain Fluff Fluff Fluffy McFluffington."

Dan snorted a laugh. The Flash didn't seem to notice.

"You may continue to call me The Flash. But that is of little importance. The Master is in grave danger."

"Amy?" He pushed himself to stand. "Do you know where she is?"

"There is no helping her until your transformation is complete."

"But do you know where she is?"

"We know where to start, and we will follow the trail until we find those responsible—" lines of sharp, white teeth flashed as he snarled "—or die trying." The mat shook as he spoke.

Dan rubbed his face. "How long will it take for me to change like you?"

"Mousebane's transformation took several hours, but his strength grows with every passing day. My alteration is also ongoing. I feel the power building inside. It is how I am able to speak with you, how I have been able to give you visions of my memories, and how I have been able to delve into the depths of your mind to conjure all you see here." The Flash raised a paw and motioned to the mats spinning in infinity. "When I tried to speak with you in your dreams, they were unclear. With the power contained in the amphibian, your mind has finally been opened to me."

"Yes, the frogs... What are they?"

"The Disappearing Woman has the answers we seek."

"You call her that too? The one from the video?"

"Yes, she is a ghost. She moves with light."

"I've seen." How *had* she just disappeared? "The man that was with her said something about a reptile?" Dan had so many questions. Asking them was like chopping heads off a hydra; dealing with one only caused two more to rise in its place.

"A reptile? When my brother and I devoured the frogs, we were sent a vision. A creature spoke to me. It showed me a moment from my past. A moment of great challenge where I could have done better if I had been different." The Flash shook his head. "I don't know what it means."

"We'll figure it out together," he said. "What about Amy? How do we find her?"

"She was taken by the one you call Parkaman."

Dan's hands balled into fists. His knuckles cracked. An unfamiliar anger rose up inside him. "I am going to smash his slimy eel face in."

The Flash grinned, his lips drawn back across needle teeth. "You'll have to beat my brother to that fight. Parkaman is the one who took us from you and The Master. I will show you."

Dan tried to speak, but the air was sucked out of him as his vision blurred and the cosmic dojo started to spin rapidly.

The room blurred, and for a moment he thought he might fall. Fall and keep falling forever through the void. The image of the room continued to swirl, and just as he thought he couldn't take anymore, the movement slowed and his vision cleared. He was inside a cat box. He felt groggy and sick, almost hungover. Beyond the grill was the red tarmac of the cycle path that ran to the industrial estate.

"I do not know how we came to be in the cages, but when we awoke, this is where we were." The Flash narrated.

The view through the bars swayed with the footsteps of whoever was carrying him.

A voice from outside the box spoke. "Red Mist, where are you?" Dan himself didn't recognise it, but somehow he knew it was Catman who had spoken.

"I am here, brother." The Flash replied. "Do not fear. We will get out of this."

The memory skipped forward and they were in the warehouse.

"We were held captive for days."

A pair of creamy marble eyes at the root of a long thin nose looked at him from the dark beyond. A ring of fur surrounded the face. Dan tried to shout when he recognised the pallid features of Parkaman, but no words came out.

Parkaman's face sunk lower. He opened the cage below and took out Catman. His long fingers gripped him tightly by the scruff of the neck. Catman lashed out. Parkaman stumbled and crashed into the box that Dan/The Flash was in. His stomach somersaulted as the box dropped and smashed to the floor. The door sprang open.

"Shit-it," he heard Parkaman shout.

With no hesitation, he was out of the cage. Catman landed ahead of him and bolted.

The Flash followed as Parkaman's foot crashed down next to him. The door at the end of the room was open and The Flash chased Catman through into the alley at the back of the warehouse. They sped through the rusted gap in the fence and into the woods. For a few moments, all was a blur of brown and green as they sprinted through the undergrowth.

"We hadn't eaten for days," The Flash continued to narrate, and the scene slowed when they reached the pool. "So, we ate well. But those frogs were different. They awoke something inside of us. Something long dormant."

"The reptile?" He was still unsure what this meant, but he could sense something growing behind his eyes. Something dark and powerful. A lurking strength. "What will it give me?"

"It will have something to do with your dream."

Dan thought back to the vision he'd had upon eating the frog. It gave him no clues.

"I can sense a power awakening inside you. It is time to find out what you are truly made of Dan, Master's Mate."

"Wait. What?"

"The power is awakening?" The Flash cocked his head.

"No, I meant the Master's Mate bit. What do you mean? Who's the master if not me?"

The Flash laughed. A strange high sound that he would have found adorable were Dan not a little annoyed by the sentiment. "You are not the master. You may bring us sustenance, but you are not in control. You are like us. We all dwell under her watchful eye. She provides. She protects. Our leader. But now, it is our turn to protect her. To fight for her. My brother and I swore an oath. We must journey into battle once more. Will you take up the call with us and free her?"

Tears pricked his eyes. "Yes." And something deep inside spoke up. *Blood will flow.*

The Flash bowed, and Dan returned the gesture.

"Then it is time for you to wake."

His limbs became lighter and his feet left the ground as his vision blurred again.

He was back in the living room. The Flash stood next to him. Dan reached out and scratched his head.

It took a lot of effort to sit up. His stomach muscles blazed. He had no idea how long he'd been asleep. He took out his phone. No missed calls or messages. They hadn't called again with instructions.

Andrew still wasn't there. He scanned the living room for Catman and Dimitri. His eyes fell on a photo next to the TV. Him and Amy on their wedding day. Huge grins shone from their faces as they were leaving the church beneath cascades of confetti. It hadn't been the best day of his life. Every day since he'd met her had been just as good. And now...

"Oh god," he said, pressing his hands to his face. He felt like someone had inflated a balloon in his throat. He held back a sob. He might never see that beautiful smile again. "Oh, Amy."

A thin red eye opened in his mind. A memory of his dream? No, something more. It seemed to search for him, then fixed him with its reptilian gaze. A voice spoke up in his head. A curious sensation, not like someone else in the room was speaking, more like they had spoken, and he was remembering what they had said. It sounded angry.

'Let's not fuck about moping. Let's find her!'

Without intention, the worry for Amy faded as if turned down like the volume on a stereo. An agitated fire lit in his belly, replacing the anxiety. He jerked his shoulders and began clicking his fingers with the new energy.

"Who are you?"

'The part of us that we don't like to acknowledge exists. The part of us that liked smashing that guy in the warehouse with a broom. You've suppressed us for too long. Something in the frog set us free.'

His mind raced. Was this really happening? Was he really about to gain some sort of superpower? He felt elated, excited, nervous, all at once. He could save Amy.

He headed to the bedroom and pulled on a fresh set of clothes.Checked the clock by his bedside table: 1:30 p.m. He'd been out for ten hours. That meant he only had fourteen to get the money.

'*We won't be getting the money,*' growled the reptile. '*We choose violence.*'

"Do we?"

'*Abso-fuckin-lutely.*'

As if controlled by an outside force, he took his phone from his pocket and sent a text to Amy: '*Got the money*'.

Sudden panic gripped him. Why had he done that?

'*Now they have incentive to call back, and it will be their undoing.*' The reptile cackled.

"What?" he voiced to the empty room.

'*They knew we'd never get the money. They are lying to us to give themselves more time to get away with her.*'

The thought had crossed his mind. Worry constricted his throat. They wouldn't do that, would they? People weren't that terrible. There had to be a chance to set things right, to fix the mess he'd made.

'*People are that terrible.*'

He realised he was making a low, croaking moan. His knees buckled and he fell to sit on the edge of the bed.

'*We can be that terrible.*'

"What do we do if they don't believe us?"

In answer to his question, the phone vibrated in his hand. A reply: '*Will send you the location of a meeting point. Be ready. And no police.*'

"We need to do something before then, don't we?" he said to himself. "Find them."

He heard the front door slam. "Dan?" Then hurried footsteps on the stairs. Andrew burst into the room wearing a set of Dan's black tracksuit bottoms and a hoodie beneath his robe. "Are you OK?"

"I've felt better," he said.

"We know where they are," said Andrew. He motioned for Dan to follow him.

"Who Amy?"

The trio headed downstairs.

"That guy with the parka, at least. He's at the old man's house. The one across the road."

"Gatsby." Dan thought for a moment. "They're at Gatsby's?"

It took him a second to fathom why, but of course, the house opposite was the perfect stake out location to make sure Dan didn't call the police. Poor Gatsby. Had they hurt the old man?

"Yeah," said Andrew. "Those thugs from the warehouse." He punched one fist into his open palm. Coming from a small man wearing a flowery black robe and sandals, the move didn't look overly threatening, but Dan guessed it was the thought that counted. "And they'll know where to find her."

"Alright, we should come up with a plan." Dan tapped his chin.

'No plan. Plans are for the weak,' growled the reptile.

"Wait. What?"

'The weeeeeak!'

Dan felt his body forced to its feet, and the reptile spoke through him to Andrew. "Let's go unleash the beasts on these pricks. Follow me."

They couldn't just barge in. They couldn't.

'We'll be fine. Trust us.'

"Sure thing," said Andrew, surprisingly, although behind his friend's eyes, Dan could see a flicker of fear.

He was forced downstairs by his own legs. "Come on boys," the reptile called as it strode Dan's body through the front door. Catman and Dimitri soon caught up. "Time to fuck shit up."

He threw open Gatsby's gate and ran at the front door. In his mind's eye, he could see the reptile's intention was to kick it in.

But what if they were wrong? What if Gatsby was just sitting in his living room watching Antiques Roadshow, or something?

'Then we'll apologise,' answered the reptile, *'but if they're here, then it's blood-bath time.'*

"No. What do you mean? You can't just—" He glanced at Andrew. "Did you keep hearing this voi—? woah—"

He threw himself against the door.

Perhaps this was it. He was going to be strong like Catman. He closed his eyes and pushed as hard as he could. But the door remained firmly shut.

'Why are we so pathetic? Haven't we been going to the gym?'

"We're an ectomorph. It's hard for us to put on muscle."

'We're a little bitch, is what we are. But that'll change.' He sensed clawed hands rubbing together. *Just give me a moment for some tinkering in here.'*

"Tinkering? What are you going to do?"

Just you wait and see... But first, let's try the window."

"You're hearing it too?" Andrew tapped the side of his head.

"What is it?" asked Dan, while his eyes scanned the garden for a large rock.

"It said it was me."

This voice was most certainly not Dan. It was a maniac.

He picked up a heavy-looking gnome and, before he could do anything to stop himself, sent it crashing through the front window.

He shuddered at the noise of the glass shattering, but still leant in, unlocked it, pulled it open, and jumped over and into Gatsby's front room.

"Are you coming?" he hissed to Andrew.

"In this?" He held up his arms to show his robe. "Can you get the door?"

Dan grunted.

A leather chesterfield sat at right angles with a dark green armchair facing a large television. The room smelt musty, but he could just make out the hint of Amy's perfume, like she'd been here recently.

"Amy?"

"Oi!" came a reply from further inside. "What you doing?"

It didn't sound like Gatsby.

Hoodyman entered from the kitchen on the far side of the living room. "Oh, it's you." He looked taken aback for a moment, then grinned and drew his knife from his pocket. It opened with a flick of his wrist. "I was well pissed when you got away the other day."

Dan's lips parted into a grin. "Find us a spoon. His eyes are coming out."

Surprised at his own outburst, he covered his mouth with both hands.

'What?' said the reptile. *'Go on. Let me.'*

"Let's just do normal fighting for now," he said, raising his fists hopefully. "No spoons."

Hoodyman wrinkled his nose in confusion. "You what, mate? You better prepare to get stabbed up, mate."

"Andrew, help!"

"What do I do?"

The man lunged forward and stabbed for Dan's throat. Relying on instinct, he swung his arm up and slammed it into Hoodyman's as hard as he could. The knife flew away as he caught the wrist. He turned, pushing his hip into Hoodyman's stomach, and pulled him over in a perfectly executed throw.

For a fraction of a second he was surprised at what he'd done — it'd been years since he'd trained, but the move had come naturally — and then he was being pelted by a rain of tiny stones.

"Sorry," said Andrew from outside, clutching another fistful of gravel. "I was aiming at him. Looks like you didn't need me, though. You've got sick kung fu powers."

Dan spun Hoodyman's arm around and locked it. His red face spluttered into the carpet, wild eyes staring up.

"Did you really think she'd be here?" he shouted. "You're not going to see her agaaaaa—"

Dan twisted the arm further and pressed a knee into his neck, squashing the hood and cap from his head.

"Where is she?" His fingers twitched, eager to twist further, to break the arm if he had to, to find out where she was.

A thump came through the ceiling from the room above.

He heard a rush of fabric behind.

"Watch out," called Andrew.

Something crunched into the back of his head. He fell forward, catching himself on the back of the old leather sofa.

Parkaman pulled Hoodyman up by his jumper. In his left hand he held a hook handled walking stick. Dan touched the back of his head. It wasn't bleeding.

"Cop a load of this," shouted Andrew, and his second handful of gravel pattered against the outside of the house. "Ah, bums."

"Maybe if throwing isn't your strong suit, try something else," shouted Dan. "Or at least try throwing something more dangerous than gravel."

"OK, bear with... Maybe just kung fu the shit out of them for a bit."

Dan scanned the room, hoping for something he could use as a weapon as the pair closed in. A decorative bucket of fire pokers sat by the gas fire. He dodged another swing of the stick, dived over the chesterfield, and grabbed the brass ash spade.

"Get 'em, Dimi," said Andrew.

Dimitri shot like a fluffy bullet through the window, claws first, and latched onto the back of Hoodyman's head. Hoodyman screamed and fell back onto the armchair. The whole thing toppled over under his weight.

"You next, big boy." Andrew heaved Catman up onto the window ledge from outside. "Attack!"

Catman's eyes narrowed when he saw Parkaman.

"No, not you." Parkaman bolted, disappearing into the hall. Catman quickly followed.

A hiss followed by a scream, and a series of bumps moved up the stairs. A sickening crunch, and the thumps reversed. A moment's silence. Then Catman brushed past the door frame and slunk back into the lounge.

Dan edged closer to the doorway, the spade clutched tight in his sweaty palms. Parkaman lay at the foot of the stairs, his skinny jean-clad legs sprawled above him on the first few steps. His head, still deep within the fur of his hood, lolled unnaturally to one side.

He gave him a poke. He didn't move. His eyes were open, staring.

Was he dead?

'Catman gets it,' said the reptile.

Dan shivered.

The doorbell rang. His heart fluttered. He opened it.

"Oh, did Dimitri do that?" Andrew bit the knuckle of his first finger and looked at Parkaman dead on the stairs as if he were nothing more than a broken vase.

"Um, no, but... That guy's dead, Andrew."

Andrew threw his palms to the ceiling. "Live like a prick, die like a prick." This wasn't Andrew as he knew him.

"O... K... I'm going upstairs," said Dan. "Maybe she's here somewhere."

"I'll stay down here, make sure that other one doesn't get away."

"Be careful."

He moved to step over Parkaman, expecting a long-fingered hand to grab his ankle.

Gripping the bannister, and with eyes closed, he heaved himself up the first four steps over the body.

A muffled sound came from one of the rooms that led off the landing. He entered, but it was empty. No sign of Amy. The red-eyed darkness within him grumbled.

The room had a single bed in the centre. On his right, a tall chest of drawers was topped with small metal picture frames containing faded photographs of a younger, happier Gatsby. In most, a young boy stood with him. Perhaps his son? In the biggest photo, both were immaculately dressed in hunting attire and wellington boots. Each held a hunting shotgun resting over one arm, and the boy was holding up a fat breasted pheasant.

A sound came from the wardrobe at the far side of the room. His hopes rose as he crossed and opened the doors.

Gatsby was sitting on the floor of the cupboard in a pair of stripy blue pyjamas. His long limbs squashed in that space made him look like he had been folded and put away like one of his pristine suits. He gazed up at Dan with tired, watery eyes and leant his head back against the wall.

"Thank goodness," he slurred.

His mouth looked strange, and Dan quickly realised why.

They'd smashed out all of his teeth.

OLD SPORT

D an took Gatsby by the elbow and helped him to stand. It surprised him how light he was, as if he were an origami model of a man. His eyes were continually drawn to the old man's mouth. His shock must have been obvious, but he couldn't hide it.

'*The bastards,*' the reptile hissed.

He agreed. Those complete and utter bastards. How could they do this to a frail, old man?

Gatsby rolled his eyes. Not at all fazed by his injuries.

'*That's one tough son of a bitch.*'

He headed to the bed and fell to a seated position. Reached for a glass on the bedside table, and fished out a set of dentures, popping them in with a lip-smacking sucking noise.

'*Oh.*'

"You look at me the way my boy does when I've not got these things in." He smiled, now with perfect white teeth. "Did you take care of those good for nothings downstairs? They caught me napping and threw me in the cupboard. Been in there all bloody night."

Gatsby's eyes flicked over Catman and The Flash as they crept into the room.

"Did they hurt you?" He looked the old man over. He seemed alright considering.

"My pride more than anything." He rubbed his legs with chunky misshapen knuckles. His eyes squeezed shut and his mouth formed an O, the way an actor in a pantomime might when feigning pain. "My legs feel like they're covered with pins."

He sat and stared at Catman for a moment, before looking sideways at Dan with a squint. "They were spying on you, you know? They were talking about you when you got back last night." His gaze returned to Catman.

Dan squatted to his haunches next to where The Flash was sniffing Gatsby's slippered foot. "What did they say?"

"They've got your wife. What did you do to get yourself into a mess like this?" He pointed a shaking finger at the door. "Those aren't the sort of people someone like you wants to mess with."

"They're the ones who've been taking the cats."

"I read something about that in the paper. They were using them for fighting."

Dan nodded. "They must have taken yours too."

"What?" He looked at Dan clearly perplexed, then blinked a few times. "Ah yes, my Tabby."

His stony gaze locked with Dan's. There was something bird like about his features. Beaky nose. Sunken eyes. Dan couldn't hold his stare.

"How did you find them?" Gatsby asked.

"These guys did it." He pointed two fingers at Catman and The Flash. "I know it's hard to believe, but they found them in one of the warehouses on the estate."

"I believe it. These animals aren't stupid. And he's big, isn't he? The black one." He pointed at Catman. "How did he get so big?"

"They found something. I don't quite understand it yet, but I think they've come into contact with some sort of—" He paused, trying to think of the right word. Something Gatsby might understand. "—elixir of strength."

"Well, you can sign me up for that."

Dan grunted. "If you're OK. I'm going to go now. I guess you can call the police. Or I can get you an ambulance?"

"Don't worry about me. But where will you go? To get your wife? You don't know where she is, do you?"

"I'm hoping the guy downstairs will." The one left alive.

Shakily, Gatsby pushed himself up from the bed. A snarl crossed his lined face, which Dan put down to the effort of getting up. He grasped his elbow and helped him to the door.

"I can do it," Gatsby said, waving him off and hobbling to the landing. "I've walked all my bloody life without help from the likes of you."

They reached the top of the stairs. Gatsby sighed when he saw Parkaman's body.

"You're going to have to clear him out the way before I can get down," he said, through gritted dentures. "He was the one who pulled me out of bed and shoved me in the cupboard." His knuckles turned white as he gripped the bannister.

He left Gatsby at the top and descended. Every step worse than the last. Until today, he'd never seen a dead body, let alone moved one.

He jumped the last three stairs over where Parkaman lay, and before he could think — because if he thought too much he'd never be able move again — grabbed the dead man's bony ankles with shaking hands. Parkaman's phone fell out of his jean pocket and Dan nearly had a heart attack.

The head flopped to one side as he yanked Parkaman along the floor. His stomach turned, and he dropped one of the legs as he fought back a gag. Looked away and did his best to convince himself that Gatsby's wall paper was the most interesting thing he'd ever seen, and backed into the lounge dragging the body behind him.

"The other one's dead, too," said Andrew, from somewhere inside the house.

When he passed Hoodyman, Dan gagged again. Blood leaked from fresh gouges in his cheeks and into the tired beige carpet.

'Nice,' said the reptile.

"Not nice," hissed Dan. "Shut up a minute." He left Parkaman on the floor next to Hoodyman. "Andrew, where are you?"

Andrew came out of the kitchen with half a baguette in one hand. "Ever since we ate those frogs, me and Dimitri have been absolutely famished."

"What's going on down there?" came Gatsby's voice.

"Oh, is the old dude OK?" said Andrew. He broke the bread and held one half out to Dan.

"Thanks." In another life, he would have thought moving corpses and being embroiled in murderous activity whilst hunting down his kidnapped wife might ruin his appetite somewhat, but his stomach was ablaze with hunger. He took a bite. "I think so. They stuffed him in a cupboard."

"Poor guy."

Dan left Andrew in the lounge then headed back to the stairs.

He flitted around Gatsby as the older man descended, conscious of his pride in his independence, but also that he may not be at his best having spent the night in the cupboard.

"I don't think you're going to be getting any information out of them," the old man said when he saw the bodies in his lounge.

"I've got a number I can call. They'll tell me where to go."

"Well, you better get ringing," said Gatsby. He allowed Dan to help him over to the chesterfield. "They are going to know something's up when those two idiots don't check in." He motioned towards the two bodies. "If it was me, and I'd sent them to watch you, I'd expect a call every few hours with an update."

Dan grabbed Parkaman's phone from the hall. "I'll keep this one's phone on me. If anyone tries to get in touch, I'll fake it."

Gatsby shrugged. He did a double take as he noticed the bloodied face of Hoodyman.

"A right pig's ear you've made of that one." He nodded in Hoodyman's direction. He'd collected his mahogany walking stick from somewhere and folded his hands over the handle. His long fingers in that position made him look like a praying mantis. "You don't look like you've got it in you."

"That was my, Dimitri." Andrew leant proudly on the back of the armchair. "He's a natural born killer."

Dan nodded at Catman. "I think they had a score to settle."

Gatsby hummed. "Not sure if anyone'll believe that. When they ask, I'll say I took them down when they invaded my home." He shook his walking stick in the air. "The papers love an underdog."

He sat there in his stripy blue pyjamas. His hands shook, sending tremors all the way down his stick. Andrew frowned, and Dan could tell what he was thinking, because he was thinking it too. It would probably be easier to believe that a cat had murdered the two thugs.

"I can tell what you're thinking and don't." Gatsby pointed a finger. "Just 'cus you see an old man in front of you now, doesn't mean I'm old up here." He tapped his temple. "I wasn't born this way you know." His voice rose and fell like an angry wave. "I've had my fair share of scraps. The things I've seen would—" He stopped himself. Shook his head. His train of thought hanging mid-sentence. "Any normal person would have called the police by now, why ain't you?"

"I can't. They won't let me. And... I'm not sure I want their help." Dan thought back to the second time he'd spoken with Gatsby. "What you said before, when you saw us out front, you were right."

Gatsby's mouth quivered into a smile. "I don't remember a lot of what I say these days. You'll need to remind me." A mischievous gleam in his eye made him look like a sly, old imp.

"You said about finding my dragon to fight. *This* is my dragon. This is my chance to change. Whoever has Amy is going to sell her tonight, and it's down to me to stop it." He paused. He knew this was right. "I need to be the one to fix this." He took his phone from his pocket and held it up. "I just need to meet them where they send me and I'll get her back."

"That's a lot to wager." Gatsby chuckled. "But you're right. I've been on this earth eighty-five years and the police have never done nothing for me. They'll only get in the way." He looked Dan up and down. "You're very confident in yourself though, boy. It's admirable, but what makes you think you've got what it takes?" He nodded at Andrew. "Snowman over here is hardly going to back you up in a fight."

Andrew scoffed. "Uh, it's snow*flake*."

"I have Catman and The Flash with me," said Dan.

Gatsby shook his head.

'Maybe the old man wants to come along for the ride,' said the reptile. *'He might have less to lose than us. Although I resent the use of reptiles as the bad guys in this metaphor, let's give him one last dragon to fight.'*

"If I told you I could give you the opportunity to give these guys a taste of their own medicine," said Dan, "to get revenge for what they did to your cat, but it involved doing something a little bit gross, would you say yes?"

Andrew raised his eyebrows and looked at Gatsby.

Gatsby scrutinised Dan out of the corner of his eye. Then his gaze drifted across the room to Catman, The Flash, and Dimitri. He rubbed a hand across his cheek with a rasp of new stubble.

Another moment passed before he turned back to Dan.

"Has this got something to do with your elixir of strength?"

"It might."

"Well, I ain't gettin' any younger. And I did say sign me up." He held his hand up. "So, you might as well show me. At my age I've got nothing to lose and everything to gain."

Amuse My Bouche

D an returned home with Andrew to retrieve the frogs while Gatsby dressed.

Now, the three of them sat around Gatsby's kitchen table with the two frogs between them on the wipe-clean table cloth. A damp brown ring of swampy water circled each. That natural earthy smell filled the kitchen. Dan was starting to like it.

Despite the frog's slight blue glow, Gatsby, whose name they soon learned was George, seemed a little reluctant to believe them.

Which was fair enough. It was all a bit out there.

Gatsby sported a black turtleneck jumper with a soft black beret set at a jaunty angle on his head. With his classically handsome features, and his tiny well-groomed moustache, he looked like a retired milk tray man.

In his outfit of black hoody, black tracksuit bottoms, and black trainers, Dan looked more chav than chick magnet.

That reptile voice in his head had been quiet, but he could sense its presence as a background gnawing in his belly and brain. Similar to the presence of a grain of sand in a wound. What had it said before? *Tinkering.* He was worried what that meant. Other than that, he didn't feel any different since eating the frog.

Another part of him worried that the extent of his powers might just be an overconfident lizard-like passenger who liked to threaten people with spoons. He'd managed to fight off Hoodyman, but something told him that the reemergence of his Ju Jitsu skills was The Flash's clever doing.

While they sat at the table, he and Andrew filled Gatsby in on their week. Dan told him about seeing Catman and The Flash sneak through his bathroom

window, the cat abductions, the men at the warehouse, the dog fight, the pool
that he and Andrew had found in the woods and the man and woman who had
chased them from Andrew's house, culminating with their separate accounts of
eating the frogs and what it had done for them. It felt good to share the whole
story with another.

But something here was troubling him. They couldn't ask Gatsby to eat the
frog, could they? While it had lasted, the pain had been awful. What if the old
man didn't survive it?

'It'll be good for him,' said the reptile. *'He needs it. And we need him. Think
about it...'*

But what if the frogs killed him?

*'Nah, he'll be fine. And we stand more of a chance of finding Amy with three
of us.'*

As they shared their story, Gatsby had nodded along in all the right places.
He'd shown particular interest in the pool and its location. He appeared to be
taking it well, but Dan wondered if that was because he wasn't quite getting
exactly what it all meant.

"What is it? Some kind of drug?" he asked. "How do you know it's safe?"

Dan opened his mouth to say that he didn't.

"It's definitely safe," said the reptile through his lips, before Dan could voice
his concern. He tried to cover his mouth to stop himself from speaking — he
couldn't just lie — but his fingers gripped the table and he couldn't lift his hand.
"In fact it's brilliant. Best thing I've ever done. Ten out of ten, would eat a frog
again."

Andrew coughed, then spluttered. "Yeah, George, you said it yourself, what
do you have to lose?"

He gave Dan a wide eyed look, which suggested those weren't his own words
either. Dan returned it. This wasn't good.

The old man, not cottoning on to their shared look of horror, considered
their words for a moment, his eyes fixed on the frogs. "At eighty-five, and as frail
as a wet paper bag, not much. How did the pair of you feel after eating it?" He
glanced up.

"I took mine a couple of days ago," said Andrew, and with the cheesy chuckle of a juice cleanse diet influencer raised both thumbs and added, "I've never felt better."

"And you?" Gatsby looked expectantly at Dan.

He had to stop this. Tried to fight it.

"Not much different yet," he said. At least that was true. "Maybe they vary in the time they take to work? But I know something's changed. I have this voice inside my head... It's right about everything, and very clever."

'...and should be listened to on all accounts.'

"And I've been able to talk to The Flash. He helped me remember my Ju Jitsu training from when I was a teenager. When I stopped that guy in the hoody, it was like it all flooded back in that instant. I knew exactly what to do to take him down and it's been years since I trained." His stomach rumbled. "I'm hungry too, which I think is a sign..."

Of what though he couldn't say.

Gatsby leant his head to one side. "A voice?" His lips pressed into an upside down U. He looked more curious than disgusted.

"It's a part of me, I think," he said.

Gatsby poked the nearest frog with a leather-gloved finger. "And you're telling me you just ate it? Raw?"

"I sautéd mine in olive oil." Andrew spun his wrist in quick circles, mimicking the stirring of a pan, with a delighted little frown of chef-like concentration on his brow. "Added a little fresh rosemary, salt, pepper. Wasn't bad."

Dan's mouth fell open. "I didn't know that was an option."

"I did wonder why you just ate it raw." Andrew wrinkled his nose and scratched his chin. "You had this look on your face, I didn't want to stop you." He clenched his fists and shimmied his shoulders. "You were kind of in the zone."

"Still..."

"I'd planned scampi and chips for dinner last night." Gatsby leant back a little in his chair. "But I've never been shy of trying new things. I've been around."

He picked up the lighter coloured of the two frogs, and held it like a burger. He turned it over in his hands. Its colouring was similar to the one Dan had eaten, with white squiggles covering its back. It looked more appealing than the second, which was covered in darker markings, like someone had pressed a handful of minuscule black snakes into its back.

"Did it just work?" Gatsby lifted a nostril at the frog. " Will it change me before we have to go?"

"I don't know," said Dan. "I passed out for a few hours. But we have a bit of time before they call."

Gatsby looked between them. "Will it make me young again?" He moved to place the frog back on the table, but didn't let it drop.

"Whatever you need, it'll give you," the reptile said. Dan looked again at Andrew. Those had been his words. He bit his lip. This was awful. They couldn't make Gatsby go through this.

'We stand a much better chance with all of us.'

They did, it was true.

"It might sound crazy, but these things—" he picked up the last frog on the table and shook it "—can make you stronger. They can heal you."

"It could be a second chance for you," said Andrew. A small whine escaped his throat that only Dan appeared to hear.

Gatsby's nostril twitched and for a silent moment he glared at the frog in his hand. An anger burned behind those bloodshot eyes that sent shivers down Dan's back. His mouth tightened to a thin line, and for a second Dan thought the old man might leap across the table and bludgeon him to death with the cold, dead frog.

He shrugged. "Fine. Give it a once over in the pan." He pointed at Andrew.

Andrew jerked upright and took a frying pan from next to the oven. Poured in a glob of oil and turned on the hob. With a sharp knife from a drawer, he chopped the frog in half and set it to sizzling with a pinch of salt. Dan's stomach flobbled remembering his earlier dining experience.

Andrew tapped his chin. "Have you got any garlic?"

Gatsby snorted. "What do you think I am, Jamie bloody Oliver? Just salt."

It smelled something like chicken.

"That's probably enough," said Gatsby, after a moment or two.

"But..." Andrew hesitated.

"Before I change my mind."

Andrew scraped everything onto a plate and set it before Gatsby. The shrivelled heap of meat and bone didn't take up much space. With most of the water cooked out, it was hardly anything.

Gatsby picked up each half and placed them both in his mouth, and, with a crunch of denture on bone, chewed them and swallowed. Then he opened his mouth.

What had they done?

'He's only gone and bloody done it.' The reptile beamed.

"S'all gone. So, what happens ne—" His words cut off as he doubled over and slammed a fist on the table with a hammering crash. The cutlery he had set out for the previous evening's dinner jumped off the table and clattered to the floor. His beret slid off his head. He turned his furious, accusing eyes towards Dan. "What the hell have you done to me?"

Dan and Andrew both rushed around opposite ends of the table, and helped him up. Gatsby pushed them away with surprising strength. Dan fell against the fridge, and Gatsby stumbled into the living room, where he landed heavily on the chesterfield. Another spasm caused him to cry out.

"It will end," Andrew promised. "This happened to us, too."

But how could he know? Could Gatsby handle what was about to happen to him?

Gatsby winced and let out a gasp. It looked like he was trying to talk, but he couldn't get the words out. He curled into a foetal position, closed his eyes, and lay still, seemingly asleep.

"Do you think he'll be OK?" asked Dan.

Andrew nodded. "I hope so."

"What do we do now?"

"We wait." Andrew stretched his arms over his head. "I don't know about you but I'm shattered. I've been up for over twenty-four hours. We need to be ready when they call. You should try and get some sleep."

"I don't think I'll be able to. Not with her out there. But you should."

Andrew smiled. "We'll find her." He patted Dan on the shoulder then headed upstairs.

While he waited for the call, Dan moved around the living room. There were more photographs of Gatsby and his son. In an earlier photo, black and white, possibly from before the boy was born, Gatsby stood with a crew of well-dressed men and women. It took a while for Dan to pick him out. He had his arm around a young lady, who was smiling at the camera. Gatsby's concentration was elsewhere.

He thought of Amy and sighed. Tears filled his eyes and he wiped them away. His body stiffened against the sobs. He had to stay strong, focused.

Avoiding the red Hoodyman shaped patch on the carpet — Andrew had moved the bodies into Gatsby's downstairs toilet — he flopped down into the armchair opposite Gatsby. The cats stretched out on the floor.

"Are you still there?" he said to himself, to the reptile.

There was no reply. Just a rumbling in his stomach. He suddenly realised he'd never felt so hungry. He moved to the kitchen. And rifled through the fridge. Ate everything there — yoghurts, sliced meats, vegetables raw from the crisper, drank deeply from a carton of orange juice that had gone slightly fizzy, before doing the same with a pint of milk. Nothing seemed to satiate him fully, but it felt good to eat. Better than it ever had. Something was changing.

As he searched for calories through the barely lit kitchen, he felt a terrifying juxtaposition in knowing that Amy was somewhere scared and alone, and he was here stuffing his face with nothing he could do but wait and hope. Everything was going to come to a head at the last minute.

He looked at Gatsby. At least he wasn't alone. He'd felt so alone.

The text with the meeting point would come soon. The catalyst for whatever was to come next. He had to be ready.

COLD BUTTER

Night came. He checked the phone for the thousandth time. It was nearly eleven and no text yet. Nervous tension coiled around his stomach like a snake. They had to call. They had to.

He span the phone between index finger and thumb and watched Gatsby sleeping on the sofa. His breathing seemed less constricted than before, steadier, deeper. There hadn't been a peep from Andrew upstairs.

The phone lit up. Amy's number.

He answered. "Hello."

Red eyes opened inside his mind and the reptile surged forward. *'I'll get it!'* it said.

"You somehow got my money." The man on the other end's voice was still jovial, though more abrupt than the previous night.

"I— I— I did." Although the words left his mouth, it wasn't him speaking. He was merely a mouthpiece, the reptile stuttering through him. "I had to go all over town, but I m-m-managed it."

"Oh, ho, ho," said the man, saying the words rather than actually laughing. "I did not expect that. That is excellent indeed. Looks like you and I are going to end up square after all."

"Oh, I sure hope so. I just want my wife back, please"

'Gee whizz golly! This dick is lapping it up.'

"There's a little motorway bridge near the warehouse. I'll drop a pin on maps. Meet my boys there. If you really have got what you owe, then we'll make a trade," his voice darkened. "If not you'll die, and she'll watch."

"I'll be there. Please don't hurt her."

"That's up to you. Remember, I'll know if you've called the police. If they show up and my men are arrested. I'll be safe, but you will never see her again. She'll be coming in a second car when I know it's clear."

He looked at Gatsby. His wrinkled eyelids fluttered independently of each other as if he were trying to simultaneously keep them open and shut.

"Don't worry. It's just me. I promise."

The man hung up.

"What are you doing?" he said, regaining control of his own mouth. "We don't have the money."

'No, remember, we've chosen violence.'

"Have we? We're not going to be able to fight them."

'No, we probably won't be fighting. But he will...'

Dan felt his eyes shift towards Catman stretched out on the floor.

'How do we feel about torture?'

"Uh... no, definitely—"

'Well, not torture per se, more psychological manipulation.'

"Um... I don't know"

'It's not really torture if it doesn't hurt, right?'

"I suppose we do whatever we have to."

'That's the spirit. When the time comes, just do what comes naturally.'

"Do I have a say in this?"

'Ha! Nooo.'

Every time they spoke like this, he could feel himself and the reptile becoming more a single organism. Like cold butter slowly melting over a piece of toasted bread, becoming one.

"So what's the plan?"

'We'll go, we'll hide the cats in a bag pretending it's full of cash, take out all but one of the pricks at the rendezvous, then squeeze him like a sponge.'

"Sounds like you've thought this all through."

'What do you think's been going on back here?'

The reptile faded back into his subconscious leaving him with a coil of nerves in his stomach. He staggered to his feet.

"Are you talking to me?" croaked Gatsby. How long had he been awake for? He coughed. Brought a hand up to rest on his forehead. "Was that them?

"How are you feeling?" Dan moved closer.

"It feels like something is wriggling inside my guts, but—" He held his fingers before his eyes. "My hands aren't shaking. Not so much as a tremor."

Dan picked up Parkaman's coat from the back of the chesterfield. He had removed it earlier, with great difficulty and almost constant retching.

Gatsby eased himself up. "And I can see. I've not been able to see without my glasses for nearly thirty years."

He was steady on his feet, his trademark totter gone.

"Sorry to force you to move so soon after waking, but we've got to go." Dan held out the parka. "You could wear this, pretend you're the one they called Leeroy. He was about your build."

"He was." Gatsby slowly held a hand out to take it. "It'll make the perfect disguise." He took a deep breath, then slipped the coat on. "I'm more than ready for this," he said. "I feel..." He shook his head and paused for a moment. His eyes locked on Dan's. "I feel fantastic."

"We have to meet them at the motorway bridge." His stomach and neck ached from tensing. "I'll get Andrew then we'll go."

"I need to call my son," said Gatsby. "I was supposed to be seeing him today and if we're going on a mission then I'll need to cancel." He then put a hand to his stomach and started walking towards the kitchen. "And I need a snack. Bloody starving."

Obligate Carnivore

Situated at the far side of the field bordering the industrial estate was the meeting point. A small motorway bridge that Dan knew well. He and his friends had discovered the hidden gem once while out exploring the Surrey wilderness, like an Aztec temple in the jungles of South America. A concrete archway overgrown with brambles and weeds, and daubed with the spray-painted tags of long-forgotten teenage artists. It had been the perfect place to drink and make noise where no one could hear them, but now—

"This place stinks." Gatsby wrinkled his nose.

"It does," added Andrew. He was wearing Hoodyman's hooded top, with the hood pulled up and a cap from Gatsby's that left his face in shadow. He'd added a black scarf to the ensemble to hide his beard. With his robe bunched up beneath the hoody, the disguise was actually quite accurate.

Th bridge wasn't quite how he remembered it. Instead of that secret hideaway, that temple to the gods of youthful merriment, it was a dank, mouldy hole in the woods. A strong stench of stale urine filled the air, along with burnt rubber and exhaust fumes. An abandoned shopping trolley lay on its side by one wall, covered in wet strips of paper and plastic that had blown in and caught in its grill. Thin, stubby plants thrust out of the ground around the base of the concrete walls resembling the fingers of the freshly resurrected dead. The walls themselves were covered in a crumbling layer of crusty silt, and every time a car rumbled overhead, a shower of muddy flakes would fall like brown snow.

There was nowhere to hide, so they stood in the open and waited.

After roughly five minutes, he turned to Gatsby. "What if they were expecting a call from the guy in the parka? What if this is just a trick, and they were never going to bring Amy back?"

"They'll be here, boy," said Gatsby, his eyes not once leaving the far end of the tunnel. A rough dirt path snaked through the woods, just big enough for a vehicle. "If you said you had money, they'll come just to take it. They might kill you both and still keep the girl, but they'll come for the money."

Dan and Andrew shared a worried look behind Gatsby's back.

"Thanks for the reassurance," said Andrew.

Headlights shone through the forest, like a white sun rise, reflecting off the muddy puddles that covered the road.

Gatsby pulled the furry hood over his head. "Here they are."

Dan's heart sped up, and he stretched his shoulders back. Tried to look confident despite feeling everything but. The large duffle bag that he carried suddenly felt too heavy, but he held it up. Though he'd never touched £100,000 in his life, he hoped the bag felt like it weighed approximately the same. Dimitri and The Flash were waiting patiently inside. Catman, who hadn't fit, was lurking somewhere nearby.

The car stopped just short of the tunnel. He shielded his eyes from the dazzle of the headlights. Next to him, Gatsby and Andrew kept their heads down. Three men stepped out and strode forwards, silhouetted in the glare. He found himself thinking how strangely normal they looked. They weren't dressed in smart suits, nor black jackets and tight beanie hats, the clothes that all denizens of comic book criminal underworlds wore. They just looked normal. Dressed like his dad. Clean-cut family men with a wife, two kids, and an uninspiring nine to five. Like someone you would pass on the street without a second thought.

"Alright, Leeroy, Dean," said the man on the right to Gatsby and Andrew. "What you doing here?"

"Bossman told them to keep their eyes on this prick," said the man on the left, nodding at Dan. "Looks like they tailed him all the way here."

Gatsby nodded. He and Andrew stood back a little so as not to give themselves away.

"I've got the money," said Dan, hoping to divert their attention.

The guy in the middle stepped forward holding a hand out to Dan. "Hand it over then."

"Where's Amy?" He pulled the strap of the bag tight against his body. "The guy on the phone said she'd be here."

"Oh yeah, she'll be here any minute now." His face was a shadow. Dan couldn't see his eyes. He stepped forward and grabbed the bag from his shoulder. "Oh, nice and heavy. He will be pleased with you." Then returned to the car.

The other two grabbed him by the arms, bending them behind his back.

Out of the corner of his eye, he sensed Andrew move, but Gatsby motioned for him to stay where he was.

The pair pressed Dan up against the wall of the tunnel. His brow hit the mossy brick, sending flakes of dirt into his eyes. Tears began to well as he tried to blink the dust away. He strained to free himself, but only managed to pull his hoody tighter around his neck and edge the bottom of it up, baring the skin on his back to the cold air. They held him firm.

Something clicked. The cold of a blade pressed into his exposed skin, the soft part around his right kidney. He flinched forward. His cheek brushed more mud from the wall. Musty smelling dirt filled his nostrils.

"Wait. You told me there would be a trade. What about the second car?" The panic rose in his voice. "Where's Amy?"

"Second car?" The man holding the blade barked a laugh. Dan could feel the heat of his breath on his neck. He smelt of stale sweat and something like straw.

The other man twisted his arm and kicked the back of his leg. The knife skimmed painfully up his back and his face grated on the rough concrete as he fell awkwardly to his knees.

"I got you the money." His voice came out high and shrill. "Just check the bag."

He could hear the ruffling sound of the bag's toggles, followed by a shocked shout.

"What?" said the man holding the knife. The cold of the blade briefly pulled away from Dan's back.

He took his moment and jumped, pushing with his legs against the wall, hoping to force the two men back. Instead, they just let go and he shot like a rocket past them, landing with a thud on the packed mud floor. He rolled away and backed into the shadows at the end of the tunnel.

'Time to disappear.' The reptile's voice was quieter than it had been before.

Dan's skin twitched in strange ways beneath his clothes. Tingled with tiny bubbles like a pot nearing boiling point.

"Where the hell did he go?" The man with the knife span in a circle.

Dan pressed himself up to his haunches, ready to spring away, but somehow they couldn't see him in the dark. The car's headlights illuminated them like actors on a stage. Gatsby loomed by the right wall of the tunnel like a phantom in the wings, watching, not moving. He looked frozen. In fear perhaps? Who knew what his reptile might be doing or saying to him?

Andrew lingered just behind.

The bag lay open — seemingly empty — on the floor of the tunnel. To its left was the man who had taken it, his head propped uncomfortably against the wall of the tunnel. Catman sat atop his chest, busy pummelling his face with his paws.

"Get it off me," he screamed, doing his best to protect himself from the barrage.

"Leeroy, if you're not going to do anything, just watch out for that guy." The man with the knife called back as they rushed to help their fallen comrade.

Dan started forward, but Gatsby appeared by his side and placed a hand across his chest.

"Let's see what your boys can do," he said, the top half of his face hidden in shadow under his hood.

Each man drew a pistol from beneath their jackets as they approached Catman. Behind them, the bag came alive. The Flash shot out and swept the legs of the man with the knife, flipping him over. He landed hard with an "oof".

In a panic, the remaining assailant fired, indiscriminately hitting the dirt floor, the bag, the walls, blasting chunks of concrete into powder. But The Flash was too fast, an orange blur bounding up the side of the tunnel. Using his momentum, he leapt high off the concrete, and like a majestic ball of amber fluff, sailed through the air to hit his attacker square in the face. He followed up with a backwards somersault to land on the chest of the man he had tripped.

It was over quickly. All three men incapacitated in a matter of seconds. Two were unconscious, and the other pinned to the ground by Catman. Hidden in the shadow, Dan felt redundant.

"Leeroy," called the man beneath Catman. "Don't just stand there. Get this beast off me." His voice echoed off the tunnel. Spit flew from his swelling lips.

"Watch him, Catman," said Dan. He brushed Gatsby's hand away from his chest and hurried towards the car.

It was empty. He ran around to the boot and popped it. Inside was a long black bag. A body bag. He touched it. Knew it was meant for him. The muscles in his jaw tightened and he slammed the boot down causing the whole car to bounce on its suspension. He glared at the only man left conscious.

"Where is she?" The shout burned his throat.

The man watched him through thin crescent eyes. His jaw jutted defiantly, and for a second all Dan could think about was digging his fingers around the bone and ripping his chin off.

He blinked at the violent image. His mind was changing, melding with that of the reptile.

"He won't let this slide." The man's voice grated on him like quick strokes of sand paper. "Don't go thinking you're any better off now. You're no closer to finding her."

"Is she alive?" Dan's mouth twitched into a snarl.

"Of course," he said, lisping through swollen lips. *Ofth corth.* "We wouldn't let a prize like that go to waste." He thrust his head forward off the ground. "You're not gonna see her again."

Catman hissed, flashing his oversized fangs.

"Where is she?"

The man laughed. "I'm not telling you. Run and hide, little man, because he's going to come for you. You really screwed him at the warehouse, and he's not the forgiving ty—"

Catman batted him hard across the face again. His jowls shook in that embarrassingly undignified way it does when someone is slapped mid-sentence.

"Get this fucking cat off of me." His swollen face was red with rage, but Dan could see the fight in him had gone.

He shook his head. "Why would you people do this over money?" he said. "You can't just hurt people and expect to get away with it."

Behind him, Gatsby spoke up. "Different people have different priorities."

He looked back. The old man stood, arms folded and backlit by the car headlights. Like some ghostly monk, his face was completely hidden in the shadow of the deep parka hood. Andrew stood at his side with the hood down and the cap removed.

"You ain't Leeroy, are you, and you sure as shit ain't Deano?" the man said. "Where are they?"

"Dead," said Gatsby, his tone flat.

"What are you going to do, Dan?" said Andrew.

Dan felt a compulsion to kneel at the man's side, so he did. The reptile had something to say.

"Do you own cats?" he asked the man. His voice came out low and clear. Not the question he'd been expecting. He smiled in what he hoped was a menacing way, though he'd never practiced looking menacing before. The skin of his face tingled as he did, and the man's eyes widened in horror.

"What are you?" The man screwed up his face, afraid and confused.

"Have you ever watched a cat play with a mouse?" The reptile smiled behind his eyes.

"No." The man's voice lowered.

"I have, and I have cleaned up the mess afterwards. It can be..." He paused for effect. "... very messy. Now, do you know what an obligate carnivore is?" Dan tilted his head to one side.

"No." The man began to wriggle. Catman hissed in his face again and he quickly settled.

"An obligate carnivore is a creature that can only survive by eating the flesh of others. Catman here is an obligate carnivore." He stroked Catman's back. "Flashy over there, sitting on top of your unconscious friend, he's an obligate carnivore, too. Most people forget that the domestic house cat, the cute little companion that lives in their house with them, is instinctively a killing machine. They forget that cats are sadistic little murderers evolved to lack any sort of empathy for a creature they see as food. You can't reason with them. If they see you as a meal, that's all you are." He smiled again. "And cats love to play with their food."

Beads of sweat popped on the man's brow.

'He's putty in our hands.' The reptile grinned, but the presence behind his eyes had almost faded completely.

"I once caught Catman in my garden playing with a mouse," he said, his mouth his own now. He felt he knew what to say. "The mouse wasn't really playing. Both of its eyes had been scratched out and Catman was toying with him as he ran blindly around my garden path. Catman was having a lovely time. The mouse, on the other hand, was not."

"What... why are you telling me this?" The man was doing his best to move his face away from the black mass of fur on his chest.

"What do you think Catman is likely to do to someone who kidnapped and imprisoned his owner, kidnapped and murdered his friends, and won't tell his other owner what he wants to know?"

Catman rose to his full height atop the man's chest.

"You wouldn't leave me with this thing." He looked between Dan and Gatsby, his breathing rapid and shallow. "You wouldn't dare — you're not a killer."

"I'm not, no." Dan gave Catman another stroke. He closed his glowing eyes and nuzzled against his owner's hand. "But I know someone who is. How do you think Leeroy met his end? Or that other guy you sent to watch me? Now, do you want to tell me where your boss is holding Amy, or shall I see if Catman can help you remember?"

Catman's claws extended slowly from his paws. He began to purr.

A strangled groan escaped the man's mouth. His eyes darted wildly. "I'll tell you where she is — just get this thing off of me." His legs spasmed, drawing arcs in the dirt.

"Go on then." Dan didn't move.

"Here." He fumbled in his pocket and passed over his phone. "His address is in the contacts under Martin Shields. You don't think you're just going to sneak in though, do you? You and your mates with a couple of cats. You won't survive the night."

"We'll see." Dan took the phone. "You better not be lying, or we'll find you." Catman pressed a claw through the man's shirt.

The man's legs squirmed again, and his breath escaped in blubbery, wet sobs. "I swear it on my mother's grave." He closed his eyes. "Please, just take it away. Please."

"Thank you." Dan patted Catman on the head. "I'm glad we could make you see the benefits of helping us out. It'd probably be safest for you if you stayed away from Martin Shields' place tonight."

The man nodded enthusiastically. Tears rolled from his eyes.

"Come on, Catman."

Catman punched the man again, this time hard enough to knock him unconscious.

Dan breathed out a sigh of exhausted relief. Felt his shoulders relax.

"That was impressive, boy," said Gatsby, bringing him back to the moment. There was something about the way he watched him that put Dan on edge.

The old man moved to the car. He stood upright and strong. Already a different man from the one he'd been earlier that day.

"Thanks."

Catman and The Flash were sniffing at the bag in the middle of the tunnel. "Come on, you two," he said.

"Wait, where's Dimitri?" asked Andrew, he hurried over to the bag, then fell to his knees beside it. "Dimi?"

Dan felt like he'd been kicked in the chest. The bag moved slowly. He rushed past Gatsby and knelt by Andrew's side as his friend peeled the cloth back. A rose of red had bloomed on the canvas. Blood. Dimitri's.

He couldn't speak. With all the action, he'd forgotten.

A large bloody tear ran the length of Dimitri's side. Through a gap in his fur, Dan could see bone. He was obviously in pain. He had been cursed with a strength that meant he had to live through what might instantly kill any normal cat. His eyelids fluttered, and he tried to raise his head from his paw. His chest rose and fell slowly.

"Dan, he's been shot." Andrew's voice wavered. "Dimitri?" His hands shook with indecision. "What do I do?" He stroked Dimitri's head. "What do I do?"

The Flash looked up at Dan. He didn't need to hear what the cat was thinking, he could read it in his face. *Do something!* But he didn't know what. He glanced at Gatsby.

The old man remained silent.

"I'm sorry." Dan swallowed. It was hard to speak. "I don't know."

Dimitri's breathing slowed, and finally his eyes closed. Andrew's head dropped and he let out a sob. The Flash climbed into the bag and gently bumped Dimitri's head with his own. He let out a pained whimper. A prickle formed behind Dan's eyes. His vision blurred and he blinked away the tears.

"I'm sorry, Andrew." He put his hand on Andrew's shoulder.

Andrew's hands curled into fists. He carried the bag to the side of the motorway bridge and placed it down by the wall. He put his hand on the canvas and whispered something under his breath. Then he stood with lips pressed together and looked at Dan. "Let's go." His voice was hard.

Dan wiped the tears from his face with his cuff and followed Andrew to the car. He climbed into the front seat while Andrew got in the back with Catman and The Flash.

Gatsby was already buckled in. He had a jar of peanut butter on his lap and was spooning it into his mouth. He appeared to be having no trouble eating it despite his dentures.

"Where'd you get that?" Dan said to Gatsby, whilst moving the rearview mirror so he could see Andrew's face. His friend's dry eyes stared at nothing. The muscles at the side of his jaw jutted and jumped beneath his beard. His breathing was slow and deep.

"I can feel it," Gatsby said, ignoring Dan's question. "I can feel myself getting stronger."

Dan gritted his teeth. He didn't feel strong. He didn't feel anything.

He opened the phone the man had given him and mapped the directions to Martin Shields' address. It would take twenty-minutes. They would be there by midnight. He hoped they weren't too late.

MOUSEBANE

The death toll rises. First my love, now Scratchtacular.

The Jester knows where we must go to free The Master.

Red Mist believes he will fight by our side. I am not so sure. I may have to go it alone.

Either way, there shall be no prisoners.

Behind You

Dan kept asking himself if it was all really happening. Dog fighting. Human trafficking. Things like that only ever happened in the mystical lands of somewhere else. Only ever far away, on the news or in movies. Not in quiet English suburbs, not in Walton-Upon-Thames, not in *his* town.

But here he was heading for an address not ten minutes' drive from his own front door, where his wife was being held against her will.

The only thing that kept him from going insane with worry was the hope that they wouldn't hurt her if they were trying to get a good price. A buyer wouldn't pay as much for spoiled goods.

God. Spoiled goods, he thought. My wife.

He squeezed the soft leather around the steering wheel. The last streetlight passed overhead, and he turned down a dark back road surrounded by fields and remote farmland.

He glanced at Andrew staring out of the window in the back seat. Catman and The Flash were together on the parcel shelf, watching through the back window. Dan sighed as an oppressive sense of guilt rose. This was all his fault. If he'd never followed them to the warehouse, none of this would have happened.

Martin would pay for taking Amy. One hair out of place on her sweet head and he would destroy him! *Rip him apart with his teeth! Crush his skull with his bare hands!* He felt something tear and realised he'd pulled a chunk from the steering wheel's covering.

He cleared his throat. Shook his head. Pushed the anger back. Since the moment he'd watched Dimitri die, the separation between himself and the reptile had ended. They were one now. And with his anger came a primal, cold sub-layer to his thoughts. It wanted carnage. It wanted to rage. To tear and rip and kill. He didn't want to know what would happen if he lost control. What might he be capable of?

He blew out a long breath to calm himself. Anger, as we all know, leads to the dark side.

Catman and The Flash were quiet. Surely, if they felt the same urge, then the fight in the warehouse would have been an absolute bloodbath. No one would have survived. Maybe the effects of the frog were different for them. Perhaps their more primitive brains had always felt urges, and so they could quash them more easily.

Next to him, Gatsby had finished the whole jar of peanut butter. His hood was up and Dan couldn't see his face. Only his nose was visible. He'd been very quiet. What was his reptile telling him? What might be going on in his head?

The Satnav on the phone beeped to inform him the destination was coming up on the left. His stomach rolled. It wasn't nerves as he'd expected, but anticipation.

"We're here," he said, but there was no reply.

He pulled up next to a high chain-link fence. No lights or buildings were visible inside the perimeter, which suggested a large estate beyond. Roughly a hundred metres ahead the fence dipped in where a short drive led up to a gate.

"Bugger." He pointed. "There's a camera above the gate."

"They'll recognise the car," said Gatsby in a cool monotone. As he spoke his jaw jutted forward. It was more angular than he remembered. "Drive straight up. They'll open it."

Dan pulled the sun visor down to cover his face and did as the old man said.

They waited at the gate. The car engine rumbled. He looked at Gatsby. He didn't seem worried. Didn't seem worried at all.

"Are you both still OK to do this?" Dan asked.

"Uh huh," said Gatsby.

"Andrew?" Dan glanced in the rearview again.

His friend looked up, catching Dan's eyes in the mirror. He nodded grimly.

The gate didn't open. Nobody came out. He was just about to slam the car into reverse and begin a search for a different entrance, when the gate jerked then slid open. Casting furtive glances around to make sure no-one was nearby, he drove through.

A smooth tarmac drive meandered through the low-cut lawns towards a large white mansion in the centre of the gardens. Rabbits sprang away as the head-lights caught them. The house reminded him of an old New Orleans plantation he'd seen in a textbook with large pillars supporting a long balcony across the first floor. Fitting considering its owner's occupation.

"Stop here, and turn off the lights," said Gatsby.

Dan slowed the car to a halt halfway up the drive.

"There'll be someone watching. We can't just drive up to the house." Gatsby looked out, surveying the surrounding gardens.

"Won't they think it strange if we just stop and leave the car here?"

"Yeah, but if we drive right up, they'll see it's not who they are expecting. We get out here, and we come at the house from two different sides." He moved his arms diagonally towards each other in a pincer movement.

"Split up? Are you sure?"

Gatsby nodded. "Best way to find the girl, and best way to make sure we don't all get caught."

Made sense. He was relieved Gatsby was taking control. He'd had no idea what they were going to do when they got here.

"When I say go, you and the orange one head for that tree." He pointed to a large willow looming in the darkness roughly thirty metres away. "The black one, Andrew, and I will head around the house from the other side."

"Sure," said Andrew.

Gatsby climbed out with very little effort and opened the back door. He motioned to Catman, who turned to Dan.

He nodded. "Go on. It's OK."

He heard Gatsby mumble something to Andrew about the direction that they'd go.

Putting one tentative leg out, Dan looked over the garden. His palms were sweating.

The old man patted the roof lightly. 'OK, let's go."

Dan ran as fast as he could straight for the willow. The Flash followed close behind. The soft grass muted each footstep. He ducked beneath the cover of the hanging branches and looked back. Gatsby, Andrew, and Catman had already disappeared.

He watched the house from the cover of the leafy fronds. One or two of the windows in the large manor were lit. Movement on the balcony above the door gave away the location of someone watching the grounds. The orange glowfly tip of a cigarette flitted up and down in the dark.

This had to be the place.

He felt a rapid tapping on his foot and looked down. The Flash was facing away from the house, instead looking towards a long wooden shed.

"What is it?" He ducked down to The Flash's level to see beneath the willow branches.

Two men were making their way towards them from near the shed. If they were heading for the car, they were going to pass straight under the tree. The soft rumble of their voices carried through the night air.

"What's he parked there for?"

"Probably drunk again."

"Idiot's gonna get pulled over one of these days. Martin'll be livid when he does."

Dan backed towards the trunk of the tree and pressed himself up against the rough bark. The Flash snuck in behind his legs.

His skin tingled once more. He looked down at his hands. It must have been a trick of the light, because they appeared to be no longer there.

"The guy's a massive liability. He deserves whatever he gets." The two men pushed through the branches, drawing his focus back.

Dan sidled around to the far side of the trunk. The Flash moved with him.

"Wait, did you hear something?" They stopped within the canopy of the willow.

He held his breath.

"Tony? Is that you?"

They were looking straight at him.

"You havin' a piss Tone?" said one.

"Did you get the guy? Is he in the boot?" said the other.

A surge of anger rose within him, as if someone had grabbed his head and dunked him under the surface of a blood red pool. Lurching forward, he kicked the nearest man in the stomach, doubling him over. Caught his arm and the back of his collar. Span him headfirst into the trunk of the willow. The other fumbled with a holster on his hip, but before he could draw, The Flash crashed through his legs, knocking him to the ground. Dan rushed forwards and kicked him full force in the face, relishing the way his head bounced back. Neither man got up.

Submerged in that dark, red pool, he watched himself fight. He was holding the gun to the man's temple before he regained control.

Disgusted, he threw the gun to the side. He didn't want to kill anyone. He just needed to rescue Amy and leave.

"But what then?" The question came from out of the blue. A different voice in his head this time. The Scottish voice of his sensei.

He looked around and was surprised to see The Flash clinging to his shoulder. He hadn't noticed him climb up.

"They aren't going to leave you alone after you've saved Her." The Flash's lips didn't move, but he could tell it was him talking. "They want you dead."

"How is this possible?" He lifted The Flash down and placed his hand on his head. "Do I need to touch you so you can speak with me?"

"Our powers constantly evolve and strengthen. Now you are finally one with your reptile, as I am, we can communicate through them when we have physical contact."

He took a moment to comprehend The Flash's words.

"What do you think will happen once you've saved Her?" asked The Flash.

"The police will sort it. You do know what the police are, don't you? We'll get pictures or something. Make sure these guys don't get away."

"But what then?" The Flash cocked his head to one side. "No one can guarantee your safety. You'll spend your whole life looking over your shoulder. Unless you finish this tonight, you'll always wonder what's waiting for you around the next corner."

"But I can't kill them."

"Physically you can. Just let go. Enjoy it. It will take care of itself. That's what your reptile wants."

"I'm not going to let them change who I am."

He moved away. The Flash clawed up his leg and onto his shoulder again.

"There is no other way. Destroy them so they cannot hurt you further." The Flash bared his teeth.

Dan felt a sudden urge to retrieve the gun, but it left just as quick as it had come.

"No. We're going to sneak in, get Amy, and leave. And once we're out, we'll go. Leave the country if we have to."

"You'd give up the life we knew before?"

"It was hardly perfect."

"You humans are so foolish. What you want and what you do are never in alignment."

"I'm not going to be like them. I'm not going to turn into a killer. I can do without you up there like the bloody devil whispering in my ear." With that, he brushed The Flash once more from his shoulder.

He looked around. Couldn't see anyone else in the garden. He stalked across the grass, using the trees spread around the lawn as cover. The Flash followed behind. He didn't want to argue with him. There had to be a middle ground. His thoughts turned to Gatsby and Catman. They may have bumped into other guards. He wondered whether Gatsby or Andrew were experiencing the same urges. Hopefully, they would be able to control them.

He approached a lit window and looked through into a kitchen. The room beyond was empty of people, but the lights were on. It looked like a perfectly normal home. Dishes sat dripping on the drying rack, a collection of brightly coloured cereal boxes were stacked atop the fridge, and an overflowing bin sat by the door. It was too normal. It looked like his parent's house. Hell, if he was a couple of million pounds richer, that could be his kitchen.

But it had to be the place. You didn't have armed guards at just anyone's home.

They moved around to the back of the house. A long glass conservatory ran along the length of it. The interior was dark. A set of double doors stood in the middle, and Dan was surprised to find them unlocked. He stepped through.

The conservatory smelled of sandalwood, fresh and natural, and was decorated with an assortment of potted plants and furnished with a faded wicker three-piece suite. Three further sets of double doors led from here into the house.

He picked door number two, the centre, thinking it would give him the best scope of the property.

He entered a brightly lit hallway with dark wood panels on the walls. On the far side was the main front door to the house, and leading up through the middle of the room, a grand oak staircase with red carpet running up its centre.

While he tiptoed across the hard wooden floor, he held his breath and listened. It sounded like the house was empty, but he knew Amy was here somewhere. He could feel it.

Next to the front door, he spotted two jackets hanging from coat pegs. A ladies' padded riding coat, and a little yellow rain mac, the owner of which couldn't have been more than six-years-old. They hung over two sets of matching boots. A third peg remained unused, underneath which was a crumble of mud on the floor.

The Flash scurried past and hopped up the stairs. He looked back as if asking Dan to follow.

He crept up behind him. The third step creaked. He paused, feeling naked in the bright light of the hall. If anyone was looking in from outside, he was sure to be spotted.

He glanced over his shoulder towards the jackets on the hooks and once again doubted that this could be the right house. Perhaps his feelings regarding Amy's presence were misguided. Nervous adrenaline mistaken for premonition. This could be a young family's home. The men outside simple gun wielding night time gardeners.

And he'd broken in.

He recalled a story from a wedding he'd played once on a particularly large farm. The father-of-the-bride had told him, in a thick west country accent, that, 'all well to do country folk sleep with a loaded shotgun within arm's reach. Just in case'.

Was a wife nudging her husband awake in the master bedroom above?

"Did you hear that?" she'd say. "The third step creaked."

The husband would come out with that under-pillow-shotgun and, thinking Dan was nothing more than a burglar, blow his head off, no questions asked. The police would arrive and find him dead with The Flash by his side. They'd tell stories of the weird burglar with a ginger tom cat and crazy octogenarian side-kick.

Despite his hesitation, he climbed the stairs. No one appeared. The Flash led him to a door. It was decorated with little wooden balloons that held letters. 'David's Room'.

Before he could stop him, The Flash jumped up and pulled the handle down. The door swung open, and he disappeared inside.

The room ahead was dark. Dan waited on the threshold, not knowing how to proceed.

A child's voice came from within. "A cat. Hello." There was a pause. "Daddy, is that you?"

His initial reaction was to lie.

"No, I'm a friend of your Daddy's, David." He tried to make himself sound more confident, like he was supposed to be there. "Do you know where Daddy is?"

There was no answer. Dan pulled his hood down, conscious that his outline might be frightening.

"Hello?" he said. He couldn't see the boy in the room. Perhaps the bed was behind the door. "David?"

A little boy dressed in blue superhero pyjamas stepped out of the dark. A yellow blanket clenched in his tiny fist trailed behind him. The Flash flanked David on his left. His glowing green eyes momentarily flashed in the light of the hall behind them. Dan was reminded again of the Siamese twins in Lady and The Tramp.

"Probably in the garden." David raised an index finger to his lips and flicked them as he did so. "In the big shed. Workin' so he couldn't tuck me in." The boy's eyes glazed over.

Dan was worried he was about to cry, so knelt to his level. "I'm sure he'll tuck you in tomorrow," he said, doing his best to placate the boy. "Is it the shed in the front garden, or is there another one?"

"At the bottom of the garden." He pulled his blanket up to his mouth.

"Thank you, David." He felt rotten inside.

"Can the cat stay with me? I like him." He bent down and stroked The Flash. The Flash moved his head into the stroke and miaowed playfully.

"He likes you too, matey, but I'm afraid he has to come with me. We've both got a meeting with your dad."

David smiled. His nose wrinkled as he breathed out a little giggle. "A meeting with a cat." He put a hand next to his mouth, about to tell Dan a secret. He lowered his voice to a whisper. "Watch out. Daddy doesn't like cats. He likes big, woofy dogs, but I like cats better. Sometimes he brings me one to play with, but then they have to go away again."

"You go back to bed, David." He smiled. "Is mummy around?"

"Downstairs, I think, having a big drink."

"Ok, promise me you'll stay tucked up in bed, and get to sleep." Dan didn't want him venturing out and getting hurt. "Pretend like Santa is coming, and no matter what you hear, you can't get up until the morning. OK?"

"Ok, will Granddad still be here then?" A floorboard creaked.

"I don't know. Is he here now?"

"Yes." He said, his eyes flicked over Dan's shoulder. "Behind you."

DUD

Dan followed David's gaze and turned.

"Do as the nice man says, David, and head back to bed," came a familiar voice. "And if you can't sleep, put on the headphones I gave you."

Gatsby stood at the top of the stairs no longer wearing the parka. His previously loose turtle neck jumper was pulled tight against his torso. He looked broader, stronger. With the parka covering him, Dan had not seen the extent of his change.

He opened his mouth to speak. Gatsby hushed him.

"Not in front of the boy. Have some decency," he said. "Off to bed, David." Gatsby leant past and shut David's door.

Dan glanced past Gatsby. In the hall below was another man. He held a double-barrelled shotgun.

The Flash rushed forward and leapt for Gatsby's throat. With an impossibly quick movement, the old man caught him by the legs and swung him into the wall. He dropped The Flash limply to the ground.

Dan ran to his side. "Flashy." He picked him up, he wasn't moving. He glowered at Gatsby. "What have you done? You've killed him."

Gatsby laughed. His eyes had changed. The whites were now a pale yellow, and the black pupil had slimmed to a thin reptilian diamond.

"He's not dead. I know it. Can't you hear his heart beating?"

Dan pressed a hand to The Flash's chest. He could feel a pulse, just. Something else was terribly wrong though. His back legs hung limp, broken. He tried to support his whole body in his arms.

Gatsby smiled, his mouth stretching impossibly wide. "I feel amazing Danny boy, and it's all thanks to you."

"Where's Andrew?"

"He's safe outside."

He didn't know what to say. Nothing made sense. "What about Leeroy? And the other guy? They put you in the cupboard. You were looking for your cat?"

"I'd been looking for cats alright, just not mine. Believe it or not, when you first broke into my home, I couldn't have done anything to stop you." He raised a limp wrist and shook it. "I genuinely was a weak old man until about an hour ago, so I hid in the cupboard when I heard you coming up the stairs. Then when you found me, you thought you'd saved me, so I just went along with it."

"But you let those guys at the motorway bridge get beaten to a pulp. You could have done something then."

"Tony and the others?" Gatsby rolled his yellow eyes. "You saw how pathetic he was. I'm not surprised you made him talk."

He smiled, and this time Dan noticed the dentures were gone. His gums were bleeding. Thin white spikes pushed out through them. "I wanted to see you and those kitties in action. I wanted to know what made you tick."

Gatsby grabbed The Flash out of Dan's grip.

"Please don't hurt him."

"We'll see about that. I think it's time we reunited you with your lovely wife before she goes on her little trip." He narrowed his eyes. "And please come quietly. David is a fragile boy; I don't want him to hear me get angry." His face drew up in a smug half smile. He had a nasty twinkle in his eye. "It wouldn't do you much good anyway. I can tell your frog hasn't given you what mine has given me. Looks like you got a dud."

"What about Catman?"

"The black one ran off as soon as we got out of the car. He's an animal. He doesn't care about you. Now, get downstairs."

When Dan reached the foot of the stairs, the other man grabbed him and the hard barrel of the gun was pressed into the small of his back. He was shoved forward. Gatsby walked past, and they followed him outside.

Andrew was on the lawn with another two men.

"Dan?" he said. "George is the guy on the phone's dad."

"I know."

"We're in real trouble now."

"I know."

"What are we going to do?"

He didn't know.

They forced the pair of them across the dark expanse of the lawn, towards a group of barns that loomed at the end of the garden.

"When I spoke to you two on the street, I had no idea you actually had the balls to do anything. You looked so ridiculous with your flyers." He smiled and bared the sharp stumps in his mouth. "Looks like you've found your dragon, and it's going to eat you." He chuckled.

The night air in the garden smelled sweetly of wood smoke and fallen leaves, but as they drew closer to the sheds, and the thick grass gave way to a broken mix of dirt and stone, the smell became meaty and rotten. A mix of muffled barks and growls came through the thin walls of the nearest building. A shabby construction of corrugated iron with a wooden frame. They headed between it and another building, through a slim alley lined with broken pallets and rusted farm tools. A carpet of dirty cobwebs and dust covered the walls, and overgrown plants grew in and out of the shack's supports.

As they came to the end of the passageway between the buildings, a bright motion sensor light flashed on illuminating the complex. A row of ramshackle wooden structures ran to their left and right along a gravel road that stretched perpendicular to the alley. This side of the track looked like a small town in an old western. Breaking the illusion was a modern brick and metal building opposite. A large warehouse much like the newer ones at the industrial estate.

"Where's Amy?"

"With Marty, in the office." With the hand not carrying The Flash, Gatsby pointed at the building across the road. "He's making sure she's calm for when Lyam arrives to pick her up."

They forced them across the gravel path and into the brick building. A short unlit corridor led straight ahead, the floor carpeted but muddy. Voices floated down from further up the hall.

"Down here, Dad." Dan recognised the voice from the phone call.

They shoved them in the direction of the open door and into a small brightly lit room. Anatomical charts of dogs hung on the walls. The red exposed muscle on the paper a stark contrast to the clinical white walls.

And in the centre was Amy, sat in a chair, her sleeve rolled up to her elbow. Two men were hovering over her. One wore a wax jacket. The other held an empty syringe. He had a bandage wrapped around the top of his head and one eye.

Amy looked up and blinked slowly. "Dan?" It was clearly an effort for her to speak. Her head fell to her chest and bounced up again. Her eyes rolled in their sockets. She looked possessed.

He stepped forward wanting only to touch her, but was pulled back. His arms were twisted up his back into a lock that shot fire into his shoulders. The man in the wax jacket turned to stand in front of her. He mashed a cigarette out into a full ash tray and rubbed his hands together. His pale, blotch ridden face creased into a smile.

Dan had seen this man twice before, as a boy in the photos at Gatsby's, and on the street the day Gatsby had moved in. Martin, his son.

"Father," he said, a frown curling across his brow. "You been working out in that little hideaway I put you up in? You look much fitter since you left the retirement home."

"That I am boy. I've got something to show you." He reached into his pocket.

Martin cut him off with the practiced wave of an impatient hand. "Later," he said. His eyes caught Dan's. "You must be our man with the cats. I'm aware you've caused more trouble this evening." He glanced at Andrew. "And you've brought a friend."

"What have you done to her?" Dan struggled. It was no use; his arms were locked in place.

"Just a little sedation so she's easier to deliver. I was wondering where Leeroy had gotten with you, then Dad rung me to tell me to pick you up."

Gatsby must have rung when he'd gone to get the frogs.

The Flash began to wake. Gatsby dropped him on a table next to a tray of sharp looking instruments. He yowled in pain. Dan's heart cracked.

"I see we've caught one of yer little buggers. Where's the black one? He's really got some of my boys spooked."

The man holding his arm murmured something to the one holding Andrew. His grip loosened and Dan chanced a backwards glance. One of them was missing an ear, the other had scratches across the left side of his face.

"What was that, Carl?" said Martin.

The man with the missing ear coughed. "I said just cus you can't see him, don't mean he ain't here."

Martin rolled his eyes. "I'm pretty sure he's not in the room." He looked around for support and the man with the bandage around his head nodded quickly. "Now you," he said, turning back to Dan. "It's time for you to come clean. Who put you up to it?"

Dan shook his head. "I don't—"

Martin held up a hand to stop him. He closed his eyes and rubbed his forehead with his knuckles. Took the syringe from the man with the bandage and put it close to Amy's closed eye.

"I don't want to hear your lies. Who do you work for?" He emphasised each word with a tap of his index finger on the syringe.

Dan swallowed. His throat clicked. He couldn't take his eyes from the needle hovering perilously close to Amy's face.

"He doesn't work for anyone," said Gatsby. "He just happened to be at the warehouse that night."

Martin glanced at his father. "Did he tell you that?" He eased closer, moving his face to within an inch of Dan's. "Have you been taking advantage of my elderly father? Feeding him bullshit. I know the Baliks were trying to set up their own fight as well as running their own line."

"Don't. Please." He could only beg. "The Baliks? I don't know."

"He doesn't know anything," said Gatsby. He rolled those yellow eyes at his son.

Martin squinted and angled his head back, gaze tracking down his nose at Dan. "Hm? Only one way to be sure though, isn't there?" He nodded towards Amy. "Lyam doesn't need her to be able to see with both eyes as long as everything else is in working order." His lip curled as he looked over her unconscious form.

The anger rushed on like a tidal wave and Dan lost control. He lurched forward, almost breaking free of the arm lock that Gatsby's man held him in, and flung his leg out. His toe missed Martin's face by centimetres.

"You don't touch her," he seethed.

Martin flinched back, pulling his arm across his pasty face like a vampire hiding behind his cape. A little squeal left his throat and he dropped the syringe into Amy's lap.

When he realised Dan couldn't get close, he quickly composed himself. "Oh, ho, ho. That was stupid." He shook his head. Little beads of sweat flung from his balding head.

"Hurt her, Jimmy." He passed the syringe to the bandaged man.

Jimmy looked at the needle in his open hand, then at Martin, and then at Amy sleeping in the chair.

"Wait," cried Dan. His knees gave way. They wrenched him back to his feet. He turned his face towards Gatsby. "I told you," he pleaded. "I was just there by chance. I followed my cats."

"Marty?" said Gatsby. He put a hand on his son's shoulder, but he shrugged it off.

"Followed his cats?" Martin threw his hands in the air. "Are you hearing this?" He turned back to Dan. "I don't believe you." Martin paused a moment. "You've had your chance to cooperate."

Dan reeled back. His stomach flipped. He was going to be sick.

"In the eye, Jimmy."

Jimmy looked towards Gatsby. His face said, "help."

"Don't look at him. I'm the boss. You do as I say."

Gatsby sighed. "Son? Come on, Lyam's not going to want her if she's only got one eye."

Martin squeezed his eyes shut and rubbed his forehead. "Uh, Dad." He said, whining like a teenager with a new games console being asked to hoover the lounge. The patchy blotches on his face were fading as his whole head turned pink. No one else in the room moved. "Are you deaf?" Martin's eyes popped open, and he glared at Jimmy. He turned towards the man missing an ear. "Carl, you do it."

Carl hesitated for a moment before stepping forward. He took the syringe from Jimmy. Dan noticed his hands were shaking too.

"We'll talk about this later, Jimmy." Martin pointed a rigid finger at him.

With his one good eye, Jimmy looked at the floor, hands held by his stomach.

The man behind Dan took his free arm and held both locked. His shoulder creaked in protest.

"I don't know the Baliks," he screamed.

He cast his eyes around for anything that could stop them. The Flash was looking intently at him, and suddenly, in his mind's eye Dan was back in the dojo, in a memory. He was twelve and watching a demonstration. Sensei Martin was in the same lock. He had taught them how to break free.

A low growl built in his throat. His body shook as he tensed.

He took hold of his own left wrist with his right and with the force of both arms pushed down, breaking the lock. He raised his right leg. Slammed his shoe on to the man's foot, and followed up with an elbow to the face. He turned and stabbed his opponents Adam's apple with the tips of his fingers. The man's hands flew up to clutch his neck as his face turned purple. He fell to his knees choking.

Using the back of the man he'd just throat punched as a boost, Dan jumped up and threw an arm around Gatsby's neck, hoping the weight of his fall would pull him down. It didn't.

Gatsby stumbled back with Dan clinging on like a gibbon. Slammed him into the wall. Gatsby's steel-like fingers gripped his forearm, slowly peeling the headlock away. His other arm shot back between Dan's legs, hoisted him up, then threw him down next to Carl and Amy. He followed up with a loafer to the chest forcing the air out of his lungs.

Dan wheezed. He couldn't breathe. His chest felt like it was crawling with hairy legged spiders. He coughed. Fought to regain his breath. He climbed to his knees and felt a punch land on his face. Couldn't tell who it was. His nose sprayed blood onto the white floor.

Gatsby's breath was hot on the back of his neck as he leant and whispered in his ear. "Maybe it's not the frog that's the dud, but you, boy."

Martin gazed at his father in awe. "Father, what *has* gotten into you?"

Gatsby gave his son a cocky half-smile. "I'll show you once we have this business taken care of."

"I wasn't really going to let him do it, you know," Martin said to Dan. "Of course Dad's right. It'll only devalue her." He rubbed his hands together, and turned to Carl. "Now, about my message. We only need one of them for it. Just kill the snowflake." He flicked a hand towards Andrew.

Andrew's face went deathly white and he pressed himself backwards against the man that held him. "Wait. I didn't do anything."

Martin scrunched up his face. "You came somewhere you weren't invited."

The man with the patch over his eye joined the man holding Andrew and the pair bundled him out through the main door.

"Dan," Andrew shouted from the hall.

"You can't—" started Dan.

Martin continued over his protests as Andrew was lead away. "You guys film his bit," he pointed at Dan, "and I'll do mine later." He clapped his hands together. "Come on. Chop, chop."

Dan looked around the room. Everyone else seemed to know what Martin meant. What message? The man with scratches on his face was back on his feet, but still purple. He rubbed his throat and glared.

"But," said Carl, "if he's not with the Baliks, like George says, then won't they think it's a bit weird if they get a video with some random guy in it?"

Martin shrugged. "Doesn't matter. They'll know we mean business." He looked Dan over. "Besides, we've got him now, might as well put him to some use."

"Take this and chuck it in with him." Gatsby handed Carl The Flash.

Carl held the cat out at arm's length, even though The Flash wasn't awake enough to do anything.

"Now, Dad," Martin said, "what is it that's got you all excited?"

Gatsby fished into his trouser pocket and withdrew a frog. The last one from the kitchen. The one with the black marks on its back. He placed it on the table.

Martin scratched his head. "What the hell is that?"

Dan felt an arm wrap around his neck, and was pulled into a headlock. They dragged him away. Andrew's pleas bled down the hall from outside.

Behind him, Gatsby said, "This is something that's going to make us a lot of money. And I think I know where to get more."

And ahead, he heard a shotgun blast.

THE MESSAGE

Andrew twisted in the air and hit the gravel track hard. Dan knew he was dead. A chunk was missing from his right shoulder. The man with the gun, seemingly not convinced by the amount of damage he'd done, reloaded, then aimed at Andrew's prone form before deciding against firing again. He shoved the gun into the arms of the one called Jimmy and headed after Dan and the two pulling him along.

Over his shoulder he called, "You sort that out, Jim Jim."

In the past, Dan had imagined that if he found himself in a situation like this, he'd somehow find a way out. Fight his way through. Save everyone. Overcome the odds. He must have spent hours on long drives, sat at his desk, even in bed waiting for sleep, running through scenarios and fake fights. His dormant childhood martial arts training would come alive and power him through.

But this was real life.

Until today, he had no idea what it was like to be hit, hit so hard that all the air rushed out of your chest, hit so hard that your nose exploded. He could hardly breathe through the thick, bloody mucus that dripped from his swelling nostrils as the men dragged him across the gravel path away from his dead friend towards a barn where the guttural sounds of barks and growls grew ever louder.

He tried to look back, but one of the men shoved his head forward.

"Is the tripod still in there from last time?" asked Carl.

The man with scratches on the side of his face, the one Dan had throat punched, fished a Canon SLR out of a satchel he was wearing around his neck. He took off the lens cap and gazed through the viewfinder.

He opened his mouth to speak. "Huurrr." Cleared his throat. "I didn't move it," he croaked. He cleared his throat again, and spat at Dan. "You've messed my voice up."

Dan fought to steady his wobbling knees.

Why had he thought they stood a chance? Like it was some sort of game he could win. There were no winners here.

He'd been stupid to put all of his faith in something he had no idea would work. Insane if he thought he could do anything but lose in a situation like this. And now, Andrew was dead, Catman probably the same, Amy was about to be shipped off to some hellhole, and The Flash was a crumpled version of his former self, broken beyond repair.

Martin had said something about a message. What was his fate? The only thought that came to mind was of some sort of Lovecraftian ritual sacrifice. Sharp blades. Strange symbols carved in flesh. Blood and fire. Goat-headed priests chanting a dark god's name.

The one with the camera pushed open the door to the nearest barn, and Carl shoved Dan through. A cacophony of barks and whines exploded as he entered and for a moment his vision was filled with snapping jaws and foaming spit. The air was thick with the wretched stench of decaying meat, excrement, and filth, a post-apocalyptic slaughter house.

He gagged and fell to his knees. The men stood over him.

The one who'd shot Andrew gripped the back of his neck and leant in close. "What did you think was going to happen coming here?"

Carl held up The Flash, who lay limp in his hands, and waggled him in front of his face. "Not so scary now, are you?" The Flash's chest moved up and down. His eyes were half open. He didn't look well. "Anyone for a game of footy first?" He motioned launching The Flash up in the air and drop kicking him.

"Ain't got time," said the one gripping Dan's neck before shoving him down into the dirt.

A naked bulb hanging from the centre of the ceiling blinked into life as some-one hit the switch. The dirty light cast grim shadows that danced around the room. Now he could see slavering dogs with their insane staring eyes, chewing at the chicken wire that held them back. Under the swaying orange glow, they appeared as demons fighting to escape the roasting fires of hell.

The shed was roughly twenty feet across. This section was about six. Around the edge were three fenced off enclosures. Each cage held two large dogs. Dan thought they were either pit bull or Staffordshire terriers. He wasn't very good with dog breeds. The circling light made their mouths look like they were teeming with living, swarming teeth.

The camera guy removed a tripod from an old 70s style kitchen cabinet that had clearly once been white, but was now a blotchy, creamy brown. He attached his camera and aimed it towards the cage on Dan's left. The dog inside was thinner than the rest. Its ribs stuck through its brown fur like an organic marimba. Despite his emaciated look, he still jostled against the fence of his cage with furious energy. Strings of saliva dripped from the rusted wire.

The man with the camera set up his shot. "You looked like you were going to shit yourself when Martin asked you to put that needle through her eye, Carl," he said with his eye to the viewfinder.

"I've got a thing with eyes," said Carl. He shuddered. "Don't like watching people touch 'em. Don't like stabbing 'em with needles." He stuck his tongue out.

Dan wondered if he was telling the truth.

"Ha! Didn't think you were that squeamish," said the cameraman.

"Everyone has their things, mine is eyes."

"I don't really like noses," said the one who'd shot Andrew. "You know, like getting something shoved right up your nose." He jabbed a finger towards his nostril. "Yuck."

"Such pussies." The cameraman sighed, then flicked on another light.

The glare turned the starving dog's wild eyes into yellow candle flames and illuminated the full enclosure behind it. A metal armchair stood in the centre of the cage. Each leg was padlocked to a metal rung that had been sunk into the concrete beneath it. The concrete was covered in rust-coloured splotches. A tacky liquid caked the seat. It was was hard to discern exactly what it was in the gloom. It glistened in the roving light.

Dan shivered.

He brought his knees under him to stand and something hard hit him in the back of the head. A sound like rushing water filled his ears, and he fell face first onto the packed earth.

"Chuck us the tape," said Carl.

Dan's hands were wrenched behind his back. He heard the rip of tape as they bound his wrists. Carl opened the cage door. He felt like he was floating as they lifted him up and in.

He felt the vibration of the dog close by, barking into his left ear. It sounded far away, but the flecks of liquid hitting him on the cheek and the stench of hot meaty breath brushing his face told him otherwise. They dumped him onto the chair. Another creak of tape as first his calves, and then his arms, were fastened to it. He didn't have the strength to struggle. He could hardly keep his head up. His face, once more, felt all tingly, like fizzing bubbles were popping against his skin.

A small red light flashed under the gently swaying bulb. "That's weird. I can't see him on the camera." The voice was barely audible over the incessant barking from the other two enclosures. "It's like he's in a shadow or something."

A sweaty finger prodded Dan's cheek. All the muscles in his body gave a reflex jerk, but he was stuck fast to the chair. The poke woke him enough so that his focus started to return.

Carl was staring at him, mouth open, brow furrowed. Dan couldn't take his eyes off the ragged nub of flesh where his ear had once been.

"What's going on with your face?" Carl curled his lip and poked him again, hard enough to hurt. He turned back and shouted to the others over the din of the dogs. "It's not the light. His skin's gone weird."

Dan jerked his head away. What did he mean?

"Whatever. Adam turn on the light in there. Mart'll be pissed if you can't see what's going on."

The third man flicked a switch and another bright light came on above them. Dan squinted against it. His hands braced against the tape. He looked down to cut out the glare, and spotted The Flash, lying limp at his feet. He looked so small.

"Got him now." He raised a thumb. "Come on out Carl, and Adam, be ready to let Biffa go."

"He's ravenous. He'll go for anything," said Adam, who was fumbling with a rope tied to a peg outside of the cage. The other end was looped around the skinny dog's neck.

Carl gave Dan's face one more poke. "So weird." As he moved towards the cage exit, he jabbed a thumb towards the door of the shed and said, "Are you guys alright to do this without me? The wife's packed me off with spag bol for dinner—," he waved a hand towards Dan and the dog, "—and this is all a bit close to home, if you know what I mean? Might put me off."

"The intestines?" said Adam with a wrinkled nose.

Carl pointed a finger at him. "You got it."

"Whatever," said the cameraman waving a hand.

Had they done something like this already? Dan peeled his legs away from the chair with a sticky click.

Biffa suddenly jumped towards him, but, thankfully, the rope attached to his collar halted his progress and he jerked to a stop roughly a foot away. When Carl shut and locked the cage door, Biffa came as far as his rope would allow, but didn't strain against it this time. He stood gazing at the floor with sad, bloodshot eyes, and, for a second, Dan almost felt sorry for him.

"Hey," he said, leaning awkwardly in the chair in a bid to stay in Carl's peripheral vision as he walked out. "I'm scared now."

He struggled at his bonds. The chair rocked to the side and he had a mini heart attack as it rolled. The padlocks clanked and pulled it back to rest. "You can let me go. I've got the message. I won't tell anyone." Carl didn't look back.

No one said anything. Adam, fiddling with the knot that held Biffa back, and the one operating the camera had stopped talking to each other, each too engrossed in their task to respond. Or at least pretending to be.

"Please, just let us go. I've got the message, I promise. We can get you the money." His eyes shifted to both men in turn. "Over time we can pay you back."

He paused. Despite the cold, sweat dripped into his eyes. "I won't tell anyone." He felt awful saying it, with Andrew dead. "I won't tell anyone about Andrew."

They didn't care. He tried a different tack.

"Why do you work for someone that makes you do these sorts of things? Surely money can't be that important to you."

The little red camera light started to flash again. The cameraman gave Dan a quick, indecipherable look.

He pulled with all his strength on the tape. His eyes felt like they were going to fly out of his head with the strain. Adam was having no luck with the rope that held Biffa back. The knot had been pulled tighter by the dog's struggle and Dan could see the man's hands were shaking.

"Please. Adam, is it? You can't be serious." He could hardly get the words out.

"Shut up." Adam didn't look up.

Dan screamed, his voice rising half an octave. "You're going to feed me to this thing?" He slammed his whole body backwards and then forwards, forcing as much weight as he could into his bonds. They didn't budge. "That's inhuman. That's insane. Please, just kill me now — like Andrew — shoot me."

Where was the reptile? Where was Catman? Why had he thought he could achieve anything here?

He rocked backwards again, desperate to rip the tape from his sweating hands. He wanted to scream, but his throat had finally given up.

Adam sighed in annoyance. He turned and headed to the kitchen cabinet where he pulled out a small hand axe. Dan's heart skipped. All he could see was the blade glinting in the various light sources around the room. For a moment he thought the man was going to take him up on his plea.

But no. Adam didn't look at him as he returned. Just knelt by the rope and cut it through.

Dan's heart sank. He closed his eyes, anticipating the flurry of teeth. When it didn't come, he opened them again. The dog just stood there.

"Come on, boy. Do your thing," said Adam. He lifted the rope attached to Biffa's collar and shook it before throwing it in so the dog could see it was no longer holding him back.

The dog edged forward. But he wasn't looking at Dan.

A strange noise was coming from Dan's feet. A constant yowl that didn't waiver. He looked down. Still positioned on the floor, and propped up by his head, The Flash had his eyes locked on Biffa's. The dog whined, and stretched his body back, and in a strange moment of unrelated clarity, Dan realised where the yoga term downward dog originated. The other dogs started to settle, and gradually, as if someone was turning an overdriven amplifier that had been slammed up to eleven back down to zero, the room calmed. The contrast almost made time slow.

"Biffa?" Adam put the axe down and rattled the cage with both hands. The reflection of the light bulb shone in the beads of sweat on his hairless head. His mouth moved, but made no words as his gaze travelled around the room to the other enclosures.

Dan was just as confused. The dogs were all quiet, all watching The Flash. Wrapped up in his ball at Dan's feet, he had their full attention, but was only looking at Biffa.

Biffa whined submissively. He lay down. Rested his head on his large paws. His tired eyes softened. He looked as if he might fall asleep. He barked quietly at The Flash, who yowled again, this time softer, in a way that was almost soothing. Then the dog stood and moved behind the chair. Dan felt the wetness of gooey saliva on his fingertips as Biffa chewed through the tape that bound him.

"Carl, get in here," shouted Adam, not once taking his eyes from the scene.

As soon as Dan's hands came free, he began to wrestle with the tape around his legs. The door to the building opened and Carl re-entered.

"How'd he get free?"

"Biffa chewed the tape!"

Carl touched the hole on the side of his face where his left ear had been. "Stop him before he lets the cat out!"

Adam unwound the wire that held the enclosure gate closed. Biffa growled and pounced towards the door, holding it shut. He snapped at Adam's fingers, forcing him to retreat a step.

Dan released his feet and stood.

He scooped up The Flash.

"Put me on your shoulder," said The Flash. "You'll need your hands free, and I cannot walk."

Dan did so. The Flash gripped onto his hoodie with his claws.

Biffa bounded back from the gate and Adam, who was now trying to push it open, fell through and landed on top of him. Biffa flipped him and pinned him to the ground, jabbing his head forward, trying to bite his face. Adam pushed against the dog's throat with his forearm, but could barely hold him back. The dog flicked his neck and caught Adam's wrist between his teeth. Adam screamed.

Dan had a strange and deep desire to ram something pointy up the man's nose, but kept the urge under control.

The dogs in the other cages started up again, and the room filled with furious barking once more.

Dan felt a paw on his stomach, then heard the husky Scottish voice of The Flash inside his head. "Get them."

Once again, he felt like he had been pulled from his body and dunked underwater. This time, he didn't fight it.

He leapt over Biffa and Adam as they wrestled and flew out of the enclosure. Carl stepped away from the fence and put his fists up.

Without slowing, Dan swung his leg in a perfectly executed front kick, catching him in the stomach. Carl bent double and Dan struck the back of his head with a hammered fist, pushing him down to the dirt floor.

The cameraman swung and Dan blocked. Caught his arm. Span under it like a dancer performing a turn. Twisted him around into a straight arm lock, then picked up the axe from the shelf beside him. In a moment of lucidity, he flipped it around so that the blade was facing himself, before he brought the weighty shaft crashing down on the cameraman's head with a deep thunk. The man dropped to the ground, unconscious.

Dan raced to each of the other two dog enclosures and, one after the other, hacked through the twisted wires holding each of the doors shut. They swung open. The dogs were out almost immediately. Two rushed into Biffa's enclosure to help him, though he didn't look like he needed it. Adam was still screaming, his head trapped in Biffa's jaws. The others rushed Carl, who was making a move for the door. The first dog gripped his arm and dragged him down to the ground. He fell screaming under a blanket of fur and wagging tails.

Dan stepped past without looking back.

He threw open the door.

"Stop." It was Jimmy, the one with the eye patch. He stood outside, holding the shotgun.

"Uh." Dan put his hands up. Behind him, the bone crunching sound of animal liberation quieted.

Jimmy looked nervous. The barrel of the gun shook with his hands. His gaze kept twitching between The Flash on Dan's shoulder and the dogs that he could sense were gathering behind.

"Make them go back in their cages," he said.

"I can't do that. I can't talk to them."

"Do it." He gave the gun a threatening shake and his lips became thin white lines.

"I—"

"Who's the bloody snowflake now?" came a wheezing voice. A plank of wood swung into view and connected with Jimmy's head. The gun went off, blasting a chunk out of the wall just to Dan's right.

Jimmy fell to his knees, and Andrew staggered into view. He raised the plank above his head and knocked Jimmy to the ground, unconscious.

Andrew leant his whole weight on the plank like a crutch and took a deep breath. "Dragons shmagons."

"Andrew?"

"Oh man, look at this," he said, holding up his arms. The front of his robe was torn to shreds. The skin beneath pink and new. "This is my *second* favourite piece of leisure wear. Remind me to stop wearing robes when I'm out with you."

Dan rushed forwards and threw his arms around his friend. "Andrew? I thought you were dead."

He took another wheezing breath, then cleared his throat. "I think I was for a bit."

He stretched his right arm above his head and glanced down at his shoulder. Part of it was still missing, but it wasn't bleeding. The surrounding skin looked fresh. Dan could swear it was healing as he watched.

"Do you feel OK?"

"Hurts like a bugger," Andrew said, pulling what was left of his robe over the healing wound. "Must be the frog." He met Dan's eye. "Don't worry about me. We have to save Amy."

The Flash miaowed from Dan's shoulder, calling to the dog pack. The dogs poured from the shed, surrounding them with barks and wagging tails.

"I can't ask you to risk yourself again."

"You can't stop me," said Andrew. "Dimi's gone. They shot me." He punched his fist into his open palm once more. This time, with the spatters of his own blood covering his face and his clothing in shreds, he looked like he meant business. "I'm getting payback."

HURT THEM A LOT

Dan helped Andrew into the building where Amy had been sedated. The Flash was still on his shoulder. The dog pack followed.

The room she had been in was empty. He was too late.

A thin glowing line on a table in the room caught his eye. He stepped forward and picked it up. A frog's leg. The Flash's nose snuffled up and down. Dan held the leg up to him so he could sniff it.

"Do you think Martin's eaten the rest?" he asked, not knowing whether The Flash would answer.

"Let's hope not," said Andrew, leaning against the wall. He looked shattered.

"I believe he has," answered The Flash inside his head.

Dan didn't know whether to tell Andrew that he could speak with him. Didn't want to rub it in with Dimitri gone. Now wasn't the time.

"Are you sure you're OK?" he said to Andrew. "You look done in."

Andrew waved a hand. "I've just been shot by a massive shotgun. I think I'm doing OK considering. Could do with a nap, though. I expect it's very energy intensive, resurrection."

"Mm. I expect so."

Something in the corner of the room had caught his eye. An arm poking out from behind an open cupboard door. He moved to see better. It was a man. Another of Martin's henchmen, no doubt. He was dead, his throat a mess of red leaking out on to the linoleum floor.

"Did you do this?"

Andrew shook his head. "Not me. Catman?"

Someone — or something — had backed him into the corner and killed him. He looked so wretched and small, the way he was curled up on his side. Dan rubbed his face and groaned softly. He felt sick. Was this how it had to be? Was killing these people the only way to stop them?

"These are bad people," said The Flash.

The nausea quickly subsided as the muscles in his jaw tensed. His hands curled into tight fists. This wasn't his fault. This was Martin's fault. His muscles twitched. He wanted to punch a hole through the nearest wall, or flip the table, but held it in like a growing electrical charge.

"This isn't my fault," he whispered through gritted teeth, as if the dead man could hear him.

"Mousebane did this," said The Flash.

"But where's Amy? How can we find her?"

"She might be down the corridor," said Andrew, jabbing a thumb towards the hall. "I overheard one of them say someone called Lyam was going to be picking her up soon."

"They must be doing the deal right now."

The Flash let out a short call. Biffa and the dogs crowded through the door and surrounded them. Dan stepped back nervously. The cat called again, and the dogs formed a line.

"Give them the frog leg," The Flash said. "It may still hold the old man's scent."

Dan picked it up and held it out. The dogs all squashed in to sniff. Their enthusiastic panting filled him with anxious energy. The Flash miaowed and Biffa stalked out of the room. He followed as the dog sniffed his way up the dark corridor to the door at the end. He let out a short bark when he reached it.

"Shhh," said Dan.

He squeezed past the other dogs. Each lay waiting, their noses pointed at the door. He pushed it open just enough to see what was on the other side.

A tarmac backlot ran the length of the brick building. Bordering it was a back fence that was roughly twice a man's height. A wall of dark, neatly clipped laurel bushes stood tall beyond. It was like the deliveries depot behind the supermarket where he had worked as a teenager.

"How big is this place?" said Andrew.

Dan pushed the door open further, conscious another motion sensor light could give their position away if he wasn't careful. To his left, roughly twenty metres away, four large halogen lamps bathed the area in bright white light. Two stood on posts by the fence. Another two were attached to the main building. Men in overalls were carrying crates from the building to a lorry parked at the end of the row of cars.

Shady men loading trucks in the middle of the night, deep in the English countryside, didn't fill him with hope as to the legality of the operation. What other nefarious activities were Gatsby and Martin into? Drugs? Guns? Organs? He'd read somewhere that kidneys could fetch a high price on the black market.

Beyond the idling lorry, several 4x4s and white vans were parked up against a fence.

"What are you waiting for? Move to destroy them," said The Flash inside his head.

Dan looked to his shoulder and whispered so that Andrew couldn't hear. "We need to make sure we're not spotted. What happened in the kennels was a one off. You can't just go around beating people up."

"Why?"

"You just can't." Dan felt like he was talking to a robot. The Flash just didn't understand.

"You think too much. You will lose her if you idle."

He was right about that.

He crept through the open door, followed by Andrew and the dog pack. To his relief, there was no sudden flash of illumination, no hidden security light. From the shadows, he studied the men loading the truck. They moved back and forth like ants taking food to their queen.

"What's the plan?" hissed Andrew.

Dan looked at him and shrugged.

He remembered his father's words from the dreamed memory the reptile had shown him.

'*When you're the one in the dark and they are out there in the open, you have the control.*'

Especially if you have a load of riled up fighting dogs on your side, he thought.

A car engine grunted to life, and the tail lights of one of the 4x4s lit up. Next to it, an SUV did the same. He could hear two men talking between the cars.

The 4x4 reversed and turned. Gatsby was in the driver's seat, his elbow resting on the open window sill. He took one final look at the operation, threw a wave towards the SUV, and pulled away. The car disappeared through a gate and out of sight.

"He must be going to the pool," said Andrew.

"Do you think he has Amy?"

Andrew shook his head. "She must be in that other car."

The SUV reversed and followed Gatsby's car through the gate. He couldn't see the driver through the dark tinted windows.

"Forward before we lose her." The Flash yelped, and the dogs began sprinting towards the truck and the men there. He gave a clear paw-signal for Dan to charge.

"Oh crumbs," Dan said, giving chase. "Come on."

Andrew limped behind. "You go on. I'll catch up."

Unsurprisingly, the first of the workers to notice five vicious attack dogs, a man in a tracksuit brandishing a tiny axe with a ginger cat clinging to his shoulder, and a limping hippy with part of his torso missing, dropped the crate he was carrying in surprise. The man following him, seemingly so engrossed in the sound-system bangers pumping through the large pair of headphones covering his ears, didn't notice and, in true slapstick fashion, careered straight into the first man's back, knocking him flying.

Biffa went for the headphones guy first, jumping high and tackling him to the ground.

"Hey!" Came a shout from inside the building. Several other thugs in overalls came running through a larger roller door. Behind them were hundreds of short green plants.

One man clicked a radio on his belt. "Lads, we've got a situation in packing. A couple of nobs have let a bunch of Martin's dogs out."

Five more men came running from the room that contained the plants. Dan looked back towards Headphones and The Dropper. Both lay unconscious on the concrete, but the dogs had silently ninja'd away. Dan span. They were stood back up the way they had come, surrounding Andrew, watching him and the oncoming men.

Andrew tried to step forward, but the dogs didn't let him pass. He shrugged, helpless.

"Flashy?" Dan said, not taking his eyes from those coming his way. "Why aren't they helping?"

"Looks like your pet pals have done a runner, Dr Doolittle," said the man with the radio.

"A true warrior must learn to stand on his own four paws, Dan. It is time to unlock your potential."

"Oh no, not now." Dan turned and sprinted for the truck. "We haven't got time." Heavy boots chased him.

He threw open the passenger side door and jumped inside. Tried to shuffle over to the driver's seat, but someone caught hold of his leg and tugged. He gripped the edge of the steering wheel with both hands. His whole body lifted as someone else grabbed the other foot. His sweaty fingers slipped, and he was pulled from the cab, scrabbling with his arms to slow the inevitable meeting between his face and the tarmac. He landed hard, but managed to block his head from hitting the floor with his forearms. He curled up and rolled beneath the lorry. There were too many of them. He couldn't get away, but he couldn't hide either.

Tingles covered his skin and he looked down at his hands. Strange waves of darkness rolled up and down his fingers before coalescing and growing up his forearms, turning them black with little flecks of white and grey to match the tarmac under the truck.

He wriggled out of his hoody and his T-shirt. The tarmac froze his naked skin, but he didn't notice. His whole body had changed colour and, with his black trousers on, he was almost invisible, even to himself. He rolled so that The Flash was hidden from view behind him and lay as flat as he could.

One man knelt and looked under the truck. "Where's he gone?" he said, looking straight at him.

"Don't tell me you lost him," said another. "You were holding his leg."

The man stood while the others spread out to search.

"You guys go round there. He's got to be somewhere."

"Probably some animal activist."

Dan was no longer paying attention to what the men were doing. He was too shocked by his own flesh. It felt like thousands of feathers were falling softly all over his skin as it changed colour, reacting to the surrounding light levels and his movements.

Holy effing flip — he was invisible!

This was the reptile's gift.

He edged to the far side of the truck with The Flash cradled under one arm and the axe ready in the other. He stood, then lay The Flash down on the driver side step. He needed both hands free.

"Martin's not going to be happy if he finds out we had someone in here. They definitely saw the farm; we can't let them get away."

Scuffled, unsure footsteps moved around the front of the truck. Dan crept towards them, flipping the axe around so the sharp end was facing him. He didn't want to hurt anyone else, not seriously. He looked down at his body. His skin continually changed as he moved, depending on what was behind him. Every cell was like a sequin on a thread, spinning and changing colour with the wind.

The first man stepped into view less than two feet away. He looked right through Dan as if he wasn't there.

His eyes twitched as Dan brought the axe up past his face, and he just had time to utter a soft syllable, "what?" before Dan clonked him on the head. He fell to the ground.

The man who'd been following close behind screamed. "It's a ghost!" He stumbled away.

Dan didn't hold back. There wasn't time. He rounded the truck. A pair of jogging bottoms and a floating axe.

"What the hell are you?" said the nearest man. He was broad, rugged. Taller than Dan by a few inches. His nose looked like it had been broken and set again using a banana as a guide. "Get him." He said, lunging forward.

He remembered his father's words once more. *'If you ever come up against someone bigger than you, you have to hurt them a lot. Hurt them so they can't get back up again.'*

Before he could come any closer, Dan hit him across the jaw with the blunt side of the axe. Just like before at the warehouse, that primal feeling washed over him. This time, it was closer to euphoria.

The man gritted his teeth and swung for where his head should have been with such force that when he missed, he put himself off balance. Dan stomped on his knee — it crumpled like a paper bag — and as he went down, punched him in the mouth.

Another took his place, this one skinnier. He threw wild and fast punches into the air. Dan managed to duck beneath them and, driving himself up with all the power of his legs, uppercutted the guy in the chin. He screamed as he stood, giving the blow as much force as he could. The skinny man lifted off the ground, already unconscious before he fell, like a rag-doll, to the floor.

From there, instinct took over. He jumped forward and caught the next man by his wrist. Threw him to the ground. Hammered a heel into his face.

The others, faced with an invisible assailant, just turned and ran. He gave chase and managed to grab another by the neck of his overalls, before he realised what he was doing. He found himself staring into the frightened eyes of a man who couldn't have been long out of his teens. The boy whimpered and Dan released him. He rushed after his fleeing friends, none of whom looked back to check on him.

Dan tucked the axe into his waistband. His fists were throbbing and already beginning to swell.

"Wow, you're... *amazing*, dude."

He jumped around. Andrew stood watching him with the dogs.

"Thanks."

"And you went invisible."

Dan grimaced. "I have to catch up with Amy, but we can't let Gatsby and Martin get any more frogs."

"You take the truck. Get Amy. I'll go get the car we came in. Maybe I can find that woman who's looking for the frogs. Maybe she'll be able to help stop George."

"Are you sure?"

"Yeah."

"You have to be careful. There might be more of Martin's men around."

Andrew jabbed a thumb over his shoulder. "Ten minutes ago, I got totally marmalized with a shotgun." He shrugged. "What are they gonna do that's worse than that?"

Dan fished in his pocket for the keys to the car he'd left on Martin's drive. He threw them and Andrew caught them awkwardly with his left hand.

"Please don't go to the pool alone. I'll meet you there once I've found Amy."

Andrew nodded. "Give 'em kung fu hell."

"Will do."

"Good luck."

"You too."

Dan returned to the truck and jumped in through the passenger's side. He crossed to the driver's seat, opened the door, and scooped up The Flash, placing him carefully onto his lap. He started the engine.

Biffa climbed up looking to get in too, but The Flash put up a paw. There was a moment's silent communication between them. The dog dipped his head in submission before stepping down. Dan watched through the windscreen as the pack disappeared through the open gate up ahead.

"Mousebane is tracking her," said The Flash in his head. "I can smell him."

Dan slammed the axe down on the dashboard. "They're in a car. He won't be able to keep up."

He wrangled the gearstick into first and powered the truck through the gate.

To the left, he could just make out the dog pack as they disappeared into the dense wood that surrounded the road.

"You do not know what my brother has become. He will catch them. And they will die screaming."

Amy In The Boot

Amy knew she was dreaming — she had to be dreaming — but she just couldn't seem to wake up. Having a nap in the day was never a good idea. Her head throbbed and her throat was dry, but she didn't have the energy or moisture to swallow. She must have slept for hours. Her limbs felt so heavy that she couldn't bring herself to move. Catman and The Flash were nearby. She could hear them purring. The soft rumble seemed to vibrate the entire room. She smiled. She was safe. They were close.

The dream of the man in the parka, the one who had pulled her into the van, and the other in the wax jacket, who wouldn't stop touching her leg, was fading. Their faces covered by the mask of waking. It had been an awful dream.

The sound of voices and the radio came from behind her. Odd? They didn't have a radio in the living room. She tried to call for Dan, but the tape that covered her mouth muffled the strangled moan that came from her lifeless vocal cords.

Her eyes sprang open.

A firm yet clammy hand patted her roughly on the head. She couldn't move. Her body was numb. She'd only ever felt this way once, the morning after she'd gotten so drunk at a house party that Dan had to give her a piggyback all the way home.

She was in some sort of box. No. She was lying in the boot of a large SUV. She could just see the back window above her in the corner of her vision. The car was moving. Her nose, pressed to the carpet, caught the scent of rich, fruity shampoo with an underlying hint of something else, something she didn't much care for — an iron tang.

She tried to look down at her hands, but couldn't move her neck. Her muscles felt burdened. In her lower peripheral vision, she could see the glimmer of reflected light in the silver tape that bound her wrists together.

Her arms were heavy, her hands, like dead weights, pressed into her pounding chest. Her body was locked in a foetal position, and for a moment she nearly couldn't breathe, panicking as her mind frantically grabbed for answers.

She took a deep breath and let it out slowly. The frayed tape covering her mouth tickled her nose with the vibration of the escaping air.

What was the last thing she could remember? Had she really seen Dan in a white clinical room? That was where the man in the wax jacket had taken her. She'd spent hours tied up. There had been no way to tell how many. It had been dark and there were no windows.

Who was the man in the wax jacket?

She trawled through her memories, trying to unravel what had happened. Dan had gone to his gig, but he'd seemed distracted. He'd been acting strangely ever since the cats had come back. She'd planned to cook him a roast on Sunday. A nice dinner always cheered him up.

She had gone to the shops to get supplies, but when she arrived home, Dan's van had still been there. Parking had been a bit of a squeeze, but the man in the parka had guided her into the spot. She had opened the boot to unpack the food, and that was when he grabbed her and forced her into the old man across the road's house. He'd pulled a bag over her head, and she'd felt the duct tape being wrapped around her hands. Then, sometime later, she'd been shoved into a van and driven away.

Dan had come just before she'd passed out. He'd been brought by some brute of a man dressed all in black. She thought she recognised him, but couldn't quite put a finger on where from. Dan looked exhausted. Worse than she had ever seen him. His shoulders slumped as if not just the whole world, but the entire universe had been thrown down upon them. For the seconds that she had been able to focus on him before passing out, she remembered wanting to tell him she loved him, if only to make him smile. It was harder to see loved ones in pain than suffer yourself.

And now, where was she? And who with? She forced her eyes to look as far to the left as possible to try to glimpse whoever had just touched her head, but she was stuck facing the interior of the car boot. Her eyes stung from the strain, and a slow tear ran down her face, sliding into her ear. It was no use. She couldn't see anything except the heavily tinted back window of the car above her. And through that was blackest night.

She listened. That was all she could do.

"Good morning to those of you who are sharing the early start. Or maybe for some, it's the late finish. We've got some lovely mellow tunes to take you into sunrise."

There was no other sound. The voices she had heard before had stopped.

Something thumped on the roof.

"Bloody branches." This voice had a thick French accent. "I still don't know why we had to come all the way out here to pick up one girl."

"Martin's just doing it cus he can." The second voice rumbled through the chair behind her. Possibly the voice of the man who had touched her hair. "He's got no respect."

That was it. The man in the wax jacket was called Martin. He was creepy. He had repeated the words "don't touch the goods," under his breath a number of times while he sat with her in the room. She had caught him leering at her with the tip of his tongue pressed against the groove under his nose. Her stomach turned at the thought of what was going on behind those eyes. Then groaned audibly.

A swish of cloth on leather. "Hungry, are we?" came the deep voice. "Don't worry, you'll get to eat something soon enough." The man snorted as if he'd said something funny.

A second thump on the roof elicited another groan from the Frenchman. A light pitter patter followed, but instead of going from the front to the back, as you would expect from branches scraping across the roof, they moved in the opposite direction. The sound reminded her of home, but she didn't know why. Tears came. Where were they taking her?

"Jesus Christ," shouted the Frenchman.

The car halted abruptly and she was thrown on to her back. She could now see the ceiling, and the back of the head of the man in the backseat. He sat in the middle. The long, brown hair pulled tight into a ponytail at the base of his thick, red neck caused her to shudder. The thought of him putting his hands anywhere near her was revolting. The uncomfortable clamminess of his touch still resided on her skin like a slug trail.

"Vince, did you see that?"

"What was it?" He leant forward out of sight.

"Something slid down the windscreen off the roof. It's in front of the car."

"Well, flatten the bastard. We don't want to miss our crossing."

Something hissed and the right side of the car started to subside as if it were sinking slowly into mud.

"That's the god damn tyre." The Frenchman's voice rose. "It's popped the tyre. Do you know how much those cost?"

There was another hiss and the left side of the car sunk too.

"What was it?" said Vince. "What was on the windscreen?"

"I don't know. It was big. Like a black cloth fell off the roof on to the glass and then slipped off the bonnet when I hit the break. But it had eyes. Glowing green eyes. It looked right at me." There was a quiver in his voice. "Sabine, wake up."

A patting sound, a hand on someone's coat, preceded another French accent, a woman. There were at least three of them in the car.

"What?" She sounded sleepy at first, before becoming more coherent. "Are we here?"

"No," said Vince. "Lyam hit something and now the tyres are flat."

"I didn't hit anyth—"

Something struck the boot door with a thunderous clang, and for a second Amy thought another car had rammed them.

"Is that her?" said Sabine. "Shut her up, Vince."

The man turned around fully. He leant over to look at her. She held her breath as his staring eyes darted up and down her body. His face was red, and full veins stood out at his temples. He looked like a bodybuilder that had eaten too much beef and was well on his way to gout town. He frowned. "Nope, she's still wrapped up tight."

Vince jumped as another clang rang out on the back door. Amy sensed a movement from the plush leather lining as the metal behind it dented inwards.

"Something's banging on the boot," said Vince, turning back.

He opened his door and started to get out. There was a high growl from outside, a momentary panic in Vince's eyes. His spasming fingers fought desperately for purchase on the headrest as he was ripped through the door. His scream was cut short with a terrible, wet gurgle.

The night air came in through the open door, cooling the tears on Amy's cheeks.

She tried to blink away the snapshot of Vince's final moments. She closed her eyes and listened. A soft crunching came from outside, and once again she was reminded of home, reminded of making dinner in the kitchen with Dan and the boys.

"Sabine, shut the door." Lyam's voice wobbled.

"You shut it," came the fearful reply.

Amy imagined the two of them at the front of the car looking at each other with wide eyes, hoping the other would take the risk. Whatever it was out there, it was hungry. Had Vince been enough to sate its appetite?

The crunching stopped, and she strained her ears for the slightest sound. The door that Vince had opened creaked slightly. She held her breath, sure something had climbed onto the back seat. Whatever it was, its movement was barely audible. Her only chance was to run. She closed her eyes and concentrated. She was starting to get some feeling back in her fingers, and her hands were no longer as numb as they had been. She wiggled the tips. They didn't move much. The same went for her toes. But the more she focused, the more they responded.

The front door of the car opened.

"Lyam, don't leave me." Sabine's voice rose in a hushed whine. "It's on my side."

"Climb over here. We'll make a run for it."

Amy continued to wiggle her fingers. The rustle of fabric from the front of the car told her that Sabine was doing as Lyam had suggested. The rear door creaked again, and through the gap between the headrest and the chair back, she saw it close ever so slightly. Whatever had been there had left.

The delicate sound of claws scratching on dirt travelled around the back of the vehicle. She would have mistaken the sound for dried leaves blowing in the breeze if she didn't know it so well.

"No, no, get back in quick," said Lyam. The sound of a scuffle followed before the door slammed shut. A powerful hit shook the left-hand side of the vehicle and the whole car rocked on its suspension. "I saw it. I saw it." Each sentence surfaced between deep, laboured gulps for air. "Panthère."

"Can't you just drive?" shouted Sabine.

"We won't get far on the rims."

"Just get us out of here."

The engine started and shifted into gear. An unbearable grinding sound came from the wheel arch behind her head, and the car lurched forwards as what was left of the rubber around the rims gained traction.

The back left door slammed shut as their speed picked up, but Amy sensed slow, careful movement on the other side of the seat. It was already inside.

Two large black paws, about the size of her hands, popped up on the headrest, similar to the way Vince's had minutes before. It took her a few seconds to recognise his face, a face she had seen almost every day for the last few years. It had changed so much.

Catman leapt over the seat and into the boot with her, the fur around his mouth slick with blood. His body was roughly the length of Amy's curled form, making it a squeeze for both of them in the back of the car.

There was no shout from the front to indicate Lyam or Sabine had seen him. Amy sighed. As Catman snuggled into her chest, her fears dissipated, flowing away on her exhale.

"Is this far enough, do you think?" said Lyam.

"Whatever it was, it's probably not going to follow us if it's got Vince back there. Let's get her out and walk until we find the nearest house. There's a couple of nice places up here. We'll steal a car and continue to Folkestone."

Folkestone. They must be heading for the Eurotunnel. Amy had done it once before with Dan. You just drove the car right inside the train. There were hardly any checks.

"Go get her," said Sabine.

"We'll go together."

Both front doors opened and she heard them head towards the boot.

Through the tinted windows, they wouldn't have been able to see the danger that lay in wait for them on the other side of the door.

The handle clicked. Catman started to purr. To Amy, it sounded more like a jackhammer. She closed her eyes. She didn't want to see what happened next.

What she heard was enough.

Following The Trail

The interior of the truck was filthy. The storage holes in the door were stuffed with chocolate and crisp wrappers, and the footwell was littered with old coffee cups. Crusty bits of food and dust filled almost every crack and crevice Dan could see. Littering the dashboard was a selection of not so reputable newspapers, the kind with more nudes than news, as well as not one, but four old McDonald's bags. Dark grease stains soaked the brown paper. The smell of fat and salt sent his stomach into a rumbling frenzy.

He was ravenous. For a few seconds the hunger was all he could think about, and in a moment's mania he opened all the closed compartments in the cab in a bid to find something without a bite taken out of it or a dusting of mould. He wasn't going to be picky. Not less than 24 hours ago, he'd eaten a raw frog. Anything would do.

A half-eaten packet of beef jerky was all that met the criteria, and he split it with The Flash.

"Is Catman nearby?" he asked, as he raced the truck along the road as fast as he dared.

The Flash stared at him from his place on the double-sized passenger seat, his poor broken legs curled up beneath him. He raised an eyebrow as if to say, *if you want to talk to me, you know how.*

Dan reached out and touched a hand to his head.

Immediately, The Flash spoke. "He is not far ahead."

He couldn't take his eyes from the road for long. The slim country lanes wound treacherously between bushes and overhanging trees, but he didn't want to take his foot from the accelerator, not with Amy still out there. He kept one hand on The Flash's head as he drove.

"Was Hitler... um, the cat that we found at the warehouse, were they... you know... together?"

"She was his mate, yes. His life partner. He has sworn a blood oath to destroy all who had a hand in her death and all who threaten harm on The Master."

"And you?"

"I will aid in any way I can. But my body is broken. I have shut off the pain, but I doubt I shall walk again."

"Couldn't you just eat another frog? It'd heal you like it did Dimitri."

"I don't think they work like that."

"Oh... I'm sorry." He took a deep breath. It shuddered as it left him. "How are we going to handle Gatsby?" It was beginning to dawn on him that although he had fared well against the men at the compound, Gatsby might be a very different story. And if Martin had eaten the other frog, then he would have to contend with them both. "You saw him. He was massive."

"He and his son must be put down. No emotion. No pity," answered The Flash. "They are bad humans. There is no other way of dealing with them."

Dan glanced down at the hand holding the wheel. His skin was still fluctuating, trying to camouflage with where he was. At the moment, it looked like it had been run through with a black bar the same colour as the steering wheel. He didn't know if he had it in him to kill Gatsby, mentally or physically.

The Flash seemed to sense his thought. "It is not your duty to save everyone. It is your duty to save those you care about."

He nodded, unsure. "I can't believe I trusted him." He slammed his fist on the steering wheel.

The roads were starting to straighten, so he put his foot all the way down. His leg jiggled uncontrollably as he willed the truck to fly faster along the deserted country road. Far to the east the sky had lightened, the onyx of night gradually fading to the cool blue of the morning.

He wrestled the truck around a tight bend that he had been going too fast for. Several loud thunks crashed on the trailer behind as he swerved under a low hanging tree. Once straight again, something in the road made him slam his foot on the brakes. The truck stalled to a halt and The Flash slid off the chair and into the footwell.

The thing in the road looked like someone had dumped a bag of clothes. He turned on the full beams. A large man lay sprawled in the gutter, his white shirt covered in dark spatters of red.

The Flash squeaked from the footwell, and Dan leant down and picked him up.

"Mousebane did this." The Flash watched out of the window with keen eyes. "We are on the right track. Keep going."

Dan started the truck up again.

THE DISAPPEARING AMY

It wasn't long before Catman returned to Amy's side. She opened her eyes to look at him. He sat over her, licking his paw, and using it to clean the matted fur around his mouth. In the corner of her vision — still unable to move as she was — she could see that the flatness of the country lane outside was broken by a hump of white that didn't look like it belonged.

A cold breath of wind blew in. She could smell the blood.

"Oh, Catman. What did you do?"

Catman stopped preening and looked at her. The muscles around his shoulders stood out, chiselled and solid. His collar was tight on his neck. It looked very uncomfortable.

She concentrated on her numb arms, imagining them as melting blocks of ice, and forced them up. A dull ache built in her biceps and forearms and, with great effort, she brought her hands up slowly to Catman's neck. She hooked a finger around his collar and removed it.

"That's better," she said.

Something caught her eye. A little black coin had been stuck on the inside of the collar. It had a flickering S shape that shimmered on its surface in the dim interior light of the boot and a raised area that looked like a button. She pressed it with her nail, just as the road beyond filled with light — a truck coming around the corner.

With the press of the button, something, or everything, strobed white, as if lightning had suddenly shot from the heavens. The air surged around her, filling her ears with hissing static, and she felt a sensation much like the hurtling rush of a big drop on an extreme roller coaster. Her stomach lurched. The air around her thickened. She couldn't see anything but Catman standing over her like a guardian as the world went mad. A black sentinel against the blinding flare. His fur whistled around him. The blistering wind forced her eyes shut.

A deep sub-bass note sunk lower into a grinding throb, which vibrated the teeth in her head. Catman hugged himself tightly to her chest as the floor beneath them hardened. She opened one eye. Tiny coloured dots speckled her vision, but as things came into focus, she realised it wasn't her eyes playing tricks on her. The space all around them had changed. Hundreds of tiny multi coloured LEDS twinkled like millions of stars where the ceiling of the SUV had been.

She was no longer in the car.

So Close

Further along from the man's body, chunks of black dotted the road in two parallel lines, bits of tyre, as if someone was leaving breadcrumbs for them to follow.

Around the next corner was the black SUV. It had a French number plate. It stood there in the middle of the road, its red tail lights still on. The engine puffed out plumes of exhaust smoke, which hung in the still night air. Two more heaps lay in the road.

He stopped the truck roughly fifteen feet away. Climbed out. "Wait here," he said to The Flash.

Somewhere in the distance, he could hear the descending moan of a large vehicle at speed. The night smelled familiar. That melting plastic electrical aroma. The one left over after the woman had disappeared at Andrew's house. The air felt charged. Heavy like a storm was building. It had to be a coincidence. Surely The Disappearing Woman and Simon hadn't been here, too.

He'd left his hoody back at the complex when he'd lain under the truck, and his naked skin prickled with goosebumps. He rubbed his arms.

The boot of the car was ajar. Could Amy be inside? Had Catman saved her? "Amy?" he called. There was no answer.

He didn't want to look at the bodies as he stepped past, but his curiosity got the better of him. His eyes flicked over them. A man in a tight-fitting leather jacket and white T-shirt. The woman in a light pink peacoat. They were in better condition than the big man, but both of their throats were still a red mess. Blood had washed down their fronts.

He covered his mouth as his stomach somersaulted. Took a deep breath and turned his attention to the boot.

"Amy?" he said again.

He swung the boot open. His anticipation such that for a second he thought he saw her there, lying on her back with Catman over her chest. But like the after image caused by looking at a lightbulb, he blinked and she was gone.

He hurried to the driver's side of the car and searched through the storage compartments, anxious to find some clue. He pulled open the glove box. Two passports sat inside.

He opened the first. The man. Lyam Garnier. He recognised the first name from something Martin had said.

Had she really been here? Could she be somewhere nearby?

"Amy," he shouted. He held his breath for a reply, but none came. "Amy, are you there?"

He rushed back to the van and touched The Flash.

"Can you smell her? Is she here?"

"She was, as was Mousebane," said The Flash. His little nose twitched. "But now they are gone, and the smell is the same as that left by The Disappearing Woman."

It wasn't a coincidence. They'd been here. They'd taken Amy and Catman.

"This doesn't make sense. How did they find her way out here?" Dan pressed both hands to his forehead as panic threatened to overwhelm him. "What do we do?"

The Flash reached out and touched his bare stomach, reconnecting their telepathic bond. "If the Disappearing Woman has her, and if she and Andrew cross paths, then he will give her what she wants and bring her to the pool. We must go to face the old man there. Now." He bared his teeth. "That is our only option."

Dan took a deep breath to try to calm himself. Closed his eyes and began to count to ten. Stopped at eleven. Didn't feel any better. "Ok."

He hoped they were doing the right thing. He jumped in, ground the truck into first, and slammed his foot on the accelerator.

CHAMELEOMAN VS EGGSACK

B y the time they pulled up on the dusty road outside the warehouse, the sky had brightened considerably, and the last stars were fading into the dark blue of early morning. Pink swathes of cloud crossed the sky, their edges shadowed with deep red, as if God himself had dry brushed them.

Birds sang. Their perky chatter declaring to the world that it was time to wake and make the most of such a glorious Monday morning.

Dan wanted to stomp on their tweety little heads.

For those who haven't yet slept, the sound of birds in the morning is the audible equivalent of sand in your eyes. Sand is fun for building castles, and between your toes it's just lovely, and eyes are useful to see said castles and look out across glorious oceans, but bring the two too close, and disaster occurs. As such, bird song is often a wonderful soundtrack to the morning, but mix that with a sleepless night, and it suddenly becomes grating at best. Birds starting up before you've slept, stands for an opportunity to rest missed. An unpleasant day ahead. Usually, if he was awake at this time, it was because he had driven through the night to get home, maybe made a few wrong turns, and had been hit by road closures and traffic on the way. He hated this time in the morning with a passion, and the sound of the birds having a lovely morning tweet was like nails on a chalkboard.

He parked next to four grassed-over piles of gravel that marked the point where the road ended and the field began. Next to the gravel mounds was Gatsby's jeep. The back left and driver's side door were still open.

He placed The Flash once more onto his shoulder.

"You going to be OK up there?" he said, climbing out of the truck, conscious it would be harder to hold on without his top.

"I'll manage." The Flash gripped his bare shoulder. Dan tried to ignore the sharp pain of his claws.

As he skirted around Gatsby's car, a movement caught his eye. Broken police tape, streaming from the warehouse gates like a long flag in the wind. Everything that had happened here had been forgotten. The dog fight, the pain, the suffering. The criminals had somehow escaped justice. They were here even now, back at the scene of the crime. And where were the police? Too busy fighting the symptoms of a sick society, burdened by never ending budget cuts and time wasters.

There had to be a better way.

Perhaps The Flash was right. In a civilised society, how did you deal with people like Gatsby and Martin who would kill for money?

He pushed the driver's side door fully open and leant inside of Gatsby's car. The smell of rot and stagnant water was nearly overwhelming. The back seat was an absolute mess. For a moment, he thought an ambitious and busy spider had constructed a home, stringing thick webs between the front and back seats. But it wasn't web. A clear, viscous liquid covered the cream leather interior. Dangling from the strings of goop were strange black spots which reminded him of the S shapes that had covered the back of the final frog. They were moving.

He threw up his beef jerky across the window of the car.

The spots were fat, writhing tadpoles.

He cleared his throat and looked at the warehouse. What had happened to Martin? What would he find here?

He stalked around the fence and into the shadow of the ancient and gnarled oaks that stood at the edge of the forest. His skin tingled as it changed again, rippling to a mix of lush greens and autumnal browns. Striped colours of the forest shifted and changed as he moved.

The transformation felt more complete than before. He felt he had more control. He rubbed a hand over his skin. It felt dry and scaly. Similar to passing your hand over a sequinned dress.

To make the most of his camouflage, he hitched the ankles of his jogging bottoms up to his thighs, creating puffy, thigh hugging shorts the likes of which Shakespeare might covet.

The Flash sniffed the air. "Gatsby first moved to the warehouse where he left his son. Then he proceeded into the forest."

"No Amy?"

The Flash sniffed again. "She is not here, and neither is Andrew."

Dan rubbed his face with his free hand.

"We'll find her," said The Flash, "together."

He glanced at his pet. For some reason, up until now, he'd expected him to have all the answers.

"We will deal with these two now," said The Flash. "Martin first. We might catch him before he wakes."

Dan nodded.

He snuck through the fence, careful not to catch The Flash on the wire, and stepped into the alley between the forest and the warehouse.

Discarding the police tape that covered the back door, he crept inside and along the corridor until he reached the open doorway to the main room.

"Are you sure he's here?" he whispered.

"Yes."

Only the pit in the centre remained intact. Several pieces of MDF roughly screwed together and held up by rusting iron props. The table where they had been counting money was overturned. Flung aside in the riot the cats had caused. The floor was covered with a mix of dead leaves, dust, and glass. Even though the sun was nearly up, the place was filled with a haunting grey gloom that made the hair on the back of his neck stand on end. This was the sort of place where you felt watched. A place to keep your back to the wall for fear of cold dead hands reaching for you from the shadows.

The generator had gone. The two large metal jerry cans sat forgotten behind the long, waist-high counter where he'd hidden before.

He stepped into the room and eased his way along the wall behind the counter, trying to keep an eye on everywhere at once. He lifted a can with the hand not holding the axe. It was heavy. The liquid inside rocked from side to side.

Something smashed in the centre of the room. He looked over just in time to see fragments of glass from a window above splash across the floor.

"I see you," came a voice from above, followed by an unsettlingly high titter.

Something moved outside one of the windows that circled the top of the warehouse. He thought he'd caught sight of a skull watching him. A skull with dark-rimmed, staring eyes. The Flash hissed. His head followed the quick thud of footsteps across the warehouse roof.

Dan scanned the windows above and listened. With the axe gripped tightly in his hand, he stepped out from behind the counter into the open room. Took The Flash from his shoulder and placed him on the countertop. If there was going to be a fight, he didn't want him to get hurt.

"Shout if you see anything."

The Flash's head jerked from side to side as he scanned the windows above. Dan slipped across the room, creeping like a ninja. He backed up to the far wall, stood opposite The Flash, and waited.

Another titter, and something wet hit him in the face. It gripped his chin with what felt like hooked little claws and tried to force his lips open to get inside his mouth. He grit his teeth and batted it to the floor with his free hand.

It began to crawl towards him. He stamped on it. It writhed under his foot and he pushed harder until it burst and the squirming stopped. He crouched to investigate, keeping his eyes on the ceiling windows as he lowered.

His stomach turned. It was a large black tadpole, its head roughly the size of his fist. Parasitic and unnatural, and glistening with a jelly-like wetness that made him itch all over.

It had been trying to get into his mouth. Why had it been trying to get into his mouth? He spat and spat and spat to try to rid himself of that jelly-like feeling of its head pressing against his lips.

Something man-sized flopped down from the ceiling. It landed in the shadows to his right, then rose to stand. In the gloom of the warehouse, it looked a little like a large potato, one that had been kept for too long in the cupboard and was covered in arm length shoots.

"I can fix it," it said, its voice whiny, restricted, as if speaking was a challenge. "I'll kill you myself. He'll be proud of me then."

The figure straightened and turned to face him. Two arms and a head curled out from beneath the potato-like growth that had sprouted on his back. His face was haggard and slim, the skin drawn tight to the bone, but Dan recognised him by his torn wax jacket and wellingtons.

"Martin?" The change had been fast.

"What's the matter? Do I look a little different?" He stooped under the weight of the growth on his back, like an English country Quasimodo.

"You sold her." Dan pressed his lips together. He'd never been more furious.

"She'll be well on her way to Europe by now. I told Lyam to sell her to the filthiest Arab he could find."

Martin made a shrieking noise. Dan realised he was laughing.

"Lyam is dead," he said. "Catman got him."

Martin turned his head to consider this. A rapid, inhuman movement. "Dead?"

Dan's hands came up, but this time it wasn't the *'I just want to talk'* Ju Jitsu stance. He readied his axe. Clicked his knuckles. This was his *'I'm done talking, I'm going to beat the absolute fuck out of you'* Ju Jitsu stance.

Martin spluttered and made a sound like a vomiting Wookie. Another fist sized tadpole oozed out of his mouth and onto his hand. Although it was possibly the most revolting thing Dan had ever seen, he didn't gag. His lip curled into a sneer.

Martin curled his arm and threw it. Dan ducked. It careered over his head and splatted on the floor just behind him. With caterpillar like movements of its dextrous tail, and a surprising and unsettling amount of speed, it scrabbled across the floor towards him. He booted it like a football and it smashed into another wall before continuing at him — this time at a reduced pace.

Martin coughed again.

Dan sprinted and rugby tackled him. His shoulder connected with Martin's soft stomach and he rammed him into the wall. The blow was softened by Martin's cushiony back. He let out a pained gasp, and a strange *cusssh* noise escaped him as they fell back further, almost as if the wall had given way under the force of Dan's attack.

The confidence in his wall smashing ability quickly evaporated as he felt a gooey wet spray across his arms, and his nose was assaulted by an all-encompassing stench of putrid water.

The doughy shape on Martin's back had burst.

He looked up into that pasty white face. The tight skin across his angular features made it look like he was wearing some phantom mask. Martin winced in pain; his breath smelled worse than the swampy water oozing from his back.

"Bad idea," he smiled, revealing black gums.

Martin gripped his waist and held firm as half a dozen or so writhing tadpoles eased their way out of his cracked back sack. Dan's arms were trapped beneath him. He couldn't move.

"Don't fight it." Martin's grin widened. His eyes gleamed - dead white orbs surrounding black pinprick pupils. "Just let them inside."

Dan rocked his body up and down in a bid to break free, only managing to squeeze more of the ooze out of Martin's back. Fist sized jellies wriggled up his bare skin. Cold and wet and travelling up his spine like the decaying fingers of a long dead lover, until they were at his face. He felt them squirm across his ears towards his mouth. Pressed his lips and eyes closed as the tadpoles slid down his cheeks.

Martin laughed and gripped his waist tighter. "The reptile told me each will lay eggs. Each will grow inside of you. It is my duty to care for the spawn, my spawn."

Dan wanted to scream. Tell Martin that he had gone insane, but he couldn't. Frantic, and half-mad himself, he jerked his head from side to side, trying to flick the tadpoles off, but they gripped on with those itchy little claws.

The first began pushing through his sealed lips, firmly butting at his teeth trying to get through. He could taste the salt of the oozing slime.

Just as another began to press his teeth apart, a slap of warm fur brushed across his face and the tadpoles were batted aside.

He opened his eyes. The Flash lay protectively over him. He slashed at Martin, catching him with a claw, and the taught skin across the man's pale face split, peeling back like an unfastening zipper.

Dan jerked his head forward, butting Martin on the nose with a jarring crack. His grip loosened, allowing him to roll free. There were several pops as the rest of the tadpoles climbing up Dan's body burst under his weight.

He pushed himself up and slapped at his face to remove the rest.

Martin reeled, delicately touching the flaps of skin on either side of his nose. Dan chose that moment to kick him square in the nuts. All is fair in love and war, and this was both.

He scooped up the axe as Martin dropped to one knee. He pictured Amy as he held the weapon ceremoniously high — this was for her — and embedded it into the top of Martin's head. Martin twitched before going limp, then fell to the ground, dead.

The mutated sack on his back sagged out on the floor around him. Its limp yellow surface, with its black stalks, similar to a gruesome asparagus omelette that Dan had once burnt. He wrenched the axe free. The body jerked again as he did and he sprung back ready, but nothing more happened.

The thing that Martin had become was grotesque. A blubbery lump that looked more like the frog he had eaten than a man.

Dan flicked the axe clean, and tucked it into his waistband, then patted Martin down. A packet of cigarettes in his left coat pocket. He opened them. Tucked securely next to the remaining two was an orange lighter. He discarded the box and the cigarettes, and slipped the lighter into his pocket.

He picked up The Flash and secured him to his shoulder, then stepped around the cabinet and picked up the two fuel cans.

"What are you going to do with those?"

"If that woman doesn't tell me where Amy is, I'm gonna burn the pool, the frogs, everything. No one gets to use them."

A Dragon To Fight

The birds were up and really going for it now. Their incessant dawn chorus both sweet and infuriating. Dan jogged along the broken trail towards the firs, hoping Gatsby wasn't hidden somewhere, watching. Behind, he could hear the sub-bass rise and fall of the industrial estate coming to life.

"Is Gatsby still here?" said Dan.

"Yes, he has moved towards the pool," said The Flash from his shoulder.

"How did he know where to go?"

"I don't know."

As he jogged, the bones in his nose ground together. Broken when Gatsby had hit him earlier. Sticky, drying blood encrusted his top lip. It hurt like hell. Most of his body hurt like hell.

"I am proud of you, Dan," said The Flash. "You didn't hesitate in the final moments. You did what needed to be done."

"I don't really want to talk about it."

Fighting for real wasn't anything like he'd practiced with Sensei Martin. For a start, there hadn't been mats or head guards, and no one to call time when it became too rough. It was the difference between practicing songs at home and playing them at a gig. Everything was faster, more frantic. Errors were easily made.

"It was either you or him. In those situations, the actions take care of themselves. You did right."

Dan shook his head. He wasn't sure.

"That could have easily been you lying there, dead at Martin's hand," he said. "But you prevailed."

Dan gulped. "Is that supposed to make me feel better?"

"I will tell it like it is. You need to be ruthless if you are to defeat the old man. Why hide from the fact? You'd only be hurting yourself."

"I'm fully aware. It's just easier to keep moving if I don't think about it."

It was getting harder to breathe. His chest ached. Every inhalation seemed to hit a block, like the deepest section of his lungs had been closed off. An unpleasant tug in his left side made him want to cough every time the fuel cans bounced in his hands. Perhaps he'd broken a rib or two as well during the fight back in the sedation room. For a moment, his shortness of breath was all he could think about. The forest began to spin around him. He slowed and placed his hands on his knees as stars started to dance before his eyes.

He took a few breaths as deeply as possible until the feeling passed, then started to walk again.

Eventually, he reached the firs. The floor was like a security alarm, drying leaves and fallen sticks crackling with every misplaced step. He lay the fuel cans down as he reached the line of trees, and brushed through the needle covered branches. That now familiar tingle travelled across his skin, as his whole body turned a dark green.

Gatsby was there.

Only now, he looked wholly different. Tattered shreds of black jumper were stretched and ripped across his muscular back, which was now half the size of a garage door. An intense heat radiated from him. Even though he was still a few metres away, it warmed Dan's skin as though he was standing directly by an open fire.

Gatsby was kneeling by the side of the pool, facing away, busying himself with something in the water. By his side a duffel bag sat open. Several filthy plastic bottles were visible inside. The mouth of the bag glowed with tadpoles and spawn.

Dan felt for the axe in his waistband, but compared to the wall of muscle hunched by the edge of the pool, it was a mere toothpick. He knew he couldn't take him. Not like this. Not unless he struck the blow just right. Gatsby would crush him like a coke can.

His hands shook. He considered dousing Gatsby with petrol and lighting him along with the rest of the pool. The thought was barbaric, but the outcome was the same. Burning someone alive or hitting them with an axe, in the end, what was the difference?

In the time it had taken him to weigh up his options, Gatsby had filled another bottle and set it by his side. The care with which he scooped up the tadpoles was almost sweet, like a big bear collecting honey. Dan had to force himself to remember what the man had done. Force himself to look past the fact that, at the beginning of the week, he had just been another ageing neighbour. If Martin was anything to go by, Gatsby was a murderer, and a human trafficker. And from what he had learned at the barn, this was *his* operation that *he* had started. He deserved everything Dan was about to give him.

He returned through the firs and retrieved one of the canisters, then stepped carefully out onto the soft mud, until he was nearly in arm's reach of Gatsby.

Petrol fumes filled his nostrils as he took a long, shuddering breath. He held the can above his head. He had no idea what would happen if the fire from the lighter burnt up towards the canister and lit the petrol inside. Would it explode? Would he accidentally douse himself and burn to death while Gatsby continued filling bottles? Would Gatsby laugh?

He'd need to time the action perfectly. Withdraw the canister before he lit the petrol.

Pour, withdraw, light.

Dan rehearsed it in his head. All the while, Gatsby continued to fill the bottles.

Pour, withdraw, light.

He eased closer, pulled the lighter out of his pocket.

Pour, withdraw, light. Just do it.

He poured. He withdrew. A loud - whumf - and an eyebrow obliterating flash of flame sent him ducking backwards with his arm in front of his face. He hadn't lit, but the petrol had erupted into flame.

Gatsby blazed. But he didn't even turn around. A deep chuckle shook from inside the burning boulder that was his back. His skin blackened and cracked.

He stood and rubbed a hand over his bald head. Dan took this to mean he had at least been mildly inconvenienced.

Gatsby stepped away from his bottles, as the petrol burnt away and the fire on his back died out.

"I was scared of dragons when I was a boy." His voice was deep, like a truck engine. He stretched his meaty arms above his head and rolled his neck. "My father had always told me stories about the beasts. Told me I had to fight my dragons or they'd devour me. It was only when I got older that I discovered he was talking metaphorically. I suppose he didn't want me ending up weak like you."

Gatsby turned his head slightly. Studied Dan out of the corner of one eye. The white was a cautionary yellow, and the pupil, nothing more than a black slit.

"You sold my wife. You took her from me."

"Did I?"

"Don't play dumb." Dan gripped the axe in a way he hoped appeared threatening. The truth was his hands were sweating so much he feared he would drop it.

"You were the one who stuck your nose in where it didn't belong. Take some responsibility for your own actions." He laughed. A short series of growls. "You must be quite the disappointment. Look at you. What the hell's going on with your trousers?"

Dan looked down at his joggers which were still piled up around his thighs. Sure, he might be a mess, but he was alright, wasn't he? Amy wouldn't have stuck with him otherwise.

"He's teasing you," said The Flash.

"I'm—" he started.

"They always want more than you can give, women," Gatsby cut in. "Take Cathy. I gave her a son, a house, money. She was never happy. They always want more."

"Amy and me, we just like being together. We don't need anything more."

Gatsby scoffed. "How sweet. Well, seeing as you're here, I assume you've put Martin out of his misery. I don't blame you. He was always a sickly thing, and your elixir really did a number on him." He shook his head. "He was so pale when he was born. The first night I had him home from the hospital, I thought about just putting a pillow over his screaming face. Be done with it. But I didn't want to let Cathy down." He chuckled. "And in the end, she still left." His voice softened. "I grew to love him. He was all I had after all. And there were times when I was proud of him."

He looked inward a moment. Then turned to face Dan. He looked very different to the man Dan had met a week ago. His face had elongated almost to a point. Bony ridges rose up either side of his chin and forehead, which gave his face an angular lizard-like shape. Short horns broke through the skin on his head just above his elf-like ears, and his eyes were enlarged yellow ovals. The skin around them had hardened into darkening scales.

Dan held the axe up by his shoulder with both hands. The classic 'I'm going to die' stance not regularly taught to age twelve Ju Jitsu students.

"You'll never get old, so you won't know what it's like," continued Gatsby, "but you make one mistake and then your kids are all over you. They take away the things you like to do, take your business away, slap you in some little house where they can send someone to keep an eye on you. They say it's cus they love you, but they just want to make it easier on themselves."

Dan cleared his throat. He had the urge to say something super-hero-like. Something along the lines of "that is no excuse for your crimes" or "justice takes no prisoners", but he didn't have the confidence. And of course, justice did take prisoners. That was literally one of the main things it did. As a result his mouth opened, and shut again.

Gatsby screwed the top on to the last bottle. He held it with only his thumb and index finger, as if the bottle were filled with something hot. Strange black marks covered his fingertips.

He dropped the bottle, letting it land perfectly in the duffel, then made his move. Dan ducked Gatsby's swinging arm, but only just. The old man's hand skimmed across the top of his head, knocking him off balance. He fell sideways, stumbling into the pool as the mud gave way beneath his feet. The Flash yowled as he was dragged into the pond too.

Thick jelly-like water came up to his waist, and though the coldness of the early morning should have chilled him to his bones, the freezing water felt comforting on his skin. Insubstantial creatures writhed against him. Their rapid movements tickled his bare legs and stomach.

Arms wide, and with a fiery snarl on his face, Gatsby stalked around the edge of the pool.

"Come out and fight me like a man."

"Are you kidding? You're huge."

Dan span, tracking Gatsby's movement, before wading towards the small central island. The frogs which had made their home there, leapt away and into the water. His hands slipped and sunk into the gloopy mud as he pulled himself up using tufts of hardy reeds.

Gatsby continued to circle, but didn't come within a foot of the water's edge.

It wasn't deep.

Something was stopping him.

"Why don't you come and get me?" He frowned and tried to get a better look at the marks on Gatsby's hands. The ends of his fingers looked like black drooping ash. The sort you'd get on a cigarette left to burn.

"I'm not going to bother myself by coming in for you. I'd rather watch the hope die in your eyes when you realise you've got nowhere to go."

"Why wait?"

He gave no answer.

"Look at his fingers Dan," said the Flash. "The water has marked him."

Dan dipped the toe of his trainer into the pool and flicked a little water in Gatsby's direction.

Gatsby flinched back, and a low groan swelled in his throat. "Don't."

He was scared of it. The water hurt him.

Dan jumped. Cannonball!! As he splashed down, liquid filled his ears and nose, and from above the surface he heard Gatsby's muffled groan.

"You could have warned me." The Flash spat water from his mouth, his sopping fur slicked smoothly to his body.

On the bank, Gatsby was kneeling, hunched over on the floor. Steam billowed from his baking skin.

Dan brought his hands together and pushed as big a jet of water as he could muster. The resultant wave crashed over Gatsby's back with a thundering sizzle. He howled and hissed with steam, and a burnt earth stench filled the air.

Gatsby rolled out of the splash zone. "You'll wish you never came here," he seethed.

He crawled through the dirt to the fallen petrol canister. Gluts of petrol still drained out across the surrounding mud. He picked it up and poured the rest over his head and the nearby firs. His body exploded into flame, and several trees caught too. Very quickly thick black clouds of smoke billowed around him as the petrol burned. Out of the cloud, the second full canister flew. Dan dived out of the way as it splashed down leaking its contents into the pool.

Snake-like licks of flame ran down from the trees. The petrol in the mud around Gatsby caught. He was now surrounded by the fire, a bright orange aura. A halo of black smoke, crested over his dragon-like head.

He roared, and moved to the nearest burning tree. Pulled a long branch from it. The wood screeched as it broke free. He held it above his head like a spear, trained on Dan.

Dan waded as fast as he could to the nearest edge of the pool. Pulled himself out, as the fiery branch splashed into the water, and the spot where he had been moments before burst into flames.

His skin felt like it was boiling. His eyes streamed from the smoke. He held a hand over his face and blinked it away.

"Watch out," said The Flash, but it was too late.

Like a steam train he came, bent low and running at top speed, hot, and billowing with water vapour. Gatsby's shoulder connected with Dan's stomach. The Flash was thrown clear. The pain in Dan's left side detonated as he was carried backwards. His stomach wanted to climb out of his mouth, and the rest of his digestive tract wanted to escape in the opposite direction.

Gatsby slammed him into the ground. His yellow eyes glared down, diamond pupils slimmed to fine knife cuts. His hands closed around Dan's neck. The raging heat from those fingers burned his throat like a brand.

"If you know anything about what the hell is happening to me, you tell me now before I kill you."

He looked afraid, but Dan didn't know what to say. Even if he did, he wasn't going to tell him. Just stared hatefully back into those yellow eyes and kept his mouth firmly shut.

He wrestled with the claws around his throat as his vision started to blur.

"Tell me." Spit flew from Gatsby's toothless gums, as he rattled Dan's head against the muddy ground.

A dark shape leapt through the firs and landed on Gatsby's back.

Gatsby stood up. Tried to swat at him, but Catman was too quick. He clambered across his body like a parasite, cutting and tearing wherever he moved.

Dan rolled over and pushed himself up. Moved forward to help if he could.

"There he is!" said a familiar voice.

He turned to see Andrew coming through the firs on the other side of the pool.

"Dan!" Andrew's eyes were wide. He looked back over his shoulder into the woods beyond. "Quick! They're here."

The Disappearing Woman emerged behind him. She held her camera ready. Clicked a button on the top.

With a *fwutung* a long silver needle flew into Gatsby's neck.

His head bounced. Eyelids fluttered. He shook his head and raised his hands. Continued to stretch his fingers towards Dan's throat like a zombie. Catman jumped from his back to land at Dan's side and growled.

Fwutung.

Fwutung.

Two more darts appeared in Gatsby's chest. He blinked. Leant forward like a drunk walking into a powerful wind.

Dan stepped forward, and with every last ounce of his strength spartan kicked him in the chest. The mud under Gatsby's feet gave way, and he stumbled backwards into the pool. The water all but exploded with a hiss of steam as his skin touched the surface. White clouds of vapour billowed up from where Gatsby had fallen. The fire on the surface of the pool was extinguished, and the whole clearing was blanketed in an impenetrable white mist.

Dan looked around, but he could no longer see Andrew or The Disappearing Woman. He could hear Catman yelping ahead, so he crouched low, and followed the sound. Found him with The Flash who was clinging to the mud at the pool's edge, his back legs in the water. Dan scooped him up and cradled him in his arms.

The water continued to fizz and boil as if the world's largest effervescent vitamin tablet had just been thrown in.

"Andrew?" called Dan. But he did not hear a reply.

The mist began to thin. Gatsby's body floated in the pool, face down. Aftershock ripples rocked his drifting form, pushing him closer to the edge of the water. His back was black and cracked, like crumbling ash. Catman approached. Stretched and tapped him with a paw. No reaction.

Steadily, Dan placed a foot on Gatsby's shoulder and pushed. His body drifted away and eventually washed up on the island in the centre, scattering the frogs that had once again sought refuge there.

The water no longer glowed.

Another rustle from the bushes, but this time to his right. *Fwutung.* Something punched into his neck. He blinked and looked around. The Disappearing Woman stepped from the undergrowth.

With the last of his energy, he placed The Flash down next to Catman.

"Where is she?" he said. He realised he was falling as if in slow motion. He hit the the soft mud, unable to fight the oncoming grey.

THE SOURCE

As he woke and moved, lamps faded on over where he lay. He shielded his eyes with his arm.

He was lying on what appeared to be a hospital bed inside a square room with pure white walls. There were no windows. The far wall contained floor-to-ceiling glass cabinets, several of which contained test tubes and bottles filled with unknown liquids in varying colours. Another contained a large fish tank with about three inches of murky water inside. Skittering around in the water were several large frogs. Next to the fish tank, an unusual looking cylindrical machine hung from the ceiling. A long robot-like arm protruded from it. And next to a desk holding a computer monitor was a large screen covered in multi-coloured scrawls and algebraic equations. He stared for a moment, but couldn't understand any of it.

Someone else was in the room. His heart raced when he saw her. He felt almost giddy with relief.

Amy sat on his right, fast asleep in a one-seater leatherette chair. Her head rested on one hand, her hair a scattered mist that hung over her face. He always thought her most beautiful when she slept. He watched her for a second as her chest gently rose and fell. The relaxed curve of her face made her look so innocent. That sweetness always gave him butterflies. It made him fall in love with her day after day.

His throat constricted and for a few seconds, he forgot to breathe. There had been many moments when he'd thought he'd never see her again.

He choked and coughed, and she sat upright, immediately awake.

"Danny." She threw her arms over him, resting her head on his chest. His ribs howled and he held back a gasp. He closed his eyes. It was the most painful, most welcome hug he'd ever received. He pushed the pain away so he could remain in her embrace a moment longer.

"Oh gosh. Sorry," she said when he eventually gasped at the ache in his ribs. She picked up a metal cup from a side table next to her chair and brought it to him. "Drink this."

He did. It tasted awful. An unexpected fizzy, salty sweetness. "Yucksville." He stuck his tongue out and looked at her, betrayed. "That is gross," he choked, handing it back to her.

"Potassium," she said, setting it down by his bed. "You're low on electrolytes. Simon told me to give it to you. It'll help build your strength up."

He coughed again. "That wouldn't be gifted bio-chemist Simon De Fraine, would it?" He looked around. The room span. "How are you here?"

"It's a long story." She picked up his hand and held it firmly. "He and Pippa work here. They are nice. As soon as they found out what had happened to me, they wanted to help."

"Am I in the hospital?"

"No. I think this is where Simon and Pippa work. It's some sort of laboratory. I think we're underground. There aren't any windows anywhere."

He pressed his eyelids, hard. His brain felt like it had been shrink-wrapped. He couldn't think.

"Pippa? She's the disappearing woman, isn't she?"

"The what?" Amy frowned. "They didn't tell me much, so it might be best if we wait for them to come back. We have to leave soon. They said they wouldn't be long. They were just having a look at Andrew's shoulder, then they're sending him home. Apparently, he was shot or something."

"He was. Is he alright?"

She nodded. "He looked fine to me. When Pippa was taking me home, there was a note stuck to our front door for her which said to go to his. It was all very strange. He took her to the pool where they found you, then we all came here. He told me about your little adventure."

Dan snorted. "Uh, it was a pretty big adventure."

She gave a cheeky smile. "You know, I think he's a keeper."

He folded his arms and gave a casual shrug. "We're just, like, friends who fight crime and stuff."

She laughed. "Ooo, crime fighter friends." She looked genuinely pleased.

He scanned the room again. A screen on the wall behind him showed neon green peaks and troughs on something similar to a heart metre. None of the numbers or figures made sense. In fact, a lot of the symbols on the screen were completely alien to him. Little wireless suction pads dotted his bare chest. Two more were stuck to his temples. He lifted his blanket. A thick silver bandage surrounded his ribcage. It throbbed. The blood and the dirt that had accumulated over the last few days had been washed away, and he was wearing blue polythene boxer shorts. They rustled when he moved. He looked at Amy, eyes wide.

"No need to be embarrassed. I put those on for you." She smiled and patted his hand. "No one saw anything."

"Are you OK?" He gripped her hand tightly. "Is everything alright?"

"Yes. We're fine. We're safe. Catman and The Flash are safe."

His head tipped to the side on its own.

"You'll be a bit woozy while the tranquilliser wears off."

She was right. Whenever his eyes stopped moving, the room seemed to wonk off on the diagonal.

"Tranquilliser?"

"Pippa thought it'd be easier on you if you just woke up here, after all you've been through."

A click at the door made him jump, and Amy placed a gentle hand on his shoulder.

"It's OK Danny," she said. "It's just them."

The door opened and in strode The Disappearing Woman. She stepped briskly across the room and smiled when she saw he was awake. Simon, the man from Andrew's house, followed close behind. He glanced back through the door nervously before closing it with both hands on the handle, as if he were scared of making a noise.

The woman stepped close to the foot of the bed. She held a tablet in her hands and looked between it and the display behind him. She tapped the tablet screen, and checked her watch before nodding to herself.

Simon took the thin, almost invisible, pair of glasses from his face, and cleaned them on his lab coat. He cleared his throat and opened his mouth to speak, but Pippa beat him to it.

"Daniel Dixon, the name's Pippa Clarke," she said. "And this is Simon De Fraine."

"We've met," said Dan, looking at Simon.

Simon touched the bump in the centre of his forehead.

Pippa frowned and turned angry eyes to look at him. "You have, have you?"

He smiled, sensing Simon hadn't told Pippa about their little rendezvous.

Simon mumbled something Dan couldn't hear.

She moved closer to the scientist and, in a hushed, almost aggressive tone, hissed, "I told you if I was going to help you sort out your little mess, you had to share everything with me."

"Sorry Pippa," he said, with his chin placed firmly on his chest.

She turned back and smiled as if nothing had happened.

"I'm going to serve it to you straight. You've put us in a bit of a predicament." She jerked a thumb towards Simon. "This nincompoop lost his latest science experiment, and asked me to help him find it. Unfortunately, you got there first, which makes things slightly tricky for all of us. It's been twenty years since an outsider found out about our organisation and luckily for that guy, his mother worked for us, so we couldn't exactly erase him." She shrugged.

"Erase him?" said Amy. Her hand tightened around Dan's.

Pippa waved a hand, as if she were swatting a not particularly bothersome fly. "Don't worry, we're not going to erase you. We stopped doing that sort of thing in the nineties. You're too important to us as you are. In fact, Daniel, you're too important to the world." She hunched her back, lifted both hands in front of her face, and wiggled her fingers at him. "You and your cats are like a little petri dish of discovery. You could save hundreds of thousands of lives the world over."

"What do you mean? What's happened to me?"

Pippa turned to Simon and, with a jerk of her head, suggested it was now his time to speak.

Simon stepped forward. "We're not going to lie to you, Daniel Dixon." He paused.

"Good," Dan said, narrowing his eyes, waiting for whatever came next.

There was a moment of silence. He looked between Pippa and Simon. "And...?"

Simon looked at Pippa, suggesting that was all he had. Then added, "It's very complicated." His lips perked into a slight smile as if his job were complete, then he stepped back.

Dan raised his palms to the ceiling. "Is that it? *It's complicated?*"

"You realise that everything we do here is highly confidential," said Pippa.

"But you must be able to tell me something. Is this permanent? Is it dangerous? What are you going to do with me now?"

"We don't really know," said Pippa. "You're the first human to go through it."

"To go through what?" said Amy. She looked around at the three of them.

Simon looked at Pippa. She nodded, then looked at her watch and twirled her fingers in a hurried 'go on' gesture.

He took out a cloth from his breast pocket and wiped his face with it before folding and tucking it away. "As I said before..." His apologetic eyes momentarily flicked to Pippa, "when we met at Andrew Giles's house, the frogs contain something I like to call The Reptile."

"The voice I heard in my head," said Dan, sitting up. "It said it was me."

"It technically is you." Simon nodded. "Humans are said to have three brains, reptilian or primal, emotional, and rational. My frogs are test subjects. I loaded them with a serum designed to embolden the reptile part of their brain, the part that is in control of their self-preserving behaviour patterns. The reptile would be allowed to take control."

"Why would you want to do that?"

"The main aim was to eventually make the serum safe for humans. I've hypothesised that having a stronger reptilian brain should make a body more capable of adapting to and overcoming stressful situations. It was originally meant to help victims of certain diseases heal faster, but," he cleared his throat, "it appears to have other applications."

"It certainly does," Dan agreed, then frowned. "But what happened to Martin? How was that him adapting to a stressful situation?"

Simon looked down. "I believe Martin Shields came into contact with one of my Mother Toads. The dark batch, as I said to you at Mr Giles' house, were different. I had done a little more tinkering with them. My aim with those was to coax the frogs into passing the serum down via their genetics to their offspring."

Not for the first time, Dan felt like he might throw up. "You're telling me that if I'd have just used a dark frog instead of a light frog, then what happened to Martin would have happened to me?" His lips itched with the feeling of those creeping, clawing tadpoles.

Simon wrinkled his nose and nodded. "I'm sure the lighter ones have limited negative side effects."

"But I found and touched one of those frogs," said Amy. She looked at Dan. Her innocence plucked at his heartstrings. "And I don't feel any different."

He wrinkled his nose. "Um, yeah, I kind of ate one."

She looked horrified. "You what?" She let go of his hand for a split second before grabbing it again.

"It was in the heat of the moment." He held her hand tighter.

She looked at Simon. Concerned frown lines crept across her forehead. "Will he be OK?"

"Simon will be keeping a close eye on you and will guide you through any following transitions." Pippa looked at him with raised eyebrows. "Won't you, Simon?"

He nodded quickly. "Yes, yes of course."

"In the hope that you will both be completely honest with us going forward," said Pippa, "I want to make you aware that our superiors here at Source do not know about this breach. They do not know Simon lost his specimens. And they don't know that you are here now. If they did, we would all be in a world of trouble. We hope that together we can keep it that way."

Amy nodded quickly. "We will."

"Sure," said Dan, glancing at her as she stared with wide, trusting eyes at Pippa and Simon. As long as they weren't going to hurt either of them, he would agree to whatever they wanted.

"We also want you to have this. We feel you deserve it." Pippa stepped to a nearby shelving unit and removed a briefcase. "It was in George Shields' car when we found it at the warehouse." She placed it on the end of the bed and glanced again at her watch. "There's no more time here. We must send you back."

"Wait, are Catman and The Flash OK?" said Dan.

Pippa smiled, softening at the mention of the cats. "They are waiting for you at home. Quite the handful."

Amy smiled back. "They are."

Simon came forward and handed Dan a battered old Nokia. "I will need you to keep me up to date with any other changes that happen to you or the cats. My number is the only one on there."

"Or if you have any questions about anything," said Pippa. "This must have been frightening for you both and we want to be as helpful as we can."

He frowned and slowly picked up the phone as if it were a bomb about to go off. "But isn't this a top-secret lab? Aren't you supposed to keep us in the dark or have us murdered or something?"

"Dan?" hissed Amy.

Pippa crossed to the head of his bed and pressed a section of the wall there. With a hydraulic hiss, a small panel slid out of the wall. It glowed bright blue, reminding him of the pool.

"Would you prefer that?" she asked, while pressing several holographic projections there. A section of the ceiling above the bed slid backwards into the wall. Behind it, the ceiling flickered with hundreds of multi coloured LEDs. An increasingly intense hum built up, and his whole body started to tingle.

"No, not really," he shouted over the noise. "What is this?"

"Give it a few days, then call us if you have a problem," said Pippa. "We'll be watching over you." She smiled. For a moment, her tone seemed more threatening than comforting, but it was hard to hear her above the escalating noise in the room.

He opened his mouth to speak, but before he could get the words out, there was a bright flash. He squeezed Amy's hand. Air rushed past him.

His body was a dandelion clock. A collection of seeds blown away one at a time by the wind.

It wasn't an unpleasant sensation.

Home Again

The low descending hum ground away into nothing.

"Wait—"

Dan looked around the room. They were home. He patted himself down to check he was still all there. Looked down. Still naked save his shopping bag pants. At least he was visible.

Amy stood next to him. He pushed himself up to stand, ignoring the dizziness that came to claim him, and threw his arms around her. Together they stumbled, propped against the wall of their hallway.

He took her face in his hands. Kissed her over and over. His heart fluttering like a frightened bird as she held him tightly.

"Amy." He held her for a moment at arm's length, just to look at her, to take in all he thought he'd lost. His breath hitched in his chest. "I thought I'd never see you again."

"Me too." She looked him up and down. Brushed her hands over the skin of his arms and chest. Those frown lines, the ones he'd always loved, appeared on her brow. "You feel different."

He swallowed. Took a breath. "I am... I am different." He didn't know how to tell her.

"But you're OK?"

He nodded. Hummed in the affirmative. "Think so."

Something squeaked behind him. They turned to see The Flash, legs up in some sort of wheeled contraption, pawing towards them from inside the living room.

"Alright, Prof X," said Dan, squatting down to meet him. He brushed a hand over The Flash's head. Despite his poor legs, he looked OK. "Where did you get that?"

"The scientist made it for me."

"That was nice of him. It's pretty bloody cool. Where's your bro?"

"Hold on," said Amy. She turned her head and gave him a sideways squint.

"Oh yeah, new development," said Dan. "Me and The Flash can talk now."

"What?" She crouched beside them both. "How is that even possible?"

"I think it's more him than me." He shrugged.

She put a hand out to touch The Flash's head. "Can I?"

"Don't think so. You might have to eat a frog to be able to."

"I think I'll pass."

He grinned and waggled his eyebrows. "Now I'm gonna be in on everything that goes on around here. You'll have to think twice about inviting your secret boyfriends over. He's going to be my little spy."

"As if." She giggled.

"I would die before I betrayed The Master's trust to you," said The Flash with a snarl. He nuzzled against Amy's leg, and she bowed her head to hug him. He began to purr, and in his mind's eye, Dan received a wave of pure contentment.

"What?" scoffed Dan. "After all we've been through together?"

"What did he say?" said Amy, watching The Flash.

"He said, of course he would spy on you for me."

The Flash nipped his finger. Amy laughed again.

"Why didn't you tell Simon and Pippa?" she said.

"I have a feeling it would be a good idea to keep a few things to ourselves for now."

He held his breath a moment and looked at her.

She leant her head to one side. "What else are you hiding?"

"Um..." He held his hands up. Started to sweat a little. "I don't know if it'll—" His whole body tingled and suddenly his skin changed colour to match the magnolia of the wall behind him.

Amy gasped and stepped back. "What?"

"It's OK," he said. "It doesn't hurt or anything. Like Simon said, it's just an adaptation to the stress I was in."

"And you don't think we should tell them?" She gently picked up The Flash and his wheels and backed into the lounge.

"Not yet," he said, following her. "We don't know if we can fully trust them."

She nodded as she sat on the sofa. "I agree." She sat with the cat on her lap, stroking him while she looked over their living room.

He smiled, watching her. Then realised he was freezing. "I'm just going to put some clothes on." He turned to head upstairs, and in his haste, kicked something hard. It clattered into the wall. He caught himself on the banister and looked down to find what he'd tripped on. The briefcase from Gatsby's car. It had burst open upon hitting the wall.

"You OK?" said Amy.

"Um... yeah," he said, trying to remember exactly how much Martin had said he'd been able to get for an English girl. Fifty thousand pounds, wasn't it?

The cash that had spilled out of the briefcase covered the floor.

"What is it?" she said as she crossed the living room towards him.

"You know you said you wanted me to take some time off?" he said. "How does a year sound?"

"Why—?" She gasped when she saw the money. Then turned up her nose. "Is that all I'm worth?"

"No, they don't know you. They should have probably haggled a bit."

She poked him in the back. "Shut it you."

A moment's silence passed as they stared at the money. Then she said. "We're safe from them, aren't we?"

He swallowed, then nodded. "Yeah. Me and the boys sorted them both right out. We don't need to worry about Gatsby and Martin ever again." He didn't take his eyes from the cash. "Except for the attention of the apparently benevolent secret organisation of world-class scientists that turned me invisible, Catman into a puma, and The Flash into a genius, we should be able to just go on with life as we'd planned."

"Is that what you really want?"

He paused. Chewed the question over. The answer that came surprised him. He shook his head, then put his hands on her hips and looked her in the eyes. "What I really want is another dragon."

"What do you mean?"

"I want to make sure what happened to us never happens to anyone else."

"Oh." She wrinkled up her nose, looking a little miffed. "I thought you might say we could just take all this money and blow it on spa trips and new clothes."

He snorted. "Oh yeah. Before I go off saving the world, we're definitely getting you some new threads. A superhero can't be seen going out with just anybody."

She flicked him on the ear. "A superhero are we now? You do realise you can't do that without talking to people, right?"

"Quite the opposite. We superheroes dwell in fortresses of solitude. We work only at night. We are silent and deadly." He grinned. "For me, it's perfect."

A knock on the door startled them both.

The smile that had been on Amy's face slipped away. "Who is it?" she whispered.

"It's me, Andrew," came the voice from the other side of the door. "I have exciting news."

Dan smiled and pulled the door open.

Stood on the door in a bright red pair of dungarees, a vest that said 'Not your mother, not your milk', and a yellow bobble hat, was Andrew. He held something cradled in his arms, which for a brief moment Dan mistook for some sort of furry hand warmer. Then a pair of golden green eyes opened.

"Dimitri?" Dan couldn't help but laugh.

Andrew smiled wide. "He was there when I got home." He lifted Dimitri high into the air like a Disney baboon showing off a baby lion. There was a bald patch on the cat's side where he'd been shot. "He's just like me, like daddy, like son." He snuggled Dimitri to his chin and happily closed his eyes.

The Flash joined them on the front step. Dan picked him up. "Look Flashy, Scratchtacular's here."

The Flash began to purr. "This pleases me."

"Now, where's your brother got to? He'll be happy to see his friend's OK."

MOUSEBANE

They call me The Night. The Shadow That Stalks Behind. The Dark One.

The battle is won, but the war is far from over.

I still smell him.

Beyond the grey smoke that belches from the back of the people movers; beyond the tempting salt and fat aroma of their food; beyond the sweet, wet mould of the leaves fallen from the trees. Deep down below the earth, like a drop of blood in a great river, I still smell him.

He lives.

The Disappearing Woman has him. Buried beneath metres of earth and walls of white stone.

She is not to be trusted. I can tell this by smell alone.

Does she pose a threat to The Master? I know not.

But she has the answers to why I am strong and why Red Mist is intelligent.

This bothers me not.

All that dwells on my mind is revenge.

Once I find the old man, I will have it.

I will have it.

THANK YOU

Thank you for reading my book 'There's Something Wrong With The Cats'. I hope you enjoyed it.

Please leave an honest review on amazon and goodreads to let me know what you thought. As an indie author in a sea of traditionally published and indie authors, reviews can really help my books get noticed!

Sign up to my no-spam mailing list at my website
https://cjpowellauthor.com/tswwtc

In the past I have given away full free novels and short stories, and will also let you know about any deals and updates I have!

Use this QR code to go straight there.

Thank you for taking a chance on my books!

Chris x

Also By C J Powell

A More Perfect Human

It was supposed to be easy money. But trying to keep a centenarian alive may be the death of him.

London, 2035. Nige Davies just needs some extra cash to visit his grandkids. So the recently widowed sixty-five-year-old doorman takes a security guard job for the world's oldest man... who happens to be tanned, toned, and on the eve of his 135th birthday. But when the venerable health guru's impending global birthday celebration triggers a cadre of religious nutjobs to threaten a nuclear disaster, Nige finds himself fending off eight-foot-tall ninjas and a winged assassin.

Fleeing through the cyberpunk city with his client as the cultists call for his death, the former club bouncer panics when the fit antediluvian begins to feel ill. And with their enemies hot on their heels, he fears this simple job has ensnared him in a murderous conspiracy.

Can Nige get his client to safety before his birthday candles are fatally snuffed?

A More Perfect Human is the fast-paced first book in the Chrysalis science fiction series. If you like action-packed thrills, witty dialogue, and unexpected twists and turns, then you'll love C J Powell's darkly humorous manhunt.

Grab it on Amazon!

"A perfect balance of tension and comedy..." - **DK Pike (Author of Fauxville)**

"A wonderful cast that literally jump off the page..." - **Amazon Review**

"One of the best books I've read..." - **Goodreads Review**

"I truly am stunned to see that this is this young author's first book because it really is a masterful work of fiction" - **Amazon.fr Review**

THE DEMON HUNTER'S WIFE
COMING SOON

Dirk Kilmore is one of The Bureau's top demon hunters. Rumour has it he
saved the world from eternal damnation a couple of years ago. But no one talks
about that...

And this isn't his story anyway.

When Dirk doesn't come home from work one weekend and strange creatures
come for their daughter, his wife, Sadie, is forced to drop the baby off with her
demon possessed mother, grab one of his spare wands, and go hunting for him.

Turns out Dirk hasn't been entirely truthful about what he does for a living.

Sadie will discover this and more in this darkly funny urban fantasy novel.

Coming Autumn 2023.

AFTERWORD

Hi, thanks for reading 'There's Something Wrong With The Cats'. I hope you enjoyed it. It was the second book I ever finished and was originally very different. Andrew wasn't in there. Gatsby wasn't a bad guy... That sort of thing. You can review the book on Goodreads and Amazon. I'd love to hear your thoughts!

<u>Pop Quiz</u>

Some parts of the book are based on true events. 2 of the next 3 statements are true... can you guess which?

1. I own a cat.

2. I'm a musician in a wedding band.

3. I once heard screams coming from my neighbour's house so went round to save the day only to find them doing it in a bush.

Send your answers on a postcard.

All the best,

Chris x

Printed in Great Britain
by Amazon

31551411R00169